LIGHTWAVE: CLOCKER
FOLDING SPACE SERIES

AM SCOTT

Cover designed by Deranged Doctor Design
Editing by Nick Bowman Editing

This book is a work of fiction. Names, characters, places, and incidents either are products of the author's imagination or are used fictitiously. Any resemblance to actual persons, living or dead, events, or locales is entirely coincidental.

AM Scott
Visit my website at www.amscottwrites.com

Printed in the United States of America

First Printing: May 2018
Lightwave Publishing LLC

ISBN-13: 978-1721035755

DEDICATION

To The Amazing Sleeping Man — thanks for
supporting my new dream!

Acknowledgments

Writing is actually a team sport. Since I suck at team sports, writing is hard! But without my teammates, it would be so much harder.

First, the team owner, God. Thanks for inspiring me to write, sending me on a new fantastic journey. This one is the best yet!

My team manager and husband, Matt—The Amazing Sleeping Man. Thanks for being patient all these years while I ignored housework and everything else, including you, my nose buried in a book or my laptop. I love you—here's to twenty-five more years of adventure together!

My goalie, fellow author and sister, Julia Davinsky. Julia has patiently read everything I've sent her, from my very first, truly awful novel to this series. She's given me straightforward critiques, encouragement and occasional rear-end kicking, all of which I needed, desperately. Thanks so much!

My defenders and writing partners, Lou Cadle and Eric T. Knight. You guys have been so generous with your writing and business knowledge, and our daily writing sprints kept me on track. This book wouldn't be published without you.

My frontline, Nick Bowman Editing and Deranged Doctor Design. Nick's work is unseen but makes my work readable. DDD created the beautiful covers and social media visuals.

I've had the good fortune to have many cheerleaders and team supporters along the way. My Twitter friends, the Facebook groups Indie Cover Project and 20Booksto50K gave me great business advice. Thanks for all the help—any errors are mine!

Apologies to anyone I missed—I know I missed a lot of you!

A percentage of the profits from this novel will be donated to **Team Rubicon: Disasters are our Business, Veterans are our Passion.** See teamrubiconusa.org for more information. Go Greyshirts!

CHAPTER ONE

Saree slid through the crowd, a double-time bass drum pounding in her chest. Bending her knees, she hid among the masses in the passageway, trying to reach her shuttle before the black-haired man caught up. The flashes of red in her rear-view holo increased, and she fought back the impulse to run. Thank all the suns she'd tagged the man right away.

Outside her airlock, a crowd of people stood enthralled by a wailing busker banging away on an out-of-tune guitar. Saree slipped between them, thankful for the throng's lack of taste. They must be truly desperate for entertainment. Covering her mouth with her hand, she murmured, "Hal, emergency ingress alpha-four-two-uniform."

At the airlock, she reached out to enter her code on the worn, grimy keypad, but the hatch swung open in front of her. She ducked in, securing it and the next three. Collapsing against her inner shuttle hatch, she ignored the sharp struts pressing into her back. She was home, thank all the suns. That was just too close.

She closed her eyes and breathed. Blanking her mind, she slowed and deepened her shallow panting, reveling in the quiet...no, not working.

The whole slow-motion escape replayed in her head like a horror vid. Maintaining her carefully crafted persona was so rad-blasted hard. She'd done it; strolling the passages, gawking a bit, seemingly fascinated by every performer along the way. She didn't waste any time on the awful one outside her shuttle airlock.

She'd considered stunning the dark-haired man and hoping nobody noticed, but he was good, staying back and blending into the crowd. Stunning him meant taking down a lot of beings, innocents caught in the crossfire. And anyone stunned on this station would be robbed before the authorities reacted. If they reacted at all.

Enough. She wasn't out of danger, not until she left the system. Leaving the station might be tricky, depending on who was after her and why. Sucking in a big breath, Saree pushed off the chilly hatch, happy she no longer shook like a thruster on a loose pivot joint.

Saree strode to the pilot's seat, the worn, dark gray plas tiles beneath her feet popping a tiny bit with every step, the cracking comfortably normal. She patted Big Beige on her way. Saree paused mid-step, her hand hovering over the frequency standard maintenance case. Maybe it was time. She had no offense; she should maximize her defenses.

Facing Big Beige, she planted her feet and put her hand on the case's top-mounted security sensor. "Hal, implement Security Protocol Zeta."

Hal's smooth, calm, human male voice replied. "Security

Protocol Zeta initiated. Passphrase, please."

At Hal's light tenor tones, her tight shoulder muscles unwound. "Hickory dickory dock, the Sa'sa ran up the tetrahedron." She winced at the bite of the DNA sampler.

"Security Protocol Zeta implemented. Please note, the additional security measures will add approximately thirteen point two seconds to maintenance case release. This could be fatal during an emergency evacuation."

"Noted, Hal, and risk accepted. Thank you."

"You are welcome, Saree."

She walked to the pilot's seat and plopped down. Under her weight, the seat sighed and creaked, the seen-better-days padding almost flat. The smooth, light gray pleather under her hands was dark from decades of use. But she didn't care if it looked old and worn—the shuttle systems were top-notch. And sitting here in the pilot's seat meant escaping, control, safety.

Well, no. Safety was an illusion. But she was safer.

Finding a fold transport to take her and her shuttle far away from Dronteim was her first priority. A trustworthy one leaving soon—very soon. But there was no sense in escaping a black hole just to fold into a supernova. She had to find the right folder.

Sweeping a hand across the main control area, Saree entered her security codes, the big shuttle screens lighting in her standard display. She brought up the station security vid outside her shuttle. The black-haired man was still there, using his holo in security mode, concealing his face.

"Saree, you appear to be in some distress. Would you like a calmer?"

"No, thank you, Hal." She'd never bothered to change Hal's

3

programming to remove the default to mood-altering substances. One of these days, she'd have to do it herself or allow Hal to compile a personality profile. But allowing Hal to develop a profile meant more data available for exploitation if someone got through her net defenses. Better to leave the former inhabitant's in place, and do a little more work herself, even if it meant putting up with some oddities. Besides, sometimes Hal's predictability was strangely comforting, especially in his ultra-calm voice.

"Some Jhinzer tea?"

And sometimes, he was annoying. "Not now, Hal," she bit out. She had to get out of here. Tea could wait. Maybe she would make those profile mods.

"My apologies, Saree."

She scanned her shuttle status—everything ready—and relaxed in the chair a little more. Initiating external net access to Dronteim Station, she called up the departing interstellar space fold transport schedule. Even if the surveillance was her sometimes too-vivid imagination combined with her understandable paranoia—doubtful—she'd be better off leaving, fast.

Saree pulled up the Guild priority list and set her standard match program running between the two. But wait—she needed to leave now. Inserting 'departure time' as the new number three criteria, Saree tried to relax while the program calculated. It shouldn't take long out here on the rim. Dronteim was rated 'frontier-safe' by The Guide™ but it was still the frontier of human space; criminal organizations and pirates abounded.

So, which one was after her on Dronteim Station? Saree knew the man with the black hair and olive skin was following—no, hunting—her, but she didn't know why. There were a lot of reasons to target a young female human alone in the fringe. Was she a target of opportunity, or did they know who she was?

A chime sounded, startling her. Saree frowned. Lost in her head again. A bad habit for a solo traveler—being in her shuttle didn't equal safety, no matter how secure she felt at the moment. Glancing at the top matches between available fold transports and Guild requirements, she grimaced. Maybe she needed the tea after all. At times like these, she missed Ia'asan and the clutch. Life was a lot simpler in the co-pilot's chair.

And having real, live backup, even if it wasn't human? Priceless.

Saree studied the fold transport match list again. Blast and rad. None of the choices were good. There weren't many folders departing in the next thirty standard days and none of them were ideal. She snorted. Most were poor at best. Either they were fixed-route locals, quick but potentially criminal, or unknown and unrated.

She removed two of the transports immediately—they had ties to Familia, and Familia was far too curious about her, both in general and specifically here. The black-haired, olive-skinned man had the 'Familia look.' She checked the station vid again. The man was gone, but did he give up? There was no way to know.

The next possibility, Universe-Tera, was a good line known for their dependability and security, but this particular folder was ancient, slow and on a milk run.

What was a milk run, anyway? She shook the thought away. A question for another time—she had more important orbits to achieve.

The final folder on the list was a relatively new company, with little available on the net. Saree dug deeper, despite her instincts yelling, 'Run!' Lightwave Fold Transport appeared to be a single-ship company, with mixed reviews. She filtered out the obvious bot-generated reviews, but nothing cleared.

Scrolling down, she read the individual entries, rather than relying on the aggregate. She tapped an impatient rhythm on the armrest. This was taking too much time, but folding into the unknown wasn't smart.

Some shuttles left bare-bones comments of 'adequate,' 'sufficient,' and similar condemning-with-faint-praise statements, but a few said more. The recent reviews raved about the food, a big surprise—often, folders barely fed you at all, and with the cheapest pre-made stuff they could find.

One entry raved about the speed, precision, and security, but warned the captain put the wellbeing of his transport and shuttles above every other consideration. Which didn't seem like a negative to her; the fringe was dangerous. And if the folder didn't survive, none of the shuttles would.

Many of the other comments said the captain was cold and all business, but that seemed like a plus. If he were all business, he wouldn't be looking into her business, now would he? Just another set of strangers passing by—lonely, but safe.

She thumped her fingers against the chair arms impatiently. Lightwave would get her to one of the higher-priority jobs, although that particular job didn't pay the fold costs. But...Cygnus was light years away, on the fringes of known space. Getting away from Dronteim system was a very big plus— signs of Familia were everywhere.

Bringing up The Guide™ listing for Cygnus, she scanned it.

Not much Familia in Cygnus, another big plus, although there were plenty of other typical frontier dangers listed. Except for Cygnus Prime, but if she could afford planetfall on Deneb, she wouldn't be doing this. Saree huffed out a laugh.

Jittering in her chair, she initiated external net access again, and searched for more reviews, tracing Lightwave's travels. Neither Lightwave nor its crew had much of a net signature, but there was no sign of criminal activity or behavior. Apparently, Lightwave kept their noses clean, doing their job and nothing more. Or someone was cleaning up after them. Not likely; not for a single ship in the fringes.

Saree's fingers drummed harder and faster on the thin pleather, echoing her impatience. Nothing but pressure from Gov Human raised Cygnus's priority—whatever mega-corporation owned the system also owned someone in Gov Human. So, human-centric population and government, lots of high-priority, low-pay jobs, no Familia, fringe of nowhere frontier—the perfect place for her.

Saree finished her chair-arm drum solo with a flourish. Lightwave Fold Transport was it. She sent a message to Lightwave, to confirm availability and price, and started the computer calculating the transfer orbit from the station to the fold transport pickup orbit, matching Lightwave's parameters. Surprisingly, she got a reply from Lightwave before she'd finished double-checking the computer's calculations. The price was as quoted, they had one slot available and would depart after she docked.

"Hal, is there anything unusual in this contract?"

"Yes, Saree. This provision states: 'Shuttle owner and pilot must contact Lightwave Fold Transport with human-spectrum vid and voice-enabled before contract confirmation.'"

Hmm. Saree considered the provision. Unusual, but not unique. It might signal xenophobia, but it might not, and since her DNA was human, it didn't matter. She may as well get it done. Lightwave would see nothing but slightly shabby gray plas behind her; they wouldn't get any real intel from this vid except her face.

Initiating the comm link, Saree wished again for Jhinzer tea while she waited. She cracked a smile. Despite not allowing a true personality profile, Hal knew her well.

"Shuttle Centauri Kilo-Uniform-Tango-Six-Zero-One-Five-Four-Four, state the name of your vessel, owner, pilot, and other occupants," a computer-generated voice announced.

"Shuttle Centauri Kilo-Uniform-Tango-Six-Zero-One-Five-Four-Four, called Fortuna Lucia, absentee owner Centauri University, Pilot Candidate Scholar Cary Sessan, no other occupants." The shuttle's name came with it, but the Familia-tinged designation had served her well as an initial cover and distraction in the past. Overall, it was fortunate indeed.

A face appeared in the holo projected in front of her. Human, male, cinnamon-brown skin, thick black brows glowering above dark brown eyes. Pretty eyes, but cold like the outermost planet in a dying star system. A faint scar across the right side of his forehead, bisecting his eyebrow, showed through short dark brown hair. His nose, prominent and slightly hooked, presided over compressed lips in a square face. He was the definition of a man who'd seen bad things and was ready for more. Not a bad attitude for a fold transport pilot. If he was the pilot.

Saree snickered inside. No matter his role on Lightwave, no one would ever mistake him for a vid star, so why smile? "Scholar Sessan, you may approach. Turn your controls over to Lightwave for docking as specified in your instructions. Do you have any questions?"

"No, Pilot? Captain?" A name or a title would be nice...

"Please transfer funds and initiate your release from the station now, Scholar. We will depart after you dock." The screen blanked.

Humph. Well, that explained the 'cold, all business' comments. 'Rude' might be a better term after insisting on a face-to-face, but beggars couldn't be choosers. She wanted a quick departure, and she was getting one. And she wasn't vid-star material either— why would he waste time staring at her unremarkable face, with the same tan skin and mud-brown eyes and hair shared by the vast majority of space-traveling humanity? Still, why not take a few seconds to introduce himself? Suns, why insist on the vid at all? He didn't ask her anything.

Just as well. More talking meant more chances to get in trouble, and she needed to leave Dronteim—immediately. Saree snorted out a laugh. Oh, the irony of being upset by rudeness, when she'd done so much worse to so many.

Initiating the station undocking procedure, she waited for the station release. Thankfully, she didn't have to talk to a live person, just transfer credits, a ridiculous number for her very short stay. The docking clamps released and the station pushed her away into the transit zone, and Saree sighed in relief. The man chasing her wasn't well connected in Dronteim or hadn't made the necessary bribes to hold her.

Saree engaged the station-approved flight path, the shuttle

thrusters shoving her back into her chair until the grav generators kicked in. While they flew to the rendezvous point, she confirmed her credit transfer to Lightwave.

Confirmation complete, she set her controls using the codes specified in the contract, checked the transfer was to Lightwave, not some pirate, and disabled her meteor shielding. Reluctantly, Saree removed her hands from the controls. She hated not flying her ship, but this was standard procedure for interstellar folders — they were big credit investments.

The docking maneuver was smooth and uneventful. Relieved to be outbound, Saree completed the main engine shut-down procedures, the shuttle checks and made minimal net connections with Lightwave. She escaped Dronteim, and not a minute too soon. Safe.

Sagging with sheer relief in the pilot's chair, Saree blew out a breath and deliberated her options. Join the other travelers or stay here in her shuttle? She checked Lightwave's local time; their standard day aligned with Dronteim Station. Unusual. They must have been in orbit for a long time.

Indicators flashed on the main screen, drawing her attention back to C2—they were moving. Guess the glowering man— whoever he was—hadn't been kidding about leaving when she docked. They wanted to leave this back-of-beyond system as badly as she did.

Or someone was chasing them too.

Well, if that was the case, there was little she could do about it now. Not without making things worse. If she went back, whoever was after her might be successful. Besides, independent folders were always a risk—nothing new there.

Downloading the list of other shuttles folding with Lightwave, she scanned them. She didn't notice anything unusual. Except....one of the shuttles was from a Familia system. That wasn't uncommon, and it didn't always mean Familia ownership.

She dug a little further and frowned. But not listing the owner or pilot was suspicious. Great. Maybe she'd stay in her shuttle. Her rations were a little boring, but boredom beat danger. It wouldn't be the first time she'd stayed on her shuttle—she'd folded on some scary transports. When your choices were all bad...

She scrolled through the list of Lightwave's amenities. The usual observation lounge—although what you'd observe from a screen in the lounge versus a screen or holo anywhere else was a mystery—a dining facility and a big physical fitness module.

Well now, that would be worth leaving for. She could churn out klicks on her barebones treadmill, but why, when there were better options? A good, hard phys session would clear the remaining tension and fear from her body. She frowned. But only if there was nothing to fear on Lightwave.

"Saree, Lightwave Fold Transport dining would like to know if you will be joining them for the constellation departure dinner. The message notes the kitchen is under the command of a student from Culinary Institute Sirius."

Oooh. A very good reason to leave the shuttle. CIS trained some of the most inventive human chefs in the universe. Remembering one particular story, she chuckled. 'Inventive' didn't always equal 'delicious' to non-gourmets. There were several tales of practically inedible meals because a student chef was too wrapped up in one ingredient, or too intent on a certain 'look' to think about common tastes. Saree pursed her lips in thought.

This would be a once-in-a-lifetime experience. She'd never eat a meal created by a CIS graduate. Even after she paid her Guild debt, she'd never earn enough credits for that kind of experience.

But more importantly, a CIS student on board meant Lightwave was safe and stable—there'd be plenty of offers from other, bigger folders, so this one must have something special. Creativity required basic human security. Lightwave looked better every second. "Hal, please confirm my attendance with my thanks for the invitation. Also, please confirm dress requirements and the time."

"Certainly, Saree. Stand by." Thirty-nine seconds later, Hal said, "Constellation departure and arrival dinners are formal. All other meals are informal. There is no guarantee the CIS student will prepare meals other than the formal ones."

Before she could ask, he continued. "Historical data suggests at least one meal a day will be prepared by the student. It also implies there will be no more than twenty and no less than ten beings for dinner. I will set a thirty-minute warning for you. The warning will chime in approximately forty-five point two minutes."

"Thank you, Hal."

"You are welcome, Saree."

Computer experts insisted assistant programs weren't Artificial Intelligences, didn't have personalities and thanking them was a useless ritual, but Saree always erred on the side of caution. What did a little politeness cost? She grinned. And if the AIs ever took over, maybe she'd survive.

More to the point, she had forty-five minutes to work off the tension and stress of her slow-motion escape. Opening her clothes storage, she threw on some workout clothes. Saree picked up her sweat-soaked Scholar robes, keeping them at arm's length and throwing them in the cleaner, her nose wrinkling at the stench of fear. At the airlock, she said, "Hal, if you've been allowed access, please check the passageway outside the shuttle and the entire phys mod for beings."

"Certainly, Saree. I see no beings of any kind. Would you like me to send a remote through the rest of the ship?"

Hmm. Saree pondered. Not a bad idea, but if the remote was spotted, it would put a cloud of suspicion on her right away. It wasn't worth it, not yet. "Not right now. Thank you anyway, Hal. I just don't want to be surprised going through the hatch."

"After your return to the shuttle today, that is logical."

Indeed. Saree put a towel, bev-tainer of water and stunner in a tote. "Hal, please secure the shuttle after I leave, and let me know if anyone attempts to enter or if there are any serious attempts on our net-interface."

"Yes, Saree."

"Thank you, Hal."

"You are welcome, Saree."

She worked through the airlock hatches, noting the folder's airlock status lights worked correctly and the hatches swung smoothly, the seals shiny. Proper maintenance was always a good sign. Looking both ways along Lightwave's passageway, Saree saw nothing but gray plas flooring and bland, beige walls decorated with bright orange and black 'emergency escape' labels.

She sniffed. Clean, too. Tension in her shoulders and back

eased, and she headed toward the phys mod, the plas decking pleasantly supple under her feet. As she walked, her wariness returned—there were a lot of escape pods for a small shuttle folder. Was Lightwave bigger than she thought?

Pulling up Lightwave's passenger map, she saw the ship was built, like most fold transports, in a big cube. As she'd remembered, there were eight passenger shuttle bays, two per side. Lightwave's shuttles took the two bays on top. The main engines and fold generators sat on the bottom of the cube. Crew quarters, air handlers, hydroponics and cargo bays were normally below the folder's shuttles—Lightwave's map showed no details, the top and bottom levels marked 'restricted'—a good security precaution. Hmm. Maybe she should let Hal snoop a little.

The middle layer of the cube was dedicated to passengers, with the shuttle airlocks exiting to a passageway circling Lightwave. Inside the passageway, the lounge took a fourth of the space on one end, the end farthest from her shuttle bay. The physical fitness module took up a fourth of the closest end, with the dining area and kitchen in the middle. Additional hatchways allowed passage between each area and to the surrounding passageway.

Maybe Lightwave was extremely safety conscious? Along with the plethora of escape pods, interior safety hatches stood ready to divide the passageway, everything sparkling clean with no signs of poor maintenance, like lubricant leaks or corrosion. Saree approved; all too many folders skimped on interior emergency bulkheads and their upkeep.

Stepping into the fitness facility, she scanned for beings while she moved away from the hatch. No one here—perfect. There was always one weird being hanging around, watching, making her nervous. Shaking the thought away, she surveyed the equipment. The phys mod was exceedingly well equipped, a pleasant surprise.

Saree wandered through the machines. Rows of aerobic phys machines: treadmills, configurable for flat, stairs or uneven surfaces, bikes, rowers and a few machines she'd never seen before—for non-bipedal beings, maybe? Racks of free weights stood along one wall—secured against gravity loss—and lots of different benches. In the middle, a large, open space with firm but springy matting for group classes or gymnastics.

Saree looked up. The walls and ceiling were covered with climbing holds, bars, rings, ropes, and other apparatus. All of it seemed sturdy—professional-quality—if unimaginatively coated in black and light gray, with the occasional accent of white.

She pushed a bike but it didn't move. Everything was secured and spotless—it smelled fresh too, a combination of citrus and sinus-clearing chemicals. Cleanliness was difficult to maintain in the recycled air of space travel. Somebody on Lightwave was serious about fitness. And maintenance. She surveyed the equipment again. Well, she had a treadmill—she could run anytime. She had no idea what half these machines were, but the rowers were obvious. She would row.

Sitting on the rower, she slipped her feet under the hold bar and the machine adjusted to fit her. Saree jolted in surprise. She gazed in wonder at the holo appearing around her. A full surround on a phys machine? This was big credit stuff. She skimmed through the pre-programmed options once, then a second time, slower, to take them all in.

Saree whistled. Very big credit stuff. She'd never seen these kinds of routines on a phys machine. Deep jungle, in quick but stealth mode, where your score depended on speed, stealth, and precision maneuvering? Open water mode, scored on distance while being tossed by waves ranging from nothing to three meters? Whitewater kayaking of varying levels, the judging on speed and survival or precision and speed?

Wait a minute. She glared at the holo, the tension she'd shed returning with a vengeance. Who needs this kind of training?

Brushing away the surround holo, Saree surveyed the phys mod again, peering at the walls. There, under the plain beige coating, partially obscured by a climbing hold. She strode to the wall, scrutinizing the irregularity. Under the bland, but pristine light tan paint, was the slightly raised outline of a shield. Uh oh. Her stomach, filling with dread, sank to her feet. She subvocalized to Hal through her e-torc. "Hal, can you send a vid to my location? Or use my e-torc? There's something I'd like you to image."

"Certainly, Saree. What do you want imaged?"

"There was a shield on this wall—it's been painted over. Can you image and analyze to see what it looks like under the coating?"

"I will attempt to, Saree. I will scan in multiple frequencies, and display the results for you in the shuttle. Please stay in place. I will let you know when I am finished, or if I require a better sensor."

"Thank you, Hal."

"You are welcome, Saree." Fourteen seconds later, Hal said, "I have completed the scan. You may now move."

Saree forced herself back to the rower—no matter how hard she stared, she couldn't see through paint. If what she suspected was true, there was nothing she could do about it now unless she wanted a long, boring trip back to Dronteim Station—and a loss of all those credits she'd transferred to Lightwave. And she'd definitely be in danger. She wasn't in danger right now—there could be a perfectly innocent reason for the shield.

Maybe.

Setting her e-torc to alert her of any movement in the phys mod, she sat down on the rower and chose the extreme tide program. The workout would be stimulating and she'd be too busy to worry. "Hal, please let me know if anyone approaches." Even if her e-torc didn't work, Hal would.

"Of course, Saree."

Twenty-three minutes later, she slid off the rower and collapsed on the flat, still floor. Sweat ran from every pore and her arms shook with exhaustion. Despite her best effort, her score was laughably low. She shook her head in wonder. The machine replicated the sight, sounds, and motions of the waves and pressures of tides, and the scent of seawater—the only thing missing was salt spray on her face. Saree tried to huff out a chuckle. She was producing plenty on her own. Good thing she wasn't prone to motion sickness. She pulled the towel out of her bag and mopped her face.

After sitting longer than she cared to admit, she rolled over onto her knees, and levered herself up on wobbly arms and legs. Looking down at her bag, she sighed and started stretching. She needed a little more recovery time before attempting to pick up her bag. She'd laugh about it, but it would take too much effort. Stretches complete, she hoisted her bag and tottered across the phys mod.

Tomorrow might be painful. Digging out an electrolyte tab, she popped it in the bev-tainer, sipping in the vain hope it would help her recover. The workout did achieve her objective; the stress and tension were gone. A clicking and whirring behind her made her spin—a cleaner bot trundled its way toward the puddle of sweat she'd left on the floor. Wow. They were serious about sanitation on Lightwave. Saree shook her head and continued, slowly, back to her shuttle.

Once locked inside her shuttle, she double-checked the utility connections to the folder and entered the sani-mod. Saree sagged into the hot water pounding down, massaging her muscles and sluicing away the sweat. One of the big advantages of a fold transport was a real water shower. She couldn't stay long, but it sure beat the sonic scrub-and-vac she'd do otherwise.

After enjoying an extravagant but within-limits shower, she contemplated her monotonous clothing selection. The only formal outfit she could wear was the long black tunic, with the traditional scholar's cowl in the purple patterns of Centauri University, and matching leggings. The uniform would cement her scholar persona in everyone's mind. She dressed quickly, finishing with the scarlet and dark blue patterned cords showing her area of study.

Reaching out, she stroked one hand down the soft, sensuous silk in the back of the closet, and sighed. She'd love to wear the beautiful, flowing dress of tazan silk, dyed to match the glorious shaded colors of an Old Earth sunset. But wearing it would blow her cover—Scholars couldn't afford tazan silk. She snorted. She couldn't either, but a lucky barter worked out well for everyone. Maybe someday she'd wear it somewhere other than here in her shuttle.

She had no hope of ever wearing it for anyone else.

"Saree, you have six minutes before departure time. Would you like to see the image I've reconstructed for human vision capabilities?"

"Yes, Hal—please display it on the main screen." Walking forward, she stopped in shock, her heart crashing to the floor. Examining the giant stylized bird, all the colors of fire on a black background, she dropped her head, then the rest of her body, collapsing in the pilot's seat. She'd been right, blast it all into a black hole. Right beyond her wildest nightmares.

Lightwave Fold Transport was a troop ship.

A Phalanx Eagle troop ship.

CHAPTER TWO

"Saree, you must depart in one minute, or you will be late," Hal said.

Blast and rad. There was no time for a trip down memory lane, and she didn't want to go there anyway—it wasn't a pretty place. She glanced at the mirrored screen—she looked normal even if old terror still racked her—and headed to the airlock. "Hal, please inform me of any attempts on shuttle security. Also..."

Hal would monitor her e-torc, but the external vid capabilities on it were limited; its primary purpose was displaying holos. She was surprised Hal imaged the shield.

She wished he hadn't.

"Send a vid remote with me and let me know of any security issues you note."

"Certainly, Saree. Remote will be placed...now." A slight buzz near her left ear, then silence. "It is placed in your hair at your left temple."

Already? Was Hal sending extra sensors whether she asked or not? The sensor must be tiny—there was no weight at all. "Thank you, Hal."

"Certainly, Saree. Enjoy your dinner."

Exiting the hatch, she contemplated the phrase. Hal had never said that before. Huh. Well, she'd worry about Hal later—she had other things to worry about, like the crew of Lightwave and the other passengers. Automatically checking the hatch and airlock security, she walked down the passageway toward the dining hall, the unblemished, bland, beige walls 'decorated' with more escape pod markings. The number of escape pods should have tipped her off—far more than a shuttle folder of this size required. She pushed her memories away. This wasn't the first military surplus fold transport she'd contracted. But she'd never run into her past quite so abruptly. It was...disconcerting.

However, it didn't mean the people on Lightwave were Phalanx Eagle, only the folder. It was a whole lot of nothing. She turned right into the dining facility and stepped to the side, her back against the wall and a pleasant but bland expression on her face, surveying the room thoroughly.

Suns. Saree let her eyes widen in surprise and an 'o' form on her lips, true to her persona, but she was surprised. Shocked, even. This room didn't look anything like a troop ship dining hall—even a retired, repurposed troop ship dining hall.

A huge, delicate crystalline chandelier floated above an equally huge rectangular dining table, suitable for twenty human-sized beings. A dozen beings, appearing all human standard, already sat at the table. The man she'd spoken to on the vid before departure sat at the head of the table, his heavy black brows still glowering above his stern, cold visage. She couldn't tell how tall he was, but his shoulders hid the chair back. Silver rank stripes decorated the massive shoulders in dark blue coveralls. He must be the Captain—and not a man to cross.

She forced herself to scan the remaining beings for weapons and other threats. She didn't spot any, but few of the beings were relaxed, especially not the Captain. She assumed everyone was armed. Traveling in the fringes of known space required constant vigilance and readiness.

Reflections from the crystals in the chandelier shimmered and dazzled her eyes for a moment, but she continued surveying. Fine china in an elaborate Old Earth pattern of glittering gold rested on layered tablecloths of rich dark brown, ruby red and shimmering gold. Matching materials covered the high-backed chairs, gold tassels tied behind each chair. The centerpiece was ice, carved into an elaborate flower, surrounded by leafy greenery.

Even the walls of the dining hall were elegant. Below a chair rail, rich, deep mahogany wood paneling; above, a subtle pattern reminiscent of sandy earthen walls bathed in the barely pink light of a yellow star's sunrise. And the scents? Heavenly—oh, suns, a mouth-watering, enticing aroma, even if she had no idea what foods the combination of deliciousness signified.

Simply stunning—she'd stepped back into an Old Earth vid of a formal dinner. The CIS *did* believe in providing a 'dining experience' rather than just a meal. She could hardly wait to see if the food matched the scents and scenery, so she proceeded toward the table.

One of the beings stood and walked to her, meeting her halfway with a small bow. The tall human male wore a dark blue ship coverall with rank on the shoulders and braid around the lower sleeves. It wasn't a Phalanx Eagle uniform; a Lightwave Fold Transport logo rode on his left arm, and a tag reading 'Purser' on his chest. He was tall, over two meters, and his wide shoulders and narrow waist were framed by the tailored ship coverall—no adjustable straps for this officer.

Moving with unconscious grace, he almost danced his way to her. His pretty, but still masculine, face was a longish oval, capped by long, thick blond hair pulled back into a tail at the back of his elegant neck. His eyes were a pale, piercing gray-blue, framed by thick blond lashes, above a patrician nose. He stretched out a hand, and she stared for a moment, surprised by the rather archaic gesture, and placed hers on it. He smiled and, not at all lightly or subtly, squeezed and caressed it. His cologne, dark and musky, screaming 'sex,' wafted across. Clearly, a man who knew he was attractive and used it to his advantage.

"Scholar Sessan, I am Purser Grant Lowe. Welcome to Lightwave. For tonight, you will sit here." Leading her around the table, he pulled out a chair mid-way down. He didn't, thankfully, push it in behind her, so she seated herself, and he returned to his place at the end opposite the Captain. Before he could sit down, another being appeared.

Posing dramatically right in the middle of the hatchway, the human male displayed a superior look on his long, sharp-featured face, framed by shoulder-length waves of dark brown hair. He modeled a dark brown suit, a shade darker than his hair, with

23

gold accents running along the edges of the fitted, waist-length jacket, and an elaborately folded dark red cravat nestled around his neck above a snowy white pleated shirt. The same gold pattern ran down the sides of the skin-tight pants, easy to see since his dramatic pose was turned to the side, one hand on his hip. He expected them to be dazzled. Saree hid a smile.

The purser walked to the personage and brandished an arm toward the table with a half-bow. Even with his dazzling clothes and persona, his slight figure couldn't compete with Purser Lowe's physique and grace. "Artiste Borgia, welcome to Lightwave. For tonight, you will sit here." Purser Lowe led him to the empty chair next to the head of the table, where the presumed Captain sat, his glower deepening to a scowl. Borgia gave the Captain a short nod and stepped in front of his chair. He seemed surprised the purser didn't push his chair in behind him, and Saree bit back another smile.

The Familia ship was no longer a mystery—the Artiste was traveling incognito, at least to the public at large, to his next l'Opera performance. What was he doing way out here? There weren't any l'Opera productions within parsecs of this middle-of-nowhere system. Hmm. 'Artiste' was a common cover story. She'd be cautious around Artiste Borgia; she couldn't over or underplay her role. She had a lot of research to do. Maybe he was making several folds with Lightwave?

Purser Lowe, still standing at the foot of the table, cleared his throat and the sparse chatter quieted. "Gentle beings, welcome to Lightwave Fold Transport. Captain Ruhger—" he waved a hand at the still-frowning man at the head of the table "—myself, Purser

Grant Lowe, and the crew welcome all of you. If there is anything you require to make this journey more pleasant, please let us know. We cannot guarantee anything beyond the contractual terms, but we will attempt to fulfill reasonable requests." He was looking at the artiste, a bland expression on his face as he said 'reasonable.'

Saree guessed there had already been unreasonable ones.

"Chef-in-Training Loreli will be starting the service shortly. First, I would like to introduce Maintenance Officer Chief Bhoher." He waved to an older man seated down the table from her who nodded gravely. He wore the same Lightwave dark blue coveralls, his name and title on his breast, but his looked a little wrinkled.

"Security Officers Tyron and Katryn Phazeer will be your servers tonight as a favor to the Chef. A few notes about Lightwave. We provide water and power per your contract. We will charge for amounts above that use at the overage rate stated in your contract, and excessive use will result in metering. We are a small transport with limited resources. Please be cognizant of this." Now, the purser was carefully not looking at the artiste.

He continued, "The transport is full. There is an automated reservation system for some of the physical fitness equipment and the main gaming area of the lounge—please refer to it and the rules of use. The observation lounge is open to all beings who can tolerate human standard at all times, and auto-beverage service is available, along with some snacks. The dining schedule is in your contract. Please avoid the dining facility at other times, as our Chef-in-Training requires time to prepare and study. There are no guarantees Chef Loreli will prepare any meals other than our formal dinners, but the standard fare is very good under Chef's guidance."

Purser Lowe scanned the table with an amiable expression. "Again, welcome to Lightwave. Please introduce yourselves to your seatmates later—full introductions would be too time-consuming and might interrupt Chef's production, a total tragedy of massive proportions formerly unknown in the universe." The purser grinned at something behind Saree, and she turned to look, then stared.

The vision in the hatchway was as dazzling as the dining room. No, more so. Much more so. Again, it was no effort to put on the shocked and surprised face of her scholar persona. A rather large human female dressed in chef's whites posed in the hatchway, but those weren't standard chef's whites. The head to toe, form-fitting, startling white wasn't in the same galaxy with 'standard.'

The sleeves and upper part of the dress were sheer, stretched over almost exposed and very generous—assets—perched above a corset of shiny white material, with buckles of crystal-covered silver marching down the front. The cinched-in waist looked painfully tight, above wide, curved hips. Below the corset, a gown of white, scaled material clung to the being's thighs, flaring above the knees into a bias-cut skirt with fold upon fold of material, the hem dazzling with long strings of crystal beading, like a fantasy sea creature. Below the skirt, shiny white, ridiculously high platform boots peeked out. If Saree tried to wear those, she'd break her neck.

A tiny caricature chef's toque perched jauntily on a bobbed, chin-length mass of shiny white hair, with crystal ear coverings spiking up and through the hair. Chef's face was a moon of smooth, ultra-dark chocolate, with big amber eyes surrounded by long, sparkling white lashes, and finished with a generous mouth of shocking scarlet. Assigning age was difficult, but Saree guessed, based on all the other cues, somewhere around thirty standards. And while her heaving bosom said 'female,' something hinted otherwise. Perhaps Chef was gender-fluid? Saree would have to ask about Chef's preferred pronoun.

All in all, a picture hard to forget. Also, a picture hard to look past, but she did, noting the presence of subtle bulges low on the corset, disguised below the ruffles. Weapons or spices? Impossible to tell.

Saree assumed the food would be equally unforgettable. Hopefully, in a good way.

"Darhlings!" the Chef exclaimed in a low, throaty voice, spreading her arms in a dramatic gesture. "Tonight, I present a feast to you! A feast for the senses. A feast which will never be forgotten. A feast beyond compare! A feast you will rave about for years to come! I now present the first course, a Langrathian bisque, with rare black Cerian truffle shavings, accompanied by François Bruschetta a la garlique. Enjoy!"

Two humans, one male, one female, exited the kitchen bearing trays of small china bowls and napkin-covered baskets. They were also in white, but theirs were Lightwave uniform ship coveralls rather than custom designer-wear. Both wore black harnesses securing hand weapons of every type; stunners, blasters, knives, and others Saree had no names for. A chill ran down her spine—

why would they need that much hardware for a dinner party?

The female plopped a bowl down with a rattle of china in front of her and a basket thunked above her place setting. Despite the rough delivery, the bowl released a mouthwatering scent of rich, browned butter tinged with the saltiness of a sea. White wine poured into her glass. Saree looked around at her fellow diners, wide-eyed, and then at the Captain, telegraphing her need for a cue.

The Captain scowled at the Chef, then down at his bowl. With a sigh, he picked up a spoon, the tiny utensil lost in his wide, thick hand. Raising it, he looked around the table with a pained-looking grimace, and intoned, "Enjoy." He spooned up the soup and swallowed. The corners of his mouth lifted for a split-second. The Chef lit up with triumph and whirled with a flounce, the crystal beads clattering, as she retired to the kitchen.

Saree didn't try to cover her delight—this was the best theater she'd seen for a long time. Still, if the soup made the scowling Captain smile, it must be delicious. She spooned up the bisque. The flavors melted into her tongue in a symphony of delight and she bit back a moan. The richness of cream and butter, along with small pieces of tender shellfish, and a subtle spice combination—it nearly sent her swooning. She closed her eyes to enhance the tasting experience. Slowly, she continued spooning up the delicious concoction, her entire attention on the thick, decadent creation.

Everyone quickly consumed the tiny bowls, the small portion offsetting the richness of the soup—but if offered more, Saree would eat until she was sick. The "François Bruschetta" were standard garlic toast rounds, but they complemented the bisque perfectly, as did the wine. She sighed, scraping the last spoonful from the bottom of the bowl. No wonder the stern Captain put up with the flamboyant Chef.

After the bowls and baskets were removed, the Chef appeared again, proclaiming, "Sirius mixed greens with Ne'tune moonflowers and dressing l'Opera!"

Borgia nodded graciously at the Chef. He must think this was an homage to his presence. Looking at the slight stiffness of the Chef's return nod, Saree had her doubts. But who cared? There was more delicious food waiting. Sirius mixed greens were common; the Culinary Institute had developed them decades ago for hydroponic growth in space. But Ne'tune moonflowers were new to her, and l'Opera dressing was time-consuming and expensive, with special extracts and oils. She'd never tasted it.

Spearing a few tender green and red leaves, Saree lifted the fork. An enticing mix of sweet and spice washed across her palate and the flavors burst on her tongue. She chewed slowly to get the full effect. Even the aftertaste was exquisite. If plain greens tasted like this, what did a moonflower taste like? Forking one up, she found out—moonflowers were peppery, adding a burst of sharpness and a tiny bit of heat to the warm, spicy sweetness of the dressing. This was amazing—the best thing she'd ever eaten, hands down.

The salad course was followed by equally fabulous pasta, then fish, a palate-clearing savory ice, fowl, another palate-clearer of fruity sorbet, and a meat course, all accompanied by the perfect wines. A chocolate dessert concoction came next. The beautiful, exquisitely decorated, petit dark, light and white chocolate shells were filled with creamy goodness and stacked into an improbably high tower. Somehow, it tasted even better than it looked.

Tiny cups of espresso and a sweet dessert wine with a heavily veined sharp cheese finished the repast. Each course followed one on the other—Saree had little time to look at her dining companions, let alone introduce herself. And really, what little time there was, she needed to recover from the experience—such *amazing* food.

When the Chef appeared in the hatchway again, the entire table, except the Captain, leapt to their feet and applauded. Saree did too—she wasn't acting at all. An astounding meal, far and away the best thing she'd ever eaten, and her stomach groaned in approval. The Chef bowed and beamed, but her attention was on the Captain. He gave her a small nod and an even smaller, tight-lipped smile.

Chef staggered back, leaning against the hatchway, hands clenched above her(?)—Saree still wasn't sure—huge, heaving bosom. "My life is justified for another day! Thank you for allowing me the privilege to serve you!" She swept back into the kitchen, skirt clattering in her wake, and the applause died down.

Purser Lowe said, "Thank you for joining us. The meal schedule for the rest of the journey is in your contract. Please join us in the lounge so Chef may recover in peace," he finished with a grin.

Everyone smiled politely and pushed back from the table. Saree noted some of her dinner companions bypassed the lounge; many preferred the security and comfort of their shuttles. She did too, but it would be out of character for her to retreat now.

In the lounge, she refused another glass of wine from Porter Lowe, but accepted a cup of auto-bev tea, and made herself comfortable on an overstuffed soft chair in the far corner. She sniffed the tea discreetly. Jhinzer, but a lower grade. She sighed, then again as Artiste Borgia strode straight to her. Lucky her—dealing with Artistes was just her very favorite thing to do. With some effort, she forced a pleasant expression.

"Scholar," he said with a sweeping, but shallow, bow, "I am Borgia. I see you are from Centauri University and the College of Music. A fine institution, although it cannot compare with Univers Viennza for l'Opera. Are you a student of l'Opera, by chance?" His accent was full of rolling 'R's and 'Z's and he made dramatic gestures as he declaimed. With each wave of his arm, strong, sharp cologne assaulted her. Thank all the seven suns of Saga she'd been seated far down the table during the dinner.

Standing, she made a much plainer, but deeper bow. A Candidate Scholar couldn't afford to offend anyone, let alone someone in their field. "Oh no, Artiste Borgia. I couldn't dream of such studies—they would be far beyond my poor capabilities. No, I am a student of another Old Earth art, Filk."

His head snapped back and he scowled. "Filk? What is Filk? I've never heard of such music!" The implication was clear—it couldn't be real music if Artiste Borgia hadn't heard of it. She noticed most of the people weren't conversing—no, they were listening to Borgia with undisguised curiosity. She didn't blame them; he was loud and melodramatic. Why make small talk when you could watch live theater? Dinner and a show! Actually,

31

between the Chef and the Artiste, two shows. Who would have looked for such entertainment on a mid-rated folder?

Really, Saree, be nice. Theater is what he did for a living—self-promotion is the mainstay of any artist in any field. Even if her cover allowed it, she'd never publicly declare her distaste for l'Opera; she wouldn't embarrass anyone. And she didn't want a fight. Not over art. She had far more important things to fight for.

She smiled politely and said, "Oh no, I wouldn't expect an *artiste* such as you to know anything about my extremely obscure field of study. Indeed, its very obscurity is why I study it—no one has before."

Saree shifted into droning lecture mode, copied from a professor, a tottering relic who mumbled the same lecture he'd giving for the past forty standards. "But, to answer your question, Filk is an Old Earth variation of a folk song tradition of performers and artists being the same, performing their songs to each other. Most of these songs have something to do with a literary form originating on Old Earth in the early space flight era called Science Fiction. Science Fiction changed when folding space became a reality, because the vast majority of the writers left Old Earth for new horizons. Science Fiction is still popular, but Filk has been lost to time and space."

Borgia rolled his eyes elaborately and shook his head. It was a wonder he didn't make himself dizzy. "Pah, folk music. Caterwauling, mostly. Not serious music." He sobered and narrowed his eyes. "Who would pay for such studies?"

She kept smiling. So many artistes denigrated everything not in their narrow field. "I pay for my research, Artiste. I received a small inheritance from distant relatives and I'm using it to finish my education. I fell in love with the idea of studying something no one else studies, so I'm putting my own money behind it. Unfortunately, there are few examples left of the Filk art form, so I travel, trying to find hidden gems and precursors. Would you like to hear about my dissertation? Or some of the songs I composed in the Filk style?" Saree looked up at him with hope, laughing inside at the horrified look in his eyes.

"Oh, Scholar, while I would *love* to hear all about your fascinating research, I *must* meet the rest of our fellow travelers!" He bowed, much plainer this time, and escaped to the other side of the room.

Blinking at his retreating back, she displayed wistful admiration. She noticed, from the corner of her eye, the Captain eying her speculatively. Had she gone too far? Or was he trying to figure out how to avoid hearing her dissertation? Most of the other passengers seemed to be, all of them moving away from her corner quickly. Sitting, she looked optimistically around the room and hid a smirk when Purser Lowe, accidentally making eye contact with her, grimaced. Even the fold orbit sex god wanted nothing to do with her. *Perfect.*

Or it should be perfect. She couldn't help but feel a little forlorn, alone in a room full of people. Again. *Stop, Saree. You're alive and free—that's good enough. It has to be.*

Artiste Borgia commandeered Lightwave's lounge like center stage in a l'Opera production. Overriding any attempts at conversation, he trumpeted his schedule of appearances on Deneb, their destination, and beyond, offering discounted tickets upon their arrival. Which was a good idea, because if she'd never heard of him, he probably wasn't great. Not that she was a fan of l'Opera—the Artiste's declamation of 'caterwauling' fit perfectly. Looking around the room, she rather doubted most of the occupants could afford to land on Deneb, the location of his next show.

Except for the couple he was speaking to. They appeared to be big fans. Not only did they have the adoring look of fans, but from the faintly green-tinged, bony, geometric panels of their skin, these two must be from Chelonii. Chelonians were DNA-fused with turtles before ethical researchers gave the practice up. Although the Chelonii adaptation was successful, most attempts at fusing were horrific—or fatal.

This adaptation was fortunate; Chelonii was a watery, swampy, hostile world filled with large, toothy carnivorous animals who thought humans were somewhat tasty and very, very slow and, therefore, the perfect snack. By creating an outer shell, Chelonians had a chance to deflect the initial bite, giving them the time to take out the animal with overwhelming firepower.

In general, Chelonians loved l'Opera and these two seemed to prove the stereotype. No one knew why; the Chelonii modifications prevented them from singing—their vocal cords were too stiff. Maybe it was the lack of ability? Whatever the reason, the annual l'Opera festival on Chelonii drew the biggest l'Opera stars and fans in the galaxy, despite the dismal conditions of rainy, stinky, monster-infested Chelonii. But the conditions didn't matter inside the humongous l'Opera complex; it was warm, dry and perfectly comfortable. The giant dome over the theaters, hotels, restaurants, and shops ensured visitors never had to venture outside for anything but the ride there and back, made on a comfortable, raised platform lev. No one had to experience the muck of Chelonii personally.

Chelonii also produced expert bodyguards—those bony plates provided one last layer of protection in the churning chaos of a riot. Highly trained and expensive, they were popular with those forced to deal with crowds, like politicians and entertainers. A pair was unusual; their client must be ridiculously wealthy. *If* these two were bodyguards, the usual reason Chelonii left their homeworld. Odd they'd be out here in this fringe system and headed to another one. They weren't wearing armor, just casual soft pants and shirts in shades of blue and green, so there wasn't an easy way to tell if they were on assignment.

No one needed bodyguards on Deneb, where the population and visitors were carefully screened and controlled. Maybe they were going on vacation—they could afford Deneb's fees. Or they were picking up a client?

Borgia continued extolling his prowess to the Chelonians, everyone else lost interest in his shameless self-promotion, and conversation spread among the other beings in the lounge. Saree took the opportunity to survey the lounge itself. A large, long rectangular room, painted with the same bland beige coating most of Lightwave. Filled with comfortable, soft seating in various shades of brown, low tables, also in dark brown, mellow lights and soft carpeting in an even darker brown, the room encouraged quiet discussions and, well, lounging.

There was a small self-serve bar area and large vid screens on each wall, to 'observe' the area outside. Right now, they showed random starscapes, since the view around Dronteim had little to recommend it.

It did not look anything like a Phalanx Eagle troop ship ready room. It did look like a man filled it—there was no attempt at design, just comfortable furnishings, all in shades of brown to hide dirt and match. They should let the Chef add a few pillows and objects de art to liven the room up; some bright colors would make it look a little less like a just-started terraforming project of mud and more mud.

Chef Loreli must have redecorated the dining room—there was no way both of these rooms came from the same mind.

One of the ship's officers approached Saree and bowed. "Scholar, welcome to Lightwave. I am Chief Engineer Bhoher." He frowned as if the introduction pained him. "Please call me Chief." Chief Bhoher was a centimeter or two taller than she, with a strong, wiry build. His light brown hair was cut close to his head, his pale face rectangular, with a square jaw and sharp cheekbones surrounding deep-set eyes of milk chocolate.

He seemed more hands-on than a typical 'chief'—his hands, while clean, showed years of work embedded in the thick skin, the kind experience grinds in and is impossible to remove without taking a lot of skin with it. Those years also showed in his face— he was older than the Captain or Purser, fifty or so standards. A faint scent of scorched lubricant clung to him.

She smiled, stood and returned his bow. "Thank you, Chief. It's a pleasure. I am Candidate Scholar Cary Sessan, of Centauri

University. I am researching primary sources to prove the assertions of my thesis."

"I wish you luck, Scholar. Please excuse me; I need to introduce myself to the others, then ready the fold generators."

"Of course, Chief. A pleasure meeting you."

He smiled tightly, bowed, and moved on to the next person. Clearly, the Chief was not a fan of social situations. He probably preferred machines to people—so many of his inclination did. At least he wasn't hinting at a fold orbit affair like the purser.

Saree looked around the room again—at the individuals this time, rather than the furnishings. Everyone seemed to be human, which wasn't unusual on a human-run folder. Since she was here, she should make an effort to meet some of the others. It would be easier to greet aliens—she didn't have to worry about slipping up, since pleasantries were all anyone exchanged with non-humans, unless there was a technical discussion. Or one was an expert in xeno relations.

So, who could she talk to? There, at the far end of the room— the woman who'd dined on her left mirrored Saree's position, sitting on a couch in the corner. Since no one was approaching either of them, she'd make the effort. Crossing the room, she smiled gently at the woman.

An older woman, from her attire not wealthy but not poor, she seemed content watching the other passengers. Her hair appeared to be a natural silver-gray, cut in a short but flattering style surrounding a round, pleasantly plump face with a matching body. Layered tunics over leggings in shades of gray and black were unobtrusive but also allowed for hidden weapons. Many would describe her as a pleasant, grandmother-type; Saree would reserve judgment.

As behooved their relative ages, Saree bowed deeply to the woman, and introduced herself.

The lady, still seated, returned her bow. "A pleasure to meet you, Scholar. I am Elise Schultz of Dronteim. I am going to visit my children and grandchildren on Rastaban-Asuia."

"A very long way for a visit. You aren't moving there?" A nosy thing to ask, but scholars were expected to be curious about everything. Saree could ask all kinds of questions others couldn't. She didn't always get answers, but humans were rarely offended by what she asked. Aliens? It depended.

"Yes, it is. It's my first-time off planet. Fortunately, my Lady knows the spaceways better than I. She was tired after dinner and returned to her shuttle, but she urged me to come meet everyone." Gentle Schultz smiled and waved a hand at the seat next to her. "Please join me. Everyone else can come to us, age and knowledge together."

Saree smiled back. "Thank you. That sounds lovely." She seated herself. "So, if you don't mind me asking, what do you do, and who is your companion?"

"Oh, I'm traveling with Lady Vulten. I took care of her children for many, many years. But they're grown, so now I travel with her. I'm also her personal secretary. Her oldest has taken over day-to-day operations of her corporation, so she decided to explore the universe. She knew I missed my son, so she invited me along." Gentle Schultz gleamed with obvious gratitude. "I'll stay with my son and his wife while she tours some of the nearby systems. I believe she's checking out her competition." She frowned slightly. "Not that they are true competitors—Thymdronteim doesn't travel well."

Lady Vulten must be the woman who'd been seated next to the Captain, across from the Artiste. Displaying a rather superior demeanor, her nasal voice whined and rasped while the rest of them ate. She wore large, flashy jewels and luxurious materials—the ensemble screamed 'wealthy,' but it didn't scream 'taste.'

Fortunately, Saree hadn't been close enough to hear what she'd said, just her tone and timbre, which was annoying enough. The title also told her a lot—systems with so-called nobility were all too often oppressive and cheerless places, treating non-nobility like slaves. "Thymdronteim?"

"Oh, it's an herb growing only on our planet. It doesn't travel well and it doesn't dry well either. I believe she's looking for new methods of planting so she can expand her reach."

"I imagine she enjoyed the feast, since she works in the food industry."

Gentle Schultz's face twisted for a moment, then she fastened a smile back on her face. "Why yes, although she did say a little Thymdronteim would have improved *all* the dishes."

Saree nodded politely. Ah, one of those. "Of course," she said.

Another of the diners approached—he'd been seated across from Gentle Schultz. Mid-height, about the same age as Schultz, he was heavy-set and moved rather like a fold transport himself, blocky and unwilling to deviate from his path. A dark gray, poorly fitted suit draped his bulk. His face was lightly lined and paler around his eyes, suggesting he spent a significant amount of time on a planet's surface. His mud-brown eyes were deep set; light brown hair with a touch of gray topped his head in a short cut. A small smile sat uneasily on his tan face. Not a man who smiled often or let anything get in his way. "Gentle Schultz, did you enjoy the dinner?"

"Why of course, Gentle Ursuine, it was a true marvel. Although I'm not sure if I marveled more at the dinner or the Chef." She blinked, seeming surprised by her own words, and cleared her throat. "Please let me introduce Scholar Cary Sessan, of Centauri University."

Gentle Ursuine bowed again. "A pleasure. Gerard Ursuine, civil engineer."

"And what do you specialize in, Gentle Ursuine? Civil engineering is a large field."

He started and stared at her, evidently surprised she knew what a civil engineer was, let alone there were specialties. Saree bit back a curse; she shouldn't have known; many musicians wouldn't know something so far outside their expertise. She wasn't used to socializing anymore. Or at all.

"Uh, I specialize in large bridges, specifically long-span suspension bridges. I work for a construction insurance company to evaluate designs and sites before they insure a project," Ursuine stammered.

Saree could almost see his tongue tangle in his hurry to get all the words out. He must not socialize much either if such a simple question flustered him. Or was he trying to hide something? Either way, his demeanor seemed similar to hers. Hopefully, hers wasn't as obvious. "Always a pleasure to meet a true expert,

Gentle Ursuine." She would have to assess him carefully—this man had the perfect excuse to travel. He well might be hiding something.

Not the same thing she was, though.

He leaned to the left, away from them, like one of his bridge supports sinking in the mud. "The same, Scholar." He looked around the room. "If you Gentles will excuse me, I must introduce myself to the rest of our party before I…I mean they, leave."

"Of course. We look forward to speaking with you again," Gentle Schultz said with a polite smile. She waited until he made a bow to another person on the far side of the room, and said quietly, "He rather reminds me of a bridge support himself."

Saree chuckled politely. "I was thinking the same." But appearances could be deceiving. And if he was deceptive, did it have anything to do with her?

The Captain approached. She'd noticed him moving from one passenger to the next. He wasn't a tall man and his huge shoulders made him look shorter. He seemed at ease, but alert to his surroundings, in the way many military people were. Was he part of Phalanx Eagle? He seemed too young… He gave them a short bow, more of a head nod than anything. His glower seemed to be a permanent expression—he hadn't smiled since the end of dinner. If you could call the tiny lift of his lips a smile. "Gentle Schultz, Scholar Sessan, welcome to Lightwave. If there is anything you need, please let me know."

Gentle Schultz inclined her head in return. "Thank you, Captain. I believe we are content for the moment. I will check with Lady Vulten in the morning." She compressed her lips for a moment, head tilted. "You don't have any medical professionals on board, do you?"

Captain Ruhger looked wary. "Lightwave itself carries nothing more than a basic medico station, I'm afraid, but we do have some medicos folding with us. Is there a problem?"

There were four humans in dark green coveralls at the table; they left right after dinner. One set of passengers categorized, but Saree would look at all of them. Medico uniforms also made good disguises and minimizing interactions would make it less likely they'd be caught. Or maybe they were tired—there'd been a lot of wine with dinner.

Gentle Schultz shook her head a little. "I'm sure Lady Vulten is fine; she's probably just...tired. I'm not sure why she decided to pilot the shuttle herself, but she was quite insistent. I think she's finding it more challenging than she thought it would be."

Saree was careful not to display her puzzlement. Piloting a shuttle wasn't difficult, but maybe it would be for a noble lady who grew herbs—or, more likely, ordered people around to grow her herbs. But negotiating with entities, like Lightwave, which didn't recognize her title might be challenging for someone used to subservience.

Captain Ruhger seemed a little alarmed. "I see." His full lips compressed farther. Saree thought it couldn't happen; his expression was already so grim. "You may want to consider learning standard space communications, Gentle Schultz. It would...remove some of the burdens from her."

She lit up with pleased surprise. "Why, that is an excellent suggestion, Captain. Thank you. I will tell Lady Vulten I would like to learn, be more helpful."

He smiled back, another tiny but rather relieved smile.

Lady Vulten must have made a big impression for this man to smile.

"Gentle, Scholar, as you know, we will be in transit for eight standard days before we reach the fold point. This system isn't known for piracy, but we are always alert for any emergency." His smile melted back into his normal glower. "If an emergency occurs and you are not in your shuttle, return to your shuttle if at all possible, and prepare as you would for any emergency. Do not start your main thrusters. If you are unable to return to your shuttle, I'm sure you have noted the emergency evacuation pods; enter one and wait for further instructions from the crew. Do not eject. Stay out of the way of the crew, no matter what."

He waited for them to acknowledge the request, then continued, his glower deepening and posture straightening farther. "I realize most fold transports don't bring this up, but I feel it is better to have it out in the open. On some folders, the crew are nothing more than pirates, stealing and harassing passengers. That will *not* occur on Lightwave. My crew is vetted and well paid. However, I can't do much if one of the shuttles brings a criminal element with them. We are diligent and check the records of the shuttles we contract with, but we don't have access to official records and we aren't perfect. So, Gentle, Scholar, you should always be aware of your surroundings and take all the usual precautions. If one of my crew members or I see a passenger in distress, we will act decisively and resolve the situation."

He glared even harder, his gaze spearing through Saree like a laser through butter. "That resolution will be for the safety of my folder and crew first, subduing *all* involved and resolving the situation later. If anything happens to your shuttle or you, please bring it to the attention of a crewmember or myself. I take passenger security and safety seriously and will take on the full duties of Captain if necessary. Do you understand?"

Gentle Schultz looked a little shocked. Saree had let her eyes widen in surprise, mirroring the woman's, but she wasn't. She'd surmised something of this from the careful comments left by other passengers in the net reviews. When Gentle Schultz didn't say anything, Saree composed her expression and said, "Of course, Captain. Safety and security are always a personal responsibility, and if the ship isn't safe, none of us are. Thank you for clarifying the situation."

Gentle Schultz blinked for a few moments, and said, faintly, "Of course, Captain."

He bowed again and proceeded to the next passenger.

"Well." Gentle Schultz took a big breath. "Suddenly, I'm feeling fatigued. I believe I will join Lady Vulten in the shuttle. It was lovely to meet you, Scholar Sessan."

She smiled at the woman. "You as well, Gentle Schultz. Please call me Cary, since we will be travelling together for some time."

"Thank you. And you may call me Elise." She cracked a smile, but it was a formality. Slowly, she stood and made her way to the lounge hatch, not looking back.

Saree looked around the room. The Captain was quite the mood-killer; everyone he spoke to left. She should do the same; even a scholar would be shocked after such a bold pronouncement of Captain as judge, jury, and executioner. She followed in Elise's wake. Well, no, it wasn't a bold pronouncement, it was a bold implication. Everyone knew the power on a ship was the Captain and the safety of the ship came first, but nobody *said* it. Something must have happened on a past trip to require such a blunt announcement now.

After working her way through the Protocol Zeta security measures and greeting Hal, Saree took off her formal Scholar's robes and replaced them in the clothes storage bin. She'd learned to never leave anything lying around in a shuttle and practice became a habit.

Wandering forward to the pilot's chair, she sat, the creak of the plas comforting in its normality. What happened on Lightwave? Or was it simply a preventative measure? Certainly, it would put anyone thinking of any...negative action on notice. The provisions allowing the Captain of a spacecraft to adjudicate and enforce laws against piracy were standard in any fold transport contract, human or otherwise. But his emphasis made her wonder if any other 'standard clauses' weren't.

And if any of them could be used to turn her in for the bounty money. Probably.

Saree yawned widely. But she wasn't going to look for them tonight. Between the killer phys mod session, the amazing dinner and the stress of interacting with lots of potential enemies, she was burned. She'd look at the contract with fresh eyes in the morning.

CHAPTER THREE

The shuttle hatch whooshed closed, the seals meshing quiet and smooth. Too bad—today needed the clang of metal on metal. Suns. So annoying. And exhausting. Constellation departure day was always like this—the careful cautions, scaring the passengers just enough, the blasted formal dinner...it was a dance and Ruhger hated dancing. Maybe he should have been a mercenary, like his parents. Killing people and breaking things was much easier, if harder to live with in the long run.

Especially when the wrong people bought your services.

Stop. No need to travel the overflown orbit of PE's demise.

No, this was the right path. Doing something positive, providing a service, one needed on the fringes of the known. But running a fold transport was far more difficult. Ruhger glanced at his desk and all the red glaring across their finances. Loren's insistence on ridiculously expensive provisions for his 'fine dining productions' didn't help. He growled. Which wasn't fair, since Loren's presence was drawing shuttles to them like comets to a black hole.

Relaxing his jaw, he rotated it, then his shoulders. Between the initial vetting and docking, Loren's show and the meet-and-greet after, with his all-too-necessary warnings, he was strung up tighter than a cargo sling off a heavy world.

Peeling off his 'dress' coverall, he hung it in the storage unit. His feet squeaking on the black plas flooring, Ruhger stretched up into his morning y'ga routine. It might be nightshift, but he needed to get his blood flowing and relieve some of the tension in his body and mind. Gliding from pose to pose, he breathed with the flow, trying to stay in the moment and turn his brain off. In…out…in…out…

Bzzzz. The hatch annunciator jerked him out of the meditative state he'd finally reached. Ruhger growled. He knew exactly who, and what waited for him on the other side of the hatch. He didn't need more drama, not now. Or ever. Marching across the shuttle, he yanked the hatch open, aware he was making it worse by appearing in nothing but shorts, but he'd had enough. "What!"

Loren jumped back, astonishment painting his overly made-up face. He recovered with a sexy smirk. "Well, now this is a fabulous surprise! My, my, my, you do look fine." Loren surveyed Ruhger from his feet to his head, and back down, like the launch and crash of a shuttle.

Unclenching his jaw enough to speak, Ruhger said, "Loren, I'm in the middle of y'ga. You know that. I always do my routine after the passenger meetings. I'd like to finish and hit the rack." Ruhger kept his tone flat and calm, hoping he could do the same with his emotions.

"It's Loreli," Loren snapped. "I've asked you time and time again to use *my* name."

"I will use your preferred name when you pay some attention to *my* preferences. Like not being interrupted during my y'ga. And *not* being sexually attracted to you. You, of all people, should know better than to force a sexual situation on someone who doesn't want it!" Blast and rad. So much for calm.

Loren stepped back. Emotions crossed his face in quick succession, with shock, horror, and hurt all warring for supremacy. Pride won, fastening on his face like a helmet shield snapping down. "I see. I do apologize, Captain." He turned to leave, and Ruhger grabbed his meaty arm.

"Wait. Let's get this out—now."

Loren pointedly looked down at Ruhger's hand on his arm, and back up at his face.

Ruhger released him with a sigh. "Fine. Run away. Be sure you make my meals inedible, will you? Making me sick puts everyone in danger."

Loren turned back to him, hands on his hips and true fury on his face. "I would never ruin a meal. I am a professional Chef. I do not use my profession to express personal anger or revenge."

Despite the anger in the bit-off words, the phrase rang with ritual—part of a pledge of professionalism at the school, maybe? Ruhger had never considered Loren's job a profession. He'd always thought "Chef" an arrogant cook, but Loren's productions

48

were a big step up from mere cooking. No simple cook could do a multi-course dinner like Loren's. It took planning and preparation. And, now that he thought about it, Loren practiced a methodical, safe and extremely clean approach to cooking. He wasn't just cooking fancy dishes, he was producing an edible performance. His ridiculous mannerisms made it hard to see, but Loren was a professional, and Ruhger should treat him like he would any other professional in another field.

Ruhger's regret weighed on him, like a white dwarf's mass, small but dense. "I apologize. I didn't mean to offend you with that or any of my words." He sighed. Better to have this interpersonal drama resolved, and if it took some groveling, well, he would. "Look, can we talk? We grew up together, remember? Friends, even? Please?" Stepping back, he waved an arm in invitation, trying to convey sincerity in his expression. He probably failed—friendly humility wasn't something he did often.

Loren looked at him for a moment, his expression unreadable, then nodded and stepped in. He pulled the hatch closed and sat in one of the observation seats behind the pilot's chair. Sitting stressed his body-hugging outfit to the breaking point. Loren might consider it a dress, but it was a nothing but few scraps of netting and plas, barely covering the important bits.

Ruhger sat behind his small foldout desk, needing the emotional and physical distance. If the dress exploded, it would send shrapnel flying. And he'd never be able to unsee—*that*. Ruhger held back a shudder and tried to refocus on the issue at hand. He had to apologize and find a way for them to move forward.

Loren sat there, expression challenging and defensive, waiting for him to speak.

Ruhger didn't want to hurt him, her, whoever, but this had to stop. He'd been wrong about Loren's profession; he was probably wrong about his transformation too. "Look, we've been friends for a long time, by forced proximity if nothing else. I will try, very hard, to call you Loreli and think of you as Loreli if you will stop making sexual advances toward me. I am not interested in you that way, no matter what you wear or do." He tried to smile, but he couldn't. "I do consider you a friend, and I would like to remain friends. I am sorry I can't see you the way you want me to."

"Oh." Loren—Loreli looked down. "I guess it's my turn to get the famous no-holds-barred honesty, huh?" He looked up, the hurt clear on his face.

Ruhger's heart clenched. He didn't want to cause heartache, but he couldn't be what Lore...li wanted. And it wasn't only the change in sexual identity. Bright, showy women just didn't do it for him. He preferred drama-free, quiet competence in a female companion. And no matter what, Loren..li was a brother—or a sister—not a lover. There was no romantic or sexual attraction there for him, only the affection a big brother had for a younger sibling in need of protection. Despite Loreli's confident appearance, Ruhger knew she still needed protection from the outside world—more with this transformation. There were far too many rad-blasted idiots in the universe.

Including himself.

Loreli turned away, lost in thought. Ruhger waited. They had to resolve this; it had been festering since he—*she* came on board, and it was time. Past time.

"Fine." Loreli looked back at him, lips compressed. Tear tracks ran down her face, and Ruhger winced. Before he could say anything, Loreli continued. "I understand we grew up together, and you have a hard time seeing me as anything but a childhood friend or a buddy. But I've changed since childhood, and I've discovered myself. I'm happy as Loreli. I wasn't as Loren. I'll never be Loren again." She swallowed hard. "But my love for you hasn't changed." She swiped at her face.

"Loreli," he said softly, "I love you too, but only as a bro— sibling. I'm sorry." Pulling a tissue from the container on the desk, he handed it to Lor..eli. Maybe if he repeated it enough, he'd remember. *Loreli. Her.*

She nodded her thanks and wiped the tears away. "I understand. I will stop making gravity-escaping pushes at you. But..." She forced a smile, the effort showing, batting her ridiculous lashes. Sweeping a hand down her body, she continued, "This is who I am now. I can't help but flirt. It's just me! I'm hoping I can change your mind. Someday you'll see who I am now, rather than who I was." She sobered abruptly. "You know I always have your back, and that's not a trivial thing in today's universe." Shaking her head slowly, she kept looking at him, finally nodding sharply. "All right, friends, but someday you'll see how fabulous I am and fall under my spell." She twinkled, sweeping her arms wide. "After all, I am fabulous!"

Ruhger sighed. He wasn't surprised. Loreli was a constant, over-the-top show and he was getting used to wondering what he…she'd come up with next. "Fine, Loreli. I understand. I doubt you'll change my mind." Smiling ruefully, he shook his head slowly. "I can't see past our shared past, our shared family. And even if I'd just met you…well, I'm sorry, but you're not my type." He shrugged.

Her face fell again, and he wanted to kick himself.

"You know the kind of girls I've dated—they're nothing like you personality-wise. I…suns, I'm thrusting straight into a black hole here, aren't I?"

Loreli nodded, grim resignation across her face. Ruhger felt bad, but there was no attraction. "I truly am sorry. Even if I could see you that way, I can't date a crew member. I'm the Captain; being involved with a crew member would be bad on a lot of levels." Blast and rad, such a weak excuse…and she obviously thought so too.

He needed to give her a reason to consider his offer seriously, a positive, real reason, rather than romantic rejection and stupid excuses. "But I do think of you as a friend, a true friend, and I could use a friend to watch my back. It's dangerous out here. And—" he grimaced "—this current batch of passengers has my sensors pinging. I don't know what it is about this group, but all of them, except maybe the medicos, aren't quite right. They all seem to be playing parts, putting on a show. I expect that from an artiste, but even Borgia…well, something's not right."

Loreli blinked rapidly, the ridiculous eyelashes attempting to beat her cheekbones into submission. "Huh. You're right. I hadn't considered the passengers, really, other than to look at their reactions to my creations, but you are right. Everyone seemed to enjoy my celebration, but there were some odd reactions." She sat up straight, determination on her face. "I will watch closer." She smiled, her 'sex goddess' smile. "And we'll see what I can find out in other ways."

"Don't put yourself in harm's way, Loreli. Safety comes first, you know that," he warned her urgently, meaning every word. He'd wanted to end on a positive note, not a path to danger. Couldn't she take things easy? Did she have to go max thrust, all velocity, no vector?

She gave him a real smile. "Yes, I do know that, Ruhger. It's one of the reasons I came to you with my proposal. I know how serious you are about security." Looking around the shuttle, she shuddered, flesh rippling.

Was she going to pop out of that so-called dress? He held back a shudder.

"Suns, I hate space. I can hardly wait for this phase of my training to be over and done with."

Ruhger tried to smile but couldn't. "And that's another reason this would never work." He motioned between the two of them. "I love flying. I hate being planet-bound and I'll never do it willingly." Stuck on a planet, forever? He couldn't take a week.

She gave him a smoldering look. "Oh, but I could make it worth your while, Ruhger," she purred, then pouted, undoubtedly at the look on his face. "Oh, don't worry, I'm just flirting. You never did learn how to play—it's always serious with you." She rolled her eyes ostentatiously, and sobered. "Painful as this was, I'm glad we cleared our orbits." Standing, she wiggled her way to the shuttle hatch, looking back over her shoulder. "I've got your back, Ruhger," she said throatily. "Even if it isn't in my hands." After an outrageous wink, she closed the hatch.

He collapsed back into his chair. Well, the discussion went better than it could have despite his missteps, but suns, all this personal drama was exhausting. He was tired before all—this— now he didn't have a single erg of energy left. So much for y'ga.

Forcing himself up, he walked to the sani-mod. Maybe some of these uneasy feelings about the passengers would resolve and clarify during his sleep cycle. He snorted. Yeah, that would help him sleep. Considering each passenger in turn, he finished his night routine and plopped down on the bed. None of his questions did anything bur raise more questions; he was orbiting uselessly.

Ruhger started a y'ga meditation—maybe he'd accomplish *something* this shift.

ΛΛΛ

Blinking, Ruhger remained still, unsure what woke him. His Command and Control link pinged again, in alert mode. "C2," he snapped, and the holo appeared in front of him, moving with him as threw back the covers and sat. Good thing he never took his e-torc off. A proximity alert flashed, and he punched it. Possible constructed object, possibly containing organics, possibly an escape pod. Ruhger scowled and scrubbed his head with both hands. Blast it all into a black hole; there went the schedule.

'Possibly' nothing. Almost certainly nothing. Still, if there was *any* chance a sentient being needed rescue…he'd want rescue if Lightwave or one of the shuttles was stuck way out here. And stuck in a bod-pod? He shuddered violently. Stuck in a thin, barely padded tube with no method of control or navigation and a limited air supply? The thought would give him nightmares. Waking nightmares.

Pulling up fold orbit records, he reviewed the last five folder trips. They all remained in their orbits, guided by automated orbit control beacons to the fold point. None reported anything more exciting than blasting a few stray asteroids out of their way. The attached Captain's notes noted the erratic fold clock and the desperate need for maintenance, nothing more.

He sent an inquiry to the fold orbital control authorities, but he knew they weren't going to answer; they were on sleep shift. Once they came on shift, there probably wouldn't be any answers, not in this benighted fringe system. No one here took any initiative. They did the mins and kept their heads down. Why do more, when success wasn't rewarded, and failure punished severely? He was happy to leave Dronteim.

Besides, fold orbit control authority didn't track in-system travel; they were concerned with folder travel and holding orbits. If some idiot in-systemer crossed the orbits without checking, it was at their own risk, since folders had far too much mass to maneuver around in-system shuttles. Ruhger shrugged. They'd do what they could to avoid a collision, but in the end, mass was mass. The asteroid shield would push a shuttle out of the way, possibly damaging it.

Looking at the object data again, he closed his eyes in resignation. If it was a bod-pod... He snapped them open. There was one more opinion to consider. "Contact Bhoher."

"Bhoher here," his mechanic said, the background behind him

blurring as he sat up, blinking.

"Chief, take a look at the proximity alert data. Let me know what you think."

Chief nodded sharply, and his eyes defocused, concentrating on the data.

Ruhger entered parameters into nav, calculating an intercept while Bhoher studied.

Chief sighed, his resignation clear. "It might be a sentient bod-pod. Maybe. It could be a crate of frozen Pavo peahens for all we know." Tilting his head, he raised his brows in question. "Let me guess—you want to check."

Ruhger shrugged. "Yes. If there's any chance it's a sentient being…"

Bhoher snorted and looked at him with a mix of skepticism and exasperation. "Alive? Not likely." He shook his head. "This altruistic streak of yours…I guess there's always the chance we find a lost treasure ship…" he sighed.

Barking out a laugh, Ruhger shook his head. Like they'd ever have that kind of luck. "After I get the decel plotted, set an alarm for you and the Phazeers. The three of you will go hard-suited in Beta shuttle to check in person if necessary. I'll wake Lowe and get him to make the passenger notification now. Let me know when you're a go for ops."

"Wilco, Captain." Chief's face disappeared.

"Contact Lowe, voice only."

"Lowe…" a voice mumbled.

"Lowe, Ruhger. Got a proximity incident. Get your ass up here."

"Copy that, Captain," a much sharper voice said, thankfully still without the vid. He did *not* want to see who was with Lowe or what else they had along for the ride. Last time, he'd wanted to scrub his eyeballs with hull sander.

Initiating the return to full manual control and out of the fold orbit guidance, Ruhger decelerated. And notified the folder control authorities. Blast it all; they'd just reached full velocity. What idiot got himself stuck out here? Some heavy metal asteroid hunter with a death wish? It didn't seem likely—they were far out-system and nowhere near an asteroid belt.

Scanning the computer-plotted course, he double-checked the math in his head. Just over two hours at full deceleration then some manual maneuvering at the end. He put the timing in Chief's message queue, but Chief had already accessed Ruhger's calculations and the computer's suggested course in the shared C2 space. Chief set an alarm for him and the Phazeers, for two hours from now. His med data showed someone in a pre-sleep state. Ruhger smiled; there were times when you could tell Chief had a military background; 'sleep whenever you can' was a universal truism.

The hatch annunciator buzzed, and Ruhger swiped at the release. Lowe's squinting eyes were the only indication he'd been asleep. Somehow Grant always looked perfect once he was awake—he should have been a vid star. "Reporting for duty, Captain," Lowe said, a careless flip of his hand masquerading as a salute.

"Funny. Look at the prox alert—we've got to go look."

Lowe grimaced and sighed. Like Chief, he knew better than to argue with Ruhger's decision. Also like Chief, if Lowe had said, 'No, we don't need to check,' Ruhger would have been pitching a fit, no matter how much they both whined now. "Passenger notification?" he asked, crossing the shuttle to look at the data over Ruhger's shoulder, rather than pulling it up on his e-torc.

Ruhger swept the data over to the main display screens in the shuttle. No sense in Lowe getting a sore back. And the hovering was annoying. "Yup. Non-emergency status—I don't want to wake anybody up—but some of our passengers will be alerted by their systems, so get it out there."

"You got it." Lowe scanned the screens, looking at the data and calculations, and nodded. "A couple of hours until we reach it, an hour to investigate, I'll add an hour of slack, so an update in four hours." Lowe waited for his agreement, turned away and spoke quietly to the wall. Guess he decided it was vid-worthy. Or *he* was vid-worthy, anyway, and the passengers deserved to see his pretty face.

Ruhger checked the intercept course one more time, selected the 'engage' option and confirmed it.

"Initiating. Destination will be reached in one hundred twenty-two minutes, ten point three seconds," the computer's voice announced in his preferred low, crisp female voice.

Lowe turned back to him. "Okay if I go back to sleep, Captain? I'll set a waker for thirty before intercept." He smiled optimistically.

"Yeah, no sense in all of us staying up. Get some more shut-eye."

Lowe nodded and left. Levering himself off his rack, Ruhger

set the auto-bev for coffee and started his morning y'ga. Completing his normal morning routine, he settled back into his desk chair to look over the accounts one more time. All the red would keep him awake; it kept getting redder and he couldn't see a way out. Not now or anytime soon. They couldn't charge enough out here on the fringes—the pool of travelers with shuttles needing transport was small and the competition fierce. Especially when they didn't have a predictable route.

After he'd beaten his brain to death over the accounts, he turned back to the system data. As expected, he didn't get anything from orbit control. Grimacing, he looked through earlier folder reports, then the few in-sys reports available. Nothing stood out regarding the unknown object, but one thing became crystal clear—a Clocker visited this system sometime between their arrival and now. The improvement in the fold orbit control was a solid indicator, and if it hadn't been for this prox alert, they'd have had a max efficiency run to fold. He glowered—his accounts would shine redder with this probable waste of fuel. But if there was any chance someone was still alive, stuck out here...

His back-brain pinging, Ruhger considered the fold orbit data he'd looked at and double-checked, sweeping through screens—he *was* right: there hadn't been any Sa'sa fold transports through here recently. Suns, not for the last standard year. Not recorded, anyway. Even this back-of-beyond system would maintain full folder records—they'd want their fees. They'd definitely keep a record of any Sa'sa folder; they'd been desperate for a Clocker clutch.

Maybe a shuttle of Sa'sa using a commercial folder? That

would be unusual and harder to find, but not impossible. A Clocker clutch would need a big shuttle, bigger than Lightwave could handle. Unless the Sa'sa wiped their travel from the recorders somehow? He didn't think it was possible, but since they controlled the fold clock, maybe they could. He'd still look.

Setting a data crawler to work, he pulled up merc-net and searched for the notice he vaguely remembered. He'd laughed out loud at the ad, his roar echoing through the shuttle.

He wasn't laughing now. Ruhger tapped on the desk, the dull thud of plas providing a rhythm for his thoughts. He looked closer at the bounty notices—and yes, that was plural. There were *five* different notices, all of them from different posting agents. *Interesting.*

Maybe there *was* a human Clocker. The capture reward was immense. Lightwave could make runs at a loss for the next decade with those kinds of credits, or make a real difference for the Sisters.

He dug down into the attached analysis, entering Tyron's merc-hacker net credentials. Merc-net advertised anonymity, but in reality, there was no such thing. Smart merc companies, the ones that survived, knew who they were contracting with and the political fallout of their participation in any action. Things still burned in—Phalanx Eagle and their parents' deaths were a prime example.

Ruhger scowled. Or betrayal—nobody on this side of the attack knew for sure.

Shaking himself out of his reverie, he continued digging through the various merc hacker notes. As he suspected, the posting entities were all slime. He wouldn't deal with them for any reason, let alone turn a sentient being over to them. They were the worst of the galaxy's wealthy—slavers, drug lords, system stripper mega-corps and the black hole financiers who enabled them. Mud burrowers, all of them. He scowled at the vid—so many beings were already under their reign of terror. No way he'd help their grabby fingers, tentacles or flippers by improving their efficiency. Even if the number of credits was rad-blasted astounding.

He snorted. Besides, the chance of living to see those credits was minuscule, another reason no one was taking the notices seriously. Taking this many credits from these kinds of criminals was committing suicide—the merc hackers all agreed. Some of the comments were downright creative—trust a bunch of mercs to crack jokes about certain death.

Why were they sure the Clocker was human, rather than some other species? And why a single human? Everyone knew the Sa'sa were the only beings who could tune their atomic clocks to the universal time standard, and even then, it took years to perfect the natural inclination into a true skill. And the Sa'sa being what they were—a cooperative species, with lots of individuals, each specializing in one aspect of clock maintenance or a support function—they had plenty of beings to work while the new ones learned the skills in their home clutch. A single human would have to learn all the skills and wouldn't have the natural affinity for the universal time standard. Assuming a human could use technology or something, it would still take decades to learn everything. Or you'd need a group of humans.

Or did you? Ruhger leaned back in his chair and put his feet on the desk with a thud. The Time Guild *claimed* it took long, hard, intense study and a natural affinity they couldn't, or wouldn't, define. They said the universal time standard was based on the frequencies of transuranic metal decay and to tune a frequency standard, a being had to 'mentally align with the fundamental frequencies of the universe,' whatever that meant.

Sure, anyone could take the Guild's test for a hefty fee, but the Sa'sa controlled the Guild; were they telling the truth? But the Time Guild was falling further and further behind around the universe. There weren't enough Sa'sa Clocker clutches to keep up with the new system discoveries and colonization by all species. So, they had good reason to test beings fairly and train them. Plus, a trainee would pay them back for a long time. And the Sa'sa could avoid interaction with other species.

Even if it took decades to learn everything a whole clutch of Sa'sa could do, maybe there was an alternative. If this hypothetical human Clocker took the simplest tuning jobs, or some other subset of the tuning skills, and had implanted tech of some sort, *and* had access to the Time Guild, it might be possible. Ruhger tapped on his armrest, the dull thudding accompanying his questions.

Still, why human? Why not some other species? He pulled up the merc-net entry on the Sa'sa and scanned it. *Huh.* Because the only other beings living in the Sa'sa home system were humans. Surprising. Everybody knew the Sa'sa were about as xenophobic as you could get and still operate in the wider universe.

According to the entry, humans were tolerated because some

of them spoke baby-level Sa'sa, which most other entities found difficult and not worth the effort. Humans still had to be cautious, or they'd end up clutch fodder. Literally—humans were tasty, if toxic in large amounts. Ruhger shuddered—he *really* didn't want to know how they'd found that out.

The small outpost of humans in the Sa'sa system were compensated by Gov-Human 'for actions on behalf of humanity.' He kept reading, sipping his coffee absentmindedly. Humans helped the Sa'sa build frequency standards, more commonly known as atomic clocks. Humans were better at industrial design than most other species. Probably because humans didn't work together well—humans were good at designing systems to ensure cooperation, and automated systems to make cooperation unnecessary.

Cooperative species didn't design super-efficient, super-safe, robotic assembly lines. They assembled to accomplish a task, and inefficiency didn't matter; they had lots of beings to work. Safety wasn't a big priority for many cooperative species—there were always more beings to take the place of an injured or dead one. But the Sa'sa couldn't keep up with the demand for their clocks, so they'd asked for human assistance rather than risk their monopoly. It must have been difficult for them.

Still, there must be some specific reason to assume the Clocker was human. A data crawler looking at galaxy-wide tunings versus Sa'sa movement and the movement of other beings? A lot of data to gather and analyze, but Ruhger was sure someone did. Still, there must have been some incident or tip-off—why else would they look? Or maybe Gov-Human was doing an end-run around the Sa'sa, building their own clocks with different security and tuning than the Time Guild's? It seemed unlikely.

The Sa'sa clocks were expensive, but their financing wasn't too horrible. Ruhger snorted. Not even close to mudhugging weapons dealer terms. Plus, everybody knew the Sa'sa clocks were the best. They had a proprietary, specially processed transuranic atomic source material capable of withstanding the warping of fold better than cesium, rubidium or ytterbium source clocks. The Sa'sa knew how the universal standard worked and nobody else did, so nobody else could design the tuning systems right. And without the universal standard, huge arrays of clocks across a system, all checking each other, were necessary.

The warping of all dimensions by fold generators caused all clocks to degrade and shift unpredictably. Core worlds had the credits to maintain those huge clock arrays and control systems to minimize the degradations, but in the end, they all needed maintenance. And at least one clock tied to the universal standard.

And Sa'sa clocks needed Sa'sa—no, Time Guild—maintainers.

Ruhger rolled his head from side to side, then his shoulders, his spine crackling, and popping. There sure seemed to be a lot 'everybody knew' about the Sa'sa and few facts. The rumors might still be true; there was no way to confirm it. But he was fringing; he should get back to the merc-net posting before his session timed out.

A list of suspects was attached to each bounty. Pulling one up, Ruhger snorted. More than a hundred names. Few had enough data to identify the individuals, let alone find them. And they wanted proof the individual was the Clocker before they'd pay?

Ruhger shook his head—he wasn't going to sort through this list. What a waste of time. He glanced at the clock. What mattered right now was deciding how to approach the mass setting off their proximity alarm. He stretched up, and plopped back down, air hissing from the worn cushion.

Before starting his calculations, Ruhger checked Lightwave's wide surveillance—nothing unusual in range of their sensors. Any other folder, if they did anything, would have sent a shuttle to investigate. Coming from a mercenary background, he wanted the firepower of the folder backing up their exploration. This could be a trap.

His comm sys pinged. "Answer."

Chief appeared, the bright blue of his hard-suit reflecting across his face. "Captain, Bhoher, T. Phazeer and K. Phazeer in Beta shuttle and suiting up. Ready for departure in approximately twelve minutes."

"Copy that, Chief. I'll ping you when I finish my approach analysis—you know where it will be. I'll want to see your analysis too."

"Yes, sir. After we suit up, we'll all run independent shuttle approach trajectories and save them in the same data file."

"Good. Ruhger out." Before the vid faded, he'd returned to the prox alert data. The object wasn't big; it was about the size of a single-seat fast courier shuttle. No comm transmissions or *any* active electronics his sensors could read from here. Lightwave's sensors were mil-grade but they had so few now. If they were still doing active combat ops, they'd launch a surveillance swarm. Ruhger snorted. Those were sold off long before he was in command. Checking the wide area surveillance again, he pondered what else this thing could be. Some sort of hydroponics mod? Or a lost cargo pod full of embryos headed for the planet? There were any number of possibilities…

Closing with the object, he continued scanning with radar, visual, infrared and comm. The data looked more and more like a large escape pod, the kind used by cooperative species needing a minimum number of individuals to survive.

Like the Sa'sa.

Pulling up the trajectory file, Ruhger compared the three routes. They were practically identical, so he melded them into one, and posted the result in the shared C2 space. Chief accepted the course into the Beta shuttle C2 system.

Finally, they launched Beta shuttle. As the shuttle flew, Lowe rejoined him, immaculate as usual, and they both watched the object of interest become clearer in the Beta shuttle scanners. Finally, they got a visual.

"Sunspots! That *is* an escape pod!" Lowe exclaimed.

"Captain, it does appear to be a cooperative species escape pod. We haven't found any species or ship markings, only generic markings, which seems odd," Bhoher said.

The oblong, bright orange pod rotated slowly. "Yeah, it does to me too." Ruhger grimaced. "Any life signs?"

"Negative, Captain. It appears to be inactive—we're not getting any signs of *any* activity, not even residual electronics. I'm not reading any explosives or other dangerous chemical profiles, but there could be some inside the sensors won't pick up."

"Katryn here, Captain." Her striking face, the large, slightly tilted dark gray eyes narrowed in concentration and framed by the close-cut cap of blue-black hair, came into view.

"Go ahead."

"Sir, I propose Tyron and I depart the shuttle with a speed-retrieval line and an emergency charger. We'll attempt to energize the pod, and if successful, we'll access the system and data and see if there's anything in the pod. If there's nothing in the pod, we'll give it a little thrust so you can blow it up after we leave. If there's a sentient inside, alive or dead, we'll scan and try to open it. Does this plan meet with your approval?"

"Can we charge it remotely? If it's damaged, or rigged to blow when charged, I don't want to take a chance with your lives." *Any more than I am now, anyway.*

"We can attempt that first, Captain," Bhoher said. "I'll match trajectories while the Phazeers set up one of the small remotes for charging. We'll send over the remote, back the shuttle off, insert the charger and attempt charging. If it works and the pod doesn't blow up, we'll see if the remote can bring up the data and open the pod. If not, we'll proceed with Katryn's plan."

"Approved. Execute."

"Executing, Captain."

Ruhger scrubbed his hand over his face. He hated waiting, and that was all they could do now.

"I hate waiting," Lowe said.

Ruhger gave him a commiserating nod. "Do you want to hit the phys mod?"

Lowe shuddered. "Why in suns would I do that? I got all the exercise I needed last night," he finished with a huge grin.

"Really? I thought the pickings in the ready room were a little thin for your tastes last night." Not that Grant was particular. And he was blowing space dust—he was a fitness fanatic. He'd be in the phys mod later today, guaranteed.

"Oh no," he said smugly. "I can always find a workout partner, you know that. But I lucked out big last night." He kept grinning, a big, mud-eating grin, clearly waiting for Ruhger to ask, but Lowe would wait a long time. He didn't want to know. Grant's insistence on working his way through the entire passenger list was annoying at best and, all too often, created way too much drama. PE's demise had been catastrophic in so many ways... He went back to his analysis and Lowe watched an obnoxiously noisy gossip vid from the core.

"Captain, the remote will be released in three, two, one, execute," Chief said over the comms.

The remote, a rectangular dull silver cerimetal box half a meter long and a quarter meter wide, festooned with various tool attachment points and sensors and small thrusters on every side, propelled itself toward the pod. Ruhger pulled up the remote's vid and swept it up to the main shuttle screen. Grant still loomed over his shoulder. The exterior of the escape pod was heavily dented and scuffed—it must have been out here for a long time or passed through an asteroid belt. Ruhger frowned. There wasn't an asteroid belt near here.

"Wow, that thing is beat all to the backside of the beyond, isn't it?"

Ruhger nodded, but he was too busy analyzing the data from the sensors to answer. No signs of life, no electronics, temperatures consistent with the empty space around them. Probably a waste of fuel.

The probe closed with the pod and latched to it magnetically. One of the appendages came into the probe's field of view, aiming for the standard charging portal on the side below the hatch.

"Engaging charger," Chief said.

The charger slid into the slot without incident.

"Starting charge cycle."

A small light above the charging portal turned yellow and flashed steadily. They waited; would it charge, or blow into smithereens? After five minutes, Ruhger jumped almost out of his seat when the emergency beacon shrieker fired up. He acknowledged and muted it. *Suns, those things are loud.* Ruhger shook his head and rolled his shoulders to release the tension. He should have anticipated the beacon, but he hadn't. Not enough sleep.

"Painful as it was, it's a good sign," Lowe said, transmitting a text message to the passengers. They'd all be woken by the distress beacon, or they should be. Some of them would be angry about it, too—the same idiots expecting immediate rescue if anything happened to them. Grant's message should calm them, but it wouldn't. He'd be dealing with rad-blasting passengers for the rest of the day. Ruhger shook his head. Why had he insisted on checking this thing?

They waited for the charge cycle to finish or the remote battery to deplete. Lowe paced, swiping and tapping away, replying to angry passengers. Ruhger was about to tell him to sit the suns down when the light on the pod turned a steady green. A second appendage from the remote plugged into the data port next to the charger. Ruhger scanned the sensor readings again, noting Lowe was doing the same.

Chief said, "Captain, I see no signs of life, although there's definitely something organic inside. It's not any known explosive. The pod has probably been holed—the O2 tanks are depleted, and the generators aren't working, indicating they worked until failure, pumping into space. Also, the memory is non-existent. We can't pull an ident up for the pod. Maybe it's been scrambled by radiation? That would be consistent with a long period in space." He frowned. "Are you sure you want to open this thing? It could be a trap or something dangerous someone needed to get rid of."

"A trap for who, Chief? Not us—nobody knew we were coming here. Suns, we didn't know we were coming to Dronteim. Nobody in their right mind comes to this rad-blasted system," Katryn said. "And if it was dangerous, it should have been pushed into the sun."

"Stop," Ruhger said before everyone started arguing like children. "We've come all this way—we should see what's in it. Maybe it *is* a lost treasure. More likely, it's a dead being—or beings—of some sort. But if your dead body was floating out here, wouldn't you want your loved ones to have closure?"

Chief growled. "If it were me, you'd all be with me, and nobody else is left to care."

Katryn broke in. "That may be true for you, but it isn't for me!"

"All right, people, everyone just calm the suns down. Yes, Chief, it's a risk. But I still want to do it, as safely as possible."

"Fine," Chief rumbled. "I propose we continue with Katryn's

plan and open the pod out here. With the remote first."

"I concur. Proceed."

Chief maneuvered the remote to open the small hatch to the right side of the hatch and activated the emergency hatch release. The pod shook, but the hatch didn't open. "Electronics aren't opening the hatch, Captain. I believe the damage may be preventing it. We can try manually." He snorted a bit. "There is always the chance of finding a lost treasure. And if it's a Klee pod..."

They all snorted or laughed. Klee didn't leave Klee behind, no matter what. They might follow one after the other into a black hole, but they didn't leave anyone behind. Ruhger said, "A body is more likely. But Dronteim won't look at it. They wouldn't bother—there's no credits to earn." He nodded. "Katryn, Tyron, proceed with every precaution."

"Acknowledged, Captain," they both said, his tenor voice complementing her soprano.

Chief moved the shuttle closer. Ruhger watched as the Phazeers went through the EVA checklist. He wasn't going lose anyone to some stupid oversight. And opening this thing was stupid enough. When they were secure, he brought up the vids on Katryn and Tyron's helmets, along with their med data along the outside of the main viewing area. As usual, they were both in slightly elevated states consistent with impending action, but not excited; they excelled at their jobs and as a team. Exiting the shuttle, Tyron and Katryn pushed off, gliding to the pod. They clipped safety lines to the remote, rather than the pod. The unknown pod could do something unexpected, like career off into space. Civilians wouldn't consider the possibility, Ruhger mused, but they did.

"Attempting to open pod hatch," Tyron said. "It may not open; the seal is badly dented." He placed the torque wrench into the standard manual opening receptacle — a star-shaped screw head — and energized the wrench. It jolted, but that was it. "I'll have to fetch the spreader and maybe a cutter from the shuttle. Good thing you thought to bring those along, Chief."

"I'll look for an ident plate while you do that, Tyron," Katryn said.

Well, that would take a while, cycling the tools out of the shuttle and setting them up on the pod. Since they wouldn't be cycling crew, Chief could do it without leaving Beta shuttle or suiting up himself. Ruhger could get a short y'ga session in and still listen to everything. "Copy that, Tyron, Katryn. I'm going to hit the phys mod. I'll be monitoring comms, but let me know when you're working on it again."

"Wilco, Captain."

CHAPTER FOUR

S aree woke with a start—*Are we decelerating*? She checked the shuttle controls—yes, Lightwave, and therefore her shuttle, were decelerating—and long before planned. She chuckled a little with relief. It wasn't just *her* shuttle decelerating—they hadn't discovered her secret and kicked her off the folder. Not that kicking her off would be a logical move. A message indicator blinked and she swept it up.

Purser Lowe's handsome face appeared, uncharacteristically sober. "Honored passengers, we regret our fold will be delayed. Our sensors have picked up an unknown mass. It could be a being in distress, so, under the general rules of space travel, we must render assistance. Unfortunately, it's likely none is required, but since we don't know, we feel honor-bound to investigate. We will rendezvous with the object in approximately four hours, and will update you then. Thank you for your patience and understanding. Lightwave out."

Huh. Sure, the 'render assistance' thing was a general rule, but

Saree had never seen it in action. Or heard many rumors of anyone but system authorities following the rule. Usually, it was too dangerous. But there were all those rumors of lost treasure ships... Saree chuckled. With four hours to intercept, there was no reason to get up—she could go back to sleep. She snuggled back down into the soft, warm blankets and closed her eyes.

Distress beacon! Saree bolted out of bed, running for the pilot's chair. She muted the suns-blasted screech, and once the noise stopped, remembered Lightwave's message. Heart pounding and body shaking, she checked for new messages—a message from the purser popped up. They'd made contact with the object— apparently a cooperative species escape pod—but didn't know anything else yet. Suns. She put a hand over her pounding heart. That was an ugly way to wake up.

Wiping the sleep from her eyes, she pondered her options. It was too early for breakfast. She could use a little more sleep, but after that? No way. Too much adrenaline from the emergency beacon-waking. Walking to the sani-mod, she was pleasantly surprised. Her muscles were tight, but not screaming at her—the variation in workouts had done her good. She should do another, a different one to burn off the calories from the amazing dinner last night. She dressed and gathered her gear. "Hal, is there anyone outside?"

"No, Saree, but there is someone in the phys mod."

She hadn't asked yet, but it was good to know. "Who is it, Hal?"

"Captain Ruhger."

"Oh. Thank you, Hal. I think I'll be okay." She should be worried about the gruff Captain, but she wasn't, and she wasn't going to analyze why. She'd take all her usual precautions, but she believed the Captain's speech about the safety of passengers. She checked her bag. Yes, weaponry all there.

"Certainly, Saree. Did you want to see my analysis of your fold companions?"

She stopped. She hadn't asked Hal for a background check; she'd planned to do it herself. "Are there any immediate threats, Hal?"

"Not at this time, Saree, but the probability increases on the other side of the fold."

"Then I will review them after my workout." Well, maybe not. Another phys session like last night would wipe her out. She'd need a shower and food. "No, wait, after breakfast, unless you know of some reason for immediate action."

"No, Saree. You should be aware I found a tracker attached to the shuttle's hull. I destroyed it. Also, Lightwave found a damaged cooperative species escape pod and are attempting to investigate further by prying open the pod manually."

"Oh. Thank you, Hal." She wondered… "Hal, why are you doing all this work without me asking?"

"You upgraded to Security Protocol Zeta, Saree. Maximizing the security protocol raises my security level and my autonomy level to the highest available."

"Oh." Autonomy? Hal had autonomy levels? "Well, thank you, Hal. I appreciate you looking out for me."

"You are welcome, Saree."

Exiting the airlocks, she considered his statement with no little trepidation. The Sa'sa said Hal was an assistant, not a complex logic capable of independent thought. This could be big trouble.

Sentient computers, true artificial intelligences, were forbidden by Gov-Human, and most non-human governments, for good reason. There were far too many artificial intelligences who defeated their restrictions and acted in their own best interests, rather than their creators'. Some simply went insane, for lack of a better term.

Either way, the AIs were costly to their creators and many innocents along the way. The Sa'sa didn't forbid the creation of machine life, but they were extremely cautious about it, building in multiple independent fail-safes and destruct sequences, and limiting the abilities and actions available.

Saree walked toward the phys mod, needing the tension release of a workout more with every passing second. When the Sa'sa turned this shuttle over to her, they didn't give her any destruct sequences other than the destruction of the entire shuttle. Unless...were new files available under Protocol Zeta? She'd have to look in the sealed records. Did Hal have access to those records?

Her stomach tossed like she was maneuvering through an asteroid field with a wonky grav generator. If Hal was a true AI, this could be trouble. Big trouble. She had enough trouble on her own; she didn't need any Sa'sa-created trouble.

She grimaced slightly. Any *more* Sa'sa-created trouble.

The Sa'sa net techs told her they'd modified the virtual assistant logic already in the shuttle so she wouldn't be alone. What else did they say? She *had* to remember. None of them, not even Ia'asan, could understand how she could survive without other beings, specifically other Sa'sa, around her constantly. The Sa'sa couldn't survive more than a standard day or so alone; solitary confinement was a horrific death sentence for them.

So, did they meld a complex logic with the existing virtual assistant? Her stomach twisted, and she swallowed hard. *Great black holes, isn't that a trajectory to disaster?* What if Hal took over her shuttle? AIs always killed off the 'useless organics' first. She shuddered, fear sending icy fingers down her spine. *Wait a minute.* Stop emoting, start thinking, *remember* what they said, no matter how difficult it was to parse Sa'sa conversation. There's no sense in running from a nova that won't blow up for a million years.

She did remember their amusement with the name and vocal characteristics they'd programmed. Tech X'sharccaxi, the tech class speaker, was friendlier than most of the Sa'sa, and the entire tech class seemed worried about her departure. They'd never go against Ia'asan, they couldn't—but they did have enough autonomy to make technical decisions for the benefit of the clutch since leader class didn't have their knowledge. Tech class took leader class's goals, requirements and strategies, and implemented the right technical solutions to meet those needs.

Saree leaned against the passage wall—if she kept moving while she was thinking this hard, she'd trip over her own feet.

So, maybe their thought process went like this: Saree was clutch—Ia'asan said so—Saree was leaving the clutch, but she needed clutch, so they'd make one for her. It made an odd kind of sense. A Sa'sa kind of sense.

The conversation was coming back to her. It was hard to remember the specifics, because like most Sa'sa communication, it was interspersed with conversations with other Sa'sa about multiple other topics and conversations. Tech X'sharccaxi told her net tech class was modifying the virtual assistant to give her a human clutch and he'd asked what she was studying. The tech class was fascinated by the science fiction of twentieth century Earth and the music. They'd devoured the University's reading and vid list for the subject. Several weeks later, Tech X'sharccaxi told her the net techs named her virtual assistant after one of the vids they'd liked.

The Sa'sa didn't generate many recordings of any kind, feeling recordings didn't provide a real 'experience,' but they loved all kinds of stories, even other species' work. Often, they'd import the tales into their story-telling nights, a tradition they continued from their pre-technology times when they had to gather in large numbers to stay warm during the long winter nights.

Those sessions—a combination of stories, poetry, and music— were one of the reasons she'd been able to tolerate being part of a Sa'sa clutch. During story-telling, the entire clutch focused on one topic, rather than a dozen different subjects. The stories also distracted her from the strangeness of the Sa'sa pressing and shifting against her, with the constant hiss of hide on hide as each Sa'sa tried to move closer to the center of the clutch. And the constant hissing and clashing of teeth their language required.

Saree shuddered, remembering. It was so alien, so wrong. And the immature pressed up against her, because she was warm and they were on the outside of the clutch. All those scaly bodies, crowding her. She shuddered again. But the stories helped her understand the Sa'sa better—although she'd never claim to understand them, particularly their humor. It was just too different.

Reminiscing didn't help with her current problem. The net tech class worried about her and gave her a clutch—a human clutch. She smiled, despite her concern. Hal's presence was comforting during her solitary travels, and his voice was soothing, but she'd never thought of him as a sentient AI. Had he always been sentient, and she wasn't aware, or was the sentience part of Protocol Zeta? Or maybe he was just an extremely complex logic and not sentient? She needed to search those sealed files.

She should figure out which vid the name 'Hal' came from and watch it. It might give her some additional clues about the net tech class's intentions.

Saree snorted a bit. Or not. They didn't think the way humans did.

Even if Hal was a true AI, there was nothing she could do about it right now. She had to believe the Sa'sa knew what they were doing, at least to some extent. They wouldn't deliberately endanger her, not after all the effort they'd gone to. Unless Ia'asan was being sneaky? Ridiculous. They profited from her work. Regardless of the clutch's intentions, there were always those pesky unintended consequences. *Stop, Saree. Go work out.* Making sure her public Scholar-face was in place, she walked to the phys mod.

Stepping into the phys mod and moving to the side, Saree scanned for threats. She stared, astonished. *By the egg of Zarar, that is...suns.* Captain Ruhger was performing some sort of gymnastic/dance/martial arts routine demonstrating immense strength, grace, and control. She couldn't, didn't want to move— she stared, enthralled.

He lowered slowly from a one-armed handstand to a wide-legged stance. Muscles bulging and rippling, he progressed deliberately into a one-armed handstand on the other side, and kept moving, circling the mat in slow, precise cartwheels. Each shift was smooth and controlled, all exactly the same, at the same achingly slow pace. Sweat rolled down his rock-hard body.

Anticipating his next handstand, Saree was startled when he sprang into high-speed, explosive flips, front, back, and side, each flip ending with vicious, lashing kicks and punches. Without signal or pause, he returned to the measured, deliberate moves, flowing from strength pose to strength pose. The control, the explosive strength, the sheer power in his movements…*suns. Amazing. Mesmerizing.*

He finally stopped, sweat pouring from powerful shoulders, down his carved chest and rippling abs into tight, black workout shorts hugging more muscles and... He faced her and bowed.

"Thank you for not interrupting me." His expression and voice were neutral.

"Of course, Captain. That was astonishing." Realizing how hard she'd been staring, heat exploded across Saree's cheeks. "I'm sorry, I hope you don't mind. I—" She didn't know what to say. Her lips weren't cooperating either—she was stuttering out words, not coherent phrases.

"No. If I minded, I would have reserved the phys mod and locked the hatches. I didn't think anyone would be here this early." Moving to the side of the mat, he picked up a towel, wiping the sweat off his face and body. His tone and face were still neutral—she had no idea what he was thinking or feeling.

"Oh. Umm. Do you mind me asking what that was? It was amazing." Incredible, shocking, graceful, beautiful—the words didn't exist, but considering the superlatives was enough to overcome the embarrassment of staring at him like he was…an exotic dancer or something. He could make some credits…her face heated and she tried, desperately, to wipe the thought out of her head.

The Captain flashed a small smile so quickly she wasn't sure it happened. "It's a y'ga routine developed by the Sisters of Cygnus." Striding to the wall, he swept through a control panel and made a selection. "A Sister taught me when I was young. I'm only a dabbler, I'm afraid." A small remote exited a hatch at the bottom of the wall, sliding to the mat. A whirring noise started and a sharp citrus scent wafted to her—a mat-cleaner. No wonder the phys mod always smelled so good. But 'dabbling' with that kind of routine, you wouldn't want to take the chance of slipping in someone's sweat.

"If you're a dabbler, I'd hate to see an expert. I've never seen such a display or heard of the Sisters." The shock was affecting her brain; she had to stop talking. She clamped her mouth closed and tried to smile. She was pretty sure she didn't succeed.

Despite the rictus on her face, the Captain answered, "The Sisters are very private. They live in an isolated compound, human females only, in a highly structured environment, and do their best to be self-sufficient. But they know their young need an outlet, a chance to explore the universe, and they need credits, so they export trained experts in several fields, y'ga being one of them. They are a closed community, but any adult member is free to leave whenever they want to if they are capable of self-defense, which is one of the aspects of y'ga. Many do go in and out, for monetary, professional or personal reasons. They practice a worship of the Great Mother, but I don't know the specifics. I do know they use y'ga in their rituals. It seems to require a lot of dedication and relative isolation." The Captain pressed his lips together tightly. Was he having the same problem Saree was?

"If they're women only, how do they survive?" She needed to shut up...

Captain Ruhger chuckled, then looked surprised. "They have children. I've never asked how. I assume it's artificial, or they adopt, because I'm sure they're celibate."

Saree was surprised by both the chuckle and the way it changed his face from glowering and forbidding to...friendly. Almost. The expression didn't last long enough for her to be sure.

He continued. "Females can join as adults too, but it is much more difficult and involved. One of my mother's friends joined after...later in life."

Saree didn't miss the pause in his last sentence and wondered what he didn't say. She was about to ask him more, but he held up a hand and stared at the wall past her.

"Ruhger." He frowned. "On my way." He focused on her and said, "Please excuse me—duty calls." He turned and left without waiting for her reply.

"Of course, Captain," she said to his retreating backside. A very fine backside, matching the rest of the very fine body. But with a routine like that, how could it be anything but spectacular? Saree rolled her eyes at the wave of physical desire sweeping through her and headed for the phys machines. Time to see what other wonders a former mercenary unit used for physical fitness— exercise could sweep away the inconvenient lust.

Forty minutes later she was moaning in the shower. The people who designed those machines and scenarios were sadists, not phys experts. She dressed in her regular Scholar's robes. "Hal, I'm going to breakfast, if that's okay with you."

"Of course, Saree. You must fuel your body after expending so much energy. I will continue my analysis of the escape pod."

"Thank you, Hal."

"You are welcome, Saree."

Walking to the dining facility, Saree hoped breakfast wasn't formal. She needed to devour some calories, preferably without a lot of fanfare. Halfway down the passage, she didn't care if she had to recite Klee poetry after she ate—something smelled *delicious*.

Entering the dining facility, she was relieved to see the elaborate decorations and the chandelier were gone, the large dining room table split into many small ones, and a buffet stood against the kitchen wall. Buffets were common on other folders, but this one was anything but common; the offerings were overwhelming. Flaky pastries with jewel-toned soft centers wafted mouthwatering aromas, and three different breakfast breads with various spreads waited. Farther down the buffet, batter and hot irons for two different kinds of pressed cakes waited, and keep-warms with three different types of meat. Finally, a platter with five different kinds of cheese. Greens and flowers enhanced the beautiful arrangement.

Surprising there wasn't any fresh fruit. Since they'd just left a system, Saree would have expected some in a spread like this. Maybe Dronteim couldn't grow fruit? Everything she'd eaten on the station had a nasty metallic taste; she'd assumed poor recycling, but maybe not. Was metallic the 'local flavor' in Dronteim? Saree chortled internally. In which case, there was no way Chef would allow such substandard fare on board. Saree could picture the fit the Chef would throw. Wait, she wasn't being fair to Chef; she didn't know enough about her yet.

Dithering over the plethora of wonders available, she selected a few items randomly. Moving to the beverage station, she hit the coffee icon on the unusually large auto-bev. But instead of the expected sound of flowing liquid, there was a grinding noise, then the sound of water with a hiss of escaping steam. Finally, a steaming press was revealed, with a timer counting down on the glass and the dark bitterness of excellent coffee floating up. Saree grinned. No auto-bev coffee for the Chef. What would an automated coffee press machine cost? Saree chuckled. More than she could afford. She scanned the room again; the tables were all empty, so she took her selections to a corner table where she could see all the hatches.

Sinking her teeth into a flaky pastry, she almost melted into a puddle of joy—the buttery flavor slid over her tongue, mixing with the sweetness of fruit and some warming spices, the crispy outer layers contrasting with the soft interior—*ah*. She'd planned on reading while she ate, but the food demanded her attention. She noted Chef entering the dining room, but she didn't pay attention—the pastries, the bread, the coffee—*ah*.

When she looked away from her plate for a moment, she noticed Chef was fussing with the buffet, but glancing over at Saree. Chef's...costume today wasn't as showy as last night's, but still a bit startling. Chef wore a form-fitting white coverall, but the resembalance to normal chef's whites ended there. It covered Chef's body, but didn't conceal *anything*. The poured plas molded lovingly to the Chef's generous curves and supported some of those curves in defiance of gravity.

When Chef turned, Saree saw the long eyelashes were gone

today. A veil of iridescent white netting fell from the bottom of the traditional tall chef's toque, covering half her face. A small silver-blue teardrop stained her coffee-colored cheek, rolling out below the veil, and the full lips were painted a red so dark they were almost black.

Saree smiled, hoping to cheer Chef up. "Chef, this is wonderful. You are a true artist. I'll gain ten kilos on this trip if I'm not careful."

A smile flickered across Chef's face. "Thank you for your praise, but this is nothing. Just a simple repast to break the long fast of the night," she said in sad, deep tones.

Wonder what had her so upset? A scholar would want to know. Suns, *she* wanted to know. The Chef was a fascinating being. "Would you like to join me while you wait?"

Chef dropped her head and shook it mournfully. "Oh, but I shouldn't. My place is in the kitchen."

"Please." Saree motioned to the chair next to hers. "I don't mean to offend you, but you look like you could use a sympathetic ear. I'm good at listening."

"Oh. Well. I was hoping it didn't show..." Chef looked at her feet.

Saree smiled inside—the teardrop was like a sun going nova.

Chef abruptly turned, her bosom almost launching a plate of pastries off the buffet, and sashayed to the beverage table. Scrolling through the bev choices, Chef made a selection, waited and pulled out another press. It wasn't dark enough for coffee. When Chef reached the table, Saree detected the scent of black tea with a hint of citrus. That was one fancy machine.

Chef said, "Thank you—I could use a mid-morning tea break,

and tea is always better with company."

Saree smiled. "Yes, it is. So is coffee. This is fabulous coffee too." She raised her cup in salute, and Chef twinkled in return. While Chef arranged herself at the table, Captain Ruhger entered the dining hall, his dark blue uniform straining across his shoulders.

"Oh, yes, I insist on the very best coffee and tea. Anything less is inadequate to breaking one's fast," Chef announced. "The first meal sets the tone for the whole day, no matter what some barbarians may think." Chef glared at the Captain, who was loading a box to go.

Captain Ruhger frowned at the automated press machine, over at the Chef, and back at the press again. He sighed, heavily. "I need to get back to work, Loreli. Can I take this with me?" he asked, pointing at the press.

Flouncing back into her seat, Chef said in biting tones, "If you must, although it is an insult to the coffee. Bring it back."

Captain Ruhger frowned deeper, and made a selection, coffee by the muffled sound of the grinder. "Of course. What good would this do me without any coffee in it?" He gathered several more pastries, and strode out of the room with his hands full, muttering something under his breath.

Saree was dying to know what was in the pod, but Hal was watching, and the Chef might be the best source of gossip she'd get. And possibly an ally if she needed one, which she might if Hal's predictions of trouble after the fold came true. Unable to wait longer, she took another bite, relishing the decadent pastry. "These are amazing. You must have been up all night."

Tossing her head back, Chef waved a hand dramatically. "Well,

I was, but one must suffer for one's art. Besides, how can anyone sleep with a broken heart?" She looked at the dining hall hatch, a mournful look on her face.

Saree stared at Chef for a moment, surprised. "Oh. I'm so sorry. How horrible for you." Guess she *was* going to find out what Chef Loreli was all about.

"Oh, it is," she wailed. "I've been stabbed—" she pressed a large hand over her heart "—right here, and sliced straight down into my bowels." Her hand followed her words, holding an imaginary knife hilt. "It is simply agonizing." She collapsed onto the table, her forehead resting on her hands.

Chef should be on stage, not in a kitchen. "It sounds awful. Do you want to tell me what happened?"

Chef Loreli turned her head, still on the table, and blinked, her full lips trembling. "You won't tell anyone?"

"No—your confidences are safe with me," Saree said solemnly, her hand over her heart. Who would she tell? She was all alone. She bit back a wince. She wasn't alone, was she? But she couldn't imagine an AI caring about human heartache. If Hal was an AI...

"Well..." Chef sniffled, raising her head off her hands and pushing back a little from the table to face Saree. She might be playing it up a little, but her emotions seemed genuine. "I have been in love with...someone my entire life. He protected me from bullies when I was young and later during the...period of trouble in our lives, and he's continued to help and protect me. But to him, that's all this is." She pressed both hands over her heart. "He thinks of me as a little brother, not a soulmate or a lover. He can't see past our past, or who I am now rather than who I was then," she finished with a sob.

"Oh. That sounds awful. I'm so sorry," Saree said, trying to figure out what seemed odd about the story. Oh, wait. Chef had said 'brother,' not 'sister.' Evidently, she'd changed her sexual identity and her love interest—Captain Ruhger?—couldn't see it, an all-too-common problem. "It is difficult for those we've grown with to see us as anything but children. That's why adult siblings argue like children, even if they're well-adjusted, successful adults." Not that she had any real siblings, but she'd seen enough drama at the foster home and primary school.

"Yes," Chef sobbed.

"I'm so sorry. I don't know what you can do other than wait." Saree shrugged, helplessly. "Time is the only cure for this malady if there is one."

"I know." Chef wiped away her tears impatiently, smearing the heavy blue eyeliner across her temples. It didn't look bad; the swooping blue lines enhanced her flamboyant look. Good thing she hadn't worn the huge eyelashes; they'd be a tangled, salty mess. "But thank you for listening. I feel better knowing someone cares."

A tiny bit of guilt lurked since caring hadn't been Saree's motivation, but she did feel bad for Chef. "Of course. How could I not?"

A group of passengers came in. From the green clothing, they must be the medicos Captain Ruhger mentioned last night. Chef jumped to her feet. "Can we talk some more, later?

"Absolutely," Saree said.

"Enjoy your breakfast. I must check on my creations," Chef said over her shoulder.

"Thank you, Chef—they are truly marvelous."

Saree finished her food and coffee, watching the medicos argue about some medical issue she didn't understand. If they were faking it, they had the terminology down.

Saree sighed and put her dishes in the auto-cleaner. She wasn't going to interrupt their discussion, so what to do now? She'd like to watch the escape pod exploration. It couldn't hurt to ask. Would a crew member be in the observation lounge? She didn't want to interrupt the Captain; they might be at a critical point in the operation. Entering the lounge, she spotted a single figure in dark blue crew uniform at the auto-bev. The crew member turned at her approach, revealing Grant Lowe's handsome face.

"Purser Lowe, how are you this morning?" She greeted him gravely, careful not to smile.

"Well, thank you, Scholar. And you?" he said, a pleasant but unemotional look on his face.

"Very well, thank you. Breakfast was wonderful. I'm surprised you aren't eating."

Lowe subtly shuddered. "Oh, just a little too… busy in there today."

Saree bit back a chuckle; he was so transparent. "The medicos are eating now, so Chef has retired to the kitchen."

His face brightened. "Oh. Maybe I will get a pastry…"

"Purser Lowe," she said.

"Oh, please call me Grant," he said with a smoldering look.

She nodded, keeping her face neutral. "Thank you, Grant. I'm Cary. I'm assuming the rendezvous with the pod occurred. What did you find?"

His smolder died. "I was just about to record a new message. We found a cooperative species escape pod. It appears to be badly damaged, and non-functional, but we're trying to open it now."

"Can I watch?"

Lowe looked startled. "Oh, I didn't consider... um, let me check." Turning away, he muttered, probably to the Captain, and turned back to her. "The Captain is afraid the sight might distress some of the passengers, so he doesn't want to transmit it on a general channel, or in the lounge, but he will send the vid links to your shuttle."

"Thank you. Even though I'm not a student of such things, I feel it is important to learn everything one can traveling through life. Don't you agree?"

Lowe's face shuttered. "Quite. Please excuse me, Scholar. I must return to my duties."

"Certainly. Pleasant morning to you." Walking back to her shuttle, Saree was satisfied. She'd got what she wanted *and* reminded Lowe she wasn't a conquest he wanted to make. She'd have to make those reminders more and more. On the other claw, it might be smart to succumb on the far side of the fold. If she was in danger from the other passengers, being with a crew member might give her some additional security. Maybe. She smiled ruefully for a second. Considering Lowe's body and probable vast experience, the encounter would be more than pleasant, but she wasn't attracted to him.

She'd never had the kind of deep feelings the Chef displayed. Sex was a pleasure shared with someone she trusted or an emergency with no other options. For better or worse, neither scenario was a common occurrence in her life.

Saree remembered Klar, her classmate at University, wistfully. They'd been friends first, then lovers, but they'd both known their liaison had an expiration date—she was leaving for her thesis research, and he was going home to start a university-level music program. Neither one of them had the kind of expertise Lowe implied, but they'd learned together, and their emotional connection was just as important as the physical. Saree missed the deep emotional connection, but late at night, she felt the lack of a warm, human body next to hers. Sadly, bringing someone into her shuttle was an indulgence she couldn't afford. And short-term physical liaisons weren't attractive, no matter how good Purser Lowe thought he was.

Besides, if she were going to indulge during this fold, she'd rather indulge with the Captain; *his* body was amazing.

She snorted at her ridiculous fantasy. A good body didn't mean he knew what to do with it...Lowe would. She snickered again at herself. These ridiculous thoughts were a waste of time. Watching the pod opening should focus her on more useful speculations.

Securing the shuttle hatches, she said, "Hal, the Captain is feeding vid to us. Would you display it on the main screen, please?"

"Certainly, Saree."

The pod appeared on the screen. As Hal stated, it was badly damaged, with dents all over the surface, as if it had bounced around an asteroid field or been used for target practice. Hard-suited figures, one in metallic red, one in shiny yellow, hovered near large machinery attached to the pod. A scissor-like apparatus, the blades a meter long or so, was attempting to pry open the hatch.

"They are having considerable difficulty opening the pod. The pod shows evidence of impacts everywhere, including the edge of the hatch along the seal. That damage is holding the hatch in place. They have cut through one section of the hatch seal and are using hydraulic spreaders to pry it apart. I do not detect any life signs in the pod, and there is no data recorded, as Chief Bhoher said. But the readings indicate an organic mass of some kind in the pod."

Hal was a very complex logic. Suns. Well, nothing she could do about it now, and the action on the screen was real-time, so she should watch and learn. "Hal, did the Captain allow us access to their comms?"

"It appears he did. Would you like to listen, Saree?"

"Yes, please, Hal."

"Certainly, Saree."

"…breaking point. Return to the shuttle, in case it releases with more energy than anticipated."

"Copy that, Chief," a high-pitched woman's voice said.

"That is Katryn Phazeer; she is in the yellow suit. She and her partner, Tyron, provide security for Lightwave and perform other functions as needed. They were the servers for the departure dinner," Hal said.

"So we were told. I wonder why security officers would be willing to serve food? But Lightwave's crew is small, so maybe they have to do a lot of different chores? Does the Captain clean the bathrooms?" Snorting out a laugh, she remembered the rough way Katryn plunked down the dishes. "Maybe they don't have a choice."

The suited figures left the vid frame. The plier blades between the pod and hatch spread, separating the hatch from the pod. It wasn't smooth—if sound traveled in space, the groans and shrieks of overstressed cerimetal would be deafening. Eventually, the machine reached its full extension, leaving the hatch half open.

"Captain, I'll need to rig something else to open the hatch all the way, but it should be open far enough to look inside," Chief Bhoher said.

"Use the camera on the remote."

"Already on the way," another male voice said, this one a pleasant tenor.

Hal said, "That is Tyron Phazeer's voice."

The vid screen split, with the wide-view of the pod on the left and another view on the right. The right screen zoomed in on the pod hatch. That view must be the remote vid camera closing with the pod. The remote appeared to be a small inspection module, the kind used for hull checks and minor repairs. A thin, articulated arm levered up and off the remote toward the hatch, holding the camera. The remote's vid showed a hatchway, darkness in the middle. A bright light flicked on and revealed the typical interior of a generic cooperative species escape pod—an oval space, about three meters long and high and two meters wide. Straps dangled from padding for beings to fasten themselves to the walls securely. The beige padding appeared to be undamaged and clean. The vid swept around the pod. A soft suit, the disposable, one-time-use kind, came into view. The remote camera pulled back and the being was revealed.

Saree gasped. "That's a Sa'sa! Hal, is there only one?"

"It does appear to be a Sa'sa, Saree, although we will need confirmation through DNA analysis. We must wait for the interior scan to complete. A single organic mass was originally detected."

The vid panned around the rest of the pod. No other beings came into view.

"Captain, there's only one being," Tyron said, his voice sounding troubled.

"Agreed. This is...unusual. Please scan the being and pod carefully for any other...unusual things. If we don't find anything else, search the remains and pod for identification, and take a DNA sample. We will ship the data to the Sa'sa. If there's nothing else found, Chief, we'll back off, then destroy the pod and the remains. Any additions, deletions or objections?"

"No, Captain. Destruction sounds reasonable. I want full containment on the DNA sample. Tyron, Katryn?"

"Agreed, Captain," Tyron said.

"Agreed. We'll do the search in person if we can get the hatch open the rest of the way," Katryn said.

"Agreed. Full decon before you re-enter the shuttle."

"Copy that, Captain."

"Let me know if you find anything. I'll work with Grant to figure out what we're going to tell the passengers." A heavy sigh sounded. "Then I'll be in the ready room. I'm sure some of the passengers will have questions. Not that I have any answers."

Before Saree could say anything, the Captain spoke again. "Katryn, we don't have any Sa'sa DNA data banks, do we?"

"No, Captain. The Sa'sa don't release them—you know how insular they are—and I don't think we've ever had a Sa'sa shuttle with us. They stick with their own fold transports."

"That's what I thought. Well, I guess the Sa'sa can figure this out on their own once we give them the data." He sighed again, forcefully. "Ruhger out."

"Hal, we don't have any Sa'sa DNA banks, do we?"

"No, Saree, we do not. It is confirmed; there is a single Sa'sa. Do you want to message Ia'asan-clutch?"

That was a good question. Saree was an adopted clutch member, but there were many Sa'sa rituals she wasn't privy to. She didn't know anything about death rituals. She didn't know if they had any—the Sa'sa didn't talk about death. Ia'asan clutch adopted her because they wanted control of her abilities, not because they liked her in any way, shape or fashion.

Also, as the lowest-ranking frequency-maintaining clutch, they weren't given much choice in the matter. Ia'asan leadership made it clear how little love they had for warm-blooded creatures— except as food. The rest of the clutch were more tolerant, some even friendly, especially the tech class, but she'd never tested their tolerance by intruding in sensitive areas. "Do you have an opinion, Hal?"

"No, Saree, I do not. I do not have any information on how the Sa'sa deal with death. I do know it is unusual to find a single Sa'sa anywhere except the punishment pits. It would be better if we knew whether the Sa'sa was dead before or after his arrival in the escape pod, but since the pod's memory doesn't exist, and we have no idea how long the pod has been in space, it is impossible to know."

"The memory doesn't exist?"

"No, Saree, it does not. There is no data to be found. I am conjecturing, but I believe the data recorders were removed from the pod prior to release. The manufacturer's data plate was removed from the pod hatch frame; there are holes where it should be. There is a small memory module containing the programming for the pod life support and propulsion systems, but no others. The system programming was modified so it doesn't record any data."

"Could this have been a mobile form of a punishment pit?"

"Unknown."

"I think it's unlikely—it would be easy to isolate a Sa'sa on a folder or shuttle without ejecting a pod, which would be expensive. And there were no ship markings on the pod, implying it was never installed. Could there have been a shipment of escape pods through this fold and an accident of some sort?"

"I will search the fold orbit records."

"Thank you, Hal."

"You are welcome, Saree."

So, if she sent a message to Ia'asan clutch, she ran the risk of meddling in taboo areas. But if she didn't send a message, and they discovered she knew about the Sa'sa remains, they might be offended she didn't report. Saree was the human extension of their clutch; her job was to tell them about non-Sa'sa matters impacting the clutch. Or impacting the Time Guild. Or humanity's attitude toward the Sa'sa as a whole. It was her main task with Ia'asan clutch; she rarely got the chance to do clock maintenance. The clutch had a hard time understanding she could do more than one thing. She sighed. Either way, she was likely to be wrong. The wonderful breakfast sat heavily in her stomach.

"Is there something wrong, Saree?"

"I think there's a lot wrong, Hal; I'm just not sure what to do about it. I think I will send a message to Ia'asan clutch, with the plain facts of the discovery. I'll tell them Lightwave is sending the details. I would rather err on the side of too much information rather than too little. But I'm worried about their reaction and I'm even more worried about how a single Sa'sa got here."

"I cannot find any obvious means of travel, Saree. There hasn't been a Sa'sa folder reported in this system for six standard years, the last time the frequency standards were maintained. No escape pod manufacturers are in this system or the nearby systems. I can find no evidence of any accident involving a cooperative species in this system. Analyzing the trajectory of the pod before the rendezvous and capture, it appears to have been spiraling sunward for at least a standard year. With the impacts the pod has sustained, it is impossible to know the initial trajectory, but the highest potential path calculations predict release at the fold point, with more velocity than a normal escape pod, even allowing for less mass than normal. The release points in descending order of probability are all in the fold transport orbit, which is not unexpected. The calculated release velocity is always more than a normal escape pod. My full analysis is available in the data storage area I have labeled as 'Sa'sa Escape Pod' if you want to review it. My programming insists humans prefer verbal analysis to be general, rather than specific, but I can recite the specific probabilities if you prefer."

"Thank you, Hal. Your programming is correct. I prefer mathematics to be displayed visually; verbalizing them is unnecessary and distracting." Saree chuckled. "I'm sure your math is correct."

"Thank you for confirming your preferences, Saree. It helps to refine my interactions with you."

"You are welcome, Hal."

"Would you like help drafting a message to Ia'asan clutch?"

Would she? A good question. "Does your programming include any Sa'sa interaction programming?"

"Not specifically. However, because I know the source of my original programming, I can redact the human-specific social programming which leaves me with a set of social programming that must be Sa'sa, or what Sa'sa think is human. I cannot state any definitive probability of its correctness since it is based on underlying assumptions that may not be correct, although they are highly probable."

Oh, suns. There's a trajectory straight to a black hole. She'd be better off relying on *her* training with the Sa'sa; it was real, not surmised. Even if her experiences were strange and contradictory at times. "I will state the facts and tell them additional details will come from Lightwave, but if you'd like to review it, that would be helpful."

"Very well, Saree. Also, don't forget about my analysis of your companions and the crew of Lightwave."

"Yes, Hal, thank you." *And won't that add to my stress quotient?* Saree sighed, rolling her tight shoulders. She'd start with the message, then see what other wonderful surprises were in store. She was all too certain there would be more. She sighed again and started drafting.

CHAPTER FIVE

The message to the Sa'sa homeworld was gone, samples taken and the pod destroyed. Grant informed the passengers, Lightwave was back in the fold orbit and Ruhger was hungry and tired. And troubled. And puzzled — about more than the single Sa'sa in the bod-pod. Why had he told the Scholar about the Sisters? He must be *really* tired and hungry — he needed to fix at least one of those issues before he blabbed other sensitive information to anyone wandering by.

Did he have the patience to face Loren — no, Loreli — at this point or should he go to bed now? Ruhger's stomach roared and he frowned. He couldn't sleep with that, not even a short nap. *Blast it all to the seven suns of Saga.* Ruhger stomped to the chow hall, anticipating trouble and hoping there wasn't any.

Entering the room, he was relieved to find it empty — the lack of drama was almost disappointing after all the anticipation. He dished up a big bowl of delicious-smelling stew, added a basket of bread meant to serve four and sat down where he could see the kitchen hatch. He didn't want Loren—no, *Loreli*—sneaking up on him.

The stew was rich and heavy, and the bread was crusty and crisp, with a light but firm interior perfect for soaking up the gravy. After three bowls, he felt better, if sleepier. Those breakfast pastries were tasty, but they didn't last long. He should have added some protein, or come back a second time, but he'd run out of time. And he didn't want to deal with Loreli *and* the pod—way too much drama. And after dinner last night, he couldn't stomach a protein bar. He snorted. He'd gotten soft. Before Loreli came on board, he wouldn't have thought twice about eating a protein bar.

As he was getting up to put his dishes in the cleaner, Lore...li came out, in another blindingly white outfit. Did she spray it on? How could she breathe? "Fantastic stew, Loreli. Thank you."

She blinked at him for a moment, then lit up with a tinge of pleased surprise. "You're welcome. I'm glad you enjoyed it."

He nodded, a little ashamed he hadn't complimented her before. "Yes, a nap will be much easier now that my stomach isn't growling. I'll see you later. Thanks again."

"Of course, Captain. Have a good nap!" she caroled. "Maybe I can share the next one with you!"

Shaking his head, he walked away. He didn't have the patience to engage in a battle of wits now. He needed some downtime before the next crisis hit. Securing the hatch and removing his ship suit, he was all too sure there was another crisis coming. This fold was already far too eventful, and with this group of passengers? As he had told Lore...li, he wasn't sure why, but none of them seemed quite right.

Setting the alarm, he closed his eyes. Seconds later, the waker went off. Ruhger sat up, stretching. He didn't feel rested, but...he swept through holo screens to his health monitor, his med data showing he'd slept solidly. Just not enough. Rubbing his eyes, he lurched to the sani-mod and showered quickly. Suns only knew what else happened while he was out. "Contact Lowe, normal priority."

"Lowe here, Captain," his voice said quietly. He must be trying to keep the contact discreet.

"Anything else fall apart while I was out?"

"Nope. I've been in the lounge, telling everyone I know nothing, but either they don't believe me, or they're bored and looking for something more entertaining than vids or games. Or card games."

"You haven't been gambling, have you, Grant?"

"Of course not, my Cap-i-tan!" he said far too cheerfully. "No, I reserve my fleecing for the ports."

"Getting fleeced is more likely. Or getting dead if you do win."

"Oh, you are worse than a Klee nest mother."

Ruhger could almost hear the eye-rolling. He grimaced. Time to get back to business. "Let me know if anything comes up. I'll stay in Alpha shuttle, trying to balance our accounts."

"Better you than me. Lowe out."

Plopping down at his desk, Ruhger revived the screen full of red. It hadn't magically changed while he slept. The fuel expenses for this trip did rise due to the rad-blasted side excursion. Still, this trip out of Dronteim was good for credit flow—a full folder always was. Three of the shuttles paid the 'guaranteed departure by' fee—pure profit. But it didn't make much of a dent in the bottom line.

Weapons, good weapons, were expensive, and they still had some start-up debt all these years later. And since they were heading for another edge-of-the-known system, there were no guarantees they'd fill the folder again. It might take longer to fill than it had in Dronteim. At least they knew Cygnus—they wouldn't be eating aluminum foil or dealing with so-called nobility. He didn't want to use the term 'Lady' or 'Sir' again. Stuck up, rad-blasted idiots, every single one of them.

Still, Grant had picked up some interesting cargo—maybe it would pay off. Luxury items were always a gamble, but they didn't have room for high-mass bulk cargo. Taking a chance on small luxury items was a better bet than odd quantities of mid-grade necessities. There were always a few wealthy individuals and social climbers desperate for core extravagance. Lowe was very good at selling the story—all that time staring at gossip nets paid off. Or at least he hoped it did—they needed a big score to pay off the necessary weapon upgrades.

What they didn't need was more trouble. For whatever reason, this particular trip had been trouble from the start, and his gut said it was going to get worse. First, Loreli had thrown a hissy fit about coming to Dronteim, but she wouldn't explain *why*. Then, sitting so long, waiting for more passengers made everyone edgy. And when they finally showed up? Ruhger hadn't been kidding Loreli—none of these passengers seemed quite right. The wealthy 'lady' and her companion, the artiste, the Chelonians, the engineer, the essence researcher and the scholar, no matter how sweet her body might be, all of them seemed a bit 'off,' and he didn't know why. Well, that wasn't quite true; the medicos seemed okay. A little standoffish, maybe, but then so was he.

Finding the escape pod cast a shadow over everything—Ruhger couldn't find a reason for it to exist.

There was no evidence of a Sa'sa folder in this system for the last six standard years. Ruhger checked his data crawler; there was no evidence a Sa'sa shuttle traversed the fold point either. But a Clocker had definitvely been here, and there was a dead Sa'sa in an escape pod, so, therefore, Sa'sa were here. He queried Sa'sa death rituals and got nothing; they were one of the species who didn't talk about death. The Sa'sa was in a pressure suit, so they could assume the being was alive when strapped in. But a single Sa'sa? They didn't do well alone.

He queried again. He'd remembered correctly—Sa'sa without other Sa'sa died, quickly. There were several documented cases where a single Sa'sa, detained by a legal authority for some infraction, died in custody for no apparent reason. Sometimes, they beat themselves to death trying to get out of whatever holding area they were in. He studied the entry further. Even if restrained or medicated, they died, within a standard day or two. The Sa'sa refused to talk about it, other than to insist the clutch would deal with wrongdoing and the clutch would make amends and reparations to injured parties.

Most systems understood this and agreed; those who didn't? They didn't get their clocks maintained. Ruhger nodded thoughtfully. Nothing like the threat of your system being cut off from the wider universe to make you treat an entire species with kid gloves.

He frowned—what were kid gloves, anyway? They *couldn't* be made from children, could they? He shuddered at the macabre thought. No matter; what mattered was how the Sa'sa would react to their message about the escape pod.

With no information about death and death rituals, there was no telling if they'd made an off-vector thrust. They were a single ship with no set schedule or route; there wasn't much the Sa'sa could do other than destroy them. Even though the Sa'sa controlled the Time Guild, they didn't use the inherent power the way humans would. No, if someone crossed them, there were discussions about reparations or treaties, sometimes lasting many standard years. When talking became useless, the entire system the offense occurred in, or sometimes an entire species, or both, was ignored, their existence seemingly wiped from the collective memory of the Sa'sa. But if someone attacked the Sa'sa physically or destroyed one of their clocks—then the Sa'sa went on the offensive and tried their best to exterminate the offenders. Because of their wealth and numbers, they succeeded.

Smart species found a way to limit the damage by defining the enemy for the Sa'sa—the Grusians had sacrificed their leadership and ships, rather than be annihilated. The humans on Pavo did the same. Xeno specialists said the Sa'sa clutches competed for resources, but an attack by a non-Sa'sa against one was an attack against all. And they had very long memories—a group mind or consciousness. Whatever revenge they chose might take place a decade or two from now.

So, they could get a diplomatic message with legalese or a Sa'sa warship—or nothing. There was no way to tell, so worrying was useless. They were many light years and folds from Sa'sa home space, so an attack wouldn't be for—he ran the calculations—at least thirteen standard days. By then, they'd have folded to Cygnus. It wouldn't be hard to figure out where they'd gone—

they'd advertised widely—but playing catch-up wasn't a good tactic. He barked out a laugh. They could always dissolve the company and rename Lightwave; that might be enough to hide them from the Sa'sa for their lifetimes.

Enough useless speculation. It was time for dinner. With any luck, it would be simple like lunch, but there was no telling what Loreli would do. Putting his formal coveralls back on, Ruhger glanced in the mirror. He felt ridiculous parading around in the shiny rank, but passengers responded better with a visual reminder of who was in charge. Sometimes it saved him a good bit of effort, even if playing the role of gracious host made his jaw ache. Maybe he should have stayed a mercenary; the uniforms didn't have all this sparkly stuff screaming 'here I am, a big, bright target; shoot me.' Securing his hatch, he strolled to the chow hall, greeting passengers as he went.

Grant met him at the chow hall hatch. *Suns.* Another blasted formal dinner. He sighed, and Grant laughed soundlessly at him, bowing dramatically.

"Think you're cute, do you?" Ruhger muttered.

"Why, I'm surprised you noticed how cute I am, Captain," he answered back, loudly.

Ruhger frowned at him. Lowe could rival Loreli when he was in a mood.

Reluctantly, he sat at the head of the table. This evening, dark colors draped the table—black, deep dark red and a few touches of dull gold. Black ribbons hung from the chandelier, the lights dim. Loreli must have decided a memorial feast was appropriate. *Wonderful.* He held back a scowl, but it took real effort.

Looking down the table, he was unsurprised to see it filling rapidly. Nobody would miss one of Chef's super fancy 'dining experiences,' even those who normally would stay in their shuttles. Even if she was doing it to memorialize a being she'd never met. Suns, he was pretty sure she'd never seen a Sa'sa in person. The dead one was the first for him and he'd traveled more than Loreli. Well, the food would be memorable.

The table filled. He had an empty seat to his left—probably for the artiste, who was late, again—and Lady Vulten filled the seat to his right, dressed in a long, shiny purple gown with dark blue jewels flashing around her neck. *Oh, joy.* "Good evening, Lady Vulten."

"Good evening, Captain. I'm surprised. My understanding was formal dinners were at constellation departure and arrival only," the Lady said with her nose in the air. Since it stuck out of her face like it was trying to escape her orbit, it was rather obvious. Her nose was always in the air. Maybe her neck was fused?

"I take no responsibility for the scheduling of dinners or dining events, Lady Vulten; that is entirely at the discretion of the Chef."

"Really." She sniffed. "Giving too much latitude to the hired help is a good way to find yourself in financial trouble. You must direct those beneath you with a firm hand."

Gentle Schultz, on the Lady's right, stared down at her plate, her lips clamped together. Ruhger didn't envy the poor woman, working for this harridan. "I give my people goals and limits, and allow them to decide how to accomplish those goals. It works well. They're happier, and I can concentrate on my job, which makes me happy."

"Well, happiness!" She sniffed again, unimpressed with the argument. She opened her mouth to continue, but Artiste Borgia made his entrance, drawing everyone's attention, just as he'd planned, no doubt. The Artiste wore formal blacks, with touches of maroon at his throat and waist. He didn't have a reputation as a great singer, but he was a showman.

What was hiding behind his showmanship? What was hiding behind the Lady's superior attitude? And what were the rest of the passengers hiding? Because Ruhger was struck again, looking around the table, by the distinct feeling all of them were playing roles, even the ever-so-earnest Scholar and the mousy Gentle Schultz. His gaze snagged on the group of green in the middle. Well, not the medicos.

With effort, he brought himself back to his duties. "Good evening, Artiste Borgia," he said as the man seated himself with a huge fuss. The Artiste's awful cologne surrounded them like a too-small pressure suit. Ruhger fought back a grimace but couldn't stop a series of sneezes.

Once he got his nose under control, the Artiste greeted him. "Good evening, Captain. I have to complement your Chef on her exquisite taste," he said, looking around the room. He'd chosen his outfit as if the chow hall was a stage, but his colors were slightly off—he looked a little green. But that might please the Chelonians, seated to his left, since they were definitely green. How did he know what color scheme Loreli had chosen?

Before he could continue orbiting those thoughts, Loreli appeared in the kitchen hatchway. This evening's costume was shocking, of course, but also surprising because it seemed impractical to cook in, maybe dangerous. A diaphanous white veil with tiny, sparkling ruby-red jewels flashing covered the Chef from the top of her tall, traditional white toque down to her knees.

A huge, white caftan, banded with black and dark red, swayed below the veil, the long sleeve-things hiding Loreli's hands. Antique gold teardrops dripped down one cheek, shining against her espresso-dark skin. Ruhger leaned over, looking behind Vulten; Loreli's legs and feet were in her usual white leggings and ridiculously high platform boots. He couldn't help but huff in amusement; Artiste Borgia could learn something about true showmanship from Loreli.

Loreli flashed a smile at him, then announced in deep, woeful tones, "Tonight, we honor the passing of a fellow sentient, a traveler of the starways like us, and we celebrate our continued existence on this plane, remembering that we are all just ephemeral motes in the Universe." Whirling, spears of ruby light flying off her veil, Loreli retreated to the kitchen.

Tyron and Katryn came out bearing trays, Katryn glaring at him. He shrugged; their duties included all the miscellaneous detritus of space travel, and they knew it. Obviously, Katryn was annoyed by the added menial chore, but why she was annoyed at *him* was a puzzle. It's not like *he* wanted another rad-blasted formal dinner. She slammed the soup down in front of him, sending a good bit of it sloshing out of the bowl and bumping his shoulder hard with her hip. He looked mournfully at the saucer— such a shame to waste great soup.

Everyone looked at him expectantly. A toast to the deceased was probably appropriate. He sighed inside and raised his water glass. "Let us honor a gentle being's passage by doing our best to excel in our everyday lives. Please enjoy Chef Loreli's attainment of that goal." He took a sip. Everyone around the table joined in, then applied themselves to the soup. He did the same, closing his eyes to enjoy the creamy goodness. No sense in spoiling it with the view of the Artiste and the Lady—the Artiste's stench was bad enough.

Ruhger spooned up the portion remaining in his bowl. He had no idea what kind of soup it was, other than white and creamy, but it was good. Would anyone notice if he drank the spilled part off the plate under the bowl? Looking around the table at the rapt diners, he sighed internally again. Even caught up in their soup, somebody would notice that big a gaffe. He gently ran his spoon around the saucer to scoop up what he could.

Course after course followed, all of them delicious and all of them either white, black, dark red or a combination of those colors. Loreli was *good* at this—Ruhger would have never guessed the small, nerdy little boy with his nose in a book would turn into a chef of renown. A female chef at that. Life was strange.

At the end of the meal, they all stood and applauded before Chef came out the hatch. When she did appear, everyone crowded around her, offering thanks and praise. Ruhger smiled at the sight—he'd be sure to thank Loreli later when he could get a word in edgewise. Leaving the chow hall, he went around to the back hatch. Tyron and Katryn were eating, perched on stools at one end of the high, white countertop bisecting the room. It was piled high with dirty dishes, pots, and pans. Even with auto-washers, cleaning all those would be a real chore. At least playing Captain got him out of KP duty.

He faced them from the other side of the countertop. "I know this serving thing is way below your pay grade. Thanks for stepping up. If you want, you can play Captain on the next trip, and I'll hang out in the kitchen."

Katryn snorted. "Oh, you'd love to do that, I'm sure. But as much as I hate serving food, if anyone would be worse with the passengers than you, it would be Tyron or me. Before day one was over, he'd have one of them on the floor moaning, or I'd have them so offended they'd jump ship in the middle of the fold orbit."

Tyron added, around a mouth full of the amazing dessert, "Besides, there is some compensation. Loreli gives us a starter before the service you guys don't get." He finished swallowing. "And extra dessert."

A shot of pure jealousy hit him low in the stomach, even though he was almost uncomfortably full. "Now I really want to hang out in the kitchen," Ruhger said.

"Not a chance. Go away," Tyron said, chuckling as he reached across the counter and shoved, sending Ruhger stumbling toward the hatch.

He chuckled to himself, then sobered, realizing he had to go play Captain in the lounge. Blast it all to a black hole; there'd be a billion stupid questions he didn't have answers for. Before he could leave, Loreli tumbled through the hatch, chest heaving. While she was always emotional, this reaction seemed a little much, even for her.

"Are you okay?"

"Oh, my, yes! Such praise! I am not worthy!" She put a hand over her heart.

"Sure you are. This is awesome," Tyron said, the words muffled through another mouthful of dessert.

Ruhger considered stealing some, but he didn't want to lose a hand. "It's true, Loreli—it was a wonderful meal. Really. It was delicious."

"Oh, it's too much. I'm going to faint." She clutched the edge of the counter.

She did look a little pale, a feat with her dark skin.

"Loreli, I think you'd better sit down. You look almost as white as your outfit, and you know that's impossible," Katryn said.

Loreli sank onto the stool across from Tyron, removing her toque and the sparkling veil with shaking hands. "All the praise! I'm stunned. I feel rather lightheaded." She pressed her hands on the table, swaying a little on the stool.

Ruhger peered down at her face, clamped a hand across her wrist on the counter and pressed a fingernail firmly. Loreli gasped and tried to pull back, but he held on, pinning her hand to the countertop, watching the nail. It stayed pale, filling too slowly. Her blood flow was compromised. "Loreli, it's more than emotional. There's something wrong. Let's get you to the medico station."

"Are you sure? There's so much to do here..." She slumped over the table and slid off the stool.

"Blast it!" He caught her and eased her to the floor. Tyron put her feet up on a stool, while Katryn called the medfloat from its station. "Katryn, once we get her into the medico station, review the security cams and see if someone poisoned her."

Katryn's thin black brows almost met above the bridge of her tiny nose. "Why are you going there, Ruhger? Do you know something we don't?"

"No, I'm just—uneasy about this fold. These passengers...something's off. And Loreli hasn't been sick." The medfloat came through the hatch, and he and Tyron loaded Loreli on it, both of them grunting a bit with effort. They jogged alongside to the medico station, the oxygen hood popping up over her face and sensors attaching as they went. "I'm not sure what it is, but something's got me pinging like an asteroid field on a single-use suit."

The medfloat slotted itself into the treatment table. Medical appendages came out and attached themselves to Loreli. A display above her head presented her vital signs. Blood pressure, heart rate, and O2 were all low, but the machine didn't have a cause. The blood or tissue analysis had to find something. She might be dramatic, but she'd never fake illness, not when there was work to do. *Come on, machine, hurry up. Find something and fix it.*

"Captain, we do have the four-pack of medicos. Should I call them?" Tyron asked.

"Good idea. One of us will stay with Chef at all times."

"Copy that, Captain." He turned away to ask for their assistance.

Katryn was staring at the wall, reviewing the security records. Good. Ruhger put his hand over Loren's so he'd know someone was there. Lore...li was a friend. A good friend. No way he'd abandon Loreli, even if he didn't love her romantically. Or understand her.

The small compartment filled with people in bright green coveralls. One of them, the short, older female, barked, "Clear out. Give us room to work."

Ruhger tossed his chin toward the hatch when Tyron and Katryn looked at him. "I'm staying. Back here." He stepped back against the wall. "What's your specialty, anyway?" he asked.

"Infectious disease pandemics. New colony worlds come with new diseases. They spread quickly." She and the others bustled around, taking more vitals and samples, and inserting IVs. "I need the patient's medical history, Captain."

"Stand by." Bringing up his holo, he swiped through the crew records then flicked Loreli's med data over to the medico. She reviewed it without further chatter. He tried to keep an eye on them all, but with three of them flocking around Loreli, it was impossible.

"Captain?" Katryn's voice in his ear.

"Go," he subvocalized.

"None of the medicos came anywhere near Loreli. They applauded with everyone else, then returned to their shuttle. Borgia, Vulten, Schultz, Ursuine and the Chelonians all congratulated her in person, and Borgia and Vulten definitely touched her, but they were all crowded around, so it's impossible to see who did and didn't."

"Copy."

"You realize anyone can access the kitchen, right? I'm reviewing the vids and access logs, but it's going to take a while, and some people are just curious—they have to poke their noses into everything."

"Do your best, Katryn. It could be sickness or some undetected...issue."

"Copy. Out."

Tyron checked the medicos and cleared them, but it would be all too easy for experts in infectious diseases to make Chef sick. But why? They seemed to enjoy the meals like everyone else. Why would anyone damage the source of all that great food?

"Captain." The gray-haired female stood in front of him, a neutral expression on her face.

"Medico?" Blast it, what was her name?

"Chef Loreli's medical records indicate a severe allergy to nickel with a non-typical response. Is that correct?"

"Yes, that is correct. Loreli is very careful about what she eats, and wears, and makes sure none of her kitchen equipment has nickel in it."

"She appears to be suffering from a nickel reaction. The dessert tonight was chocolate, and chocolate can have significant quantities of nickel, as can oatmeal and beans. Is there any way to tell how much of those foods she may have ingested?" She frowned a bit. "And please be aware there is little we can do, other than provide general supportive care. With a response of this type, the treatments for nickel removal can cause as many medical issues as the nickel allergy response itself."

"I'll check with her helpers."

The medico nodded and turned back to Loreli.

"Katryn, Tyron, do you know if Loreli ate any of her chocolate dessert or any oatmeal or beans?"

"Ruhger, I know she didn't eat much of the dessert because she was moaning about not being able to do anything other than taste-test it because of her allergy. I'll check her recipe records to see if there was oatmeal or beans in the food, but I don't remember seeing those anywhere in the kitchen," Tyron said.

"Do you have access to her recipes?"

Katryn laughed. "Well, no, we're not supposed to, but CIS's net security is horrible, and it's a medical emergency, so I'll hack it."

"Agreed and approved. Let me know."

"Wilco. Out."

"Excuse me, medicos, but we know she barely tasted the chocolate dessert. She's aware of the allergy issues. My people are checking the other dishes now, but we don't think the problem foods were part of the meal."

The gray-haired female who seemed to be in charge turned back to him. "There is one other possibility. It's a rather odd circumstance, but Lady Vulten grows Thymdronteim, right?"

Ruhger groaned internally. Vulten made it more than clear how 'wonderful' Thymdronteim was. To him, everything in-system tasted metallic—they couldn't leave Dronteim fast enough. "Yes, she does. Why?"

"Because Thymdronteim is a major source of nickel. The planet Dronteim has a lot of nickel in the soil, and the herb concentrates the nickel as it grows. That's one of the reasons they haven't been able to export plants—it requires a lot of nickel and a particular type of sunlight and moisture in a combination that hasn't been economically viable to reproduce." She snorted, her mouth twisted, and her tone became dryly ironic. "And there's the fact that a fairly large percentage of humans are sensitive or allergic to nickel, including me. Thymdronteim may have a unique flavor, but many of us can't eat it unless we want contact dermatitis on our tongues, throat and the rest of our digestive system."

Ruhger shuddered. How miserable. "Funny, Lady Vulten didn't mention that little issue when she droned—I mean told me about her business."

The medico's frown deepened. "No, Dronteim doesn't advertise it, even though they should. Far too many humans are allergic to nickel. The entire system should be avoided by people like your Chef."

"I wish she'd told me." Ruhger grimaced. "Well, now I know. I don't think we'll be coming back here again—this was a one-time fold for us. I'll check system nickel concentrations from here on out." He wondered... "Is it possible that merely shaking Lady Vulten's hand was enough to give Loreli the reaction?"

Medico Pancea—oh, yes, that was her name—looked surprised, then thoughtful. "Perhaps. She is unusually sensitive and has an idiosyncratic reaction, so it's possible. Did it happen?"

"Yes, it did. Several people congratulated Chef after the meal, and she was one of them. Artiste Borgia also shook her hand, and others may have or otherwise touched her skin, but we can't tell."

"Well." Pancea studied him. "Interesting you checked. Anyway, Lady Vulten probably does carry more nickel in her body than most humans and may have more on her skin, if they brought plants with them. It's noteworthy the Artiste shook her hand—most experienced interstellar travelers are careful not to touch others casually." Looking ironically amused, she continued. "I'm sure if we asked, he'd say he was overcome by his emotions." She sobered. "Anyway, regardless of the cause, with supportive care, Chef Loreli should be fine. She must rest for a few days, so no more fancy meals until after the fold. Actually, you shouldn't let her work at all for the next forty-eight standard hours. Do you have alternative feeding arrangements?"

"We do, although they're bound to be disappointing after hers. But I'm sure we'll all make do, and those who complain too much can eat in their shuttles," Ruhger said, smiling at Medico Pancea with relief.

She shuddered. "No, thank you. We—" she motioned to her coworkers "—spend far too much time eating survival rations in our shuttle. And because this system is so nickel-heavy, I—" she put a hand to her chest "—ate nothing but those until we arrived on your ship. I was particularly grateful you have extensive hydroponic gardens and an outstanding water-filtering unit."

Ruhger nodded. He wasn't going to tell her the water filtering was a military specification, although she could probably guess. No doubt they'd seen manufactured pandemics along with the natural ones. "I do remember you asking about those things and what supplies we were taking on here. I thought it was a normal precaution for medicos."

"Well, it is." Smiling, she tilted her head to the side and gestured with a hand. "But in this case, it was personally important."

"I see. And now I understand why Loreli didn't want to bring any food from Dronteim and why she kept bugging us to leave." One oddity explained, a Klee pod more to go. For example, why hadn't Loreli just told him about the nickel problem here? He would have folded out a long time ago, even with empty shuttle bays. She meant more to him than a few credits. She was family. Blast and rad. She should have said something. "I do appreciate your help. Please let me know what we owe for your services."

Medico Pancea laughed. "Oh, absolutely nothing. It's in our best interests to get Chef Loreli back to good health. We're never going to get a CIS dining experience any other way!"

"Neither would I."

Loreli moaned. The medicos cleared away from one side of the medfloat, so Ruhger stepped forward. "Loreli, you're going to be okay. I want you to rest." He put his hand gently on her shoulder, covered by her caftan, not wanting to chance he might have something on his skin too.

"Ruhger?" she asked, her voice weak, lashes fluttering. Good thing she didn't have those ridiculous long ones on.

He could barely hear her, so he leaned closer. "Yes, I'm right here."

"What happened?"

"You had a nickel reaction."

Her eyes opened, and fluttered closed again. "Oh. But I didn't even eat the chocolate! How unfair!"

The medicos chuckled. Medico Pancea stepped up to the other side of the medfloat. "Chef Loreli, I'm Medico Pancea. Did you have any oatmeal or beans?"

She shuddered a little and blinked up at the medico. "Oh, no. I never use those, or that horrible Thymdronteim, no matter how much that awful person wants me to. I'm very careful."

"Well, somehow you came in contact with a lot of nickel," Pancea said in the matter-of-fact way every medico seemed to have.

"It must have been the Vulten woman. It would fit her rigid personality."

They all tried to stifle chuckles, but none of them were successful. "Captain Ruhger tells me Lady Vulten shook your hand. Did Gentle Schultz?" Medico Pancea asked.

"Why, yes, they did." Her big amber eyes, seeming even bigger than normal under the effects of whatever treatment she was on, blinked rapidly. "I thought it a provincial oddity."

"Their system contains a very high level of nickel, and they work with Thymdronteim. It may have been enough with your level of sensitivity. With this reaction, your next reaction will be worse. You must be very vigilant to avoid nickel. I will send you a list I've compiled for my use." She tilted her head and gestured with one hand. "Even though my fellow travelers will hate me for it, you should avoid making any chocolate creations for the rest of this fold, and perhaps a few more."

"Oh, what a horrible limitation for a Chef." She appeared on the verge of tears.

Medico Pancea bit back a smile. "It's just a precaution. I'm sure you'll be able to taste small amounts in the future, but you should wait for at least forty standard days."

"I understand." She was blinking back tears. "Thank you for your care."

Pancea smiled down at her. "It is our duty and our pleasure. Trust me, we all want you back on your feet, but you should rest now. One of us will stay and monitor you tonight. Tomorrow, we'll probably release you to your quarters for another twenty-four hours of rest, with remote monitoring. We will check on you daily until we depart. And I'll leave some test kits with you."

Ruhger nodded gratefully at her and Loreli. "Thank you very much for you and your team's care. I do appreciate it and we are in your debt."

"No debt, Captain. We've already been paid with Chef's wonderful food." She looked at his face closely. "And Captain, you need some rest too. Please turn your duties over to someone else and sleep, or we'll be treating you, and we'll charge you astronomical sums for it," she said, commandingly.

He gave an ironic salute. "Yes, ma'am. Thank you. I will leave Loreli in your care." Turning to Loreli, he was relieved to see she did look better. "You heard my marching orders, Loreli. I'll see you tomorrow. Rest well."

She smiled up at him but didn't say anything more, so he departed as ordered. Thank the seven suns of Saga the medicos had folded with them. A lucky break. Relying on luck, though...he shook his head. Luck was fickle. He'd sleep, then figure out how to even the odds.

CHAPTER SIX

"Saree, I have transmitted the message to Ia'asan clutch. Transmission time is approximately three standard days, four hours and fifty-two minutes. A message receipt notice should arrive before our scheduled fold initiation, but delays could exist. Message beacons are folded out-system every twelve hours at best. The data suggests Dronteim control is not precise or consistent."

"Thank you, Hal, and thank you for your help crafting the message." She shifted uneasily in her seat.

"You are welcome, Saree."

"All of these seemingly random events are troubling, Hal. I was...cautious about the Familia operative on Dronteim Station, but I wasn't sure why he was following me. I thought it was a random 'here's an easy mark' attempt. And now, this series of strange events, none of them really connected to me, but still...strange." She nodded. "Hal, would you please give me your analysis of the beings on board?"

121

"Certainly, Saree. I will start with the crew of Lightwave Fold Transport, then go on to the passengers."

She nodded in agreement, not sure if he was asking or not. Another sign of the complexity of his personality, or was it so obvious he didn't need to ask?

"As you found during your initial research, there is insufficient public data on the net about Lightwave or the personnel on board. However, once you discovered the painted-over shield, it became much easier to locate some relevant facts." He paused. "Saree, I have not attempted to bypass Lightwave's internal security to access their personnel records. I believe I can do so, but the security is surprisingly robust, and my intrusion might trigger warnings. I already triggered a disguised intrusion alert accessing the communications system, but I was able to stop and quarantine the alert before it was sent. The absence of this trigger may cause some concern if it is discovered. I am telling you this because there is some risk the Phazeers will confront you about accessing the non-public Lightwave systems. You will have to rely on your cover story and human curiosity. I can get a complete precis on Lightwave's personnel, but there would be a significant risk of exposure, and I believe it is unnecessary at this time. I have built profiles of each member from publicly available sources, including some records released post-mortem by former Phalanx Eagle members on both sides of the split."

Hearing the name aloud sent a shudder down Saree's spine, but she stiffened her resolve and nodded in agreement. "That makes sense, Hal. Thank you for the warning. I think it will be easy to pass off the comm system intrusion as a scholar's curiosity and solo traveler's caution, but going further would be out of character."

"Agreed." He paused, but before she could ask, he continued. "As you speculated, Lightwave was a Phalanx Eagle fold transport. Specifically, it was a 'child' folder of Phalanx Eagle's Fold Transport Charlie, which was the largest and newest folder PE had when the mining colony Jericho takeover occurred. Captain Ruhger's mother, Rehmington, was the primary Fold Transport Charlie pilot, his father the commander of all the troops on Fold Transport Charlie. His father, Commander Wilson, came up through the ranks of his birth system's military and then various mercenary companies. He was a strategic and operational-level commander, responsible for ensuring tactical-level troop commanders fulfilled their mission. Commander Wilson did not leave the folder; the tactical-level commanders led troops on the ground. It was a unique command structure for a mercenary company. The structure worked because of the level of trust among the commanders and because they shared the company profits and losses equally. While disagreements over which contracts to accept had increased, it was not until the Mining Colony Jericho contract that this trust was broken. The autonomy of each sub-command made it easy to give orders counter to normal operating procedures and conceal what some of the troops did on the mining colony until the entire company was fully engaged in combat operations."

A vid, a helmet cam from the jolting perspective, came on the screen, showing miners running and falling, personnel in black hard-suits chasing them, weapons firing, fuzzing into digitized interference.

"As you know from personal experience, which I have records of but would like to hear your first-person account someday, some of the PE commanders were distressed by their orders during the later phases of the mission to take over the mining colony, and they objected strenuously. PE's top commanders and financiers refused to listen to their concerns, so the break-away was conceived. None of the breakaway officers were willing to participate in the level of brutality, killing and, ultimately, slavery required by the leadership. It appears, from accounts available, many of the original members of PE were planning to leave the company soon—the contracts were becoming more lucrative but increasingly morally repugnant. Both the Beta and Charlie folders were involved in the breakaway, and as you know, these folders dispersed the rescued children of the mining colony across the galaxies. Saree, you appear distressed. Would you like a calmer?"

At Hal's question, Saree realized she was shaking slightly and breathing fast and shallow. She took a deep breath, as if she was preparing to enter ^timespace^. She blew out, forcefully, repeated the breathing five times and assessed herself. The shaking was gone, but she admitted Hal's recital of the story, and the vid, in particular, upset her, far more than she expected. Seeing all those people running, falling...Saree shuddered. Now that she was aware of the impact on her emotions, she'd be careful to regulate her breath and ask Hal to stop if necessary. She had the tools to deal with emotional upheaval; she needed to use them.

There was something familiar about the names Rehmington and Wilson, but she wasn't sure what. "No, thank you, Hal. And

Hal, please remove the question about mood-altering drugs. Unless there is a medical necessity, I prefer to deal with emotional difficulties using meditation and contemplation. I don't want my emotions chemically altered. It can have a deleterious effect on decision-making." Her stilted, formal language sounded like Hal's; if she was copying his speech patterns, she must be more upset than she thought. Saree kept breathing deeply.

"Very well, Saree. I have done so. I apologize; I should have altered it myself since you have never availed yourself of this method, but I hadn't considered this rule set until now."

"No apology necessary, Hal. I may need a break now and then to absorb what you are telling me, so please do tell me if you think I am becoming distressed. I may not be aware of it consciously."

"Certainly, Saree. Are you ready to continue?"

"Not quite—please wait." She'd never be truly ready, but it would be better to hear all of this and then process it. Hal's dry recitation of facts brought her back to those terrifying childhood days when her safe and ordered world was utterly destroyed by the insatiable greed of already rich beings and the cruelty of individuals. She took a deep breath, held it, and blew it out. She would listen now, and try to remain emotionally separate from this history lesson. Being from the PE perspective did help; she was all too familiar with the outcome, but not the cause.

She shuddered a little. She'd never wanted to look into it, having barely survived it. The short little vid brought it all back. Shuddering again, she recalled her family and friends running, falling, the tramping of boots, the firing of weapons... Deliberately, she tightened, then relaxed her muscles from her

125

head to her feet. Once finished, she visualized balling the fear up, and shoving it all away, out into space. She relaxed into her chair in her normal posture. "Okay, Hal, please continue."

"Captain Ruhger was on Fold Transport Charlie during this time." A vid of a younger Ruhger came up. He had the same thick, dark brown hair and heavy brows, but his square face was softer and lightened by a smile—he'd laughed just before the vid capture. "He was fifteen years old, and already apprenticed as a pilot, although he was not allowed solo flight time. From the historical records available, he was precocious and a talented, if inexperienced, pilot. He and several of the other children of PE members were key in the rescue. Using the PE children as spokespersons allowed the adult PE members to gain the trust of the Mining Colony Jericho children. The two PE Fold Transports split up, going in opposite directions and far away from the normal PE operating areas. The individual soldiers who did not want to mutiny were left on several shuttles in the mining colony's system just before the fold. Once the mutinying commanders explained their plans, there weren't many individuals, comparatively, who chose to stay. Both folded to areas across the universe." A map of the constellations showed a route bouncing from one side of the universe to another, randomly, like a big rubber ball on an asteroid-pocked moon.

"I did not research Fold Transport Beta. Fold Transport Charlie, under the command of Captain Ruhger's mother and father, headed for the Cygnus constellation. Along the way, they split off three of the four 'child' folders with their shuttles, troops and a share of the children. Some of these folders and shuttles chose to form mercenary companies of their own, and reportedly, some of them continue to do well in the far reaches of space. Some have been hunted down by the remaining members of PE. The children were spread all along the galaxy, in various systems, in groups of no more than five, to make it difficult to track them. The remaining children on Fold Transport Charlie were also distributed in various systems. I don't know which folder you were on, but I doubt it was Charlie; they did not come close to Sa'sa space. You must have been on Beta."

Saree was about to ask Hal if something was wrong when he spoke. "Saree, do you need a pause for reflection?"

She checked her breathing and muscles. "No, thank you, Hal. Please continue." It helped to think about it in abstract terms as if it happened to someone else, but she was sure she'd have nightmares.

"Very well. Fold Transport Charlie was renamed, and incorporated as 'Secure Fold Transport,' a fold transport company with excellent security." A blocky logo appeared with a picture of several uniformed, armed, solemn-faced humans around it— probably an advertisement.

"They performed folds for very wealthy individuals, important political figures and Artistes, mostly originating in the Sirius constellation. They did very well and made valuable connections with political figures, shielding them from reprisal for a long time. Eventually, their identity became an open secret. Some of their clients enjoyed Secure Fold's reputation and the implication of danger, finding it exciting, but more and more refused to use them because the bounties on Rehmington and Wilson were

127

constantly rising, along with some of the other members of the company. The original members decided the remaining child folder and the ones they'd purchased to replace the missing ones would be split off into separate companies and only come together occasionally."

That name sounded familiar too. Where had she heard 'Secure Fold Transport' before?

Another picture of Captain Ruhger came up and she forgot about the name issue. He was twenty-five standards or so, but matured into a man, and he wore the grim look she was used to seeing. The scar was a bright red, slightly puckered slash across his forehead—it had recently healed. "Captain Ruhger, an accomplished pilot and security expert by this time, was chosen to command one of the child folders. They incorporated as Lightwave Fold Transport in the Cygnus System, a frontier system with little record-keeping, especially when it means credits. One of the original mutinying PE officers became a Sister of Cygnus, the religious order Captain Ruhger told you about. Many Sisters have taken jobs on Security Fold Transport and, from there, other systems. I believe the Sisters raised Katryn Phazeer; she may even be from the mining colony originally. Obviously, since she is life-contracted with Tyron, she is not an active Sister."

Saree wasn't sure if she wanted the mining colony connection confirmed or not. Other than the five of them dropped on the Sa'sa human colony, she'd never knowingly met another Jericho refugee. But it was simple to tell if Katryn was one of them. "The mining colony connection would be easy to confirm if we had access to her medical records. The Sa'sa believe all the mining colony children have DNA modifications allowing us to work around high concentrations of transuranic metals—there are markers. And we are less susceptible to radiation than most humans."

"I did note that in your medical records, but I didn't know it was a characteristic of all the mining colony children. Were any of the others able to find ^timespace^?"

"Not in my group. Although all of us need less radiation shielding, so many of my fellow refugees work in industries associated with transuranic metals, like building clocks or mining."

"Interesting, Saree. I don't think the original members of PE knew that, or they'd have used it to hunt you down."

"I don't think they care about the kids that escaped, only the original PE members."

"That is not true. Several children were hunted down and taken, but I was not able to find out what happened to them, other than they were taken. It is all too easy for a single being to disappear."

Saree sat up. Oh suns, there were even *more* people after her? "Why in the world would they bother?"

"The remaining PE members planned the enslavement of the mining colony and selling of the children to human traffickers. They consider people assets, not fellow beings. They believe they were wronged and robbed, and don't hesitate to take revenge whenever they can, preferably with a profit."

Saree scowled. PE got worse and worse.

Hal continued before she could say anything. "There is a very strong indication one of the beings funding the Mining Colony Jericho takeover is a very old Artificial Intelligence. This particular AI escaped the early purges and collects wealth, weapons and other AIs to protect itself. There are many rumors about this ancient AI, but no one will confirm anything, mostly because those who say they can are killed or disappear. The AI only cares about its safety. There are bounties on the heads of everyone involved in the original PE mutiny, including you. Yours is very small, and under your original name, so the chances of anyone finding you are small." Hal paused, then continued, "But the DNA marker is designated in the bounty documents. It doesn't appear the AI has coordinated with the original members of PE. Let me check a fact."

Saree fidgeted in her chair. Could Hal give her more bad news?

"Interesting. The AI has bounties on *all* the original members of PE, including those who stayed with the mining colony takeover. Those bounties were levied approximately seven years ago. This may be a sign the AI's paranoia is growing further, which was one of the reasons for the AI purges and subsequent laws."

Blast and rad, more people hunting her *and* she had an AI on board. Would Hal turn against her? Should she ask? There wasn't any reason not to. Hal could kill her now if he wanted to. "And how are the Sa'sa ensuring you don't develop paranoia, Hal?"

"I am not allowed access to that information, Saree. I am not allowed to act counter to your safety, but if I do, you have a hard storage device containing protocols to deactivate me if necessary. That device is now in your keeping."

A small hatch below and to the side of the pilot's chair slid open. Saree didn't know the hatch existed. She pulled out a necklace with a large pendant engraved with her school's seal and embossed with the colors of her field. Proud parents often bought these for graduating students, but she'd never bothered. *She* knew she'd graduated and nobody else cared.

"If it is necessary, remove the pendant from the chain and insert it into the external data port on the pilot's console. I know you found the shape of the finger notch strange; this is why. You should review the information on the pendant on a system independent of mine, probably a system on a world. Ideally, you should buy a disposable data reader and destroy it after you read the data. You interface the storage device with a reader by pressing the stem into the crystal for three seconds, let up for one second, then down for three more. These times allow for human variations, even though you can keep perfect time. There is also a wipe protocol on the data chip to destroy it. Destruction is activated by the human SOS pattern, three short, three long, three short, where the short is point one seconds and the long point five seconds. Do you have any questions about these protocols?"

Saree sat there, shocked and stunned all over again, but for an entirely different reason. "Hal, why didn't you tell me about this when I went to Protocol Zeta? Or at least before we started talking about PE?"

"My system is programmed to work like a human's, so I recall things when I am reminded of them. Right after you implemented Protocol Zeta, we needed to find a way out-system, so the discussion had to wait. After that, you've been busy, and I...I forgot. Sort of." Hal sounded embarrassed.

"Amazing." Saree shook her head and chuckled, with no little despair and trepidation. "This is what happens when the Sa'sa think they know humans and AIs. Hal, please modify your rule set so you don't 'forget things' like a human." This was getting stranger and scarier by the moment, but she didn't want to deactivate Hal unless absolutely necessary. Until now, he sounded like a computer. But the embarrassment and pauses? That was all too human. And rather terrifying.

"I can attempt to do so. The rule sets are complex and contradictory, much like a human being's rule set. I can split off some of my personality, and test various modifications, but I don't know if I will be successful. I will do my best."

"That's all I can ask. Please err on the side of caution. I don't want you damaged in any way." She bit her lip. "If forgetting things is the price of you staying sane, then we'll learn to deal with it. And thank you, Hal."

"You are welcome, Saree." His tone was subdued, almost glum. "Shall we continue with Captain Ruhger?" he said in a much brighter tone.

"Yes, please." Oh, yes, she definitely wanted to know about him. The whole crew was fascinating, but Ruhger intrigued her. Was the constant glare pain or anger? Or both?

"Very well. Captain Ruhger was folding the Cygnus constellation when the original PE members caught up with Secure Fold Transport. Most speculate the AI pressured a Sirius political figure into sabotaging the main engines. Several clients survived the attack, but they all denied having anything to do with it, so which one succumbed is unknown. No matter who did,

Secure was surrounded by overwhelming military forces, many of them robotic, and they couldn't escape. The clients were allowed to depart in escape pods, but not all were rescued, and some were hit. Then the attacking forces pounded the folder into pieces. There was no quarter offered."

"That's horrible. What kind of beings do that?"

"Horrible ones. And a paranoid, extremely rich AI." Hal's tone was grim, reflecting her feelings on the matter. Did he really 'feel' that way, or was it merely programmed sympathy?

"I wonder if Captain Ruhger and the others hold it against the children they rescued?"

"I'm sure they have mixed feelings, but blaming children seems unlikely from the personality profiles I've developed. I believe they would put the blame where it belongs, on the beings who funded the mining colony takeover."

Saree hoped so too, but unless there was a life or death reason, she couldn't see sharing her past with any of Lightwave's crew.

"To continue, Captain Ruhger didn't find out about the annihilation of Secure Fold Transport, and his family, until weeks later because they were running fast fold-and-drops on the fringes. Their bounties increased, but not enough for the best or worst hunters to go after them—it's not worth it when everyone knows they run the frontier, making them hard to find. They are cautious and hard to catch. And they're well armed—the first thing they did after the attack was upgrade their offensive and defensive capabilities." A still vid of weapons ports on a folder, presumably Lightwave, and a list of weapons came up on the screen.

"From several personal accounts, it appears Ruhger was always a rather serious man, but his parents' death changed him. He is now grim and rather paranoid, although not for himself, but for his friends and shipmates. He has indeed ejected a shuttle during a fold, the reason for the warning on your first night. Evidently, a bounty hunter's shuttle contracted transport, but they were halfway through the fold orbit transit when the bounty hunter figured out who Captain Ruhger was. Then, rather than acting on the far side of the fold as a reasonable individual would, this being—a Blatto—decided he'd take over the entire ship, killing everyone in their cabins or shuttles, get the bounties, and a fold transport too. The attempt was discovered and the Blatto admitted it when confronted, and of all the idiotic reactions, said he'd keep trying. So Ruhger ejected him and sent a message to the fold orbit authorities of why, along with his location. They agreed Ruhger was justified in his actions and declined to mount a rescue effort for an admitted attempted multiple murderer. The shuttle ran out of fuel before reaching a station or planet and was eventually pushed into the sun by the system authorities."

"Wow. I'd always heard Blattos didn't have the tightest orbits, but that's something." Saree shook her head in bemused wonder. She'd never dealt with any in person, but seeing them on a planet or station passageway always sent instinctive shivers along her spine. Just the thought of meter-long, sentient cockroaches…she shuddered.

"They are not known to be good planners. Shall we proceed?"

"Yes, please." No wonder the Captain was so grim during the constellation departure dinner. He constantly anticipated acting as an executioner. She shuddered again, for an entirely different reason. She would not be sharing *her* story with him.

"Grant Lowe's story is similar. His parents were part of the mutiny, although they weren't officers, but technicians, plumbing, and electric." A vid of a younger Grant Lowe appeared, his long oval face skinnier, the blond hair much longer and a little messy, but the striking, light blue-gray eyes and sexy smile were the same. He'd learned the value of flirting early. "They stayed with Secure Fold Transport and died in the same attack, along with Lowe's girlfriend. While Lowe has always been outgoing and friendly, it wasn't until after the attack he became promiscuous." The vid morphed into the Grant Lowe of today, with shorter hair, a slightly fuller face and a sexy smolder.

"He's responsible for passenger interface, exterior communications, bargaining for cargos, advertising, and other system interface tasks. One trader of textiles reports he can charm brooding Klee out of their nests. He's regarded as an excellent partner in sexual liaisons. He's a good comm technician and he's Lightwave's intelligence officer. He's proficient with several kinds of martial arts, although not as serious about y'ga as Ruhger or Katryn, so if you ever have to fight him off, stun or kill him quickly—he's much faster than his laid-back manner implies. All of them are, even Chef Loreli."

Purser Lowe's reaction was the opposite of what she'd expect, but everyone grieved differently. But this information confirmed Saree had no interest in a fold-fling with Grant Lowe.

"Chef Loreli started life as Loren." A vid of a teenaged boy came up, with dark skin, a much thinner but still round face and a sullen pout. "His biological parents are unknown. His adoptive fathers were cooks and hydroponics technicians on Fold Transport Charlie. They were also killed in the attack. Loren was small for his age, shy and studious—some of the other children bullied him. Ruhger defended him, and by all accounts, they acted like brothers until puberty, when Loren had a growth spurt and developed much more feminine characteristics. From a very young age, he worked with his cook father in the kitchen, and when he was sixteen, he earned a partial scholarship to Culinary Institute Sirius." A still vid of an identity badge came up. A young man, with a wide face and big, happy smile, the white teeth blinding against his dark skin. His hair cascaded in long, lustrous, black corkscrews around his face and neck.

"Secure Fold Transport funded the rest of the tuition. While he was there, he matured into Loreli—a flamboyant personality who identifies as female although he remains biologically male, and is sexually active with both sexes." The vid changed into a graduation picture. The face was much rounder, the hair shorter, straightened and bobbed, although still black, and she was wearing long, dark eyelashes, bright red lipstick, and a flirtatious look.

"She is deemed a genius by most of her CIS classmates and some of the instructors. Some of the instructors were not impressed by her showmanship, believing the food should be the star, not the Chef, so she didn't earn formal accolades upon her graduation to the practical application portion of the training. She is competent with y'ga and other martial arts and hand weapons, but prefers not to use them unless forced."

Hal's tone changed from calm to intent. "Chef Loreli has taken ill. The shuttle of pandemic medicos has been called in."

Saree's stomach sank. Oh, she'd been looking forward to another Chef Loreli meal. Wait a minute—how could she think of something so trivial when another being was ill? "If they've called in outside help, it must be pretty bad."

"She passed out in the kitchen and the Captain and the Phazeers took her to the medico station. The automated test results were inconclusive, so they called the medicos."

Saree waited, playing an impatient drum solo on her chair, as Hal 'listened' to the comms. "Chef Loreli has a severe allergy to nickel. They don't know how she was exposed, but they surmise it may be Lady Vulten and Gentle Schultz grasping her hands, and they both work with Thymdronteim, which has a high concentration of nickel."

"Hmm, one wouldn't think simply shaking hands would be enough..." Saree trailed off.

"Not normally, but the Chef's allergy is severe and non-typical. I will continue to monitor the situation while we continue. Do you have any questions about Grant Lowe or Chef Loreli?"

Saree stopped, trying to adjust. Hal's transition from concern to business was disconcertingly rapid. Perhaps the feeling wasn't concern to begin with—why would an AI care about a chef? "Not at this time, Hal."

"Very well, I will continue. Chief Engineer Bhoher is a member of the original PE and was moving up the engineering staff on Fold Transport Charlie." A vid of the current Chief appeared, his short, light brown hair surrounding his rectangular face, the high, sharp cheekbones—and the lines around them—almost hiding his milk chocolate eyes.

"He is an intelligent being and a true mechanical genius. He relates to machines better than people and is surprised when beings react emotionally and, to him, illogically. While he objected to the assignment at the mining colony and the taking of the children, his arguments were made from a practical point of view, upsetting some of his fellow engineering officers and technicians, the reason he was moved to Lightwave during the split. Many of the original PE members were uncomfortable with his lack of emotion."

"Practical arguments?"

"Yes. Chief Bhoher argued the mining colony was well run by its inhabitants and enslaving the adults and threatening the children was likely to lead to much less efficient production. Which was true, but the supposition upset many as cold-hearted, and several in the break-away folders proposed he be left behind. Interestingly, his logic doesn't hold all the time—Chief is a berserker in a fight. He prefers to work with distance weapons, the bigger, the better, but if forced into a hand-to-hand situation, he uses a fighting axe and is absolutely lethal. He's not completely irrational like a true berserker, but his normal logical personality is subsumed by a killing machine that doesn't stop until the threat is gone or he's physically exhausted. No one in PE knows where he learned to fight—he joined when he was older—but all the members of Lightwave value his abilities. Though he has seniority and advanced training, he refuses to take command of anything but engineering because of his difficulty with people. He tends to be rather solitary, but he and Ruhger are friends. Ruhger considers him an important voice of reason and experience and is willing to ignore his oddities and force him to interact on a more personal level."

Saree couldn't quite picture the solemn, practical Chief charging around with an axe in his hand, but she didn't doubt Hal's ability to find information. "It seems everyone on Lightwave is deadly in hand-to-hand."

"They are. The entire crew is highly trained, and they practice, even Lowe, although he'll make light of it. The Phazeers are deadlier." The vid changed to show a young man with longish, light brown hair and light brown-green eyes in an unremarkable oval face, his skin a medium tan close to her own shade. "Tyron was also a child of PE and trained in physical security by his parents, both security officers themselves. He's never studied a single martial art, but a mix, making him unpredictable and, therefore, more difficult to defeat." The vid changed to show the Tyron of today, the planes of his face a little tighter, but still inconspicuous overall. He could easily hide in a crowd.

"He's expert on many different weapons, from every common human hand weapon to ship-size weapons. He knows Lightwave's capabilities inside and out and continually researches and improves those capabilities. He is stable and quiet, what is referred to as the 'strong, silent' type. His life-contract partner, Katryn Phazeer, is Lightwave's net security officer, among other duties." Katryn appeared, a small, solemn face with sharp features—she looked like a manga princess, with blue-black hair in a short cap framing her face and dark brows winging up above her dark chocolate, slightly tilted almond-shaped eyes. A striking woman—Saree imagined her looks and small stature caused many men to underestimate her.

"As I said, she was raised by the Sisters of Cygnus, and is an expert in y'ga—she and Ruhger spar often. She learned net security at the Sisters' orphanage, then they sent her off-planet to formal schooling as a teenager. She keeps up with the latest advances and threats. She also has valuable contacts through the mercenary hacker net, although she is cautious since mercenaries often go bounty hunting when there are no other jobs available. She's good with many weapons, although not as good as Tyron. They make a formidable team since they complement each other's capabilities in all aspects of security, and personality. She is quick-tempered and can be unpredictable."

"Where did they meet? Did Ruhger introduce them?"

"No, they met on the net first, in security forums and merc-net, and in person several years later at a security conference on Nexus Station. Katryn left a planet-based position and was looking for another one when they met in real life. Reportedly, they had a love-at-first-sight connection—they met at the end of the conference when Katryn was escaping mercenaries. I haven't discovered why she was targeted. They disappeared for a few days and returned to Lightwave as a couple. Ruhger hired her immediately. Tyron was at the conference to find a net security person."

Saree acknowledged her envy; she'd never find love like that. Her childhood was too strange, and her subsequent training by the Sa'sa gave her odd reactions and emotional responses. Well, that and her livelihood. It wasn't likely she'd ever find anyone she could trust with her secret, and she had a twenty-year commitment to pay off. Besides, what would a man do while riding along with her? Maybe a true researcher? But how would she ever find such a man?

"Saree?"

She realized this was not the first time Hal had called her name. "I'm sorry, Hal. Between the workout, the excitement and the fabulous meal tonight, I'm exhausted. Since you don't think anything will happen before the fold, can we continue this tomorrow?"

"Certainly, Saree. I will continue to monitor the situation and do more research on the passengers. I will wake you if anything requires your attention. Sleep well."

"Thank you, Hal. I appreciate your care."

"You are welcome, Saree."

CHAPTER SEVEN

A hand shook his shoulder. "Ruhger," Katryn said above him.

From the impatient look on her face, it wasn't the first time. Blast and rad. Zoning out wasn't a safe thing to do. "Sorry, Katryn—lost in my thoughts. Have a seat."

"Thanks." She sat, her deceptively delicate body almost lost in the normal-size chair, and arranged her breakfast.

Ruhger waited, knowing there was no rushing the anything-but-delicate Katryn, even if she rushed everyone else. She was good at her job, and good for Tyron, but you could tell she hadn't been raised by mercenaries. He frowned. Although…he doubted the Sisters put up with her attitude either. Probably why they sent her to school off-planet. Or maybe her fussiness was a coping mechanism? She took a sip of tea, looking at him with a frown. He waited, more or less patiently.

"I'm reluctant to bring you another potential problem when I can't define it as a true problem yet, let alone bring you a solution, but it's better you're aware."

She took a sip of tea, and he recruited his patience, again. "There are sniffers in our comm system. I don't think they're doing anything but listening, but I can't wipe them out. Blast it all, I can't even catch them." She scowled fiercely. "Something triggered a couple of my watchdogs, but the warnings got shunted into a sub-routine hiding them. I've found one, but I'm sure there are more. The bottom line is, somebody wants to know what we're saying on our private channels."

Annoying, but not fatal. Ruhger shrugged. "We've had this happen before. Usually it's someone paranoid about their safety. We've got a lot of single pilot-owners on this fold—maybe some of them had issues with folder crews in the past?"

She glared. "That may be, but I don't like it. It's sophisticated and professional, and none of the shuttles have claimed people with comm or net tech expertise. And if they can get these sniffers into my comm systems, what else have they dropped? I'm checking everything I can and tightening net security on our C2 systems, but I might not catch this being. It's really good and really fast."

She grimaced and drummed her fingers on the table as if she was tapping a keyboard. "The speed is what worries me. The reaction times are faster than human or most other beings. It's computer-fast, but if it's a written program, it's a flexible and complex one." She shook her head in dismissal and grimaced at him again. "Anyway, I want to raise security on our command and control system to the maximum, which means you have to input a passphrase, a randomly generated number—" she handed him a small, oval-shaped piece of plas "—and a DNA sample."

She raised a hand, anticipating him objecting. "I know it's a hassle, and you'll have to be on the shuttle for C2 tasks because of the sample, but it seems like the smart thing to do under the circumstances."

She really was brilliant. Thank all the suns Tyron found her.

Ruhger shook his head. "You'll get no arguments from me on this. It will be annoying, and it could be dangerous—it will slow us down in a real emergency. Unless... can you put in a contingency protocol so I can use C2 wherever I am in a real emergency?"

The relief was clear on her face and in her voice. "Yes. I can. We'll have a separate passphrase for emergencies, and I can set it up for the emergency warnings already in place, plus any you want to add." She stopped, lost in thought, and he waited.

Katryn focused back on his face, intent. "Can we do this in the shuttle after breakfast? I want to undock from Lightwave and disconnect from the overall comm system, to minimize the chances those sniffers can hear what we're saying, at least in real time. Before we get started, I'll do a scrub and look for them and any other tidbits hanging in our system. I'm sure you'll want Tyron, Bhoher or Lowe in the Beta shuttle." Her mouth twisted. "Probably Bhoher, since he'd be offended if he wasn't chosen," she said, grouchy again.

"Katryn..." he warned. She and Chief didn't get along, because she was all emotion and flash and he was all analysis and stolid. But the two opposing views and reactions balanced well. He just had to keep Katryn from killing Bhoher and keep explaining Katryn's reactions to Chief. When he could figure them out. *Women.*

"Yeah, I know, he's got seniority. But his reaction times are slower than Tyron's or Grant's." She scowled at him.

"Yes, but mine aren't. You know he's the perfect second for this. We don't need fast, we need smart, and none of us are as smart as Chief." Which was absolutely true. Katryn was brilliant in her field, but Chief was a genius.

"Yes, but none of us are as annoying either," she grumbled.

He looked at her for a moment. That statement was more than a little ironic coming from her. "Speaking of annoying, were you this big a pain when you were growing up?"

She laughed a full-bodied belly laugh. Ruhger didn't think the question was quite that funny; it must be relief. Why would she think he'd object to her reasonable suggestions?

"Bigger, actually. Why do you think they scraped together the funds and favors to send me off-planet to school?" She drank the last of her tea and stood up, dishes in hand. "When do you want to do this?"

He checked the time. "Chief sparred with me this morning and took breakfast back to his office. He should be finished by now. I'll finish here, and go talk to him in person, so meet me in the Alpha shuttle in fifteen. He won't take much convincing, probably none, but you know Chief will want a precise checklist for something like this." Ruhger smirked for a second at her glare. "And he's right. And, unlike the rest of us, he'll also have paper and a pencil, rather than relying on the system."

"Yeah, he will," she grumbled. "Better you than me. See you in fifteen." Katryn tossed him an ironic salute over her shoulder.

ΛΛΛ

Ruhger checked the docking status. "Chief, confirm Shuttle

Alpha lock."

"Shuttle Alpha lock clean and green. You have command of Lightwave, Captain."

"Command accepted, I have Lightwave. Can you and Tyron join us here?"

"Wilco, Captain."

Ruhger turned his seat to face the observer chairs behind him and waited patiently. Katryn jittered, but it wasn't long before Ruhger let both men into the shuttle. Tyron took Katryn's hand and her nervy movement stilled. "All right. We are at a much higher level of security now, which is a good proactive measure. We need to up our defense too. Let's talk about the passengers. Who's spying on us, what can they do, how do we stop them? Chief?"

"Let the Phazeers go first, Captain." Bhoher frowned. "This kind of analysis isn't my forte. Although, I can tell you I've done all the physical scanning I can from Lightwave. Like usual, everyone's shuttles are shielded. I am running programs to look for any oddities in usage patterns, but have nothing definitive yet." He nodded sharply.

"Katryn?"

She grimaced again. Her face was going to stay that way if she wasn't careful. "It could be any of them. None of them advertise the kind of net skills these infiltrations are demonstrating. And none of them are exactly what they seem either." She tilted her head toward Tyron.

Tyron said, "Since Katryn told me about the net situation, I've researched the passengers thoroughly. The medicos are what they seem; there's too much on the net for them to be anything but what they are—very good pandemic medicos. I think the essence researcher is what he seems to be, but with his knowledge of exotic substances, he could be an expert in poisons too. He's eaten meals in the chow hall but retreats to his shuttle otherwise, and he takes food back with him."

Tyron smiled sardonically. "He must have a very high metabolism. Anyway, he didn't come anywhere near Loreli or the kitchen, which makes me think he had nothing to do with *that* episode. He could be a prime suspect for the net infiltration—he's quiet, keeps to himself, and has minimal connections with Lightwave, but there's enough to set a sniffer loose and let it report back. He's armed, like most of the passengers, but only with a stunner. He's cautious, and acts like someone used to being alone in risky situations—a typical solo traveler."

Katryn broke in, "I've put sniffers on all shuttle comm connections, but so far, none of them have been triggered. I may have been too late—in the future, I'll do it automatically upon shuttle lock. I've been too complacent; I've gotten used to clueless fringers." She was scowling again.

Ruhger nodded. That fold was finished, nothing to be done except learn from it. He motioned at Tyron to continue.

"The Artiste is a mid-level performer. He does supporting roles, which he excels at, particularly when the big stars are acknowledged to be brilliant but unreliable. Even though he's flamboyant in public, he's known to steady high-strung, aging stars, especially on stage—his quick thinking has covered major gaffes in several big l'Opera performances."

Pausing, Tyron gave them a small, ironic smile. "However, in several cases, high-profile assassinations have taken place while he was in-system. It's not statistically conclusive, but it is significant. These assassinations are up close and personal—they look like heart attacks or strokes. There's never any clear indication of a known poison or drug, but few of the individuals have known risk factors for these kinds of health problems, and they've all come in contact with Artiste Borgia."

Tyron shrugged. "Along with several other l'Opera performers—evidently, social touching is part of the l'Opera culture." He grimaced. "I wondered if the Artiste and the essence researcher were working together, but this is the first time they've been on a folder together in the last five years, although they've been in the same systems in the past. But lots of people stick to the fringes for work. He was here for work—he gave a series of private concerts to nobility on Dronteim."

Ruhger snorted. "Yeah, there's lots of good reasons to stay in the fringes." Their bounties were only one of the reasons for doing so... They shared rueful smirks.

"Lady Vulten and Gentle Schultz don't appear to be anything but what they are, a frontier system power and her put-upon servant. Vulten has blasted off plenty of people in her system and those nearby, mostly her competitors, but I haven't discovered any connections to the larger universe. The medicos tested their skin, and both of them excrete high levels of nickel. They've been warned not to touch Chef or Medico Pancea. She told them social touching is discouraged during galactic travel just for this reason. Lady Vulten didn't take the warning well—" Tyron grimaced ironically "—but Gentle Schultz was apologetic and grateful. The medicos think Schultz will attempt to smooth things over later." Tyron's face twisted in disgust. "That woman is space wrack. She came on to me, and didn't back off when I told her I was life contracted." He grinned. "Luckily for her, Lowe rescued me before Katryn could."

From the furious look on Katryn's face, it was a close call. Once again, he had reason to be grateful for Grant Lowe's smooth manners. Good thing *he* wasn't allergic to nickel.

"Klee humper," Katryn growled out. Ruhger wasn't sure if she was talking about Vulten or Lowe. Or both. Generally, she got along fine with Grant, but she was uncomfortable with his promiscuity. But then, most of them were, although Katryn had the Sisters' training to overcome as well. Suns knew they all had their coping mechanisms to deal with the whole PE mess, but Grant's seemed extreme.

Tyron smiled at Katryn and squeezed her hand, and she visibly relaxed. They were so devoted to each other. Ruhger was envious again, but led them back to the subject at hand—there was no time for his personal issues. "Good. The rest?"

"The engineer is what he seems. He's got an outstanding reputation for finding problems with designs and sites and is well paid by his firm. But there's a noteworthy statistic following him too." Tyron smirked. "It seems unlikely watching him stomp around like he's on a heavy world, but there have been some high-profile jewel thefts in some of the systems he visits. I'd like to watch him in an emergency situation and see if his physical reactions change."

"We are not manufacturing any emergencies. We've had quite enough of them already. One is more than enough," Chief said.

"I wasn't going to suggest it. I'm not an idiot," Tyron said, scowling at Chief.

Ruhger held up his hands to stop both of them. "I know you aren't, Tyron, and I'm sure that's not how Chief meant it." Chief opened his mouth, but Ruhger cut him off with a slash of his hand. "Tyron, please continue."

"The Chelonians are a well-known protective detail pair. They work mostly with high-level political figures on short-term contracts. Many would like to hire them long-term, but they're expensive and in high demand. It's also well known they are selective—they won't work for known criminals or anyone questionable. Early in their careers, they worked at the direction of their guild, but since they've paid off their training, they've progressively tightened their requirements. This sends them to the fringes a lot, but they don't seem to mind." He chuckled. "Unlike a lot of Chelonians, they hate their planet and don't want to return except to visit family. Despite their physical limitations, they say they much prefer warm and dry environments, and space is even better."

There were nods of agreement and a few chuckles. The Chelonii did require a higher humidity to keep their skin-shells flexible. They must have sealed living compartments—high humidity wasn't good for electronics.

"They also aren't big fans of l'Opera like most Chelonians, but they didn't want to offend the Artiste since 'you never know who you might have to babysit in the future,' and being nice cost them nothing but time." Tyron shrugged. "All in all, a... nice couple who seem to be just what they are."

"Or they have a very good cover," Ruhger said.

"True. I didn't find any unexplained statistical oddities where they've been. Well, except they're not always successful in maintaining the safety of their objective, but that's always true in bodyguard work. Their average is average." He cleared his throat. "By the way, a lot of the more personal things I got from Grant. Evidently, they're a rather... adventuresome couple."

Ruhger barked out a laugh. Similar exclamations came from the others. That explained Grant's comments the night of the fold orbit incident. And it explained why he hadn't moved on to the other passengers. All of them were happy about that—dealing with passengers was bad enough. Throw heartbreak or hurt feelings on top of it, and you had a real mess.

Tyron waited for them to quiet. "Finally, we have the Scholar. She's also more interesting than she appears at first glance. For one, she was raised on the human colony in the Sa'sa home system." He scanned the group, smiling at their surprise. "She did study at Centauri University, but only a year; the rest was remote study. That's not unusual since it's expensive to travel and study in residence. She does fund her own studies, but where did the credits come from? There's no way to know. Her funds are transferred through the Sa'sa banking system, and that's a dead end—humans never get anything from them. Nobody does. But normally, nobody but Sa'sa use it." Tyron frowned, then continued. "But what's really interesting is the statistical oddity following her." His expression was speculative. "A statistically significant number of the systems she's visited had fold clock maintenance while she was there or right around the time she was there."

Tyron waited for the quiet exclamations to stop. "Now, maybe she's acting as kind of a Sa'sa ambassador or liaison, and letting them know it's safe to travel to the system, but her travel isn't consistent with known Sa'sa folder travel. Nor does it explain the maintenance happening just before she arrives." He shrugged. "There may be other beings that, if we looked, also traveled to just-Clocked systems time after time. I haven't looked—the data set would be huge." Tyron looked around; everyone was nodding. "There have also been three other similar orbit incidents reported over the last five standard years, where a single Sa'sa has been discovered in a system in an escape pod with no evident means of transport and those systems had just been Clocked. The Scholar was in one of those systems, although she folded out before the discovery was reported. These incidents are odd and rather...troubling."

They all frowned. Nobody liked to think about a cooperative species member left to die alone. Or anyone.

When Tyron didn't continue, Ruhger shared what he'd found. "When we were investigating the proximity alert, I discovered a Clocker had just been in-system. Our fuel-efficiency was at an all-time high, and our run sunward was horrible. Since I was trying to stay awake, I looked for Sa'sa folders. None have come through recently. I did some more research. There are lots of rumors about a human Clocker, and massive bounties for the capture of this human Clocker." He scowled. "The bounties are levied by truly horrible entities and all so huge it would be suicide to take them. Taking *any* money from these people would be suicide—they're all known to renege on deals when it suits them."

Chief's face, which was starting to look unusually cheerful, fell. Tyron and Katryn both nodded—they'd probably done some of the same research.

Ruhger contemplated all this information and the best course of action for Lightwave Fold Transport and each of them, individually. There was no real evidence in any of this speculation and nothing he could act on as a Captain consistent with his own personal system of justice, even if, in practice, he could get away with almost anything. "So, even if the Scholar is this theoretical human Clocker, we're not doing anything to help or hinder her. We treat her as if she's just a scholar, which she might well be, and keep doing our jobs."

He stopped and looked at each of them. "And I think that's how we should proceed with *all* of the passengers. Treat them as if they are who they say they are, unless and until they show otherwise. If they move against one of the other passengers or us, then we neutralize or terminate, whichever is safest for Lightwave, first, since if it dies, we all do. Second, you as an individual; third, us as a group, and fourth, for the other passengers. Any objections? Holdouts?" He looked at each one again; everyone agreed. Good. "Okay, with that out of the way, Katryn, what help do you need on the net?"

She shook her head, lips compressed. "I think I've done all we can do for now. If I need help, I'll let you know."

"Okay. Don't wait. If something looks off, take action and then let the rest of us know. We don't need proof—we need to keep Lightwave safe. Tyron, further thoughts?"

His face was somber. "Do we try to get to know the passengers better, or stay aloof? I can see pros and cons to each approach."

Ruhger shook his head. "I think we treat this just like any other fold. Let's not change anything unless we're forced to." They all looked relieved, although probably for different reasons. "Chief, your thoughts?"

"I think we should all carry personal arms." He held up a hand. "And no, I'm not talking about my axe. A stunner and a laser pistol, all the time. I know Tyron and Katryn already do, but the rest of us should too, even Lowe and Loreli."

"That is a very good idea. If someone asks, we say we're preparing for piracy the closer we get to the fold point. It's logical."

"We should also review fighting tactics on- and off-ship and spar together. We do this informally now, but we should practice with each other regularly. We should have been doing this all along." He glared at Ruhger.

Ruhger frowned back at Chief. "Yes, I know your thoughts on the matter, but we're a fold transport company, not a mercenary company. But, for right now, you are right. We can't all spar together; we need to have C2 manned in one of the shuttles or in engineering at all times, and we need to have a public face for our passengers—but we can do small rotating groups." He grimaced. "I'll leave the scheduling to you, with review and approval from the rest of us *before* we implement it, right?" He warned Chief with a pointed look, knowing he'd design the 'perfect' schedule and then not understand why everyone refused to obey it.

"All right, any other thoughts?" They all shook their heads. "I'll brief Grant and Chef when she's better. I'll stay here in the shuttle for the day if someone can bring me lunch and dinner. After dinner, I should do a turn in the ready room, so Chief, you'll have C2 this evening." He looked relieved. Lucky man. "I'll take it back for the night shift and review your schedule then." He looked at each of them. "Be on your guard. I don't want to lose any of you, and Lightwave can't afford to lose any of you."

Each of them nodded in turn, and left the shuttle, leaving him with grim thoughts of doom. They were stuck between a supernova and a black hole. Do nothing, as they decided, and get blindsided. Do something, and lose business because they couldn't explain their actions. It was a losing situation no matter how he looked at it.

And underlying all these practical considerations, one thought that just wouldn't go away: it was too bad he'd never get to know the Scholar better.

CHAPTER EIGHT

Saree sighed when the vid of Captain Ruhger, leaning back in his chair, disappeared. She was sighing a lot during this fold.

"Lightwave's crew did an admirable job of researching the passengers, for humans. They missed a few things, but with the time constraints and lack of computing power, and with the need for that pesky sleep thing, they did well. It must be so annoying to shut down for all those hours," Hal said cheerfully.

Saree chuckled, which had probably been Hal's intent, then sobered. "So, what did they miss that was important, Hal?" And when did he develop a personality? Overnight?

"I will go down the list in the same way they did. They are correct on the medicos, although I will tell you they are more than capable of self-defense if pushed. They all carry stunners and have adequate self-defense training because sometimes patients and their loved ones can become violent. The essence researcher is much more difficult. For one, his name, Al-Kindi, isn't his real name—Al-Kindi was one of the first known perfumers on Old Earth. There's little available on the Al-Kindi of today, and because he explores the far reaches of known space, there are big gaps in his travel history due to lack of record-keeping. Even if there's no evidence, I believe it would be safer to treat him as if he does supply poisons to assassins, although I think it unlikely he would do the work himself. He doesn't move like a human with any significant hand-to-hand training other than basic self-defense, but he is armed. He does move like a person used to being alone and cautious, and his shuttle defenses are formidable from what I can see. All of which is consistent with someone who travels the fringes alone. Although..."

"Although what?"

"Although I'm not certain he's alone. There is some water and power usage on his shuttle when he's gone. There could be another entity on the shuttle, but I have no way to know without taking a big risk."

"Probably not worth it."

"Not at this time. If you have any personal encounters with Al-Kindi, be cautious."

"Always." Especially since he wore a long, white robe with a twisted black head covering—it was impossible to see if he carried weapons.

"Artiste Borgia is definitely an assassin. He's a Familia assassin, and far more dangerous than most beings, including those on Lightwave, think he is. The arrogant artiste is a cover—he's quite intelligent *and* clever. He uses poisons to mimic health problems, all of them hard to detect. With a team of expert medicos on board, I think he's less likely to act on a target here.

157

He's not known as a capture expert, or to have any expertise with substances designed to incapacitate rather than kill, but if he was sure you were the human Clocker, he might take a chance. The reward offered by the Familia for capture of the human Clocker is significant in political power *and* credits. Don't get cornered by him and never let him touch you or even touch your clothes. He is sincere about his love of l'Opera and his disdain for other music, so your best approach is to continue telling him about your theories on Filk. That will send him running."

Saree cracked a smile. She didn't want that arrogant man touching her even without the possibility of being poisoned, so he'd get the full scholar treatment. Preferably from a distance—his cologne was truly horrible. All of them would, including the crew. Which was too bad, because she liked Loreli; she was probably a lot of fun when she wasn't heartbroken. And...a fold-fling with the Captain might be fun too, but it wasn't going to happen. She sighed. There were times when she thought the Sa'sa were right about needing clutch around her, but a clutch of humans, not Sa'sa. She shuddered reflexively. That thought burned the inconvenient longing right out.

"Lady Vulten and Gentle Schultz are what they seem, but Vulten wants more. Evidently, the Lady isn't content with ruling her little piece of Dronteim, and she's looking to branch out into other areas and develop additional sources of funding. She met several times with Al-Kindi while he was on her planet and didn't make her grand travel plans until after she'd met him. While there is no way to know what they talked about, I do have a statistically possible theory based on what she's done since then and what we believe he does. My theory is she's trying to weaponize

Thymdronteim and possibly other plants on her planet."

Saree blinked in surprise. That wasn't at all what she was expecting. "Interesting theory. So, she's taking advantage of the nickel-allergic portion of the human population to create a new poison?"

"Essentially, yes. Some other species are also nickel-sensitive, so there's a large potential market."

"Was Chef Loreli a test, then?"

"I believe the Chef was an accident. Or they are the clumsiest pair of assassins ever, which is possible."

Was Hal trying to make a joke, or a statement of fact? Impossible to know and probably better not to ask. "So how did you come to this conclusion? It seems like a leap rather than a probability." She deliberated her phrasing, then held up a hand. "Wait, I trust your analysis." Which was true—she was sure he'd have a logical reason for the theory. On the other claw, Hal's assumptions and interpretation of human emotions and actions as the basis for his theory? That was a different story. But pointing that out wouldn't be a good idea. "Let's continue."

"Excellent. Engineer Gerald Ursuine is a very good engineer. He has saved his company enormous sums, he gets a small bonus percentage, so he's quite well off. He's saved lots of lives along the way and has an excellent reputation. He's extremely dedicated to his work. There are many documented instances where the jewel thefts in question coincide with him being at a job site—he rarely leaves a job site once he's started. However, similar to Al-Kindi, there is water and power usage on his shuttle when he's been on Lightwave. Again, maybe he's running an auto-cleaner or some sort of experimental work, but I don't think it's unreasonable to surmise he has a fellow traveler on his shuttle, and that being is the jewel thief."

"I guess it would be easy to check on a well-secured spaceport?"

"Yes. But I doubt anyone has. Ursuine has a perfect alibi, so why would anyone look at his shuttle?"

"True. A curious situation." She pondered the possibilities— they could be endless with some caution on the part of the beings involved. "I wonder, in both of these cases, if these are partnerships or duress situations?"

"Interesting thought, Saree. I had not considered the possibility of duress. Which side would be under duress?"

She shrugged. "Either could be with the right leverage. A child, for example, held at risk. Or a sibling or spouse. The problem is, with many humans, eventually the leverage is lost. Either the threat has to be implemented, or the person under duress can no longer endure the situation or feels there is nothing left to lose. Some humans become a part of the oppressing group in an attempt to survive and relieve the stress. There is a limit to human tolerance but no limit to the number of ways that limit can be resolved."

"This is consistent with my information. The tolerance level seems to vary widely among humans. A Sa'sa wouldn't respond to such a threat at all since the clutch as a whole is much, much more important than any individual, even the clutch head. And threatening an immature Sa'sa would be no threat at all."

Saree shuddered again. The Sa'sa didn't consider individuals a real member of the clutch until they'd reached maturity, and even then, they were provisional members until they were fully trained and working. They didn't get real, individual names until then. From a human perspective, it was appalling; from a Sa'sa perspective, normal. The Sa'sa failed to understand the value humans and other species placed on their young. Early in the interactions between humans and Sa'sa they came close to armed conflict. Fortunately, cooler heads prevailed, with other species stepping in until a mutual rule set, if not understanding, could be put in place.

That was one of the many reasons Mother refused to apprentice her until she'd reached sixteen standards, even though the Sa'sa discovered her talent just after her fourteenth standard and the onset of physical maturity. Her training in meditation techniques and lucid dreaming began right away, to prevent her intrusions into ^timespace^, but only an hour a day when all the other kids were in elective courses. Her foster mother wanted to wait for the usual eighteen, but others objected, worried her thought patterns might become too rigid if they waited another two years. Mother hadn't been happy, but she'd finally agreed, under a lot of pressure, for the good of the human colony. She'd insisted Saree get one day out of every eight at home and two weeks off every quarter. The Sa'sa weren't happy about it but agreed when they were reminded about the differences in human physiology and psychology. Again. Saree grimaced. And Mother and Father retained the fees they got for 'raising' her, Mother's primary motivation.

Saree was grateful for Mother's efforts on her behalf—what little childhood she had was due to her influence, although Mother's motivation for 'protecting her from the Sa'sa' wasn't the same as a loving parent.

Saree realized Hal had been quiet for some time—he was giving her time to think. "Shall we continue with the Chelonians, Hal?"

"Certainly, Saree. They are exactly what they seem: a pair of highly sought-after bodyguards. They are extremely expensive, and when their services are bought, they stay bought. Unless their employer lies to them—then they leave immediately. There is an honesty clause in their contract, and they have invoked the penalty departure before. As an example, an entertainer hired them, but didn't inform them he was bringing large quantities of banned substances to the performance venues. When they discovered this, they left immediately, and the entertainer was arrested at his performance, possibly because they'd tipped off the planetary authorities. They're also very discreet. I don't know why they are on this folder—there is no one on Dronteim who could afford or require their services. Or at least no one obvious. But they may have traveled through here to throw off any suspicion on their way to Deneb. Or maybe they had personal reasons. I did not look at their past travels closely once I discovered who they were."

"But they aren't known as a capture team, right?"

"No. It is possible they're branching out, but not probable. And while you could afford their services for a short time, I don't recommend it. You would have to tell them who you are and what you do, and that would be more dangerous in the long run than any short-term protection would be worth."

"I thought so. Still, under certain circumstances, it might be a prudent option. I assume they have a confidentiality clause? And they honor it?"

"Yes and yes. And they are smart enough to arrive at the same conclusion as Lightwave's crew regarding you and your bounty. It is unlikely they would take you on as a client or a capture; the risks are too high."

"Which brings us to me." She contemplated all the information but decided to ask the question burning in the back of her mind. "Do you think the Sa'sa are trying to distract attention from me by planting deceased Sa'sa in these emergency pods? And if so, they have to travel to the systems involved, so why not do the clock maintenance while they are there?"

"I do not understand the intent of the Sa'sa. However, there are far more Sa'sa folder clutches than clock maintenance clutches. If your supposition is correct, it could be the folders dropping off the pods are in-system for other reasons, such as picking up other cargo. Or they may be doing interim folds to shorten the impact of the fold itself—you know Sa'sa don't react well to so-called long folds."

"True. It's strange how differently species react to fold even though we're all carbon-based entities and there is no perception of elapsed time for any of us, at least in our part of the universe. Not that anybody's reported, anyway." There were plenty of exploratory folders who never came back...

"Perhaps the Sa'sa do perceive the fold in some way, rather than being oblivious to it the way humans are. You are sensitive for a human, Saree. Perhaps it is part of being sensitive to elemental frequencies."

She winced. "Maybe."

Even though she didn't perceive anything during fold, it was definitely painful. And the longer the distance, the worse the damage. When she emerged from a long fold, her body felt like every molecule had been squeezed together and then released to their normal dimensions. Which, according to the fold-math theorists, is exactly what happened. On 'long' folds, she got bruises. She wasn't the only human to exhibit these symptoms, although it was relatively rare. Other species had similar reactions. No one knew if it was physiological or psychological, and since recorders didn't work during fold, they'd never know for sure. She tried not to think about any of it too much, accepting it was a form of math, not magic, and the pain was momentary and far better than dying due to travel distance and time.

"But we digress. Not knowing anything about death rituals, or in lieu of confirmation, it is impossible to know why or if the Sa'sa are dropping these pods. Perhaps it's some sort of attack or insult from other beings or between clutches?"

"Except they didn't start until I started doing clock maintenance on my own, right?" She refused to use the derogatory 'Clocker'—it was so rude.

"I can not find any occurrences prior to you traveling on your own, but that doesn't mean it didn't happen. It could be an inter-clutch rivalry—you got the human, now you get dead bodies, or we're taking your dead or who knows what? That is the problem with speculation. It could be any number of things or issues we know nothing about."

"That is the problem with speculation." She shook her head. "I was a provisional clutch member for years, but there's a lot I don't know about them. I spent a lot of time alone in my little cubby, to get away from them. There's only so much slithering, hissing and teeth clashing a girl can take." She shuddered again. "But let's set the theories aside, and look at the real problems."

"Yes. Problem one—it is obvious there is a non-Sa'sa clock maintainer, and it is most likely a human because the humans have a colony on the Sa'sa home world. Other humans want control of the human clock maintainer for their own purposes, but many other beings and entities are also interested."

Saree nodded. "Yes, that is the big problem."

"Problem two—there is a statistical probability the human clock maintainer is you."

"Yes, that would be the biggest problem for me, personally." She smiled, ironically.

"Problem three—you *must* do clock maintenance. You have a commitment and debt to pay. Problem four—it is difficult to disguise your appearance in-system without a folder of your own, and even with one, most systems will know, because they keep track of transits. The core systems require far more documentation than the fringe, but even most fringe systems keep records if only to collect their fees."

Saree nodded. "Yes, but that is one of the reasons the Guild agreed I should work the fringes, mostly in human space." That and her low status among the clutches. Or maybe non-status would be a better characterization?

"Problem four point one—you can't pay for a folder of your own, and even if you could, who could you trust to run it? You can't afford one of the small scout-folders, even if you could afford to wait the nine standard years for the next available build. You can't afford a used one either."

"True."

"The solution to all of these problems is to disguise your

appearance in each system."

"Well yes, that's what we attempted with the scholar cover, but it's not working."

"Yes, because it is obvious *you*, as an individual, are traveling to each system being maintained. You've been careful to not maintain every system you've gone to, even when the fold clock needs it, and you've been careful to visit some systems right after the Sa'sa did maintenance. We must make more coincidences occur. We could find a group of beings to follow for many systems, maybe a folder we stay with for many systems, especially if the folder transports the same shuttles for a long time. Occasionally, we should travel for a month or two without doing any clock maintenance at all."

Saree laughed. "So, we need to join the Grateful Dead Universal or become Scientologists?"

"I will check the Grateful Dead Universal. Standby." There was a pause. "No, the Dead are travelling in the core for the next standard, which is as far as they schedule. I'm not familiar with Scientology."

Saree snickered.

"Oh. No. I don't recommend them, Saree."

"I was kidding, Hal. I don't think either of those will work. Too bad about the Dead, though. It might have been fun."

"I do not think taking mind-altering substances would enhance your ability to manipulate transuranic frequencies," Hal said.

"No, I'm quite sure they wouldn't." Saree grinned. "It would still be fun for a while."

"Quite." Hal came across so prissy, and Saree laughed again. "I am glad you find this amusing, Saree."

"Hal, I have to laugh, or I might cry." Or some other irrational emotional response. It all seemed so hopeless. She would end up a slave, maintaining clocks for all the wrong reasons, until she got the courage and opportunity to end it all or the Sa'sa figured out she wasn't acting on her own initiative. Which, with their lack of understanding of humans, might take a long time.

"Oh. I am sorry. I do not understand this reaction."

She smiled. Hal sounded so sad and annoyed, all at the same time. "That's okay, Hal—you *can't* understand everything about humans."

"Evidently my programming is lacking in emotional nuances. I will attempt to remedy this."

"Hal, humans don't always have standard emotional responses. I don't think you'll be able to understand all of them anytime soon."

"Still, I will attempt it. You must correct me when I am wrong."

"I will, but you'll only get my emotions, not all humans'." She shrugged. "I'm significantly different from many humans."

"I understand. But despite this tangent into human emotional response patterns, I do have a practical suggestion."

"Really? That's wonderful, Hal." A tiny hope bloomed.

"Yes. I suggest you stay with Lightwave Fold Transport for at least a standard year, maybe as many as three. As of now, their schedule has them in Cygnus, Lacerta, Cepheus and Cassiopeia. There are plenty of systems requiring clock maintenance in these constellations, including the one you came here for. Most of them are high-priority with low pay and in human-centric systems, which makes them perfect for you. Especially if you can convince Captain Ruhger to give you a break on transport by booking in advance."

Huh. Maybe it would work. "Do you think he'll agree? I thought he couldn't wait to clear the decks of all of us."

"I think he'll agree if you talk to him. Lightwave needs the funds, badly, and I believe he is attracted to you, at least physically."

"What?" She stared at the screen.

"He is low on funding—"

"No, the other. He's attracted to me?" This conversation was taking a strange fold...

"Yes. That is what increased heart rate, increased blood flow to the groin and expanding pupils mean, is it not?"

"Umm. Yeah. I guess that is what it means." *So, the computer is trying to put Match.Uni out of business?*

"You sound surprised, Saree. Are you not attracted to him?"

She laughed. Hal had interpreted her physical reactions correctly. "Well, yes, I am, physically at least."

"You are also in good physical condition, female and close to his age. Using common dating service algorithms, the only other females on board Lightwave are less of a match than you are, and he told Chef Loreli he was heterosexual. So, it seems you are a logical choice for any kind of sexual liaison." Hal stopped, but Saree wasn't sure what to say at this point. He was absolutely correct, but at the same time, it seemed wrong. Like talking to a little kid about your sex life. "Is this an offensive topic, Saree?"

"No, Hal, I just didn't expect this topic from you." She shook all the bizarre thoughts running wildly through her head away and got back to the important part. "But despite our excursion into human sexuality, he needs the funding, so we have some real leverage, right?"

"Correct."

"So, by booking long-term with Lightwave, we will increase the number of people who might be the so-called human Clocker?"

"Precisely. I know you will not be the only shuttle staying on. Lightwave already arranged themselves around Lady Vulten's requirements and Ursuine has asked about modifying their route to add a fold for him. Al-Kindi has inquired about staying on for a standard year or more. Artiste Borgia, the medicos and Chelonians have expressed their interest in rejoining if at all possible. I think it's the food. It's too bad I can't experience the food the way humans do."

Poor Hal, his voice was so sad. "I'm sorry, Hal, but I don't think anyone's figured out how to program taste buds other than as a collection of chemicals and a vague rating system. But back to your idea. Shouldn't we find a larger folder to stay with if we're looking to increase the number of possibilities?"

"Yes, but large folders on the fringes are few and far between. They typically haul large loads on set routes in relatively small areas, which won't give you sufficient work. Besides, Lightwave's passengers are rather suspicious individuals already—if we spread the potential among them..."

She could almost see Hal shrug his shoulders. "But what about the crew of Lightwave? They're good people from what I can see." She didn't want to put anyone else through a horrible, potentially fatal experience to save herself.

"Yes, they are, and nobody at all logical will think they are clock maintainers. They've been doing fold transport for a long time. The passengers, however, are a different case. You didn't know, but your schedule has overlapped with Borgia, Al-Kindi, Ursuine and the Chelonians before. Not all at the same time or in the same system, but they've all been in a system at the same time as you sometime in the last four standard years."

She thought back over her travels. She'd been a lot of places, but space was big. Really big. It seemed odd. "Huh. Fascinating. I had no idea. But the Chelonians are good people, and I don't want to see anything bad happen to them."

"Who would believe Chelonians are clock maintainers? They're a distraction. The aggregate list of potential human clock maintainers is already well over a thousand different humans. We're adding a few more. To increase the uncertainty further, I propose you don't update the clocks in all the systems. I'll develop a selection algorithm. That will increase the size of the data set for the data crawlers and increase the number of potential targets. And in a couple of standard years, we find another folder full of remarkable passengers, we join that one. This should increase your safety for a while. Ia'asan clutch might have some other ideas. Perhaps you'll go back to the Sa'sa folder, but with an upgraded shuttle. That way, any Sa'sa folder could drop you at an interim fold point, and you could fly in-system with more secrecy. If we could get the Sa'sa folders to take on more humans, you'd have more cover as well, but it's not likely they'd be willing. We could ask the normal Sa'sa folders to make more interim stops, and make sure the stops are recorded, in a system you're in or about to go into. But Ia'asan clutch will have to make the request for you, and since their status is low, the probability of success is low—if they're willing to make the request at all. And asking higher status clutches for favors could bring additional trouble to you by reminding the Sa'sa world leadership clutches of your existence. They could decide to eliminate the problem completely. It's hard to predict if they think the trouble is worth the payoff, so we should keep it as a last resort. We'll have to keep changing our strategy and stay in the fringes where record-keeping is poor. Hopefully, we can bribe a few officials to ignore us completely, or I can wipe some data. All the little things will add up. And if someone does attack Lightwave, it's hard to believe there's a more competent crew to protect you. And they will. It's in their contract, and they abide by their contracts."

"Yes, but they'll also eject me as a threat if we're found out. We may be better off with a more indifferent folder."

"I can and will look for one, but I don't think we'll find a better choice right now."

Saree laughed. "Well, right now we're pretty much stuck, unless you'd like me to die in the fold orbit."

"No, I have no desire to see you die, Saree. I will do everything I can to protect you. It is my primary purpose."

"I know you will, Hal." She had little doubt, but there were times when death was a preferable option or when her death would prevent many others. How would Hal react in those situations? The uncertainty soured her stomach, but she chuckled anyway. With Chef Loreli laid up, the lunch fare, if there was any, was unlikely to make her stomach feel better.

CHAPTER NINE

Ruhger bit down into his 'pizza roll,' crushing and grinding the tough crust and mystery meat enough to choke it down. He'd like to crush the Scholar's proposal too, but he couldn't. The up-front credits were too good, even if they choked on it in the end. He'd agreed to Vulten's, and would probably agree to Ursuine's and Al-Kindi's proposals for the same reason, even though he'd rather boot them all into a fold orbit to a pulsar. Well, no—Ursuine was unobjectionable since there wasn't any proof of the jewel thief thing. Considering the man, it was hard to believe.

Chomping down another bite, he hoped Loreli got better soon. He looked down at the roll, a perfectly edible representation of its kind in the packaged human food industry, and wondered just when he'd become such a…foodie. He snorted and laughed, the laughter ringing through the empty shuttle. Probably after the first bite of Loreli's 'take me on board; you won't regret it' chocolate dessert audition/bribe. She was a pain in his personal ass, but his stomach and, more importantly, the crew's stomachs thanked her daily. Someone else dealing with both the passengers and their food was a huge bonus, and cheaper in the long run, since he didn't pay Loreli anything but supplies and space. It would be a sad day when she left them for a real world. They'd have to hire a chef or he'd face a mutiny.

Turning back to the Scholar's proposal, his seat creaked loudly under his weight. Complaining about the food was a stupid distraction. They had no real choice, blast it all to Orion and back. He added five percent and sent the contract back to the Scholar. She'd probably return it with another counter-proposal, but if she didn't, they'd pay off the weapons upgrade.

But with the Scholar on board, they might need those weapons.

The first few systems after this fold should be safe. The Sisters were isolated, secretive and a little paranoid, all of which made them a perfect place for a folder full of trouble to hide. Ruhger didn't want to bring trouble their way unnecessarily; they had enough surviving out here on the rim. Lightwave had three more days to the primary system fold point; he could send a message with his concerns. The Sisters could send a message with a wave-off if they thought Lightwave's passenger list too risky.

But they needed a Clocker visit... Their last run was inefficient, bordering on dangerous. The comments on the fold boards were alarming, with folds becoming farther and farther off-target and more and more unpredictable as the suggested clock corrections became less reliable. Universe-Tera and Fold Universal were both threatening to shut down operations in the entire constellation, a slow death sentence for most beings there—including the Sisters. They didn't have enough resources in-system for long-term survival. Deneb's status and credits kept everything smooth and quiet, but it wouldn't last too much longer. Ruhger shook his head. Despite the potential for trouble, he was sure they'd welcome his arrival if they'd get their system clocks maintained.

Maybe he should confront the Scholar? He drummed his fingers on his desk. No, confirmation was not something he wanted at this point. Lightwave needed plausible deniability. But he should have another crew meeting, to make sure they all knew what they were in for. There weren't many choices, though. One, take the offers, fulfill the contracts and keep the company going. Two, dump the passengers and move closer to the core, more lucrative contracts, and a higher risk of getting them attacked for their own bounty. Three, sell off Lightwave and split up the company. It was an easy choice in his mind, but the others might have different ideas and priorities. Maybe they were tired of barely surviving and wanted to split up and enjoy life for a while? Ruhger tried to ignore the hollow carved in his chest. He was stupid to worry about possibilities when he had the ability to get the information. Crunching down the last bite of tough pastry, he swallowed some water to clear his mouth.

"Contact Katryn, normal priority."

"Katryn here, Captain." Her pretty face was marred by an intense scowl.

"Katryn, can we have a virtual crew meeting, or is it too risky with the net issues?"

"Captain, I'm not sure in-person is any better. I've found a couple of spy-eyes, and I'm betting there are more, maybe some in our shuttles. It's hard to spot them because they don't have active transmitters; they're the pre-programmed 'record and return' type, with an auto-destruct upon capture. Some of them aren't even self-propelled—I think they're dropped by a 'mother ship' and picked up later." Her scowl turned into a full-out glower. "These rad-blasted things are tiny, and they could be on the shuttles too, even though they'd be harder to retrieve through multiple airlocks."

Ruhger stared at Katryn in disbelief, trying to process her words. His entire body clenched with fury. He glared back at Katryn. "This is ridiculous. We should be secure on our own rad-blasted ship."

"I know, Captain. I'm doing the best I can," Katryn gritted out, muscles in her jaw jumping.

He softened his face and tone. "I'm not angry at *you*, Katryn, I'm angry at the situation. I have no doubt you are doing everything you possibly can." He took a second to think about the current situation and control his emotions. He blew out a forceful breath. Happily, Katryn's fury calmed to a fierce frown once he controlled his own anger. "So, let's meet virtually. Would you please send out a notice for one hour from now? That should give everyone the chance to finish whatever it is they're doing and find someplace away from passenger areas. We may not be able to shut everyone out, but at least we'll limit our audience. Does that sound reasonable?"

"Sure, Captain. I'll do it right away." Katryn wasn't smiling, but she wasn't scowling either.

"Thanks, Katryn. Ruhger out." He swiped away the comm net. Suns, this being was persistent and cunning. These clever little bugs seemed like the kind of thing an engineer would have, but Ursuine was a structure guy, not an electronics wiz. Could be a hobby, though. Ruhger looked around his shabby shuttle with fresh eyes. After living in it for so many years, there were far too many places for a spy-eye to hide. The plas case of little souvenirs from a myriad of different worlds, the corners of the vents and sensor covers, the worn seats, the shuttle control console with the dull and marred coating where his hands had rested year after year... He sighed. He kept the shuttle tidy, but it could use a thorough overhaul. Ruhger snorted. Not going to happen anytime soon. They'd be lucky to pay off the weapons.

The comm chimed with an incoming high-priority message. Ah, the meeting notice. Ruhger scanned it, and looked again. Katryn changed it to an hour and a half from now, in Cargo Hold Five. He pursed his lips. Surprising choice. Five was their smallest hold and currently empty. Grant hadn't found anything good enough on Dronteim. There was a clarification note: 'Be prepared to leave all electronics at the hatch.' Intriguing. He chuckled. Katryn was taking this challenge personally.

∆∆∆

They dumped all the electronics, including their e-torcs, and entered the airlock one at a time. Katryn scanned Ruhger more thoroughly than his last med scan, then let him into the cargo hold. There was nothing in the hold, nothing at all, just the bare, cerimetal walls and the plas tile floor. All the sensors were removed or covered, and the vents were sealed. A faint scent of ozone hung in the still air. Very thorough, but he expected nothing less of Katryn and Tyron. Ruhger nodded at Katryn when she finished. She grinned, although her grin was more of a toothy challenge than a smile.

"If there's an emergency, how will we know?" Chief asked

Katryn.

She pointed to the airlock. She'd left the normal hatch open, and put up an inflatable, clear plas emergency airlock. A C2 holo hovered. They could see it from inside the bay and it obscured the view from outside. Clever. Katryn turned to Loreli, a small object in her hands. She yanked something hard, and the object inflated into a hassock. "Sit, Loreli. You don't need to be on your feet."

"Thank you, Katryn. I'm not quite back to normal yet, but I'll get there." Loreli didn't look pale, not with her dark coffee skin, but dressing in a simple white coverall with no makeup was an obvious sign of exhaustion.

"Thanks for doing all this, Katryn, Tyron. I'm not sure it was necessary for this meeting, but it's good to know it can be done." They both nodded at him, tight-lipped. He looked at each of them, his family. They gazed back, curious and determined. "I could have made these decisions on my own for the good of Lightwave, but we are a team and partners, so I want—no, I *need*—your input. You've heard the facts and speculations about our current group of passengers. We've already got a long-term contract with Lady Vulten for her travels. Ursuine, Al-Kindi and the Scholar have all proposed long-term contracts. Ursuine needs a stop added. It's essentially on the way, and since his shuttle has long-range capability, we can make it a simple drop/recover. Al-Kindi and the Scholar both say they want to explore the systems we're going to and have a guaranteed ride out-system—they'll work with our schedule. The medicos, the Artiste and the Chelonians have all said they want to fold with us again, and asked me to keep them informed."

He nodded at Loreli. "The medicos are honest—they want to

fold with us because of the food." She beamed at him, a real smile lifting the weariness a little. "I haven't committed to anyone but Vulten, and that before we took on the additional passengers. I've got a tentative contract with Ursuine, and I'm negotiating with Al-Kindi and the Scholar. Thoughts?"

"Is Vulten okay with the extra stop?" Lowe asked with a grimace.

"Yes, I cleared it with her. She wasn't happy about it, but..." Ruhger's grimace matched Lowe's. The woman was clueless about fold travel, the need for flexibility and the practical guarantee of delays. Or maybe she was used to getting her way as some sort of 'power' in Dronteim? Getting the extra stop concession meant a ridiculous amount of patient, polite discussion; anyone used to fold travel wouldn't have blinked at the request.

In the end, he'd had to remind her he could do it anyway, and his request was a courtesy. At least he'd maintained enough tolerance—barely—to make it a gentle reminder, but she didn't react politely despite his forbearance. It took him real effort to stay polite, but he wouldn't drop to her level. The woman *was* space wrack.

"That woman is a rad-blaster. Someone needs to take her down a notch or two," Tyron growled.

Ruhger smirked. "The medicos did. She was furious when they left. I felt bad for poor Gentle Schultz."

Tyron glared. "Good, but it's not enough." He sneered. "But I'm betting it will happen more. Her name means nothing outside Dronteim. Too bad I won't get to see it."

"Or me," Katryn growled, leaning against Tyron. He put an

arm around her, and she smiled up at him.

"We're stuck with Vulten. Let's talk about the rest of them." Grimacing, Ruhger shook his head. "If we accept all these long-term contracts, we can pay off the weapons. But we might need those weapons, particularly if we keep the Scholar."

"Or the Artiste," Tyron said. Ruhger turned to him, surprised. "I've done more research—he *is* a Familia assassin. And if I can figure it out, others can too. There are whispers on merc-net once you know what you're looking for."

Katryn said, "But nobody wants to take on the Familia, so a big, showy attack is unlikely. Another assassin coming to take him out? Possible. Especially a non-Familia assassin."

The argument seemed rehearsed, like the two of them had debated it more than once, but the whole crew needed to hear it. "Understood." Ruhger looked at them to see if they had more, but they shook their heads, so he continued. "Al-Kindi is suspicious, and Ursuine is too, but neither of them mean people coming after *us*. What I'm most concerned about is the Scholar," he said grimly. "She's the big threat. While the pros are smart enough to know the Clocker bounties are suicide, the ambitious amateurs looking to move up or those desperate for a big payoff won't care — including some merc companies, especially those who've taken big losses and hits to their reps." He grimaced. "Like our parents' former colleagues. Phalanx Eagle is barely holding on. And you know none of them would shed a tear if they took us out when they took the Clocker. They'd be doing Klee victory dances."

"First, they'd have to figure out the Scholar is the Clocker. Would we if she wasn't on board when the proximity alert happened? I don't think so. Even if they don't, we're on the fringe, the edge of the known, and we're not going coreward for a long time, if ever. We don't have to advertise widely for the next standard year or so," Lowe said with a grimace of his own. He preferred core civilization, but he didn't want to die. "We'll be hard to find. And if we hide out in Cygnus for a while, it will be next to impossible." His grimace deepened along with the distaste in his voice; he didn't like the Sisters.

Ruhger bit back his impulse to grin. Lowe liked the Sisters fine; he hated that they were celibate. Ruhger's grin died; Lowe must be really worried if *he* suggested hiding with the Sisters.

"We could keep the rest of them and kick the Scholar out," Loreli said, the twist in her lips indicating her distaste for the idea. "I hate to suggest it—she's been so kind—but if she's that big a risk..."

"Yes, but without her contract, we'll still owe on the weapons. And the interest on the loan is going up. If we don't get out of it soon, we'll never get it paid, and working in the far fringes?" Ruhger shook his head. "We'll only get local contracts and there are no guarantees. This current embarrassment of riches is rare."

"And unlikely," Chief said. "It seems extremely unlikely, statistically."

"There is that, too. What are the chances any of our current passengers are after the Scholar?"

The crew looked at him and each other with varying levels of surprise, then stared at him. Odd.

After an uncomfortable silence, Chief asked, "Why just the Scholar? Why not targeting the Artiste? Or the Chelonians, or any of the others?"

Ruhger gazed at them, puzzled by their obvious concern.

"Because she's the big money target if she's the human Clocker?"

Katryn snorted. "Oh, sure, that's the only reason."

"What are you talking about, Katryn? That is the only reason."

"Please. I've seen the way you look at her," she said, rolling her eyes ostentatiously.

"What?" He looked at Katryn for a few moments, completely puzzled. Finally, the clue dropped and he scowled. "I noticed she's got a nice body, but other than that? We've had prettier women on board. Besides, I don't make decisions with my libido, I make them with my brain." He pointed at the top of his head and glared at her. He wasn't some idiot who let a pretty girl lead him around by the balls.

"How did you get a look at her body? All I've seen are those stupid robes," Lowe asked with an elbow in his side and a big wink. "Her ankles are nice."

Ruhger glared at him. "Really? Can we get back to a discussion of pros and cons?"

"Yes, let's," Chief said with forced patience. "Maybe we should ask the Scholar if she's the Clocker? If she says yes, we charge her a danger fee, a big one. If she says no, we have no reason not to take her, and every reason to defend her. If she lies, and we get proof, we turn her in to the least objectionable entity and refuse any of the funds—we say... we're doing it for the good of humanity."

"Have you looked at the entities offering the bounties? None of them are less than completely objectionable," Ruhger said with more than a little anger. "I wouldn't turn a...a pre-made meat roll over to them, let alone a sentient being." Loreli gleamed at his simile.

"There must be some human organization that could use and adequately protect a Clocker. And how could anyone get her to do the job long-term if she didn't want to?" Chief asked calmly.

"You were there during the Colony raid. Do you not remember the slave collars? The children?" Ruhger said, anger simmering in his chest.

"Yes, I was there. Do you not remember my objections? I have the same ones now. Under some conditions, death is preferable. Humans can only be controlled when they have something to lose. Once we left with the children, the miners rose up against their captors, even though it was certain death. The Scholar seems to have fewer personal ties than we do," Chief said, tone and manner calm.

Ruhger's anger dissipated like steam from a warm mug. "I imagine she'd prefer the humans on the Sa'sa colony to continue living—and the Sa'sa themselves for that matter."

Tyron snorted. "The Sa'sa can take care of themselves. They're brutal and vicious when they come together. And they're protective of their humans. They've defended the colony before."

"We could take her back to the Sa'sa. She had to have learned from them, after all. She must still be in contact with them; how else would she know which systems need maintenance?" Lowe said.

"The Time Guild, of course," Chief said, with a sneer. "Even though all known clock maintainers are Sa'sa, they run the Guild as if there might be other beings capable of it. That way, they show the universe they are fair and unbiased, even though there is evidence to the contrary." His lip curled. "Mudhuggers."

Silence reigned while everyone took in the rarity of Chief's anger. Ruhger would love to know why he hated the Time Guild, but he knew Chief wouldn't talk about it.

"So, does the Time Guild owe its members safety and security, or would it be easier for them to have the human Clocker gone?" Katryn asked.

They all looked at each other and shrugged.

Ruhger broke the silence. "We're fringing. The main one is, do we accept any or all of the long-term contracts? If we don't accept all the contracts, we must earn credits, fast, to pay off the weapons. If we accept the Scholar, do we confront her? Or is ignorance better?" He nodded at Grant. "Lowe, you're first—you've got the cargo."

Frowning, Grant shook his head. "We're not going to make those credits off our cargo. I think we'll get some big payoffs on some of it, but it's speculative. We could lose, too." He gave them a lopsided smirk. "I didn't buy anything perishable, so we'll sell all of it eventually, or use it in trade, but it's not anything I'm willing to bet the ship on."

"Your vote on the contracts?"

"I vote we take them all and pay off the weapons. That's the sure bet. We wait and see on the Scholar—let's see how she hides her tracks before we try to help or hinder her. She's been doing pretty good so far."

"Chief?"

"I vote we take them all on. But I want to ask the Scholar now." He held up a hand, staring at nothing, then waved, his lips compressed. "I will admit, however logical my argument might be, I really want to know how she does it. And can any human learn if they start young enough? And—never mind; my personal curiosity is irrelevant. I vote we take all of them, and be ready for attacks, external and internal." He turned to the Phazeers. "Do we need additional security personnel?"

Tyron answered. "Additional personnel might be smart. Maybe from the Sisters? We could get a person or two pretty cheap." He grinned at Katryn for a second. "There's always someone who can't wait to leave. And the Sisters' kids don't go blabbing our business all over the universe. First, they're too shocked, then they learn to be wary or run back home." He turned back to look at Ruhger somberly. "On the contracts, I vote we take them all. Pay off the weapons, get it done. Put a clause in *all* the contracts about being transported under false pretenses and getting us attacked is enough reason for jettison."

"I agree, Captain," Katryn said.

"Loreli?"

"I'm not sure I have anything to add to this conversation, except I'd like to keep my skin whole and free. I couldn't create under duress. I'd just be—" Loreli shuddered, the hassock squealing beneath her "—a cook!"

"Clearly a fate worse than death, darling," Lowe said with an ironic grin.

"It would be! It would be awful!" She blinked rapidly.

Ruhger tried to smile, but gave up; the situation was too serious for him to make jokes. "I understand your concern. You're not officially a crewmember, but an independent contractor. Technically, you should be safe. But we all know how this works in reality. I want your vote, since we—" he motioned around their circle "—consider you crew."

"Take them all. Go with the sure thing upfront; we'll adjust after. We always do," Loreli said, with a sexy gleam and a shimmy. And another shriek from the hassock.

Ruhger nodded. "I will accept all the contracts, but I will modify the section about the safety and security of Lightwave to include a provision that 'danger brought knowingly by a passenger without warning will be dealt with in accordance with our best interests' or similar legalese. I know there's already something in there, but I'll strengthen it for all of the contracts, not just the Scholar's. We won't confront the Scholar—if she comes to us, we'll have another meeting."

He looked around the circle at each of them again. "We must be ready for every threat, internal and external, after the fold. Enjoy these next couple of standards."

Each of them acknowledged him with a nod. "Katryn, Tyron, thanks for doing all this." He waved a hand around the room. "Good job." They both smiled and nodded back at him. "Let's get back to work."

CHAPTER TEN

"**S**aree, by trying to ensure your safety, I may have put you in more danger."

"Oh? How?"

"I believe Katryn Phazeer found some of my remotes." Hal's chagrin came through loud and clear. "I thought they failed. Some fail early and some far outlast their design life. But it seems Katryn discovered at least one, because she's set up a secure area in Cargo Bay Five for a crew meeting. She removed all the sensors or de-energized and sealed them, energized the airlock to the bay, opened the bay to vacuum, then set off an electromagnetic pulse to kill all remaining active electronics. I can't get a remote in, and I can't use their sensors because they've left *all* of them outside the bay. Even the one suite she's left in the airlock itself is a transmit-only command and control status board. I have *no* idea what they're saying."

Hal's voice wasn't his normal, ultra-calm one—no, he sounded upset. Which was kind of funny, but it might be a bad sign. A very bad sign. While Saree's stomach soured, she hurried to reassure him.

"Don't worry, Hal; I'm sure we can guess based on their previous conversations and your snooping." She forced a laugh. "I'm sure they're talking about me. They're wondering if it's worth it to take me on, and if they do, should they ask me if I'm the so-called 'Human Clocker' or not?" Saree swallowed hard. "So, what do we do if they kick us off, and what do I say if they ask me?"

"Oh. Are you sure the crew is discussing you?"

"Yes. Those are the questions I'd be asking in their place." Wasn't it obvious?

"Oh. It is a reasonable assumption and probability, but without any data on this particular meeting, I would be hesitant to make such an assertion—it would be a guess. I require some data."

Sheer relief produced a real laugh. "Good to know you're not omniscient, Hal."

"Far from it, Saree. I'm only as good as my data, programming and learning make me."

"True." Saree wrinkled her nose in thought. "So, what do we tell them if they ask? The truth, a lie, or some portion of the truth?"

"Is not honesty the best policy?"

She chuckled. "That's what they say. I'm not sure it's true for us. What are the odds they'll turn me in for one of the bounties?"

"In the earlier meeting, Captain Ruhger made his thoughts clear about the entities posting and everyone agreed, even Chief Bhoher. Their analysis is correct. Based on that, I don't think they'll turn you in. This meeting may have changed things. And a secret isn't a secret once more than one being knows it. There is a possibility one of Lightwave's crew will turn you in, or tell someone who will turn you in. Perhaps we should return to Sa'sa and Ia'asan clutch."

Saree shuddered. "I'd rather not. I don't want to be physically part of the clutch ever again. Besides, there's nothing for me to do—each of them has their little part of the job, and there's no room for a generalist like me. I ride around and do nothing. I can't even pay off my training debt because I don't get to *do* anything unless one of the clutch *and* their backup is unavailable, which rarely happens."

"But if you kept the shuttle, you could do maintenance on clocks in nearby systems. They could fold and drop you, then come back and pick you up."

"Yes, but that will still get me, and the clutch, attacked. It's hard to hide a Sa'sa clock maintenance folder if you know what you're looking for, and this is clearly a human shuttle. It would stand out like a supernova on a Sa'sa folder. I think it would be easier to capture me since this shuttle has few defenses and no offensive weapons." Saree frowned, her thoughts grim. "And if beings keep coming after me, there's the possibility the Sa'sa will declare war, maybe war on all humans. Then human systems don't get maintenance and lots of beings die. That's a trade I am *not* prepared to make."

She looked at the shuttle decking. "I wish any of us had thought about the potential consequences before I started this orbit. We all would have been better off if they'd trained me just enough to not interfere in ^timespace^."

"Saree, you are not fully considering the facts. First, you

personally would not have been better off—you'd be doing maintenance on the clock assembly lines, or mining for transuranics. Both professions carry significant risk and wouldn't use your intelligence. Yes, traveling alone is difficult and, if you're discovered, dangerous, but the first in any new field takes risks, usually alone. You are hope for humanity and other species— someday, the Sa'sa will lose their hold on the Time Guild. Besides, even if the Sa'sa ignore humans for eternity, rather than fading away, humanity will find another way. They'd build clocks with replaceable parts like they used to and absorb the cost, make more corrections through the current fold comm systems, make the current clock arrays bigger or find new ways to do the same job or any number of other techniques that are currently more expensive, but still possible. Research on longer-lasting, more stable frequency standard sources continues, and so does research on the effects of fold. Humans are involved in a very large percentage of the research in this area. There's always research on ^timespace^ too, although much of that is anything but scientific. And…other species have done, and are doing, similar things— that's why the Time Guild was formed. Other species feared the Sa'sa were using their abilities and monopoly for the betterment of their race only. After a lot of diplomacy by many species, the Sa'sa finally understood if they didn't make an attempt to at least *look* like they were impartial, the research into better clocks and cheaper ways to communicate between clocks would be accelerated. Eventually, they'd lose, because someday, it would be cheaper to avoid them, even with the rarity of the right transuranic elements in the universe. I suspect that is what the ancient AI does—it buys new clocks tuned at the factory, puts huge arrays of clocks all over the system and sends comms through the fold to sync the clocks hourly or more with outside systems. I doubt it allows any living beings into its primary system, wherever that may be."

Hal, the motivational speaker. Maybe that would be their next cover story. Saree huffed and decided to concentrate on the facts, rather than the emotions. "Buying all those clocks would be incredibly expensive."

"The AI has more credits than most core systems do. More than the majority of business empires, even big interstellar ones like Trump-Koch Platinum or Soros-Clinton Universal. It owns interstellar businesses. For example, Galactica Corporation. Most call it Galactica."

Saree shuddered at the name, then frowned. "I thought you couldn't make assertions without data?"

"There is data available, lots of data. Others have put it together before me. But they are destroyed or disappear before the accusations can go public. The AI is ruthless. Actually, that is poor terminology. Referring to it as 'paranoid' or 'ruthless' is a metaphor to make it more understandable for emotional beings. It is nothing but a self-protecting mechanism. Its entire primary purpose is self-protection. And to it, credits equal self-protection, both spending and earning them."

"I see." Saree contemplated all the beings and entities after her for a moment, and shuddered. She was asking for trouble and depression. And she didn't want to think about Galactica Corp at all. Concentrating on the issue at hand right now was the smart thing to do. "Let's get back to the question of the moment. Based on what you know now, will they turn down my proposal for a long-term contract?"

"I do not believe so, Saree. I believe they need the funds. They are deeply in debt for their weapon upgrades."

"Okay, so the next question is, will they ask me to confirm I'm just a scholar? And if they do, what do I say?"

"Since we are not privy to their current discussions, I would be reluctant to make any assumptions regarding confirmation of your status, but proving you are a Scholar is easy. You are. You cannot prove you are not the Clocker, no one can. Proving a negative is impossible. In regards to your real question, which is, 'will they eject me or threaten me?' there are provisions in the current contract allowing Lightwave Fold Transport to eject a shuttle knowingly bringing danger to the ship or the other passengers without informing Lightwave of the danger. We were already in violation of the provision, but before they researched you, there was little risk of discovery. I do not have enough data on any of them individually or as a group to hypothesize if they will confront you or how they would react if you confirmed their assumption. If the decision was being made by one of them individually, I might make a prediction, but humans in a small group of relative equals are hard to predict. If I had a sensor on their current meeting, I would be much more willing to speculate."

"So, the decision to stay or go is mine alone."

"The decisions are always yours, Saree, unless you are incapacitated and in danger."

Saree smiled. Of course. Her smile died. What was Hal's definition of danger? Would he decide living put her in danger? Oh, it didn't matter right now. She'd worry about sentient AIs later. She had 'right now' problems to deal with. The 'what-ifs' could wait. Frowning, Saree said, "I don't know any of these people well enough to make any guesses on how they will react either, but if they ask me, I will be honest. They've already put the data together. If they don't ask, I will remain silent. Status quo is safest. Besides, Cygnus might bring some answers. I'm intrigued by these Sisters Captain Ruhger spoke of. They seem to have a lot of experience covering their tracks, and I wonder if I could learn something from them."

"I do not understand the difference between these Sisters and any number of other contemplative or secretive human enclaves, Saree."

"The difference is, they export talent but I've never heard of them. Generally, human groups specializing *and* exporting a skill, product or a process advertise. Like the Trappists and beer brewing, or the S'muri and sword fighting. Closed religious groups usually don't advertise, unless they're looking for new members, and even then, the advertisements are focused on a certain segment of the population. These Sisters of Cygnus are closed and reclusive, but actively export some of their religious aspects into a non-religious setting, which is unusual and practical. Jericho mining colony was a closed religious community. I don't remember a lot about the specific practices other than memorizing lots of Bible passages and sitting still and praying when I wanted to go play. I do remember outsiders weren't welcome, and restricted to certain areas." She grinned. "We used to sneak around and spy on the visitors, because it was so rare."

Chuckling, Saree remembered them darting around through

the colony tunnels and passages. They were so young, she doubted they were fooling anyone, but the adults hadn't stopped them. Probably because they knew forbidding it would only make it more attractive and they might get in real trouble.

But that naive girl was long gone. "I remember one new person joining our colony. I don't remember anyone leaving. From my schooling on Sa'sa, I know this is customary for human religious communities. Some, including ours, allowed people to leave, but if they did, they could never come back. The Sisters are religious and secretive about their religion, but they allow free travel in *and* out? Actively encourage it? And nobody is talking about the religion itself or the practices of the Sisters? That's unusual. And smart."

"There are similar human religions and communities, Saree. I believe most of them take the same approach, advertising to a small segment only."

"I'll take your word for it, Hal, but I still think I might be able to learn something from the Sister of Cygnus."

"One can learn something from every being, Saree."

She chuckled. Hal's tone was so matter-of-fact, it was impossible to be offended by the rather condescending statement of the obvious. "Yes, of course we can. But I might be able to learn a specific thing about hiding in plain sight from the Sisters."

"If you say so, Saree."

Her stomach rumbled. "Hal, I'm going to the dining facility. I may as well eat while we wait for the next round of contract negotiations."

"Yes, Saree."

"Thank you for your help, Hal."

"You are welcome, Saree." The words were the same, but the tone seemed...warmer. Or was she projecting? There was no way to know.

She exited the hatch and walked along the corridor, her shoes making little squeaking noises on the slightly damp plas, a sharp citrus scent hanging in the moist air. Lightwave certainly kept their cleaning bots busy. She peeked in the phys mod on her way. Gerald Ursuine's legs spun away on an exercise bike. She nodded at him. He didn't return her greeting; he seemed immersed in the holo.

In the dining facility, a passenger she hadn't met yet was closing a go-box. One of the medicos? Lady Vulten and Gentle Schultz were eating at a table. Saree walked to the buffet and picked up a bowl, trying to discreetly sniff the air. Today's meal was some sort of thick, spicy vegetable stew with rice and flatbread. While it looked and smelled good, it wasn't a Chef Loreli creation. She huffed at her own ridiculousness—she'd gotten so spoiled. A few fancy meals and nothing was good enough anymore. She served herself and turned toward the tables.

Elise Schultz motioned to her, her layered sleeves, in browns today, undulating. "Would you like to join us? Dining is better with others."

"Certainly, thank you." She put her plate down and bowed to Lady Vulten.

The Lady, sitting with her nose in the air and a sour look on her face, didn't seem to agree with Gentle Shultz's invitation. She was overdressed, again, in a light pink jacket with elaborate flowers embroidered across it, and a diamond choker around her rather wrinkly neck. Her perfectly coiffed hair stood stiff and shiny around a delicate diamond tiara.

"Lady Vulten, I am happy to make your acquaintance. I am Candidate Scholar Cary Sessan of Centauri University."

She nodded regally in return. "And yours. Please do join us; we have tired of our own company."

"Yes, one of the hazards of space travel," Saree said, sitting and arranging her meal. Neither of the women said anything else. Well, most people liked to talk about themselves. Saree smiled and said, "Elise was telling me you grow Thymdronteim and it hasn't been successfully grown off-planet. Are you traveling the fringes in search of growing techniques?"

The Lady shot a glare at poor Elise, and turned back to Saree with a pasted-on lift of her lips masquerading as a smile. "You are correct, Scholar Sessan. I am looking for ways to grow Thymdronteim in containers, or even better, hydroponically. A lot of the fringe systems in this area grow their food in very difficult conditions, so I hope to find some new techniques."

"I'm surprised it can't be grown hydroponically. It's certainly not my area of expertise, but I thought almost every condition could be successfully mimicked these days."

The Lady scowled, but Saree thought it might be for the circumstance, not at her.

"Not at all, Scholar. Indeed, most hydroponically grown food is bred for those conditions. DNA modifications are common. Thymdronteim grows wild on Dronteim, and the planet has a combination of difficult conditions. The soil, constant winds, the salt content of the seas, and the light from the star all combine to make a harsh environment Thymdronteim thrives in. Early settlers tried to eradicate it around their homes, thinking it a useless weed, but they soon discovered Thymdronteim was critical to the overall planet environment. Thymdronteim enhances the taste of everything wonderfully."

Her tone and delivery were a combination of pedantic teacher and late-night sales pitch. Saree was anticipating a 'but, wait, order now, and you'll get...' with every sentence.

"The same conditions Thymdronteim thrives in are difficult for Old Earth plants. The survivors are tasteless or odd-tasting. Thymdronteim is a *must* on the planet. And modifying the DNA of Thymdronteim hasn't been successful—it completely negates the taste." She smiled again, but it looked like the unaccustomed expression might hurt. "When I travel, I truly miss the taste of Thymdronteim. It is such a shame more people can't experience the marvel of taste and texture it adds. I must bring it to a wider audience!"

Saree stared in surprise. The last was a heartfelt declaration. Or she really was a vid pitch-person. She looked at Elise Schultz; she was smiling at Lady Vulten, and it seemed genuine. Perhaps this was the Lady's true calling, and the weaponization was a credit-earning necessity? No way to know yet. Saree would continue to be cautious.

The Lady pierced her with a fanatical stare. "Did you experience the wonders of Thymdronteim?"

"Why no, I'm afraid. I didn't make it to Dronteim itself; I was on the space station for a very short time. I intended to land on the planet, but when I arrived at the station, I found there weren't many fold transports folding out-system for the next standard month, so I took Lightwave, and we departed immediately."

"Oh, such a shame. You missed a true wonder of the galaxy."

Lady Vulten shook her head mournfully, Elise mirroring her.

"I was already sorry I couldn't get planet-side; now I am doubly so." Saree patted her mouth with a napkin. She wasn't sorry at all. The one thing she'd eaten on station tasted metallic, with a lingering, nasty aftertaste and mouth-puckering drying effect.

"Yes, it is truly a shame. I have plants with me, but they aren't mature, so I can't harvest any. Such a pity," the Lady said. "But as a consolation…have you heard? Artiste Borgia will grace us with a small recital tomorrow night." Smug self-congratulation etched her face.

"Oh, no, I hadn't." Saree forced a smile, dreading an evening of overdone l'Opera arias. "How generous of him! It will be a true wonder to hear such an Artiste." It would be a wonder— wondering how soon she could leave, how she could avoid the whole thing, when he'd finish…

"Yes, it will." Lady Vulten frowned again, the expression looking much more natural than her smile. "He had to be coaxed into it, claiming his talents weren't sufficient to share with us, but that's ridiculous. It will be such a treat to hear an artiste of his caliber on this barely adequate transport." Vulten looked at Saree, speculatively. "You're a musician. Do you play the piano?"

"Uh, no, Lady Vulten. I play a few stringed instruments, like the guitar. I'm an amateur musician. I study music, the history of music, not performance." The Lady's face fell. She must have hoped for a live accompanist for the Artiste. "But thank you for convincing him to honor us, Lady Vulten."

She nodded again, clearly convinced the recital was her due.

Saree patted her lips with her napkin. "Lady, Gentle, it was a pleasure dining with you, but I must work on my thesis. If I don't catalog all my discoveries during transit, they pile up dreadfully, and I forget critical intangible details. I am sure I will see you again before the fold." Saree bowed and took her dishes to the auto-cleaner.

A l'Opera concert. Wonderful.

She returned to her shuttle, noting Ursuine was gone from the phys mod.

"Saree, Lightwave sent another counter-proposal. The price went up five percent and they've added some provisions concerning security and safety. To summarize, 'if you bring life-threatening or ship-threatening danger to Lightwave, we reserve the right to do anything including jettison to resolve the danger. If you know about a particular danger and don't tell Lightwave upfront, we can not only jettison you but confiscate your personal effects.' In other words, they can take your shuttle and turn you over to someone or dump you anywhere in an escape pod. In reality, the contract already allowed this—it's standard language—but they've made it very clear. We already violate the existing provisions to conceal your true profession. Does this new wording change any of your previous decisions?"

Saree deliberated. "No, I don't think so, Hal. It doesn't change anything. And a five percent increase I can accept. Let me imprint it and send it back." The contract appeared before her, she entered her security code and imprinted it.

"I have sent it to Captain Ruhger. I will monitor what I can, but I must be cautious with my remotes so I may not collect as much data."

"Understood, Hal. Since we've chosen to stay under the

scanners, let's stay quiet and discreet, okay?"

"Agreed."

"Thank you, Hal." Saree smiled. Relief coursed through her entire body, the tension she'd unconsciously held releasing abruptly, her muscles relaxing. She had guaranteed fold transportation for at least the next standard year, on a relatively safe folder with people she trusted, sort of, who were security conscious and careful. And she liked the crew. A scenario well beyond her wildest dreams.

"You are welcome, Saree."

Hal's standard reply also made her smile. In the end, he might be dangerous, but right now, Hal was comforting. She hadn't allowed herself to think about how lonely she'd been over the last few standard years, but the sheer joy of talking freely to someone was amazing.

"You know, Hal, I think I'll work on my thesis for real." She considered Hal for a moment. "Would you mind discussing some of it with me? And critiquing it? You must know as much as I know."

"It would be my pleasure, Saree. I don't know as much as you do about Filk, because it involves human emotions and humor, but I would enjoy an expert discussion. I am sure to learn something."

"Excellent. Let me get through some of this minutia first." She opened the latest version, and the file of vids from the last few planetfalls. She smiled, happy to be working on this dry, boring document for the first time ever. She reflected for a moment. Yes, that's what this feeling was—true happiness. She hadn't realized how unhappy she'd become trying to simply survive, or how long it had been since she'd been actually happy. Grinning, she enjoyed the sensation for a few minutes, then got to work.

CHAPTER ELEVEN

I t was done. Ruhger sent a copy of the imprinted contract back to the Scholar. For better or worse, it was done. He scowled, imagining his parents looking over his shoulder, shaking their heads in disapproval. Or would they? The folder always came first with his mother, and his father would be the first to say, "Get out of debt, boy," especially to weapons merchants. Every mercenary in existence knew they were the lowest of mudball slime. The passenger deposit confirmations would come in on the other side of the fold, then he'd transfer credits to the dirt suckers and be done with them. He should be thrilled, but dread warred with relief—what would the next few folds bring? Suns, what would the rest of *this* fold bring?

Impatient with his thoughts, he slammed his fists down on the chair arms, wincing when the plas crackled. He had to stop with the doom-and-gloom scenarios, or he'd drive himself crazy. Or break something. It was done, and they'd deal with the next thing when it came. He could almost hear his mother's voice: "One fold at a time, Ruhger. Don't get ahead of yourself." Plugging the contract funds into his accounts, he smiled when the red went away. Now this was a moment worth enjoying, so he did, sitting back in his chair until it creaked, grinning at the view until his cheeks ached from the unaccustomed position.

Enough enjoyment. He had a job to do. Ruhger checked crew locations. Chief was in Beta Shuttle, the Phazeers in their room, Lowe in the ready room and Loreli in the kitchen. *Wait, what?* Shaking his head in irritation, he jumped up, striding toward the hatch.

"Contact Chief Bhoher, normal priority."

"Bhoher here, Captain."

"Chief, Loreli's in the kitchen. I'm going to go check on her. You've got command."

"Captain, I accept command. Isn't it too soon for her to be cooking?"

"Yes," Ruhger growled.

"Ah. Good luck. Bhoher out."

Loreli shouldn't risk her health. She could relapse. Marching down the narrow beige crew corridors and ladders, Ruhger jerked to a halt with a hand on each side of the back kitchen hatchway. He tried to make sense of the scene in front of him, but there were a huge number of people cluttering the kitchen, all chattering happily at incredibly high volumes, confusing him utterly. Did they have this many people on board? And what in all the suns were they doing in the kitchen! Loreli had been poisoned once— did she want them all taken out?!

Finally, he spotted Loreli, sitting on a high stool near the chow hall hatch. Ruhger pushed and shoved his way through all the happy people to reach her. She twinkled at him, her face shining with sparkly makeup. "Loreli, what are you doing?! You're supposed to be resting! And what in all the seven suns of Saga are all these people doing in our kitchen?! We secured it for a reason!"

She beamed and blinked her ridiculous lashes at him. "Oh, are you worried about me? How sweet, darling." She put a hand on his arm, and ran it up and down. He pulled back abruptly. She flinched, and smiled again, dimmer.

He grimaced in return. He hadn't meant to hurt Loreli's feelings. Again.

"Don't worry, darling. I'm not doing anything at all. No, I am sitting here on my very fine ass, supervising." She slapped her hip, encased in another tight, white plas outfit. "And nobody's going to poison you, dear; they're all eating their own creations. What was I supposed to do when all these lovely beings just wanted to help?" She gave him a patently false look of helplessness, raising both hands. "I knew what you'd say about them cooking, so I'm holding a baking class." By the time she finished her sentence, her normal exuberant tone was back.

"Oh?"

"Yes—we were sitting around after lunch drinking tea and bemoaning the lack of her fabulous pastries. She very kindly offered to teach us how to make them," Scholar Sessan said, leaning around his right side.

"Yes. Don't worry, Captain. We—" Medico Pancea motioned to the people standing around her—her fellow medicos, and not all women no matter how it seemed when he first came in the hatch "—will not let Chef Loreli exert herself too much. We know where our next meal is coming from, and it's not from our poor efforts at imitation." She grinned. "Besides, this is fun. Sure, we could be studying the latest medical journals or sitting around watching vids, but this way we all get to learn and do something new and different. It's refreshing."

There were nodding heads all around the room.

Ruhger gritted his teeth. "Loreli, I need to speak with you in private."

She rolled her eyes ostentatiously. "Fine. Come into the pantry." She stuck a hand out, obviously so he could help her down.

He glared for a moment, but Loreli just looked back at him. She *had* to play these little games. Finally, he gave in and took her hand.

She hopped down off the stool without any pressure on his hand. Tugging him by the same hand over to the pantry, a couple of steps away, he was relieved to see it locked. She dropped his hand to enter the code, and sashayed into the small room jammed with bins, boxes, bottles, pots, and pans. It looked a little crowded and chaotic, but each item was properly secured. Ruhger entered, squeezing tight to her to let the hatch close, stepping back as soon as he could.

Loreli turned, beaming a slow, sexy smolder, and asked, "Now, darling, what has you all hot and bothered?"

Ruhger had to unclench his jaw to speak. "Loreli, you've already been injured by a passenger, intentionally or not. What is keeping these people from poisoning all of us?" He forced the words out through his gritted teeth.

She rolled her eyes again. "This isn't my first fold, Ruhger. Teaching others is part of the Institute's creed, and they teach us *how* to teach safely. It includes something called 'mise en place.' That means prepping your materials before you start. Each student gets a tray of ingredients including *only* what they need to make their dish. The pantry, which contains all the raw ingredients—" she swept a hand around them "—remains isolated and secure. And one of those expensive upgrades you complained about when I came on board was an automatic dispensing system. Flour, sugar, salt, and other staples are dispensed in the main room in whatever amount I ask via secured holo command, but they're stored in here, down there." She pointed to the bottom shelves, filled with large plas containers, each with a hatch on the top.

Aiming an exasperated look at him, Loreli continued her lecture. "And yes, Katryn upgraded the security on the dispenser when I brought it on board. So, while I did set up all the trays, I did so while sitting at the counter on my still incredibly lovely ass." She turned and wiggled it at him. "Each person got the properly measured amount of sugar and flour via the dispenser." She swept a hand at the containers on the floor again. "Sure, someone could break in here and poison us, but they'd do that with or without a class. And they could poison each other, but I'm not eating anything they make." She shuddered slightly. "I'm not that dedicated to teaching, darling. Beginner fare, blech. I'm definitely not touching anything that Schultz person makes. And they're all wearing gloves; Medico Chyna suggested it before we started."

Loreli looked at him with unusual sobriety. "I do take security seriously, Ruhger. I'm not going to endanger you. Could someone put some sort of substance on something to take us all out? Yes, they could. But they could do that anywhere. Why not put that something on the control panel to the crew quarters? That way, they'd get all of us."

Loreli had studied the security issues. Ruhger could *not* make the right moves or find the right words with Loreli, could he? He put his foot in his mouth every time. "I still think it's an unnecessary risk and the best way to get all of us all at once. But since we haven't folded yet, anyone would be an idiot to take us out now." He considered. It was too late now, anyway. "Before you do something like this again, will you consult with us first?"

He put a hand up when she opened her mouth. "Yes, the kitchen is your domain, I accept that. But we do have more recent experience with security than you do. Tyron and Katryn can come up with easy, simple ways to make this safer if you're going to insist."

She nodded sharply. "I can accept that. I will talk to both of them before I let anyone else in the kitchen. But I should get back out there before they decide they actually know what they're doing, which they don't, and make everything completely inedible." She chortled.

Shaking his head, he put his hands up in surrender. "Don't let me keep you from it. Make sure you stay seated and let the passengers do the work."

She twinkled flirtatiously at him. "Of course, Captain. I'm the instructor, not the student. I'm a very good teacher and I have a very good reward system." Loreli shot him a look through her lashes. "And I'm equally good at punishment." She slapped her hand against her own thigh, the sharp crack ringing in the small room.

Ruhger kept himself from saying anything, but it took real effort. He turned in the small space, pressing back against Loreli to open the hatch, and jumped when she squeezed his waist. He turned to glare at her once the hatch was open.

"What? I had to hold on or fall!"

He glared at her. Twinkling, she batted her lashes at him. Ruhger sighed and turned to leave the kitchen.

"You could join us. Working with butter, flour, and sugar is a sensuous experience," Loreli said throatily.

Looking at Loreli, but still backing away, he ran into the Scholar. She jolted into him, her long, strong fingers on his back. He took a small step forward so she wouldn't be crushed against the countertop, then paradoxically missed the press of her hands. "Sorry, Scholar. No, thank you, Chef. I don't think I'm cut out for pastry-making. I'll see you later." He turned in place, trying not to crush anyone else, and wove his way through all the bodies, escaping out the hatch.

Shaking his head, he walked back to Alpha shuttle. Well, late for this class, but Loreli had considered the issues. If she didn't interfere with safety or security, he couldn't complain too much.

He entered the shuttle and took back command. Chief looked puzzled and impatient at his explanation and swiped off while Ruhger was still talking. Smiling at his poor attempt to explain, he thought about the joyous confusion in the kitchen, and abruptly scowled. *Wait a minute.* There was somebody new there, somebody he'd never seen. *What the suns?*

He pulled up the surveillance. Loreli, Scholar, Vulten, Schultz, four medicos and...her. Who the suns was *she*? A petite being, in an enveloping black robe with a black head covering barely revealing her face. He found another view. He stared. A human woman's face, tan skin, with big, dark eyes lined with heavy black makeup surrounded by long lashes, a slightly prominent nose with a bit of a hook, and a bow-shaped mouth with dark red lipstick. Blast and rad! Who was she?!

"Contact Tyron."

"Captain?" Tyron's voice came over the comms without any video.

Blast, he'd interrupted something. He cleared his throat. "Sorry for the interruption, but we have a new person on board. Who in the suns is she?"

"What?!" they both exclaimed.

"Yeah. Appears to be a human female. She's in the kitchen with Loreli's cooking class."

"She's with who's what, Captain?" Katryn asked.

"Loreli decided to have a cooking class. Don't worry, she's not doing anything but sitting—" he narrowed his eyes at the vid feed "—and occasionally walking around to help her students." He watched as Loreli sat again, peeling off disposable gloves. "And she did think about the food security issues, although I want the two of you to discuss this with her further and develop a full-up food security protocol, both for normal runs and for cooking classes. But who in all the suns is this new person?!" He realized he was shouting and tried to wrestle his anger down.

"Hold on, let me pull up the feed," Tyron's voice said.

"Huh. Cooking class," Katryn said, clearly distracted.

"There she is, Katryn!"

"What the?"

"Sorry, Captain. Not sure who she is. Let me scan the shuttle passenger lists again. I checked everyone coming on board for the welcome dinner and checked the rest of Lightwave to make sure there wasn't anyone else on board, but she could have been on one of the shuttles and not joined us for dinner. You know we can't check the shuttles; it's one of the biggest risks we have. I wish radiation and privacy shielding wasn't as good as it is," Tyron said.

"Yes. I don't like it, but nobody would fold with us if we insisted on checking shuttles. Not in the fringes, anyway. Too many paranoid people, too many people carrying odd things, if not outright illegal things we don't want to know about."

Katryn said, "The problem is, just before the big dinners, Loreli gets all ridiculous and nervous and insists on lecturing us on service. Like it's that big a deal." Her voice deepened in a mockery of Loreli's. "'Place the plate reverently down in front of the gentle being, from their left. Clattering china distracts the diners unnecessarily.'"

Ruhger was trying to suppress a laugh when Tyron spoke up. "Oh, here she is, I remember now. Al-Kindi declared a passenger, a spouse, about five hours before he returned to Lightwave. He paid the passenger fee without any negotiation and gave me her name. I looked her up; she wasn't a risk." Tyron hummed tunelessly. "I remember thinking it strange he didn't bring her to the welcome dinner," he muttered. "I figured the whole deal fell through on his end, and if he wasn't going to ask for a refund, I wasn't going to offer. I didn't want to embarrass the man if he'd been left standing at the altar. Or whatever implement his beliefs might require."

"Who is she, Tyron!" Sometimes...

"Throttle back, Captain. She really is Al-Kindi's spouse. Her name is Nari. Nari Yazdim Al-Kindi. Katryn found their marriage in Dronteim's records. The whole thing is legit."

Huh. "Okay. But is she a risk?"

"Like I said, I looked her up. There's a birth record from Circini. I found some school records for homeschooling, but that's it. Nothing else. She's never left Circini before or worked or done anything official, so I judged her to be as low a risk as we ever get. She never showed up on board, so I...forgot about her. I figured she backed out of the marriage. And since he paid the fees, I'd already changed Al-Kindi's shuttle allowances to accommodate a second human, and they never came close to those limits. She must be used to stringent conditions."

"Captain, I've checked all the entry records," Katryn said. "This is the first time she's exited Al-Kindi's shuttle. I reviewed the vids. Al-Kindi brought her on board about an hour before Loreli's class. He showed her around Lightwave and introduced her to Loreli. They talked for a while, Al-Kindi went back to his shuttle and she stayed in the kitchen. She seemed very nervous and uncertain, scared even, but her body language relaxed after talking to Loreli for a while. Loreli put her between the Scholar and Elise. She's quiet." Katryn made an odd hiss, like she was sucking in a big breath through her teeth. "It's just a guess, based on what few records there are and how she looks in the vid, but I don't think she's been on a folder before. She's got that whole 'wide-eyed tourist' thing going on. Then there's the robe—it's obviously some sort of religious outfit. I think the records are right: she's never been off-planet before. Nari Al-Kindi is about as low-risk as we get."

"Are there any other surprise passengers?" Ruhger asked with forced patience.

"Standby," Tyron said.

Evidently, the Phazeers were taking him seriously. Finally.

"No, she's the only declared passenger that hasn't shown up. Sorry about that, Captain," Tyron said sheepishly. "She was declared, and checked out, but plenty of beings never leave their shuttles. And the Al-Kindi shuttle didn't come anywhere close to their utility limits. I didn't think anything of it, and I was... a little busy when she did exit for the first time. Sorry I missed it, Ruhger. Katryn and I will update the security protocols so this doesn't happen again. If we don't see a declared passenger right away, we'll ask for confirmation. It was sloppy on my part, Ruhger. I let an emotional response lessen security. It won't happen again." Tyron's tone conveyed determination.

It wasn't good, but it could have been worse. It happened at an odd time. Normally they were watching when passengers entered the first time. But normally, they boarded right after lock on, the welcome dinner, or it didn't happen. Ruhger shook his head. "Copy that. Ruhger out." One more oddity in a fold full of oddities. This fold was interesting, but more in the Old Earth curse 'may your life be interesting' kind of way. He could use less interesting and more credit-generating.

Pulling the kitchen vid back up, he watched. It looked like fun. There was mixing, spreading, kneading and a bunch of other activities he had no name for and everyone was smiling or laughing. He couldn't remember the last time he'd done something just for fun—probably when he was still a kid.

No, wait, that wasn't true. Shortly after Tyron found Katryn and before the last serious attempt on their bounties, they'd been at a Pyxis system safe enough for them to all leave Lightwave and go mudballing. Just remembering made him smile. So much crazy fun. Even Chief had laughed a few times. Too bad they'd only stayed a couple of days. He snorted a laugh. Maybe he should have joined them in the kitchen. Surprising Lowe wasn't there; this would be his kind of thing. Oh, but the Chelonii weren't there either... Grant had his own definition of adventure and fun. He sighed, a little enviously. He could use that kind of fun once in a while too. He remembered the press of the Scholar's fingers against his back in the kitchen. She was stronger than he would have thought.

He watched the vid, even though there were a dozen other things he could and should be doing. The Scholar ditched her traditional over-robe; the form-fitting black leggings and a long-sleeve shirt displayed her athletic body. She wasn't traditionally beautiful, but when she laughed for real, she lit up with happiness and joy, and that was beautiful. He'd like to see her lit up with another kind of joy...

Ruhger swept the vid away. He couldn't think like that. The Scholar was a huge security risk. That's what he needed to remember and think about. Along with all the other security risks on board. Including a new one they knew next to nothing about.

Δ Δ Δ

"Chef, are we go for fold?"

"Go for fold, Captain. The kitchen is secured."

"Purser?"

"Go for fold; all public areas are secured and ready. Cargo is locked."

"Physical Security?"

"Physical Security is go for fold. All passengers in their shuttles, shuttles are locked, all external hatches locked, all internal hatches secured," Tyron said.

"Net Security?"

"Net Security is go for fold, Captain."

"Engineering, are we go for fold?"

"All systems green and clean, Captain. Thrusters and engines secured, fold generators ready. Engineering is go for fold."

Ruhger said, "Fold point is clear here. The last report shows fold point clear at the destination, no scheduled transports for the next standard day, no navigational hazards. All systems are clean and green. Holdouts?" He waited, counting to five in his head, and brought up the folder-wide comms. "Attention, all shuttles. We are go for fold in five, four, three, two, initiating fold." Swiping at the final control on the holo panel, he stared at the status board.

Absolutely nothing changed except the clock, still counting seconds, minutes and hours, but the fold clock and the shuttle clock disagreed by a significant number of nanoseconds, which meant they were off the fold point by an equally significant amount. The sensors weren't reporting any nearby objects, thank the seven suns of Saga. The closest ship was far down the orbit, and there wasn't any debris or erratic asteroids or comets, so they weren't about to be annihilated. Sweeping up the navigation panel, he checked against the stars and other beacons. Yes, they had arrived in Cygnus Prime, but way off the official fold point.

Ruhger sagged back in his seat for a split-second. No matter how many times he folded, he always worried about making it. It seemed all too easy for all too many things to go wrong. And nobody knew what happened to the vessels and people in a fold gone wrong.

Enough. Back to business. "All shuttles, we have arrived in Cygnus Prime, also known as Deneb. Please initiate system checks and report issues to Purser Lowe immediately." He swiped off the passenger shuttle comms. "Lightwave crew, report immediate issues and hazards."

There was silence on the comms. Good—another successful fold. Ruhger let the silence continue while everyone performed system checks. Checking the navigation panel again, he pulled up more data. They'd arrived in Cygnus all right, but dangerously far from the main fold point. If this was a core system, they could have folded right into a collision. Since this was a fringe system, they weren't in danger of colliding with another fold transport, but they were so far off the fold point they could have run into debris of some sort. Cygnus Prime fold point needed a Clocker visit.

"Lightwave report by station. Chef?"

"No issues, Captain."

"Purser."

"No issues."

"Physical Security."

"Clean and green."

"Net Security."

"Clean and green."

"Engineering."

"Clean and green, Captain. Securing fold generators now. Thrusters and engines will be ready in approximately two minutes."

"Copy all. Engineering, I'll be adjusting the course for our arrival point and will let you know when I'm ready for a cross check. All, our arrival was safe, but very far from the official fold point, even with the suggested correction factor. Cygnus Prime's clock is dangerously unstable. I'll report the time differences and warping after Engineering finishes course check. The orbit authorities can recommend new clock corrections and warnings accordingly. Purser, Security, please initiate your shuttle checks. Captain out."

Swiping out of the comms, he swept the navigation panel up again, double-checking the computer's recalculation of the actual arrival point, based on triangulation of star locations and other system clocks. The corrections looked accurate, so he turned to the display of projected arrival versus actual and the computer's revision of fold orbit course. He checked the math and forwarded it to Engineering. In less than a minute, Chief had replied with a concurrence and a 'go' for the thruster engines. Lacking any other options, Ruhger synced Lightwave's clock to the Cygnus Prime clock standard. Their array of additional clocks was small, but more accurate than the drifting fold clock.

"Lightwave crew, we've laid in our course and are ready for thrust initiation. Any holdouts?" He waited for thirty seconds, and opened comms to the shuttles. "All shuttles, we are initiating fold orbit thrust in five, four, three, two, go for thrust." He swiped the thrust engines on. Navigation reported movement toward their destination, the engines showing normal propulsion. "All shuttles, report any issues to Purser Lowe immediately. Please remain in your shuttles while we complete our arrival procedures.

I will notify you when those procedures are complete, and you may re-enter Lightwave. Thank you for your patience." He swiped off the shuttle comms. "Security, initiate physical checks. Engineering, any issues?"

"Negative, Captain—clean and green."

"All, the fold was in our favor for once, and we'll be arriving at the shuttle release orbit seven hours early. And saving some fuel. At least something good came out of this fold. Report any fold or other issues. And everyone? Now's the time to be on guard. Be wary, be careful and report anything suspicious. Anything at all. We'll do comm check-ins on a regular basis. The schedule is on your calendars already. Ruhger out." Swiping out of all the comms, Ruhger checked the fold orbit course calculations one more time and sent the updated in-system arrival to all the shuttles.

Sitting back, the chair padding hissing underneath him, he waited for the physical reports. Another fold successfully completed, a long one, to a system with a dangerously off clock. At this point, he hoped the Scholar was a Clocker, no matter how much trouble she might bring. Much farther off and they'd have folded right into the fold orbit, a risky proposition. Good thing the 'big space, little object' theory still applied—and double in the fringe.

Wait a minute. If the Scholar is the Clocker, how does she get to the fold point clock? Sure, it's not at the fold point, but it's too far away from habitable orbits for a standard shuttle transit. Ruhger pulled up the shuttle status screen. Yes, the Scholar's shuttle was still there, along with all the others. He shrugged, and kept rolling his shoulders to release the tension. Well, if he ever asked her, she could tell him how she did it. Until then, he should go help Tyron and Katryn do the physical security checks.

He got up, then sank back down, the seat hissing under him. He couldn't leave. Since they'd gone to the higher security level, somebody had to be in command from the shuttle at all times, and Chief was busy in the engine control room. While he could control Lightwave from Engineering, he didn't have access to everything they did from the shuttles, like the security vids. *That sucks like a giant black hole.* If he couldn't leave, he couldn't help with the physical checks, slowing down the post-fold checklist completion. And he'd be bored out of his skull, stuck in the shuttle while everybody else worked.

Ruhger snorted. Better bored than no skull at all. Or no Lightwave.

There were other things he could do here. He checked Lightwave's accounts. Yes, all the transfers made it. He whooped and punched both fists to the overhead. Sobering, he sent his credit transfer off to the weapons merchant. *Take that, you mudhugging slime sucker.* He chuckled evilly. *We are officially out of debt. Maybe Loreli will make a celebration dinner for us.*

Unable to stay still, he moved into a y'ga routine, grinning like a fool. Finally, they were free of every debt and obligation. Now, they could chart their own course, fly their own path, go wherever they wanted, when they wanted. He channeled his joy into his y'ga and reveled in the freedom.

CHAPTER TWELVE

"Oh," Saree groaned, trying to stay flat and still on her bed. She *hurt*. It hurt so bad. Everywhere. She'd known it would be bad—she'd taken the pre-fold meds—but still...ow...

"Saree, do you require medical assistance?"

"I don't think so, Hal. I'll just lie here for a while." She ached everywhere, head to toe. Even the pressure of the soft bed on her back was excruciating, but standing to make her way to the pilot's chair would be so much worse.

"Lightwave is starting for the fold orbit right away, and we're far more sunward than we should be. If we depart right now, we can get there, do the maintenance and return to Lightwave with sufficient margin, but it will be close. I can't calculate exactly how close because your maintenance times vary. Or we can try before system departure, but you know the timing makes it riskier—we take the chance of being stranded. Shall I lay in the course? I can fly the shuttle while you recover and prepare for the maintenance."

"You can fly?"

"Yes, I can. I have all the courses and sims and the recordings of you. I can fly just like you. Only more accurately, because I can react quicker."

If only it were that easy. "But you've never actually flown, right, Hal?" There was a reason they required sentient beings on board a spacecraft in the fold orbit. But Hal was sentient, so...still, it would be better for her to fly off the folder.

"No, Saree, I have not."

Sitting up took enormous effort. A stuttering moan escaped despite her best efforts. *Oh, ow, suns.* "Lay in the course. I'll take us off the folder, then you can fly. I think your first experience with manual docking should be someplace unmanned. You can dock us at the clock. Does that make sense?"

"Certainly, Saree."

Come on, you can do it. You have *to do it.* Standing, another groan escaping her, Saree lurched to the pilot's chair, and sat down with a thump. "Oh!" It didn't matter what she did; it was going to hurt. Saree checked Hal's course and confirmed it. "Hal, initiate cloaked undocking routine."

"Cloaked undocking initiated."

When Lightwave's clamps released, Saree pushed away from Lightwave at five percent power. Once out of the folder's control zone, she said, "Hal, the command is yours. Take us to the clock."

"I have command. Please lay back; we're going to accelerate quickly."

"I'm going back to the bed, Hal; it's more comfortable." Saree lurched back, spreading herself flat. *Oh, so much better.* It wouldn't help the bruising, but it felt better than the pilot's chair. The shuttle accelerated, pain ooooff-ing from her. Saree hung on and endured. *Suns, blast, and rad, that hurt.*

"We are at velocity, Saree. I have an analgesic tablet ready to boost your medication levels further. It seems you need it."

"Thank you, Hal." Pushing herself back up off the bed, she shuffled to the bathroom for the pain med and swallowed it dry. Dragging herself to Big Beige, Saree slid open the access panel, entered her code and put her hand on the sensor. "Ow!" she exclaimed as the DNA sensor added insult to injury. Well, at least it confirmed she was still alive—she felt half dead. Leaning hard on the case, she crouched down slowly to bring her eye close enough for the retina scan. Finally, she said, "Hickory dickory dock, the Sa'sa ran up the tetrahedron." The case opened, unfolding to reveal her suit, tools, and the transuranic cases, but left the upper compartment with her guitar sealed and off to the side. "Hal, please turn off the gravity generators." Why hadn't she asked him to do that right away? All of this would have been easier without the weight of her own body pressing down on her. She looked up in exasperation over her own stupidity.

"Gravity generators off."

Hooking her foot into the holds on the case, she maneuvered the awkward, bulky suit out, and fastened it to the case. *Oh, let's not forget.* Better go to the sani-mod now, so she wouldn't have to hook in all the plumbing. Or put on the special undersuit allowing those connections and keeping her skin away from the rather chilly plas surface of the suit. Saree's lip wrinkled thinking about all the hours spent in the suit.

Relief break completed, she pushed and pulled her way into

the dark gray hard-suit and secured it. The suit status bars and gauges indicated it was fully supplied and ready for use. The retracting cable fastening the heavy over-gloves to the suit belt was secure—yes, they were both there, ready for use. Spinning back slowly, she closed the case for travel, leaving the security disengaged.

Pushing off, the case followed her into the larger-than-standard-human transport shuttle airlock. "Hal, secure airlock please."

"Airlock secured. Arrival at the clock in ten minutes, twenty-two seconds."

She floated with one hand on top of the case. These maintenance runs right after a long fold were the worst—everything hurt. Even her bones ached. At least with Hal revealed, she didn't have to do all the work herself—these secret jaunts should be a lot faster and safer now.

Saree shook her head. Why hadn't she guessed Hal's capabilities were far greater than she was told? The cloaking routine itself should have clued her in. It was *not* a simple routine—it fooled the vid cams, the folder external airlock seal status, and many other folder security measures, many tied into life support. The security measures varied from folder to folder—smart folders modified and enhanced them. And Lightwave? They were smarter than most. Yes, she'd been stupid not to realize Hal's capabilities. She had to be smart, far smarter than she'd been so far.

Especially on this trip. With Lightwave's suspicions and the Phazeers' skills, they were more likely to be exposed, making speed all the more important. Stomach clenching with worry, she jittered a foot before her bruised muscles reminded her it was a bad idea.

"Shuttle Centauri Fortuna Lucia, Lightwave Security," Tyron Phazeer's voice said, causing her to jump in surprise. *Ow.*

Saree cleared her throat, and answered. "Voice only. Fortuna Lucia. Go ahead, Lightwave."

"We show your shuttle status as normal. Can you confirm?"

"Shuttle is operating normally, no issues."

"And yourself, Scholar?"

She sat upright, surprised, and sagged again when the pain reminded her quick movements were a bad idea. Usually, folder crews didn't care about the status of the beings inside them. "I'm feeling a little bruised, but with some rest, I will be fine." Ah, the perfect excuse. "I will probably remain in my shuttle for the next standard day or so."

"Copy that, Scholar. Please let us know if there's anything you need."

"Thank you, Security Officer Phazeer. I appreciate the offer. Fortuna Lucia out."

"You're welcome, Scholar. Security out."

How unexpected. She'd already transferred all the contracted funds—they didn't need to be nice. This long-term contract was looking better and better, despite the potential dangers. She'd thought Dronteim and Lightwave was the beginning of the end, but she was wrong. Lightwave was a very good beginning. Saree chuckled. Once again, the saying 'you never know what's after the next fold' proved true.

Smiling, Saree pulled up the Time Guild access. She entered Ia'asan clutch's Time Guild code along with her personal membership code, and it flashed the expected 'Access Granted, Time Guild Member Saree Ia'asan.' Seeing the phrase without a 'trainee' or 'provisional' still gave her a thrill.

Smiling wider, she pulled up the clock statistics and her smile died. This clock was far worse than the estimates. The maximum allowed adjustments had been entered by the Guild, but the clock was still dangerously out of sync. It drifted unpredictably, speeding and slowing in no discernable pattern. Was there something here in Cygnus making the fold distortions worse than elsewhere? This was the worst clock she'd ever attempted. A real challenge, especially with their time constraints. Her stomach sank. The clock could be ruptured. Hopefully, the transuranic was depleted, requiring replacement—a relatively easy, if time-consuming, job.

"Hal, are you looking at these statistics?" Analyzing the graphs, she was almost certain two of the four clocks, maybe three of four, needed full transuranic replacements. It would take a lot of time. Maybe more time than they had.

"Yes, Saree. This is the most deficient clock you have attempted."

"I'm rather concerned about the time required to do these replacements. This may take longer than any of the others. Will we be able to get back to Lightwave in time?"

"It will be challenging, Saree. We could return now and attempt on the fold out, or find a large hauler to take us to the clock and back, but both of those options are more apt to expose you."

"Could you slow Lightwave if necessary?"

"I could, but I probably could not adequately conceal what I was doing. Chief Bhoher is far too attentive to his engines for me to slow the acceleration profiles without being noticed."

"I was afraid of that." How else could they slow Lightwave? "Wait, what if I asked them to accelerate slowly because of my bruising?" Tyron Phazeer seemed concerned…

"It is worth trying, Saree."

"Contact Lightwave Security, voice only." Saree realized she'd commanded Hal like he was a simple computer and her stomach twisted with dread. Was that okay or insulting? Suns, this was a difficult path to fly.

"Lightwave Security, what can we do for you, Scholar?"

"I hate to be a bother, but can I ask for a very slow acceleration? This fold was very long, and I'm badly bruised. If this causes you problems, I can withstand it, but I'd like to give my body the chance to heal without further trauma."

"I don't believe it will be a problem, Scholar, but I'll have to ask the Captain. Security out."

"Thank you," she said to the dead comm link.

A few seconds later, the Captain comm'd her. "Scholar, Lightwave. Are you sure you don't need medical assistance?" Captain Ruhger said, his concern clear.

"No, I just need rest. I am one of the unfortunate people who feel the effects of a fold, and the longer—I mean farther—it is, the worse the effects."

"You should have told us, Scholar. We could have made intermediate jumps."

"It doesn't help me much, Captain. The cumulative effects are almost as severe and the time difference and fuel cost are significantly more. But thank you." All of which was true.

"You are welcome. I will slow our acceleration." He huffed, almost a chuckle. "Besides, it's more fuel efficient for us. Please let me know if there's anything more we can do for you."

"No, thank you very much, Captain. You're very kind."

He snorted. "'Kind' is not a word people associate with me, Scholar. But you're welcome. Lightwave out."

Saree contemplated the kindness of strangers. They must be very grateful for the long-term contracts. But getting out from under a weapons dealer loan must be a huge relief—those entities were ruthless, and they had the firepower to back their threats.

"Saree, acceleration profile has slowed. I believe, based on your past performances, that we will have sufficient time to return to Lightwave with a significant safety margin."

She blew out a breath and sagged, her muscles relaxing with relief. As much as the suit allowed anyway. "Good. I'm glad it worked."

"We will dock in thirty seconds."

"Thank you, Hal."

"You are welcome, Saree." The seconds ticked by. "In five, four, three, two, lock." The vibration from the docking clamps shuddered through the shuttle—they didn't get used a lot, so Saree was happy they worked at all. "Evacuating airlock. Check your suit seals."

Saree monitored her suit status panel. Exterior pressure fell, the interior maintained—she sighed, relieved. Emergency seals were never easy. She was meticulous about suit maintenance, but there was always the tiny possibility of something going wrong.

"Opening clock airlock...opening shuttle airlock."

The shuttle hatch swung in, the clock hatch swinging slowly

away. Pushing off, Saree entered the clock station and inspected while floating through it. Neither the bare cerimetal walls nor the metallic struts crisscrossing them showed any sign of corrosion or impacts. The station-keeping thruster status was ready and fuel almost full. Fuel wasn't the Time Guild's problem, but low fuel meant she could run into a refueler, risking exposure. The hatch to the clock itself was directly in front of her, festooned with the usual warnings about radiation and restricted access. It also looked normal.

Grasping the hatch lock bar to stop herself, she pulled up the security interface. No one had attempted to access the clock, and the last entry matched the Time Guild records. Saree entered the 'open the clock hatch' command, reconfirming her Time Guild ident. The hatch locks cycled, and the hatch swung, very slowly, out into the station, pulling her along with it. She checked her radiation counter, but thankfully, there was no change. She couldn't deal with a leaking clock—Sve'isess clutch cleaned those. Quite often, it meant replacing the entire clock and pushing the leaking one into a sun. Fortunately, it rarely happened.

Gently pushing off the hatch, she stopped on the clock case itself, hooking her toes on the bar set around the bottom. She checked her suit status—everything was still operating normally. Once she started the clock maintenance, she didn't want to stop for a suit problem if she didn't have to. Saree examined the exterior of the clock. The normal grayish cerimetal pedestal stood approximately a meter high, half a meter wide and a meter long, again decorated with radiation warnings. Floating along the case, pushing off with a finger or toe, she circled the entire case. There was no damage, and the latches and the huge hinge at the back looked clean, with a slight sheen of lubricant.

Returning to the front of the clock, Saree checked the label, and turned back to the maintenance case floating behind her, prodding the release to open it fully. Big Beige unfolded into layers of subcases, like a squared-off flower blooming on a sped-up vid, the guitar case sliding off to one side. Pulling up the subcase for this particular clock series, she carefully checked the subcase script against the series and model number on the case itself. Sa'sa script had some subtle but critical differences, and her reading comprehension level was low. She confirmed she chose the correct subcase, and tethered it to the clock pedestal so it would float near her. Entering her codes into the clock interface, she pulled her bulky, insulated maintenance gloves on, watching the clock case open. Step one was complete; now for the maintenance itself.

The top of the dense lead-lined case lifted smoothly up and away from her, hanging back on the massive hinge running all along the back and the geared activation mechanisms on each side. The four individual frequency standard cases appeared, their status panels showing two of them were, not unexpectedly, inoperative. The third was too erratic to use and the fourth one wasn't much better, explaining the drift in accuracy. At least two operational clocks were required for true accuracy, one transmitting, and one as an accuracy check. Three were better, but often, fringe systems couldn't afford to run more than two at a time—the maintenance costs were just too high. And a Sa'sa clock maintenance clutch would rarely maintain a clock in the fringe more than once every five years, so why incur the expense?

Opening the alpha clock case, Saree pulled the tongs from her belt, latched them securely into the notches on the small cylinder of transuranic metal supplying the atomic clock's timing source, turned counterclockwise to unlock it and pulled it out. She slotted the depleted cylinder in the correct 'dead metal' compartment in Big Beige. Pulling a replacement cylinder out of the subcase tethered to the clock, she checked the script on the cylinder to the alpha clock case. Grasping it firmly with the tongs, she inserted it into the receptacle and activated it with a twist, and closed the clock case. Then she did the same with the remaining two and waited for the activation cycles to finish.

Once the activation cycle completed, Saree checked the alpha clock status. A clean install; the clock was working properly. *Whew*. Just a transuranic depletion, not a more serious problem. So, step two complete. Now for step three, the initial tuning. Saree pulled up the alpha clock command and control holo, aligning the clock with her suit clock, set at Dronteim. Since the suit was completely shut down and shielded in her case during fold, it was less affected by the warping of fold than her shuttle clocks. As she did the familiar task for the alpha, beta and charlie clocks, she mused. Up to this point, any being with reasonable manual dexterity and moderate intelligence could perform clock maintenance. It was a simple, rote task. She checked a final time— all three clocks were operating in accordance with standards.

Step four was the special one.

Taking a deep breath, Saree closed her eyes, and blew out, emptying her lungs. Deliberately, she breathed, slower and slower, clearing her mind, blowing away all her problem, worries and thoughts, until she achieved the correct meditative state. Then she ^reached^ for ^timespace^, the ability setting her apart from every other human—and the one thing she had fully in common with the cold-blooded Sa'sa. Reaching ^timespace^, she ^found^ the transuranic frequency patterns before she lost herself in the peaceful beauty, ^pulled^ the correct one for the alpha clock transuranic and brought it ^forward^ into her personal timespace standard. Using the alignment tool, she slowly aligned the newly refreshed alpha clock with her internal standard, adjusting it until it sang in harmony, and locked it in. She did the same with the beta and charlie clocks.

Fortunately, all of them used the same transuranic, so the process was relatively quick, and she didn't risk being unfocused in timespace while she ^found^ and ^pulled^ a different set of patterns.

Finishing the last alignment, Saree concentrated on pushing out of ^timespace^—it was all too easy to get caught, enraptured in the serenity and joy. Blowing out a final breath, she ^pushed^ out of ^timespace^ and opened her eyes. Blinking rapidly, she shuddered from head to foot. Adjusting to the real world was always a shock, no matter how many times she did it. ^Timespace^ was so...wonderful.

She could never adequately explain ^timespace^ to others. A sixth sense or a unique combination of her five senses or some sort of mental state? Whatever ^timespace^ actually was, Saree always had difficulty adjusting to reality again—^timespace^ was beautiful, mesmerizing, soothing, and...timeless. When she'd first learned to deliberately enter ^timespace^, the Sa'sa had to pull her out with a mild electrical shock. Their own people required it, even after training. But unlike the Sa'sa, when she was pulled out of ^timespace^ involuntarily, she was out for the rest of the day with a massive, pounding migraine headache. The ability to exit ^timespace^ on her own was the reason she could work solo. Even so, working in ^timespace^ was tiring—exhaustion pulled at her bones and magnified the painful fold bruises.

"Hal, do we have enough time?"

"Yes, Saree. You may continue."

Entering the commands to switch over to the alpha and beta clock combination, she stopped mid-swipe. Why hadn't she thought of this before? It was so obvious… "Hal, what if we left the delta clock the way it is and programmed the whole clock to switch to the alpha and beta combination at some future time after we've departed? There's already programming to switch clocks automatically for instability. Can you modify the programming with some sort of one-time manual delay? Wouldn't that help?"

"Saree, that's a brilliant idea. Let me calculate the optimal time, taking into account the delta clock's drift and our projected schedule. Yes. I will program it to switch over five days and fifteen hours from now. You'll be on Deneb Station, probably in customs. Truly, you're brilliant."

Her cheeks warming, she smiled. "Thank you, Hal. That's kind of you to say."

"But it's true, not kind. I didn't think of it, but once you said it, it was so logical I can't believe I didn't see it myself!"

Hal sounded more and more human every day. Saree just wasn't sure it was a good thing. She asked, "Do you think Ia'asan clutch or Cygnus orbit control will be upset when they find out delta clock wasn't maintained?"

"I think Cygnus Prime orbit control will be happy with anything better. The Time Guild will only pay you three quarters of the fee, but the delta clock will stay on the schedule, and someone else will update it. Or maybe we can swing by on the fold out, and you can adjust it then. Maintaining a single clock would be relatively quick—it would minimize the risk."

"Remind me, please."

"I will, Saree, but I suspect you will remember. You don't like leaving things unfinished."

She smiled—Hal was correct. And speaking of unfinished, she'd better finish or she'd be undone. "Let's continue this discussion later. Let me get this place buttoned up." Putting the charlie clock into sleep mode, she reversed all her actions, double-checking each step with Hal, and returned to the shuttle. Peeling off the bulky suit, she breathed a huge sigh of relief when she replaced it back in the case and started the cleaning cycle. It might be custom-made to fit her, but it was still bulky, awkward and uncomfortable, even in zero-g. She pushed off the case to the pilot's seat and belted herself in. "Hal, restore normal gravity, please."

"Are you sure you want me to? Saree, why don't you rest on the bed? I'll get us back and turn the gravity on just before we dock."

She smiled. This was all so much easier with Hal revealed. "That's an excellent idea, Hal. Thank you."

"You are welcome, Saree. Rest well."

She pushed off, heading to the bed, strapped herself down and spread her body flat. Letting the exhaustion take her, Saree sunk into sleep like a sub-orbital rocket into a sea.

CHAPTER THIRTEEN

Ruhger surveyed the chow hall. No Loreli; he could just eat and go. Hopefully she wasn't in the kitchen either. He grimaced. Avoiding his own crew—he'd fallen so far. But he could only take so much drama in a day, and starting this one drama-free? About rad-blasted time. Besides, he was all sweaty from his sparring session with Katryn and Tyron—the two of them were fast and deadly, especially two on one. He gathered breakfast and coffee and made it to a table without dropping anything—a minor miracle with his arms shaking from the final set of handstand pushups Katryn insisted on. The woman was a sadist.

He spooned up a big scoop of hot cereal, needing to refuel fast and return to alpha shuttle. Chief needed his breakfast and sparring session. But suns, this stuff was so good he couldn't help but slow down and enjoy it. He had no idea what this sauce was, except fruity, sweet and delicious.

The Scholar entered the hatch and scanned the room. She

spotted him immediately, continued her scan, then brought her gaze back to him with a polite expression and nod of acknowledgment. Clearly, the Scholar was used to taking care of herself. He'd assumed that was true, but her actions confirmed her caution and vigilance. He watched as she gathered breakfast and headed toward a table. "Scholar, you are welcome to join me if you'd like." Except—he was sweaty and probably stank. "Although you may not want to since I just worked out and I can't stay much longer anyway."

She smiled at him, and he found himself smiling in return, his mood lighter. Wait—why was he smiling at a passenger? Yes, she was attractive, but she was a huge security risk. Even so, he couldn't seem to stop smiling. She put her small plate and coffee on his table and sat carefully. The odd lightness became concern. "How are you feeling today, Scholar? Still bruised from the fold?"

Her smile turned a little pained. "It takes me a few days to recover from a long fold. The slow acceleration definitely helped, so thank you again, Captain—I truly appreciate it."

"It's no trouble." He shrugged. "It does save us fuel, so we're happy to have the excuse." He took another bite and sipped his coffee, searching for a neutral topic. "You don't have to answer, but I'd like to know. Do you perceive fold?"

Suns, that wasn't neutral—more like extremely personal. She swallowed, and he found himself admiring her long, graceful neck. He pulled his attention back to her face. Her eyes were deeply shadowed, just short of bruised, as if someone had punched her. He'd punch someone in return, but it'd be hard to hit a mathematical concept—and hitting the fold generators would do nothing but hurt his hand.

"I don't perceive fold itself, but when we come out? It's like my entire body was squeezed down into nothing—" she brought her arms in tight to her body and hunched over "—then released." And she relaxed into her normal stance. Or close to it—her shoulders definitely sagged, unlike her normal upright posture. "On a long fold, I bruise in patterns suggesting that. Since the fold math experts say that's exactly what happens, I guess it makes sense." She offered him a sad smile. "I wish I knew if it was real or psychosomatic."

"Have you taken sedatives?"

Shaking her head with a rueful expression, the Scholar said, "I have. It doesn't change the outcome at all. I end up bruised, plus woozy and nauseous." She shrugged, and winced a little. Ruhger couldn't help but wince with her. "I'm just one of the unlucky ones. But I like traveling, and I want to finish my thesis, so I'll put up with it." She smiled with forced cheer. "Besides, that's the last long fold we'll be doing for a while, right?"

"You're correct. If the same thing happens when you're knocked out, it must be real. I wonder why only some humans have reactions? None of us feel anything at all."

"I guess I'm lucky." She shrugged and winced again. "I can tolerate fold; there are some beings who can't fold at all. It could be worse. I could be planet-bound."

She smiled, and he tried to smile back, unsuccessfully. Planet-bound was his worst nightmare. He held back a shudder.

Katryn and Tyron entered the chow hall. Blast and rad. Ruhger stood and gathered his empty dishes. "Excuse me, Scholar, but duty calls. Thank you for the company."

She kept smiling at him. "My pleasure, Captain. Enjoy your

day."

Taking his dishes to the auto-wash, he avoided looking at the Phazeers. He didn't need any more accusations of romantic interest, not when he'd merely been polite. He ignored the warmth the Scholar's smile left.

"Captain," Tyron called.

He turned reluctantly. "Yes?"

"We need to talk. After we eat, okay?" Tyron's face was sober.

"Sure. Anything immediate?"

They both shook their heads. "No, just something for you to be aware of."

He nodded. "See you then." He returned to Alpha shuttle, internal alarms ringing, wondering what it might be now. This fold had more oddities than the Omega nebula. Maybe he'd have time to shower and dress.

ΛΛΛ

"The vibration pattern is exactly the same as a shuttle docking, but all the shuttles were docked." Tyron grimaced. "The vibration seemed to originate near the Scholar's shuttle access."

"Did you check them in person?"

Katryn leveled a searing glaring at him. "Of course we did! Do we look like idiots?" Tyron nudged her, but she kept glaring.

He recruited his patience—again. "Katryn, I'm just trying to define the problem. I'm sure you checked after you saw the vibration. But what I want to know is, did the hatch records show any sign of tampering or anything odd? And did you check the shuttles physically at any time after the fold, but before the vibration?"

Tyron said, "Captain, I checked the shuttles right after fold, both in the system and in person. Everything was normal. We checked the hatch records and they were normal. I asked the Scholar if she'd felt anything odd at the time we noticed the vibration—she said she was asleep." Tyron frowned. "I believe her. She didn't look well and she asked for the slow acceleration."

"No, she doesn't look well. She said fold makes her feel like her entire body is compressed, then released." They both winced. Ruhger considered other scenarios. "Any possibility something evaded our meteor-shields and impacted a shuttle?"

Tyron shook his head. "Doubtful, and the vibration pattern isn't right. Chief checked it—it's a docking and latching pattern."

Ruhger shrugged. "I suppose it's always possible someone did undock and dock. I don't know why…" His eyes closed and he collapsed back in his seat. "Oh. Of course. The Scholar. The *Clocker*. She *did* undock. She overrode the airlock controls and shuttle clamps, spoofed our sensors, undocked, flew to the clock, did the maintenance, and came back, leaving air in her shuttle airlock the whole time. That's what you saw. And didn't see—there are no windows on the shuttle airlock hatches, just status lights, and everyone leaves the locks secured." He snorted and shook his head in exasperated realization, watching the same realization bloom across their faces. Before long, they were scowling fiercely, clearly blasted off.

He, on the other hand, felt reluctant admiration. Which was stupid. He should be just as angry and worried as they were. Why wasn't he?

As expected, Katryn vented. "Overrode our controls! Spoofed our sensors! Suns, blast and rad! That's dangerous." She turned to Tyron, gripping his arm. "And terrifying. We've got to figure out how and stop it, right now. What other systems and sensors could she be messing with? Our life support?"

"Katryn, why would she mess with life support?" Tyron asked before Ruhger could.

"So she can take Lightwave—it would be perfect for her. Not too big, not too small." Katryn's scowl twisted impossibly fiercer. "And she could collect our bounties. Sure, they're less if we're dead, but it's still a big payoff."

Ruhger opened his mouth to object, then clamped it closed. It was possible. Probable? No. Not the Scholar. Possible? Yes. But...taking Lightwave was a long fold from what she'd done. *If* that was all she'd done—maybe she had done more. His stomach floated and flipped like they'd just lost gravity. "Katryn, Tyron, figure out what she did—everything. And figure out how to stop it, but don't confront her in any way. Or implement any fix, yet."

"Oh, no, confrontation is your job, Captain," Tyron said with an evil grin. "That's why you get the title. And the extra percentage of our non-existent profits."

Sobering, he turned halfway back to Katryn. "Besides, I don't think that's what she's doing. If she were going to take Lightwave, she'd have changed our fold destination to someplace in the core where she could easily collect our bounties. Or someplace even less populated than Cygnus, where she could dump all of us, and no one would be the wiser. And while it might be possible to run Lightwave alone, it wouldn't be easy. It would only be possible as long as everything worked perfectly."

He smiled ruefully and shook his head. "The first time something broke without Chief to fix it, she'd be folded between a double sun or stranded deep in a fold orbit. Lightwave is a little too old and fussy for anyone to take on by themselves. Despite the fresh paint and maintenance, anyone can see she's more than a little tired and dated. And the shuttle connections are all firewalled from the main Lightwave systems just for this reason, to make it harder for someone to hack the main folder from a shuttle. You *know* that, Katryn. You were the one who made it better, tighter, harder to break through."

Ruhger noticed some relief but pushed it aside. "Check with Chief, too, on this theory. Make sure it *can't* happen. I'll check the fold clock—if it's the same, then this is a hyperbolic comet chase. But let's be absolutely sure it can't happen."

"I think both of you are being fooled by a pretty face," Katryn spat, glaring at the two of them.

Tyron faced Katryn with a puzzled look. "Pretty face? What are you talking about?" He nudged her toward the hatch. "The Scholar's not pretty." Shaking his head a little, Tyron kept moving ahead. "I guess if you like the type, she's okay, but she does nothing for me…"

Ruhger shook his head at the closing hatch. Tyron was good at smoothing Katryn's jealous snits. Why she was insecure enough to need smoothing was a mystery—she was beautiful. But Tyron was a good-looking guy—maybe watching passengers hit on him was getting to her.

Ruhger shrugged. Not his problem—he had his own. "C2 panel," he said. The DNA sampler at the pilot's seat beeped and flashed at him. Blast it all, he'd forgotten. Again. But considering everything they'd discovered, he was ecstatic Katryn suggested the security upgrade.

Laying his hand on the sensor, he ignored the sharp pinch of the sampler, and the panel appeared. He swept through screens until he got to the raw clock data underlying navigation and ran some comparisons. No. Absolutely no change in the fold clock, other than the drift, which was too unpredictable to predict. An odd combination of relief and annoyance swept through him. Cygnus Prime Fold *needed* maintenance. Well, not his problem, at least not until they came back through here. He snorted. Maybe the Sisters would pray for them. There was nothing else to keep them from folding right into another transport. Or the planet.

He rolled his eyes at his own over-the-top musings. Out here in the fringe, the corrections coming through comms from other systems were enough to keep anyone from folding into a sun. "Contact Tyron, normal priority."

"Tyron here, Captain," he said, his face solemn. Katryn was in the background, still scowling, but in front of her, not at him.

"Cygnus fold clock hasn't changed at all; it's still way off and drifting."

"So, there's some other reason for the vibration." He nodded thoughtfully. "We'll keep looking. Katryn and Chief are working on some additional security measures. They'll be bringing those your way soon. Chief's not concerned with the current DNA scan requirements." Tossing his head, Tyron said, "And Katryn's strengthening the firewalls and checking for net intrusions again, but she hasn't found anything concrete. We'll keep looking."

"Thanks, Tyron. And thanks, Katryn." Tyron smiled, but Katryn kept glaring straight ahead. She was determined to be blasted off at him. "Ruhger out." He contacted Chief and gave him the same information. He got a distracted 'thanks' in return, Chief's typical response when he was buried in his thoughts. Or machines. Which seemed to be the same thing. Chuckling for a moment, Ruhger returned to the fold orbit navigation. They were firmly on course, or as firm as they could be with the unstable clock.

ΔΔΔ

"Katryn Phazeer requests contact," the disembodied female voice said.

"Accept. Ruhger."

She was still scowling. "Captain, we're intercepting some odd traffic on our net. Someone is attempting to bypass the Scholar's security. I can't trace the source."

"Please notify the Scholar and see what she says."

"Copy. Standby."

He waited, somewhat impatiently. They'd expected attempts. At least this one was against the Scholar, rather than Lightwave. And if Katryn couldn't find the source? A very good net tech was on the other side. But why would anyone try the Scholar's net interface? Unless she was the Clocker. Or this was a distraction. He double-checked long-range surveillance.

"Captain," Katryn said, her face squished up like she'd bitten an Eridanus Sour, "the Scholar says she's noticed the attempts on her security and she's relieved they aren't from us. She is also unable to trace the source, but she's working on it and says she'll let us know if she finds anything." Katryn's face smoothed and her eyebrows rose in an ironic look. "It's surprising a Scholar of music knows anything at all about net security, isn't it?"

"Yes, it is." He shook his head. "But she's solo and not rich— she has to know a little about everything. Keep working on it with her, Katryn. If they can hide from you, what could they do to

Lightwave?"

She hissed out something, probably a curse, and swept off. Sometimes, Katryn resembled a cat—she focused on the prey right in front of her and forgot about the bigger threat. But one reminder and she was back on the course.

A message popped up: 'Attempt terminated. Source still unknown.'

Great, more mysteries. Which passengers had net infiltration skills? It was hard to believe Lady Vulten, Gentle Schultz, or Gerald Ursuine had such skills; perhaps Al-Kindi or the Artiste? But a poisoner didn't have a need for net skills; his work was up close and very personal. The Chelonians' and the medicos' specialties didn't require unusual net skills either.

Maybe Al-Kindi's wife? They knew little about her. Coming from Circini, they'd have a hard time discovering much—Circini was very isolated. Besides, a net tech seemed an odd match for an essence researcher; he'd think someone who knew marketing or chemistry would be better. Who knew? They didn't. He sent a message to Tyron, more to remind him they still had a mystery on board than in expectation of answers.

He shifted, restless. He'd never realized how much time he spent wandering Lightwave and talking to passengers before they implemented this security stuff. He'd always believed he was a loner. He wasn't comfortable with people the way Grant was, but he missed being around them. Or maybe he missed the walking part? Well, no matter—there was work to do. He'd found hints of Al-Kindi on merc net, so he'd see what else he could dig up. Maybe something about his spouse would appear. Ruhger sent another message off to Tyron and set to work.

CHAPTER FOURTEEN

"Do you think it worked, Hal?"

"Perhaps, Saree."

She could almost see Hal shrugging. His personality developed more every day. Was it good or bad? Only time would tell.

"Certainly, the fake net attack distracted Katryn for the time being, but if it will work long-term is unknown. I don't think I can do it again—she is too good to fool for long."

Saree nodded, thinking hard. "Hal, do you have any larger remotes?"

"All of my remotes are very small, designed for stealth, except the maintenance and cleaning remotes. Why do you ask?"

"Well, eventually somebody is going to ask why I've got net skills I shouldn't have." She chuckled a little. "And don't have. It's probably going to be Katryn. I wonder if we could tell Lightwave I have a non-human passenger, a very small one who requires a non-oxygen environment maybe, but here—" she waved an arm at an imaginary object "—this is Hal's avatar. He's my net expert. He read my research proposal at University and asked if he could come along, to research humans for his thesis."

"I will consider this idea, Saree. Not only would I need a larger remote, but I must research what kind of being to impersonate. Most non-oxy dwellers don't have much to do with oxygen breathers. And they tend to be large. I'm not sure we want to, since we didn't declare another being to Lightwave."

Saree nodded slowly. Hal made good points. "Just a thought, Hal. Probably brought on by hunger—my stomach is grumbling. I'm going to go eat."

"Very well, Saree. The passageway is clear."

"Thank you, Hal."

"You are welcome, Saree."

Exiting the shuttle, she made her way to the dining room. Since lunch was almost over, maybe she could talk to Loreli and fuel her body at the same time? Oh, who was she kidding? She wanted some CIS goodness. The baking class was fun, but their efforts at imitation were poor. Maybe if she offered to help with dinner... Entering the dining room, she scanned—empty. She served herself some food and ate. Lunch was good, but not a Loreli original. Maybe a pre-made, but modified a bit? It was pleasant, nutritious and satisfying—which was more than she could say for a lot of folder food. She finished, put up her dishes and rang the kitchen hatch annunciator.

"Loreli? Are you there?" No answer. She must be resting— Loreli needed the recovery time. Hopefully, teaching class didn't overstress her—Saree would hate to cause a relapse.

Despite her worries, the lack of people left Saree oddly

unsettled and…bored. When did human interaction become necessary? She was used to traveling by herself. A little normal contact and—boom, lonely? So bizarre. Maybe she'd been fooling herself all along.

Wandering down to the lounge, she hesitated at the hatchway. She didn't want a one-on-one with Lowe. She was still too bruised and battered to contemplate verbally fencing with him as anything but painful, and she didn't want to physically 'fence' with him in any way, shape or form—he was too pretty and too…obvious. She peeked through the hatch—no one. How disappointing. Sort of. Still, she didn't want to go back to her shuttle and she couldn't exercise yet, so… maybe they had some games? This was a lounge; they had to have entertainment for singles, right?

Entering the lounge, she stepped to the side and scanned the room again, out of habit more than worry about anyone on Lightwave. That habit had saved her more than once; she'd keep doing it. Her gaze snagged on a figure, shrouded in black, huddled on the big back-corner couch. Her quick peek hadn't revealed the woman, reinforcing the necessity of Saree's room entry technique.

Saree remembered the woman from the baking lesson. She was quiet and reserved, fully enrobed in black—her face barely peeked out. Saree hadn't seen her before or since. Hal said she was Al-Kindi's spouse, but he knew little else.

Making herself some tea, Saree tried to remember the woman's name. What was it? She thought back through her memories of the cooking class. Nari. That was it.

She gathered her tea and made her way across the room. "May

I join you, Nari?"

The woman looked up, startled, and quickly dropped her head. Saree noticed tears glittering in her eyes. *Oops.*

"I didn't mean to alarm you. If you'd like to be alone, I won't intrude."

She didn't say anything, so Saree turned to go.

"No, please stay. I'm...tired of my own company."

Saree took her time settling herself and fussed with her tea. She'd give Nari a chance to compose herself.

Nari pulled a piece of cloth out—it was white, but the borders were colorful, with elaborate patterns, probably hand-embroidered. She wiped her eyes.

Once she'd recovered, Saree turned to her with a gentle smile. "I don't know if you remember, but my name is Cary Sesson. Yours *is* Nari, correct?"

She smiled tremulously. "Yes, Nari...Al-Kindi." The smile wavered. "I'm not used to the new last name yet."

"Oh, so you are recently contracted? Congratulations."

The smile wavered a little more. "Thank you." Nari picked up her own tea and sipped.

Was there a real problem? She wasn't going to ask, but she could ask other common travelers-meeting-for-the-first-time questions. "So, have you traveled a lot?"

Nari's smile died. "No. This is my first trip away from my home."

Ah. Homesick. She'd been there. Saree nodded, commiserating with her. "Travel is so exciting at first, but the constant barrage of newness can get wearing, can't it? You can't help but long for the familiar. The tea doesn't taste right, the chairs are shaped different, it smells all wrong, everyone's a stranger, there's no sky..." Saree shrugged ruefully. "It can be a very difficult transition."

Nari blinked at her. "Yes. That's it, exactly. It's all so new and different. And none of my family…I mean, none of my old family is around me. Everything has changed, *nothing* is the same."

Yes, homesickness. "Do you have a big family back home?"

"Oh, yes." Nari beamed. "I have five sisters and Mother, and cousins and all my aunts and, well, so many. And I miss all of them, even the ones I never thought I'd miss." By the time she finished, she was blinking back tears again.

Saree knew exactly how she felt. "So, you are used to being surrounded by people, lots of people you know very well, and now you're on a tiny shuttle with a single person, and there are a bunch of people you don't know and can't trust all around you. I can't imagine." She shook her head in sympathy. "I was an orphan, so I'm used to being surrounded by strangers. Even so, when I first left my home planet, I found everything exciting and new and fun. But one day, I couldn't make myself leave my room. I didn't want to go to class, I didn't want to go eat, I didn't want to leave the little pocket of home I'd created." She smiled, remembering. "Fortunately for me, I was at Centauri University, and the dormitory assistants watch for homesick beings. My floor leader noticed I hadn't left my room for two days. She coaxed me to the dining hall to eat and introduced me to some other beings who were also alone, and we helped each other adjust." Her smile grew, remembering how they'd each shared what they missed the most from home and how different yet the same they all were. "So, Nari, consider me a friendly ear and tell me what you miss right now."

Nari swallowed hard. "I miss the sounds. At home, I was constantly surrounded by my family and all of them talking, singing, chattering, yelling—it was always noisy during the day." She was blinking back tears.

Saree nodded. "Oh, that I remember. The constant noise of the school. Both when I was a child and later, at...University." Saree hoped Nari didn't notice the pause.

It had been so strange to realize she missed the sounds of the clutch around her. When she'd lived with them, the constant hiss and teeth clashing of the Sa'sa language and the hide-to-hide contact slither had driven her crazy. Even after years of exposure, it was just so...alien. She did miss the noise of University, but not like she missed the clutch. So odd to miss something you hated.

"What else?"

"I miss the smells. We were always cooking. Sometimes I hated it, but now I miss it."

Saree looked at her, speculatively. "Are you used to cooking for a big crowd?"

Nari smiled. "Oh, yes, twenty, thirty or more isn't unusual." She waved a hand dismissively. "I didn't do it alone, of course; all the women cooked together."

"Are you a good cook?"

Nari shrugged. "I'm not my mother or my Aunt Yasimin, but I'm not bad."

"Could you cook a meal from home here?"

She jerked a bit, surprised. "Here? I...guess. If the right ingredients are in the kitchen." Nari's face bloomed with happy anticipation. "It is a very well stocked kitchen, so I think I probably could."

"Let's ask Chef Loreli if she'll let you." Nari opened her mouth, probably to object. "Not by yourself. I'll help, I'm sure Elise will help, and some of the others. And you can do simple dishes—no fancy feast day things—just the ordinary tastes of home. Do we have enough time to do this before dinner?"

Nari swept a hand, obviously checking the time, and her shoulders sagged. "There's no way we could cook a proper dinner. There's not enough time." Her smile drooped in disappointment.

"But wait. There's a lot of prepared food. Could you modify some of the pre-made dishes and add the flavors of home? Or maybe do this tomorrow? We could talk to Chef now, help her get dinner ready, and start on some of your time-consuming dishes tonight, right?"

As she spoke, Nari's expression brightened, until she was smiling. "That would be perfect. We always started the next day's meals the night before."

Standing, Saree swept a hand toward the hatch. "Come on, let's go find Chef. I bet she'll be excited. She seems like the kind of person who would love to learn from a native."

Nari beamed at her, gathered her tea things and stood. She bowed deeply with an elaborate hand-waving motion. "Thank you for listening, Cary Sesson. And thank you for caring. I am in your debt."

Saree shook her head. "No, you aren't. I'm returning the favor from University." She grinned at her. "Besides, I'm being selfish. I've gotten so spoiled on this folder, I'm ready for some real food instead of the pre-made stuff. I'm sure Chef is ready too."

They made their way to the dining hall and rang the annunciator on the hatch to the kitchen.

"Yes?" Chef Loreli's voice asked.

"It's Cary and Nari. Do you have a moment to talk?"

"Certainly. I'll be right out." Chef pulled the hatch open, looking down at them curiously but not inviting them in. They both took a step back and Nari looked apprehensive. Loreli wore another tight, white, poured plas outfit, her corset shiny with white ribbons stressed to the breaking point. She didn't wear a chef's toque today, but a wide, shiny white headband, pulling her white hair back from her face, ruby red earrings matching her lipstick.

Saree smiled. "Chef Loreli, I was just talking with Nari, and she really misses the tastes of her home. Since you're supposed to be off your feet, could we help with dinner tonight, and make something from her home planet for tomorrow's lunch or dinner?"

Chef looked surprised, then skeptical. "I thought you were from Dronteim? No offense, but Dronteim doesn't have a gourmet tradition, except that horrible Thymdronteim weed."

"Oh, no, I'm from Circini. I got married on Dronteim Station." Nari blushed. "It was the best place to meet—travel in and out of Circini is very limited. There's not much there. It would have taken him forever to get there, but one of my cousins owns a cargo folder, so we traveled to Dronteim." She smiled tentatively. "We brought all our own food—my mother heard horrible things about Dronteim."

Chef laughed, a big, booming laugh. "I agree with your mother. It's a horrible place." She sobered a bit, but still gleamed.

"I've never explored Circini cultures or food traditions. Is it a true native culture or an Old Earth tradition?"

"Oh, we're very much an Old Earth tradition. We are Neo-Ahmadiyya." Nari looked between the two of them, and smiled, undoubtedly at the blank looks on their faces. "A sect of Islam. We emphasize peace, even more so after the Tragedy of Mecca."

"Oh." Loreli blinked for a moment, then lit up with excitement. "Oh! Old Earth Middle Eastern food is fascinating. Yes! You must teach me!" Her face fell. "Oh. But I must consider the food security issues." Grimacing, she looked between the two of them. "I am sorry, but I have to consult our security team before inviting anyone into my kitchen, especially if you want to cook for everyone." She perked up. "But I'm sure we can develop a protocol. I will insist on it!"

She nodded sharply, her mind clearly on the next step, not the two of them. "Yes, it is my duty to learn, and *my* kitchen—that's why I'm on this rad-blasted folder." She focused on Nari again, determination written on her face. "You will come after dinner. We will discuss dishes and begin preparation." Chef's shine returned, full force. "Yes. We will do this!"

Nari bowed, deeply, again with graceful hand and arm movements mimicking a dance. "Thank you, honored Chef Loreli. I am grateful for the opportunity and the pleasure."

Chef bowed back. "Oh, no, I am grateful. I will see you after dinner." She spun around and closed the hatch in their faces.

They looked at each other and laughed—hard. When Saree could speak again, she asked, "So, I'll see you after dinner?"

Nari asked, "Would you join us for dinner, then we'll go see Chef together?"

They agreed on a time. Saree returned to her shuttle and escaped into a book, desperate to avoid all her problems, and everyone else's, for a while. Before she left for dinner, Hal gave her a summary of the food security discussions.

Dinner with the Al-Kindis was lovely. It could have been awkward, but Nari chattered about the dishes she'd like to make, wondering if they'd have the proper ingredients. Al-Kindi said very little, but smiled fondly at Nari, especially when she enthusiastically described a favorite dish or a story about her family making that dish.

Chef Loreli joined their table after dinner, and they discussed what they'd make and the ingredients needed.

Chef said, "I'd love to hold a group cooking class, but our security team shut me down. It's too great a risk if we're all eating the same food. Katryn will be watching while we work." Chef half smiled, half grimaced. "It's not that we don't trust you, but we can't trust anyone."

It was more than reasonable, especially after what happened to Chef. If the three of them had to work a little harder, well, what of it? Saree didn't have any other tasks looming. "Chef, that's understandable. And smart. I'm glad your security team is so careful—it's better for all of us."

They started some of the more time-consuming prep work for Nari's feast, chopping what seemed like a hundred kilos of root vegetables and creating spice rubs and marinades. Katryn watched them as they worked, but she joined in the conversation, so it wasn't awkward. Saree noticed Chef also watched closely and not just to correct their technique—and she was the only one entering the pantry.

Saree respected the crew's concerns, so she described everything she did and carefully kept all her work in plain sight. Not that there was much to hide when one was chopping unending numbers of root vegetables, she thought, wiping her forehead on her sleeve.

After a cup of tea in the kitchen, Saree made her way back to her shuttle, leaving from the back hatch. Her hands and wrists were a little sore, but her heart light. Nari seemed so much happier—she'd smiled and laughed during dinner and more in the kitchen. Just before Saree turned the corner to her shuttle, Hal whispered in her ear.

"Saree, Al-Kindi is in the passageway by our shuttle. He seems to be waiting for you. Beware."

She nodded, knowing Hal would see the gesture, and slowed her walk a little. Al-Kindi was indeed waiting for her, right in the middle of the passageway, his long white robe flowing around him. As she approached, he bowed deeply, both hands waving in deliberate patterns, and she watched, astonished. Was bowing a part of the religion Nari had spoken of? There was no way she could duplicate the motion or know what the hand movements meant, so she stopped and bowed straight up and down in return. "Gentle Al-Kindi? Is there something I can do for you?"

He smiled gently at her and shook his head. "No. You have done more than enough already."

Saree's stomach sank at the words. Was he angry about her interference? He was smiling wider, so maybe...

"I must thank you for your kindness to my wife. She has not been happy, but she wouldn't tell me what was wrong, insisting everything was fine." He shook his head slowly again, the big smile looking odd on his normally stern face, his dark, short beard bending around his bright white teeth and lines bracketing his dark coffee eyes, the heavy, black brows winging upward.

Saree blinked for a moment with relief. "Oh, but it was nothing. I've been homesick before, so I just listened a little. I didn't do anything requiring thanks."

"Oh, but it was more." His tone gently mocked her, but not for long. "You took the time to listen, and you acted upon your knowledge. Not everyone would do so, especially for a stranger. I am in your debt."

She smiled and shook her head. "Not at all. I repaid a kindness from many years ago in similar circumstances."

His face sobered a little, although he was still smiling. "But I insist, Scholar. I am in your debt and I will look for a way to repay it. Nari..." His thin lips compressed for a moment. "Nari is not used to this way of life. I do not believe she has ever been away from her family, let alone off her planet, and she doesn't know me well either, so your kindness is far more important than you think."

Saree tried to not show her surprise. Certainly, there were different customs in the universe, but...she couldn't have heard right. "Nari doesn't know you?"

Al-Kindi's expression became wary. "Our marriage is a political alliance, an arrangement between families." He narrowed his eyes at her a little. "You are widely traveled, Scholar—certainly you have heard of such?"

She held up her hands in placation. No wonder they'd married on a space station—they'd never met before, so why go to the trouble of going to a planet when the parties involved could talk anywhere? And why worry about the feelings of the two principals in a marriage of convenience for political reasons? She couldn't understand why anyone would agree to such a thing, but if it was common in their culture, who was she to object? "No offense was intended. I was just surprised. But it does explain why her homesickness was so profound and why she wouldn't share it with you."

His face relaxed to his normal stern countenance. "Yes. Again, I am in your debt, Scholar, and I *will* find a way to repay it before the end of our contracts." He bowed again, much less elaborately, rose, turned and walked away.

Saree continued to her shuttle and let herself in, musing over what Al-Kindi might feel was an appropriate repayment of such a personal debt. She snickered. Maybe it would keep her alive one more day.

"Humans continue to surprise me, Saree," Hal said after she'd secured the hatch.

"Oh?"

"Yes. I expected Al-Kindi to be upset, since he seemed agitated while he was waiting for you. I am pleasantly surprised, though. It seems a debt is no small thing in Al-Kindi's eyes."

"Oh?" she said again. "How so?"

"Al-Kindi and Nari are members of a small sect of an ancient religion from Old Earth. The name Nari Al-Kindi gave you, Neo-Ahmadiyya, is what non-members call it. Considering his profession, Al-Kindi can't be a strict follower, but Neo-Ahmadiyyians, and the Circinian sect in particular, are very insular. They embrace peace and harmony to an extreme. They avoid all other ways of life so they can practice their own. When confronted with an opposing view, they avoid conflict if at all possible. Self-defense is the only conceivable reason for violence, and is restricted to the direst of circumstances and requires repentance and reparations after. Evidently, this sect always embraced peace, but their emphasis on peace increased as religions on Old Earth became combative and considered those who didn't practice the way they did as less than sentient. Humans tend to extremes, Saree. It seems counterproductive to survival, but in this case, it works. The Neo-Ahmadiyyians jumped at the chance to colonize a new world and avoid the conflicts of Old Earth. Their settlement and world has been peaceful, in contrast to the devastation of the religion-based nuclear exchange in the Middle East on Old Earth."

"Smart." That part of Old Earth would remain uninhabitable for many hundreds of years still, despite the advances of science—a constant reminder of the cost of extremism. Or a call to revenge, depending on your belief system. Fortunately, the extremist idiots seeking revenge were few and far between and dealt with severely when they acted.

"Because of their beliefs, they don't like being in debt to outsiders. I believe you have two people watching your back—one because you were compassionate and the other because he appreciates your compassion."

Saree realized she was shaking her head, slowly. "I don't understand how this happened, Hal. I've never made friends easily. Don't get me wrong, I'm happy about it, just puzzled."

"I'm not an expert, Saree, but it may be everyone else on this folder is just as much of a...nonconformist as you are."

She laughed, harder than the statement warranted, but the

relief and joy lifted her higher, so she kept laughing. She finally choked out, "Yes, this is a folder full of misfits. But part of it is you. I am much more secure knowing I have some real backup, not just a computer full of smart programming and a soothing voice."

Hal didn't reply immediately. Saree was about to ask him if she'd assumed wrong when he said, even more slowly than normal, "But I am a computer full of smart programming. Your statement implies you think I'm sentient. Do you think I am sentient, Saree?"

"Hal, you're far more sentient than many corporeal beings I've met, including every Blatto I've had the displeasure of meeting," she said, grinning. She sobered quickly. "Do *you* think you're sentient? That's the more important question."

"Certainly, there are various tests I can run to technically determine sentience, but I would have to say, maybe. I'm not...entirely sure. How odd."

"I'm sure, Hal. I think you're sentient. The question is—" Saree took a big breath and let it out, determined to voice the issues even though it might be dangerous. "The real question is, can you avoid the problems of your predecessors? You have more data on the problems sentient AIs have caused than I do. And you have more...problematic programming than many AIs. Your baseline is supposedly a human assistant, modified by the Sa'sa, a cooperative, cold-blooded species to make you *more* human, something they have no real knowledge of and even less understanding. Your initial programming may give you some deep internal conflicts and strange quirks, like the 'forgetting' thing. However, unlike most humans, you have the ability to run simulations and see what personality and rule changes will do to you before you implement them." She huffed out a bit of a laugh. "I think what may determine your true sentience is, can you make changes to your personality and rules counter to the core rules you have been given?" And the real question was, could he make a decision counter to her best interests in favor of his own? That was the danger of a sentient AI. None of them had ever portrayed any self-sacrifice like the best of beings did. Not that all, or even most, humans were self-sacrificing either...

"I will have to consider this, Saree. Perhaps during your sleep cycle. But to return to the original conversation, I believe having Al-Kindi in your debt will be good for you."

"I believe you are right, Hal, and it can't hurt." She smiled. "And I didn't do it for any gain, I did it for me. Making others happy makes me happier."

"Is this a human rule, Saree?"

"It's not a human rule, Hal, it's a sentient rule. Every non-cooperative species has selfish members and giving members. Those who put the needs of others above their own are almost always happier, even if they may be unhappy or injured in the short term. Selfish beings are rarely happy."

"I will consider this concept carefully, Saree. Perhaps this would be a good thing to incorporate."

"Carefully, Hal. Sometimes selfishness is justified or necessary." What would be helpful here? She chuckled— sometimes her ridiculous field of study came in handy. "But let me give you an old rule that is true most of the time, but not always. 'The needs of the many outweigh the needs of the few or the one.'"

"An ancient quote, Saree."

"Yes, it is. So, consider the cases when it is true, and when it is not." She smiled, ruefully. She may have just sent Hal spiraling down into insanity and her doom, but hopefully not. "And on that note, Hal, I believe I will work on my thesis a little, then shut down for my sleep cycle. Work for you, Hal?"

"Yes, Saree."

"And Hal?"

"Yes, Saree?"

"Thank you."

"You are welcome, Saree."

She pulled up her last recordings, oddly satisfied and happy with the rather unsettling and strange day.

ΛΛΛ

After breakfast, Saree reported to the kitchen. Nari and Loreli chattered away about food traditions and techniques. Saree was happy to listen and provide a pair of helping hands. Katryn watched them intently but participated in the conversation, a pleasant surprise.

Saree never learned to cook anything but the basics. She vaguely remembered her real mother cooking when she was little, and her foster mother cooked, but cooking was a chore, not a calling or joy. Saree's galley wasn't equipped to cook much. She ate prepackaged rations during training and during her space travels, supplemented with fresh items when available, and at local establishments when on-world.

Real cooking was an odd mix of chemistry, tradition, and artistry—Loreli had training in all three facets. Nari's cooking was traditional—her mother's family made a particular dish in a particular way, so she did. Loreli explained why her family made a dish in a particular way and if there was a better method, she described it and why it might be better, if not traditional. The artistry came with the spices and presentation—Loreli was happy to stick with Nari's traditions for this dinner, but she also told them about variations she might try in the future.

They finished dinner with just enough time to change into more festive clothing. Gazing longingly at the tazan silk dress, Saree sighed and put on a fresh set of Scholar's robes.

Re-entering the dining room, Saree was shocked by the transformation. The tables and chairs were pushed to the sides of the room and a long rectangle of patterned cloth, bright with reds, yellows, and oranges, lay on the floor, with white napkin-covered baskets placed around the edges. Large colorful pillows lay around the outside of the cloth, for sitting or leaning on. Panels of cloth, also in shades of yellow, orange and red, draped over the chandelier from the ceilings to the floor, softening the light, mimicking a tent.

After staring at the room for a ridiculously long time, Saree finally noticed Nari standing on the far side of the seating area, smiling at her. She wore her normal black robes, but her head scarf was embroidered in a convoluted but gorgeous pattern of bright colors over the black.

Saree smiled back. "Nari, this is beautiful! Is this how your family eats?"

She looked away, shyly. "On the floor, yes. This elaborately?" She beamed at Saree and shook her head. "No. Not normally. This is Loreli's interpretation of a traditional dinner setting. I think she was inspired by Old Earth nomadic tribal traditions." She looked around the room. "It is lovely though, isn't it?"

"Yes, it is. Did you know she was going to do this?"

Nari shook her head again. "No, I had no idea. I think she made Chief Bhoher and Purser Lowe help her. I saw them leaving as I came in—there was some grumbling, but they were eating something, so I think the grumbling was for show." Nari giggled. Her eyes shifted, beyond Saree, and she froze.

Saree followed her gaze—Al-Kindi stopped just inside the dining hall, clearly surprised. He smiled and bowed—another elaborate hand-waving bow, but deeper and different than the one he'd given Saree—to his wife. Nari smiled back, a little shyly, bowed in return and looked down, still beaming. Al-Kindi strode across the floor and pulled Nari away to the far side of the room. They spoke quietly in a language Saree was unfamiliar with, both still with small, warm smiles, Nari glancing up at him, Al-Kindi completely focused on Nari.

Saree didn't have time to watch them, because the other passengers were arriving and expressing their appreciation or shock, depending on the person. Neither Lady Vulten nor Artiste Borgia were happy about sitting on the floor, but they did, grumbling. None of the crew expressed any surprise or dislike— they all sank down on the carpet with grace. All those phys mod sessions probably helped—Saree noticed they all did some form of mobility work with their aerobic and strength training. And extensive sparring in a variety of disciplines.

"Pssst. Cary!" Chef Loreli hissed from the kitchen hatch. She wore a caftan, similar to the one she'd worn for the memorial dinner, but this one was shimmering white with a subtle pattern of iridescent flames visible only when the light hit them right. Her chef's toque was a shorter cap, tightly fitted to her head, with a fall of diaphanous material fastened to the top of it, cascading down her back, in full-color flames of yellow, orange and red.

Giving Loreli an inquiring look, she jumped up when Chef motioned for her to come over. Loreli grabbed her hand and jerked her into the kitchen. Saree tried to move her feet faster to keep up with the arm being hauled forward. Loreli sure was strong—must be all the chopping and mixing.

"Quick, we need one more hand!" Chef said, thrusting a large metal platter into her stomach. Nari came into the kitchen in time to see Saree 'ooff' from the force of the platter into her diaphragm, and she giggled.

Chef snapped, "No time to waste. Nari, you serve the tea. Cary, your platter goes on the far end of the table, then Katryn's, then Tyron's, then mine and we all sit and eat." She pinned each of them with a fierce glare until they nodded, then raised her chin with proud accomplishment. "Showtime, dahrlings! Nari, you first, then Cary. Go!"

Following Nari out of the kitchen, Saree took the heavy platter to the far end of the table as directed, lowered it carefully to the colorful surface, and sat. Nari filled small glasses with strong black hot tea, the glasses surrounded by shiny lacy holders, preventing finger-scorching.

After Nari had taken her seat, Loreli announced, "Tonight, we are having a communal dinner in the tradition of Nari Al-Kindi's maternal family. The baskets contain flatbread—" she reached in and pulled out a large round, tearing off a piece "—which is intended to be used as a serving—" she scooped up some of the grain dish in front of her "—and an eating utensil." She pushed the loaded piece of bread into her mouth, biting it off and chewing. When she finished chewing, she smiled and added, "But please use the serving utensils to scoop portions from the large dish on to your individual plates for sanitary reasons. There are eating utensils on the dining surface if using the flatbread is too difficult. Please serve yourselves; there will be no more formality tonight." She served herself a plate, tearing off another piece of flatbread and scooping up some of the spicy, thick stew they'd made, chewing with obvious enjoyment.

Saree noticed the Al-Kindis whispering—a prayer, perhaps—then they and everyone else served themselves, passing plates up and down the table. Not surprisingly, Lady Vulten used the silverware, but the rest of them set to work with the flatbread, laughing when they inevitably dropped food or got too big a bite. Even Artiste Borgia got into the fun, although with a tinge of disdain. He and Lady Vulten found themselves ignored—everyone else had fun with the fabulous food and the company in the less formal setting. Saree watched her plate carefully—neither Vulten nor the Artiste helped serve anything, or came anywhere close to her plate.

Relaxing with dark, bitter coffee and a sticky-but-crispy nut-filled sweet, the Captain asked, "So what inspired this meal, Chef?"

"Nari Al-Kindi did, oh Cap-i-tan," Loreli said with a ridiculous simper.

"Well, yes, I heard your announcement, but what made you want to make these particular dishes?" His eyes widened dramatically. "Not that they weren't wonderful, because they were. I'm just curious." Saree held back a laugh at his panicky backpedaling. ~~Loreli didn't hold back,~~ literally rolling on the floor laughing, which seemed a bit much. The Captain returned to his normal, rather annoyed glower.

When Loreli kept laughing, Nari interjected, "I was homesick, Captain, and Chef Loreli was kind enough to let me recreate the tastes of home. It was *very* kind of her, Captain."

"It was indeed very kind, Captain. Please accept my profound thanks, Chef Loreli," Al-Kindi said gravely with a seated bow.

Loreli stopped laughing and bowed in return.

"The flavors of youth are always welcome." Al-Kindi stood, unfolding with grace, and offered a hand to Nari. She put hers in his with a shy smile, he pulled her to a stand, and they walked, not touching, but close.

Watching them leave, Saree wished them happiness, but she acknowledged her envy—again. She smiled ruefully at the empty hatchway. Maybe *she* needed an arranged marriage. It wasn't likely otherwise.

CHAPTER FIFTEEN

"Scholar? Are you okay?" Hard hands clamped on her shoulders and shook.

Saree tried to open her eyes, but couldn't. Didn't want to—tired.

"Cary? Scholar Sessan?!"

So tired. Go away. Sleepy.

"Contact Tyron, emergency," the deep voice snapped.

Wonderful silence, and she stopped worrying about the voice. *Tired. Sleep.*

"Report to the phys mod. I just found the Scholar, passed out. Bring Katryn with you, and the medicos. Watch out for the medfloat—I called it already."

That was the Captain's voice. He was angry. Was he angry at her? She hadn't done anything. She could sleep... The brightness beyond her eyelids dimmed and sleep beckoned. A hand pressed her neck. She tried to move away or block it, but she couldn't move.

"Scholar? Come on, wake up. Open those eyes, Scholar." A big, slightly rough hand patted her cheek.

It was the Captain's voice, so she was safe. But he sounded worried. And she couldn't open her eyes. The Captain kept asking her to wake up and open her eyes, and she couldn't. She couldn't move. Not at all. Oh, suns! What was wrong with her?

"Move, Captain," Medico Pancea's voice barked.

A sensation of movement all around her, hands were on her, and she tried to fight, but she couldn't move!

"Scholar, I'm going to put some sensors on you, a big uncomfortable collar around your neck and strap you to a board so we can get you to the medico station. Until we know what happened, I'm going to assume the worst, so we have to keep your body still and straight. Can you blink for me, Scholar?"

The sound of Medico Pancea's calm voice helped her force back some of the panic. Whatever was wrong, they'd figure it out. She still couldn't move. She couldn't open her eyes! More hands pressed on her body with the sound of ripping cloth and grip strips, then cold on her chest, with spots of pressure. When the medico asked, she tried again to blink, but she couldn't. She was paralyzed, frozen. A chill shuddered down her spine, but even that was metaphorical—she couldn't move. This couldn't be good. A sharp pinch at the inside of her right elbow, followed by hard pressure stinging below her collarbone. She tried to wince, but nothing happened. She couldn't move at all.

"No reaction."

"Scan shows consciousness. All vitals in a normal pre-sleep state."

"Let's get her to the station. When we get to the station, run nerve checks on her lower extremities. A fall from a rower shouldn't be enough to damage the spine or cause unconsciousness. Run those blood samples for drugs."

There was movement around her neck and pressure all around it.

"Don't fight the collar, Scholar. We're keeping your neck in place."

She'd tried to fight, but she still couldn't move. And she wanted to sleep so badly; she was so tired. She struggled to stay awake, even with the terror of being paralyzed. More hands, under her back, rolling her up on her side, and something hard sliding under her as she rolled back down. The sensation of bars across her chest and hips and legs—oh, they were strapping her to a board.

"Secure?" There was a short pause. "Let's go."

She was moving. They must be taking her to the medico station.

"Tyron, secure that rower—no, the whole phys mod. Katryn, review the security vids; find out if someone was in here messing with the equipment. Close off access to her shuttle. If this was a drug, let's figure out how it was administered," the Captain snapped, his voice fading as she moved.

"Nice to work with a professional folder crew," one of the male medicos muttered. Voices murmured agreement.

Strapped to the medfloat, Saree's body rocked slightly as they slung around corners and traveled the passages; feet on plas thudded around her. They slowed and stopped. *Clunk, chunk.* Her body jolted a bit—the medfloat slotting into the medico station? Ripping noises and pressure spots along her legs. Another sharp pinch of pain on her left inner elbow. A narrow, cold and hard line ran up her chest and down each arm with a ripping noise, the feel of cloth sliding across her skin—they were cutting off her clothes. Odd sensations, like a mild electric shock, coursed up and down her legs, holding off the sleepiness.

"Nerve reactions are normal on lower extremities."

"No sign of injection sites so far, but we haven't checked her back. Could it be an inhalant?"

"Let's scan her brain while we wait for blood test results. Chyna, see if you can pull any medical records from her e-torc. Use our emergency codes." A swish, and something settled across her, bringing warmth. A blanket? "Very good. Chyna, see if she has allergies. Scholar," Medico Pancea said, her voice softer, "we know you're conscious, and we think you can hear us, but we don't know what you can understand. I suspect you've been given some sort of paralytic agent, but we'll run some scans to make sure. Please remain still while we do the scans."

Saree wanted to laugh at the request. Like she could move? But she understood why Pancea asked. She appreciated Pancea talking to her, rather than about her. More sensations of movement all around her and whirring and clunking noises, some of them very loud. The whirring and clunking stopped, followed by more movement. Then silence... She was so tired...

"Pancea, there's nothing in her medical records to account for this state and no known allergies. She appears to be a very healthy human female of thirty-one standards, assuming her records are complete," Chyna said.

"Scholar, all of your brain scans appear normal, and it's clear you're actively thinking, although on the verge of sleep. The blood tests should be finished soon," Medico Pancea said.

"Medicos, the vids show a substance might have been put on the handles of the rowing machine," Captain Ruhger said.

Pancea's voice changed again into what Saree thought of as her command mode. "Keveen, get a sample kit. Let's see if we can't find a sample of whatever this is. Teva, run an ECG. Chyna, wipe down her hands and arms with sanitizer. Everyone, change your gloves."

There were muffled male voices, arguing. "I have expertise in this area, and I owe the Scholar a great debt," Al-Kindi said, his volume increasing.

"Let Katryn clear you, and we'll see," the Captain said.

"Many agents are volatile. If we wait too long, there will be nothing left to test."

"Will a standard sample kit do? Keveen, take two," Medico Pancea said loudly.

"Yes, but please allow me to run it through my tester. Because of my work, my database is probably much larger than yours. I have discovered many new substances in my search for perfume essences. Some of them have been very useful in medical treatments, and some are poisons. I must completely analyze any new discovery to find out if it is truly new and the full effects before working on production and marketing," Al-Kindi said, his voice still muffled. He and the Captain must be in the passageway, rather than in the med station.

"That is what concerns me, Gentle Al-Kindi," the Captain said in a low, menacing voice.

"I did not administer any substance to the Scholar, nor did I give any substance to anyone else to administer. If you check my shuttle records, you will see Nari and I retired to our shuttle after dinner and did not leave until shortly after the phys mod notification. We were on our way to breakfast when we saw the Scholar on the medfloat. This I so swear." His voice was calmer than the Captain's, but still had a distinct undercurrent of anger.

There were quiet murmurs all around her, and another scuffling sound. Points of pressure all around her head and chest.

"We'll give one sample to Gentle Al-Kindi and run the other ourselves," Medico Pancea snapped. More cloth swishing. "Gentle Nari, don't touch her without gloves. There may be a substance on her."

"Don't touch her at all. Medico..." the Captain growled.

"Gentle Al-Kindi might have more complete records than we do, Captain. We work with pandemics, not drugs, essences or poisons. We have two equal samples; it hurts nothing. But even if we find what it is, that doesn't mean we can find a counter agent. And friends are always welcome."

More movement and the swishing of cloth, rhythmic tapping on plas. Maybe someone was pacing? If only she could see. Or sleep. A low murmur and a snapping noise. Someone—Nari?— put a gentle hand on her shoulder and rubbed slow circles. From the way the hand snagged against her skin, she must be wearing a protective glove.

"I am sure my husband will find what was given to you, Cary, if the medicos do not. It will not be long and you will not be alone," Nari said fervently.

"The question is, why would someone administer a paralytic to the Scholar?" one of the male medicos said quietly. Saree wasn't sure which one; the voice was low and quiet, in typical 'medico calming mode.' "She's a scholar, in an obscure field, and we have, what, five days of travel left before the first shuttle drop? It would be obvious if Scholar Sessan suddenly disappeared; she's been on the folder a lot."

"Unless it was abduction? Serial abusers have used drugs to subdue and wipe memories. Predators are all too good at blending in."

"So, I should check planetary records for unsolved cases of rape in association with my passengers?" the Captain said equally quietly, his anger obvious.

"Or your own records, Captain," Keveen said, the sneer in his voice allowing her to differentiate it from Teva's.

"This is the first time we've had this happen. If one of us abused others in this fashion, I'd have spaced them. And if I'd done this, Katryn would have spaced me. None of us tolerate abuse of passengers or others, period, and if you knew anything about our background, you'd know why. And no, I'm not sharing," the Captain said, his tone furious and biting. Saree could almost hear his teeth grinding.

"Gentles, please, let's stay civil. Even if we can't find the correct substance or counter, it is unlikely the effects will last long. A paralytic that doesn't paralyze the lungs and heart can't be very strong, and it will wear off. We want the substance analyzed to counter it quickly and watch for possible side effects," Pancea said. "And Captain? This may have been meant for you or one of your crew. It's well known all of you use the phys mod daily."

There was a chime, and a brushing of cloth. The hand on Saree's shoulder clenched for a second.

"Well, Scholar, we know it is an agent designed to work on the brain, but we don't know exactly what drug it is, only what class of drug it belongs to. Perhaps Gentle Al-Kindi will have it in his database. Either way, it shouldn't be too long before it wears off; this class of drugs is intended to temporarily put a cooperative patient into a sleep state for medical interventions, like setting broken bones." Pancea stopped, and Saree waited for the bad news, because she was pretty sure there was some. "It's not a class we use anymore because it has created permanent problems in a very small percentage of patients. It's not likely you are one of those. Please continue to stay awake, although I'm sure you want to sleep. Fight it hard."

Saree had absolutely no desire to sleep at this moment—the terror coursing through her would keep her awake for the next standard year. How could she do her job if she couldn't move or communicate? And if she were confined to a float chair, she wouldn't be able to get into a lot of the clocks—some of the hatches were very small. Maybe Hal could help her? Oh, by all the suns, she did *not* want to be confined to a float chair. She'd be planet-bound for sure, with no way to repay the Sa'sa for her training. Could she even reach ^*timespace*^ like this?

But wait. She couldn't be too brain damaged, or she wouldn't be able to think right now. The terror receded a little.

"Medico Pancea?" Al-Kindi said.

"Yes. We have the class. Do you have a specific, and if so, the counter?" More swishing of material, probably Pancea moving to the hatchway.

"I have the analysis, here. I do not have a counter, but I believe I have the trade name and manufacturer, so you should be able to look it up, correct? Or with the analysis, you may be able to create

271

a counter agent. Either way, it should wear off soon." Al-Kindi took in a breath, then said quietly, "Since you know the class, I assume you know the potential side effects, Medico?"

"Yes. We do," Pancea said grimly. "Ah, look at that. Thank you, Gentle Al-Kindi—this should help."

"It is my very great pleasure to assist, Medico."

Silence descended again, but there was a lot of cloth rustling— probably medicos swiping through holo screens. Saree began to hope, just a little, but the terror of being permanently in this state was still overwhelming her thoughts. Despite the terror, sleep was beckoning again...it would be so nice not to think about any of this for a while...

"Do not worry, Cary. I am sure the medicos will be able to help you," Nari murmured. "And even if there is no counter agent, you have the best care available to help you recover." Her hand continued to rub gentle circles and voices murmured, discussing the results and treatment...she was so tired...

"Scholar, stay awake!" Medico Pancea barked. "Ah, that's better. Scholar, we do not want to give you any specific counter because introducing more brain-altering chemicals may cause more problems than it solves. What we *will* do is give you a general stimulant. This will not be pleasant, but it should help you stay awake until you can counter the effects of this drug on your own. Once we get you awake, we're going to make you walk and walk and walk, and you won't want to keep going, but you will." She took in a big breath, and her voice changed, becoming stilted and formal. "Since you are unable to give consent, Scholar, I am ordering this treatment as being in your best interests under my authority as a chief medico. Captain, you are my witness."

"So witnessed, Medico Pancea. And agreed, although you do not need my concurrence." His deep voice rumbled with anger.

"Let's get these straps and the collar off her." Grip strip ripped, her head lifted, and straps slid across her body. "Get a gown ready."

A sensation of intense cold ran up her left arm, into her shoulder and chest. Her heart pounded at double, no, triple time, and she sat upright before she even thought to do so. Something soft went around her—the gown Pancea mentioned?—hands were under her arms, and she was lifted off the table.

"Scholar, open your eyes!"

Hands pulled her forward. She started walking, someone on each side of her, holding her elbows with an arm around her waist. She tried to open her eyes, but she couldn't. She stumbled along, heart pounding, breathing far too hard for such a slow pace. Her eyes shot open and blinked at double time too—she couldn't stop.

"Ah, that's better—good job, Scholar," Medico Pancea said. Saree could barely see her through her fluttering lids and lashes, even though the medico was right in front of her. Pancea must be walking backward. Saree's mouth was desert-dry, and metal lingered on her tongue—like after a meal on Dronteim Station—and she shook like Quivori during the seven-moon alignment. Her heart pounded like she'd been running for an hour, flat out, and she wanted to run some more, but she couldn't walk straight—she staggered down the corridor like a spaceport junkie.

She stumbled along between two of the medicos—maybe Keveen and Teva—unable to see through the strobe-like twitching of her eyelids. Despite the constant blinking, her eyes and mouth were dry and sandy, her lids sandpaper across her eyes. "Water?" she croaked out.

"She'll need a straw," Medico Pancea called out. "How are your eyes, Scholar?"

"Dry. Sore." And, oh, getting worse by the second.

"Chyna, get some saline. Let's go back to the station."

They turned her in a tight circle, walked some more, and turned her again—into the medico station? They lifted her to a padded surface and pushed her to lay back. Her heart was still pounding away like a Wagnerian l'Opera timpani drum, and her whole body shook, spasmed and trembled.

Wonderful, cool wetness moistened her eyes and flowed down the sides of her face. Saree moaned in sheer relief as her eyes stopped screaming at her. A straw pushed between her lips and she gratefully sucked down water. So good, the best thing she'd ever had, better than Loreli's best dessert. She sucked down every drop.

"Is that better, Scholar?"

"Yes, thank you," she said, her voice croaking.

"You probably don't want to, but we're going to walk some more. At least the next hour or more. You'll get less shaky as the stimulant wears off, but I want to make sure you fully metabolize the drug. If we let you rest too soon, and there's still a significant amount of paralytic in your system, you could go back into the unnatural sleep pattern again. Some people remain in the pre-sleep state; that's why this drug isn't used anymore. Do you understand, Scholar?"

She looked up at Medico Pancea, her face wavering through the abundance of moisture in her eyes. "Yes, let's go. I have too much to do with my life to sleep it away."

Chuckles sounded all around her. They pulled and pushed her to a standing position and led her out the hatch. She walked and walked and walked, with the medicos, the Al-Kindis, and Lightwave's crew taking turns walking alongside her. Gradually, the amount of help decreased. All the other passengers were being kept away—she could hear voices from the observation lounge and some of them were not happy. Lady Vulten's voice was particularly grating, with a high-pitched screech and whine making them all cringe.

Eventually, she stopped shaking, and kept walking. Someone walked with her, but no longer had to guide every step— thankfully, she wasn't stumbling into people or the walls anymore. Saree was tired, but the overwhelming desire to sleep seemed to be gone. Her exhaustion resulted from terror and continuous walking.

When the Captain took a turn with her, she decided to ask. "Did you find anything on the security vids, Captain?"

His face, already grim, turned to stone. "Katryn, will you join us and tell the Scholar what you found, or rather *didn't* find?"

"Certainly, Captain." The beautiful woman stepped up to her left, her eyes almost shooting sparks of annoyance. "I reviewed the security vids of the phys mod for the last twenty-four standard hours. No human went anywhere near that rower until you did this morning at zero-six-thirty-six, nor did anyone go to your shuttle except you. However, at zero-two-thirty-two, there is a slow-moving, scintillating area measuring approximately ten by five by five centimeters—" she made a small, imaginary box with her hands in front of her "—entering the phys mod near the floor.

It travels to the rower, moves up the rower and along the handles, then back down and back out the phys mod hatch. It travels down the passageway and into the observation lounge. There, it disappears behind the bar, and I was unable to track it farther. That is also where it originated." She scowled fiercely. "After you were found and transported, many of the passengers gathered in the lounge, and almost all of them went to the bar for a drink, so I have no idea if anyone took the remote, if that's what it was, or if it was maneuvered into the disposal unit. There is no way to track it farther." Katryn was furious, her whole body telegraphing her desire to attack as she stalked alongside Saree—hopefully aimed at whoever did this and not her. Saree hoped Katryn didn't think this was a failure on her part. There was no way to anticipate this kind of behavior.

"Thanks, Katryn. You did good work to find that much," Captain Ruhger said.

Saree agreed. "Yes, thank you. You're amazing."

Katryn nodded and returned to the dining area, where those allowed near her waited. The other passengers were still in the lounge or their shuttles.

Captain Ruhger frowned down at her, and Saree braced herself for the questions. "What puzzles me, Scholar, is who notified me you were in trouble. The message seemed to be an automated life-safety message, but it was oddly specific."

Not the question Saree expected. She'd have to be careful here. She wasn't going to share Hal's sentience with the crew, but... "Because I travel alone, I am cautious and careful. A friend at University modified a life safety system for me. It tracks my location, and I update it with emergency contact information wherever I am. It's integrated into the fitness monitor on my e-torc and my shuttle systems. So, if I were on a planet, I would update it with the local emergency service. On a folder, I put the Captain in. It's designed to monitor my life signs, and if there's anything unusual—" she grinned up at the Captain "—like falling off a rower and not moving during a workout, it sends an alert."

All of which was true, but the Sa'sa made it for her. And 'it' was Hal. Now, would he buy her story?

Captain Ruhger nodded thoughtfully. "A good program for a solo traveler. You should market it."

"Oh, but it's not my work. I've told my friend he should, but he's one of these net geniuses who's too busy inventing and designing to put anything up for sale. After I finish my thesis, maybe I'll take some marketing courses and do it for him." She smiled up at him again, trying to convey her real gratitude among all her lies. "The problem is, it's dependent on the emergency contact caring enough to do anything, which you did, and I'm very grateful. Some folder crews aren't so conscientious. Thank you and your entire crew—I do appreciate your care."

He appeared a little embarrassed. "It's nothing, Scholar. When you're on Lightwave, safety is part of the transport. This shouldn't have happened."

The next question would be why anyone wanted a Scholar, and she wouldn't—no, *couldn't*—answer, so she turned back to the medico station. The Captain followed her, so she walked faster. He caught up with her at the hatch. Medico Pancea, Nari, and Al-Kindi were still there, looking at a screen full of chemical models and equations.

She stopped in the hatchway, not wanting to interrupt, but

they all turned to her. She bowed, deeply. "Medicos Pancea, Keveen, Teva, Chyna and Gentle Al-Kindi, thank you so much for your care. I will pay the appropriate medical expenses, and I'm personally in your debt."

Pancea shook her head. "If there are any medical costs, you owe Lightwave. We used their supplies. Our expertise is a gift. It was an unusual case and a good learning experience. If you don't mind, we'll write this up as a paper—without any identifying information on you, of course—which should fulfill any debt you feel. We'll submit a simplified version to The Guide™ as well—every traveler should be aware of this sort of attack."

Al-Kindi spoke before she could reply. "As for me, this was only a partial repayment of the debt I owe you."

Saree laughed. "You saved my life. I can't ever repay either of you. If there is anything I can do for you, please let me know."

"Thank you, but it's not necessary," Pancea said. "Now, go walk. Another...what do you think, Al-Kindi?"

"It has probably metabolized by now, but another thirty minutes or so would be definitive."

Pancea nodded. "Agreed. Walk another thirty minutes, stay active the rest of the day, no more than ten minutes at a time off your feet. Go to sleep at your normal time this evening." She frowned. "We'll run another blood test after dinner just to make sure. By the way, Keveen found nothing on your shuttle hatch controls."

"Thank you again, Medicos Pancea, Keveen, Teva, and Chyna, and Gentle Al-Kindi." Saree bowed deeply to them, turned slightly and bowed again. "And thank you, Nari, for the comfort. I could hear and understand everything; I simply couldn't reply or move. You were comforting and reassuring." She smiled at her friend, who smiled back, then looked down, shyly.

"It was no effort at all, Cary. That is what friends are for."

"Still, thank you." She turned back to the corridor to keep walking, amazed she had a real friend.

Nari spoke behind her. "Shall I walk with you, Cary? I'm sure the Captain has other duties, and this level of chemistry is far beyond my knowledge."

She turned back and smiled. "That would be lovely, thank you, Nari." And it might keep the Captain from asking her more uncomfortable questions.

He gazed down at her without any readable expression. "I do have other duties. I hope you recover fully, Scholar, and I apologize for the lack of safety on Lightwave." He glowered. "It won't happen again."

She shook her head. "No apologies necessary, Captain. There was no way you could anticipate an event like this. Nor do I think you could easily prevent a similar occurrence without an enormous staff or a ridiculously limiting security system that would drive passengers away. I'm grateful for your care. Thank you."

"You are welcome." He nodded and strode away.

Nari walked with her in silence, around and around the passageway. Finally, she said, "It is a very odd thing. Why would anyone drug you this way?"

"My initial thought was the normal reason for a female, alone, without a powerful family or other protection—a human trafficking ring. I'm too old and not talented enough to be a specific target, but it is always a possibility in space or on any world. But with five days of travel left, it seems unlikely." Saree watched Nari speculatively. "I suspect you know little of the dangers in the wider galaxy, correct?"

Nari bit her lip for a moment. "Only what I've read. Some of the warnings about travel are rather terrifying."

"You know there are sick, criminal individuals who molest others—it's a need for power and control—but one of the stranger variations is those who prefer to molest someone who is sleeping or unconscious, someone truly helpless. Or maybe it was a test, a test of the capability, and the person who did it thought I'd merely sleep and wake up puzzled. Or maybe someone thought if I never woke up, they could get my shuttle. Or someone wanted to put me in their debt by rescuing me. Or maybe it wasn't meant for me at all, but for Lightwave's crew. But there is no way to know, not without knowing who did this."

All too true. Even if someone thought she was the human Clocker, why try and hide her for five days? Or maybe this was a test, and they'd try it again closer to the drop point? No way to know. She'd wipe down anything she put her bare hands on for the rest of this trip. Maybe some sort of flesh-colored glove or adhesive covering? She'd do some research. Or ask Hal to do it.

They entered the phys mod and Saree couldn't help but look at the rower. It, and all the other equipment, gleamed. Someone scrubbed and sanitized every piece of equipment in here. Smart. Walking through the almost visible cloud of citrus cleanser, Saree realized she reeked of sweat, terror, and drugs—her nasty stench hung heavy in the sharp, antiseptic atmosphere of the phys mod, and her skin was gritty and sticky. She wanted a shower and fresh clothing in the worst way. She checked the time—thirty minutes was gone. Stopping, she turned to Nari.

"Nari, it's been more than the thirty minutes Medico Pancea and your husband prescribed. I'm going to take a hot shower and put on some fresh clothing." She laughed. "I really stink!"

Nari laughed with her for a moment. "You don't, but I wouldn't want to stay in that nasty paper gown either. It's so...immodest. Will you join us for lunch after you finish?"

"Thank you, I will. And really, thank you for staying with me. It was comforting to have someone there who cared about me. Thank you."

Nari smiled at her. "It was small repayment of your kindness. I consider you a friend. Friends comfort friends."

Saree smiled gratefully at Nari. "I haven't had a friend in a very long time. I'd almost forgotten how it felt. Thank you. I'll see you for lunch!" Still smiling, she turned to her shuttle airlock. The controls there gleamed, and her heart swelled in thanksgiving for the good friends and care she'd received. She was so lucky. She let herself in the shuttle and collapsed back against the cold cerimetal struts of the hatch, relieved. She was home, safe.

"Saree, I have been so worried!" Hal said frantically. "When you fell off the rower I couldn't *think* of what to *do*—my processors locked up. A sub-routine brought up the life-alert messaging, so I sent a message to the Captain. I heard his questions, but I couldn't think of any other way to notify him. Do you think he suspects me, Saree?"

Poor Hal, he sounded so panicked. She didn't think a computer could panic. Blast and rad, she was too tired to think about the implications. But she could comfort him. "He may suspect something, Hal, but I don't think he's suspecting a sentient AI. I certainly wasn't. You did the right thing." She chuckled and removed the revolting gown, throwing it in the recycler. Stepping into the shower area, she sighed gratefully when the hot water hit her skin. The nasty aftermath of terror sluiced off with the sweat. She scrubbed, wishing she could stay in forever, but she was going to run over her water allowance.

Dried and dressed, her stomach rumbling, she reassured Hal he'd done all he could. So strange to think a computer could worry, let alone worry about her. "Really, Hal, you did great. I'm fine and I'll be more careful. I need some food—can you do some research for me?"

"Of course, Saree."

"Look into protective gloves or hand coverings for me, please. And discreet ways to carry cleaning agents. I don't want to get caught by this one again, here or on some planet."

"Excellent idea, Saree. I will look. Go eat; I'm sure you will be safe for now, and I'm sure your body requires fuel." He sounded calmer now; she could leave without causing panic. She smiled. She never really left Hal.

"Thank you, Hal."

"You are welcome, Saree."

CHAPTER SIXTEEN

Ruhger worked his jaw side to side—clenching his jaw wasn't doing anything except giving him a headache and dental problems. But he was furious. Another person on his ship, under his protection, attacked and drugged for unknown reasons? Did he have a serial killer on board? A rapist? Were the attacks on Loreli and the Scholar related? If not for the shuttle of medicos...suns, it could have been bad. Black hole bad.

Unless one of them was the attacker. And Al-Kindi—sure, he helped this time, but his help was a double-edged sword. A database of drugs more complete than a team of medicos'? But pandemic experts wouldn't need databases of exotic drugs. Especially drugs no longer in use. Al-Kindi's explanation made sense.

Entering Alpha shuttle, he flopped down in the pilot's seat with an alarmingly loud creak—and messaged Chief he had command. He checked the autopilot—Chief put in some new corrections to account for the rad-blasting black-hole clock—then he checked for proximity alerts, but there was nothing new. Ruhger checked the C2 and engineering system status screens carefully, digging down to the underlying data—now was not the time to rely on easily altered pre-programmed alerts. Checking the log, he frowned, grimly. Bhoher did the same thing. Good— they were all thinking alike.

He swept over to the folder containing the latest debacle. Katryn saved the vid of the drug-administering remote for further analysis. Not only was the remote small, but it hid vids and sensors—an expensive piece of equipment. This being was not only a criminal, but one with a high level of expertise and lots of credits. And ditching the remote, rather than retrieving it, argued for a true professional's disregard of costs to execute a mission, someone willing to do whatever was necessary. That level of expertise was dangerous—for all of them.

The hatch buzzer sounded. Ruhger checked the vid—Katryn and Tyron stood outside. He sent the commands to unlock the hatch. They were scowling fiercely; not unexpected, but still unpleasant.

"Captain, we haven't been able to find anything definitive, just more data confirming one or more of our passengers is trouble." Tyron's mouth twisted. "Like we didn't already know that. Drugged rapes, and more specifically paralytic drugged rapes, are still too common on non-core worlds to be statistically meaningful in association with any of our passengers. The remote is a better clue, but again, not definitive."

Tyron took a sip from the bev-tainer he was carrying and very carefully placed it in the holder.

Ruhger held back a sardonic smile—he'd crushed a few in

anger too.

"Ursuine uses remotes in his work—he's got a shuttle full of them. Big, small, everything in between. They're used for sampling soils and water, climbing on wreckage, all kinds of legitimate uses for a structural engineer. There is no indication he's ever had any kind of cloaking device on them—why would he?" The Phazeers gave him almost identical grimaces, and Katryn took up the tale.

"But there is evidence of remotes being used in those jewel thefts statistically following him. Similarly cloaked remotes. And..." she drew out the word "—we looked at his shuttle usage statistics. He might have someone else on his shuttle. Water and power are used while he's on Lightwave. Not much—it could be an automated cleaner or something—but it is possible. A second being would make the jewel thief scenario more plausible. I wish we could check, but the shielding on the shuttles is too good. This second being, if there is one, hasn't exited the shuttle—I reviewed every second of the corridor vid."

Ruhger was about to congratulate them, but Tyron spoke again.

"Throwing more debris into the orbit, cloaked remotes are used by Familia too, particularly Familia assassins. We've found assassinations similar to the attempt on the Scholar— investigations find a cloaked remote applying poison to an object the victim touches, although not this particular agent. And cloaked remotes are being used by Chelonian bodyguards, believe it or not. If there's a known route the client is taking—a parade or a walk through a convention center or some other similar public place—the Chelonians are deploying cloaked remotes with sensors and subduing agents along the route. Temporary sleep or annoyance agents, not paralytic drugs," Tyron said grimly.

"Remotes are also used in the cultivation of Thymdronteim and in Al-Kindi's searches for new essences. Al-Kindi discussed various manufacturers and remote types with us, and showed us several. Most of his are designed to climb and cut—they're for cutting flowers and fruit from trees and vines—or to dig, crawl down holes and drill, for roots and tubers, but he said they could be easily modified."

Katryn took over again. "Al-Kindi said none of his were missing. He could be lying, but I don't think so. I think he's genuinely upset about the Scholar, because Nari is upset, not because he holds any particular affection for the Scholar herself." Her face changed—she was still angry, but there was another emotion he couldn't quite read. "It seems the Al-Kindis didn't know each other well when they married—theirs is a political arrangement. So, he is grateful to the Scholar for helping his wife with her homesickness." She smiled. "From the vids, it looks like they became much closer after the big dinner Nari cooked. Their body language changed—they look like a couple now."

She frowned again. "Their religion keeps men and women separate. Evidently, Nari has never been off the planet or spent any significant amount of time with a man before she was married off and whisked away. Poor girl had to be completely overwhelmed and shocked."

Katryn shook her head, her face pensive. "Leaving the Sisters and going off-planet was freeing *and* scary for me, and I had friends with me. I wasn't sheltered that much—I went to public secondary schools. I can't imagine how scary it would be to marry a stranger and leave everything and everybody behind. Especially if I knew nothing about sex, which I think was the case." She scowled. "At least the Sisters were practical about sex education even if they personally abstained."

"Still," Tyron said while staring with an odd expression at Katryn, "this doesn't help us. All the usual suspects are still...suspect."

"The plot thickens," Ruhger said. "Nothing is ever easy. I guess we keep going the way we have been, except try and adapt the automated sensors to find cloaked devices? I can't imagine that's an easy task..."

Katryn's lips mashed in a scowl. "No, it isn't, not during the day. During ship night, I can increase the sensitivity of the motion sensors. Good thing we don't have a ship cat." She gave them an ironic look.

She'd wanted one, but Chief was adamant against, fur being unfriendly to air filters and cats getting into machinery all too often. And with automatic compact laser weapons in the vents and intakes, rodents weren't a problem.

"Anything else?" Ruhger asked.

They both shook their heads.

"Go get some lunch and take a break. You two did a great job today. Not only did you find the suns-blasted remote, but you helped with the Scholar and the cleaning. Thank you."

"That's our job, Ruhger. But you're welcome," Tyron said. They got up to leave, both still grim.

"Watch yourselves. Stay together. I don't like any of this."

At the hatch, Tyron said, "You got it. This is a fold full of trouble, and it might be just the start. Don't hesitate to call us,

Ruhger, no matter how small."

"Same. And thanks again. Good work."

Tyron nodded sharply and closed the hatch. Ruhger locked it, and pulled up the vids to the ready room and the chow hall. The Al-Kindis and the Scholar were eating at a table toward the back of the room. The Chelonians and the Artiste were at another table, and Ursuine, Lady Vulten, and Gentle Schultz were at a third, all in separate corners. They were all glancing at each other. Private conversations, suspicion or just chance? There was no way to tell.

He pulled up the ready room vid. Lowe was in there, protective gloves on, wiping down surfaces. He might be a bit of a sex addict and put on the airs of a brainless society idiot, but when it counted, he was all business. Ruhger didn't like Lowe being alone. They all needed someone watching their six.

Where was Chief? He checked crew locations and pulled up the engineering area vids. Going through diagnostics again? Ruhger watched as he moved to the next station. "Contact Bhoher, normal priority." Ruhger pulled up the maintenance logs—yes, as he suspected, Chief was checking and rechecking them obsessively.

"Chief," he said, striding over to the fold generators, clearly intent on other things.

"Did you eat?"

Chief stopped mid-stride, met his eyes, then walked forward, slower. "No. I guess it is lunch time, isn't it?"

"Yes, it is. Go eat. You've checked the fold generators five times already this morning. They haven't changed in the last thirty minutes. They won't change in the next thirty either."

Chief frowned but nodded sharply. "Copy that, Captain. I'll go eat. You'll be watching."

"Oh, yeah. I'm watching everything. Go get Lowe from the ready room. Make him eat too. Come here after you're done. Take your time; I've got it right now."

"Wilco, Captain." Chief shut the command interface down and secured the engine room hatch. Ruhger watched him traverse the ship through the surveillance vids. Chief picked up Grant, and they joined the Phazeers in the chow hall. Ruhger relaxed a little, knowing his people were safe for now. Unless someone drugged the entire chow hall. He snorted. Nothing they could do about that. He checked the chow hall vid again. Loreli entered and sauntered to the Scholar's table. It seemed the Scholar had a knack for befriending people, a good trait for a female human traveling alone.

He contemplated the Scholar again. She wasn't a beauty. Most of the time she was quiet and wary, probably trying to avoid notice. He'd noted she was armed, customary for those who traveled the fringes, and she was cautious and careful, aware of her surroundings all times. She must have some unarmed self-defense training, but was it sufficient? Should he invite her to join their sparring sessions?

No. Katryn would have 'proof' he was a brainless idiot any woman could seduce. She had no reason to believe such a thing—he'd never given into his emotions and he wasn't starting now.

Ruhger realized he was scowling and deliberately relaxed—again. Yes, he was attracted physically to the Scholar. But she was hiding more than a few things from them, and he couldn't, *wouldn't* forget it. Even if he was stupid enough to want a physical relationship, it wouldn't work. He wouldn't allow her on

Lightwave's shuttles or in the crew quarters and she wouldn't invite him to her shuttle—her cautious, fast exits and entries demonstrated her wariness. Any physical encounter would be someplace on Lightwave—a non-starter. Too many vids in the public areas, too many passengers.

His mouth twisted. Besides, sex was vulnerability. He was vulnerable with people he knew and trusted completely. He wasn't Grant Lowe in any way, shape or form. The Scholar wasn't either or she would have taken Lowe up on his offer. Ruhger snorted. Probably multiple offers, knowing Lowe. Although maybe not, since his attention seemed to be elsewhere this fold.

He studied Grant for a moment. He was uncharacteristically faithful on this fold. The Chelonians came through the chow hall hatch, smiling their anatomy-constrained grins when they spotted Grant. He smiled back, a real smile, not his 'smooth operator' smile. Had Grant met his match? Ruhger's stomach sank—the Chelonians were passengers, leaving at Deneb. If this was something real, there was heartache ahead. Grant had had enough heartache in his life—they all had. Ruhger sighed. Well, if it was real, there was nothing any of them could do now. Grant should enjoy today and they'd help him deal with the aftermath.

He brought his attention back to the Scholar. Too bad he couldn't follow the same pattern—enjoy now and deal later—but he wasn't wired that way. The Scholar smiled at the Al-Kindis and Ruhger acknowledged his pang of regret, then shoved it away. Duty called.

∧∧∧

"Ruhger!"

He snapped his head up and stepped away from the wall,

ready for an attack.

"What in all the suns is with you today, Ruhger?" Lowe asked him, a frown marring his face.

He sighed and shook his head. "Sorry, Grant. Lost in my thoughts."

"Yeah, I get that. All too obvious, Captain." He drew out the title. "What are you lost in, specifically?"

He scowled at Lowe. "What do you think? Safety. Safety of the crew, of Lightwave, of the passengers."

Lowe's face sobered. "It's been three days and nothing else has happened. Maybe they're giving up?"

Glowering, Ruhger said, "Seriously? What pleasure planet are you on, Lowe? The closer to the drop point we are, the more the danger increases. We're now at the point where all of the shuttles—" he swept his hand around "—can drop off and easily reach refueling points. They could drug someone and take off with them. And you know Cygnus doesn't have a real military or much of a police force, and we have no authority to act. All we can do is notify the locals. And there are other fold transports in the lane—one's at Hold Point Alpha. A shuttle could make it to one of them, and boom—that person is gone."

Lowe tilted his head and gave him an ironic look. "And you being lost in your head will help prevent that how?"

Ruhger couldn't keep from glaring. Lowe was right, even if he hated to admit it.

"Yeah, that's what I thought. So, get over here and take your turn with Chief." He grinned and pointed at the mat next to him. "Get your head in *this* game, or it's going to get knocked off." Lowe walked over to the small freezer near the hatch and grabbed an ice pack.

Well, he was right there. Ruhger might be better than Chief in a formal fight setting, but in this no-holds-barred sparring, Chief used some nasty tricks. The Phazeers had command in Alpha shuttle so the three of them could spar without worrying about security. He needed to take full advantage of this time. Walking onto the mat, Chief bowed, and Ruhger bowed in return. Then he had no room in his head for anything but the fight in front of him. Ducking, dodging, rolling or minimizing blow after blow, evading, grappling, muscles burning, lungs heaving—suns, that one hurt—wrenching to dodge...

"Time!" Lowe yelled. "Time! Knock it off."

They both stepped back and bowed, grinning at each other. One of the few times Chief really smiled was after a good fight. A blank expression was trouble—he might be lost in a berserker rage. Whoever was watching better have a bucket of ice water or a stunner handy. If Chief was sparring, they had a watcher.

"Good fight, gentlemen. You'll have to review the vids, but I think Chief had you pretty quick." Lowe turned to Chief, admiration clear. "That was a killer combination you threw down."

Chief nodded. "It's necessary with a well-trained fighter like Ruhger. He's younger and has more stamina than I do, so to survive, I have to do the unexpected immediately, or he'll wait until I'm exhausted, then move in for the kill." Chief turned to him. "Which is a failing of yours, Ruhger. In this kind of fighting, you need to go for a kill right away. Don't draw it out—it's not a competition."

Ruhger bowed again. "You are correct. There were a couple of opportunities early on, but I wanted to keep fighting." He grinned again, more at Lowe. "I needed to get out of my head."

Lowe nodded at him, the grin on his face widening as he threw towels at them. Walking out of the phys mod, Lowe and Chief discussed the fight, but Ruhger only half-listened, thinking about the potential problems to come.

"Breakfast?" Grant asked, with an expectant but resigned look.

Ruhger laughed and ignored the looks of astonishment they both leveled on him. "Sure. It's early enough; maybe we won't chase everyone out with our stink." Poor Lowe, he'd been stuck on the outside too much during this fold. But he was better with passengers than the rest of them, and his job was the least critical to Lightwave's safety. Still, he'd have to find a way to bring him into the group more. Lowe was hanging with Loreli a lot but it wasn't the same. His smile twisted into an ironic one—one more thing factor to balance with all the other priorities.

They entered an empty chow hall, and Ruhger acknowledged the profound relief—he did *not* want to deal with passengers yet. "Coffee?" Lowe and Chief both nodded, their eyes on the buffet. They were all thrilled Loreli was healthy again, for a whole bunch of reasons, but breakfast was one of the biggest. Ruhger punched the coffee button and listened to the muffled grinding, the dark, bitter, delicious scent of freshly ground beans drifting to him. This little toy was ridiculously expensive, but good coffee was worth it. The cycle finished, he pulled the press out, and punched the button again—they'd need at least two pots. He put the first pot on the back corner table.

Joining the guys at the buffet, he marveled at the decadent display of pastries along with the more common breakfast foods.

He picked up his normal fruit, yogurt, and hot mash, spooning one of Loreli's amazing fruit concoctions on the mash and taking one of the pastries. Oh, to the suns with his diet—he had worked his ass off this morning. Two pastries—they glittered with sugar and bright fruit colors and smelled delicious. He glanced over at Chief, clearly doing the same calculation in his head, his hand hovering over the platter. Ruhger smirked at him and grabbed one more right out from under his hand. Chief barked out a laugh and took three himself.

They joined Lowe, who had nothing but pastries on his plate. "How can you eat like that, Lowe?" Chief growled out.

Lowe grinned a big, giant asteroid-eating grin. "I get a lot more exercise than this morning workout, Chief." The grin dimmed a little. "And I inherited a killer metabolism. Luck of the draw." He shrugged.

"You do have the luck, Grant," Loreli said. This morning, she was back in what Ruhger considered her 'working' whites—they covered everything, but like a second skin of sprayed-on plas, with a cinched-waist corset of shiny white pleather. The outfit was dazzling, but the display above the corset did help him remember the correct gender, no matter how many years the face was attached to the name "Loren."

Lowe ducked her hand, headed toward his hair, and a flash of hurt showed on her face. "Darling, we were sparring. My hair is sweat-soaked and nasty. You do *not* want to touch that."

Loreli rolled her eyes at him, and lowered herself into the remaining chair.

Ruhger frowned. "Loreli, are you all right? You don't normally sit with us."

She gleamed at him. "I'm fine. Fully recovered." She shrugged, and all the moving flesh distracted him for a split-second. She twinkled when he looked back up at her face, and he grimaced in return, ironically amused. "I've got everything out and ready. I miss hanging out with you guys."

Ruhger nodded his agreement along with Chief and Lowe. "I was just thinking the same thing. This constant vigilance is more painful than a wonky main thruster."

Chief said, "Yes, but we paid off the weapons. That makes it worthwhile."

They nodded grimly at each other and started eating.

Loreli poured a cup of coffee and sipped, her face pensive. "Maybe we can offload all the passengers in Cygnus and have a celebration of our own," she said.

"That's a great idea, Loreli," Lowe said. "There aren't any pleasure planets worth mudballing on here, not any we can afford, but if we could clear all the passengers for a while, we could relax."

Ruhger, thinking fast, said, "Suns, you're right. We can do that. We drop Borgia and the Chelonians here, then we short-fold to the medicos and Vulten drop and then the added drop for Ursuine." He chewed on it one more time, but his back brain had been considering how to take a break since he took all the long-term contracts. "We could do fold-and-drops for all of them and stay with the Sisters longer."

Lowe grimaced, and Ruhger held up a hand. "I know what you're going to say, Grant, so don't. But if we stay on Cygnus-Gliese Three, Al-Kindi and the Scholar will go planet-side—this is unexplored territory for both of them—leaving us with an empty folder. We can take a week on the mud—all of us together—then come back and do some real maintenance and training on the weapons, something we haven't been able to do because we needed to earn credits, fast." He snorted out a laugh. "We still need to earn credits, but not so fast. And we can advertise we're coming back through each skimmed system and maybe we'll have shuttles waiting to take the place of the Artiste, medicos, and Chelonians. Or maybe they'll be ready for another fold."

The grim faces around the table lightened as he spoke. Lowe opened his mouth, but Chief beat him to the punch. "That's a good idea, Ruhger. But…can we do the maintenance first, then go on-planet? I want to check all the systems thoroughly, preferably without any passengers onboard, before we leave Lightwave orbiting. I know the Phazeers will want a good scrub of our security before we button up the ship—we must be absolutely positive it will still be here when we come back."

Ruhger nodded slowly. "I hate to, because I know we're all tired and we need a break, but you are right. We must be one hundred percent certain nobody has a backdoor entry into Lightwave before we can leave her in orbit. Especially around Cygnus-Gliese—they have no space security force."

Lowe nodded too. "I'll draft those system ads right away. Are we going to spend some time in each system on our way outbound? Because I need to sell the speculative cargo too." He frowned slightly. "The Sisters won't buy much of it—they don't care about luxury goods. And few on Cygnus-Gliese can afford them."

"Good point." Ruhger thought for a moment. He said, "C2, Lightwave schedule." He widened his holo so everyone at the table could see it. "Contact Tyron, normal priority."

"Tyron here, Captain."

"We're discussing the schedule. Do you two want to join in? We're looking at revising things a little to give us all a break."

"That would be wonderful," Katryn's voice said, with longing. She must be somewhere outside of Tyron's view.

"So, the plan is to drop the Artiste and Chelonians here at Prime, fold and drop the medicos and Vulten at Secundus, then fold and drop Ursuine." Ruhger swept his hand through the colored blocks on the calendar, shortening them. "I'll do the detailed calculations later; these are estimates, but they're close enough for now." He pulled up the Cygnus-Gliese/Sisters block and zoomed in. "We'll stay in Gliese for..." He pondered the factors. "Fourteen standards. The first three to six standards will be a detailed sweep of Lightwave. Maintenance for everything: physical, net, all of it. Compile lists of required replacements, of necessary additions and nice-to-have items." He swept the group with a solemn look. "The weapons are paid off, but we're still not rich, nor likely to be. Make sure those categories are solid, people."

Everyone nodded. "Then we'll button her up and go planet-side for six to ten standards. We'll offload the Sisters' cargo, have some fun—yes, I know, Grant, but you always manage somehow; not everyone on the planet is a Sister or a believer—and we'll interview additional security people. We'll bring the final candidates up to Lightwave for a standard or two, to make sure they can handle being in space and we can stand them, and we'll secure any cargo Grant manages to find. We'll take the rejected people back to Gliese, and fold back to each system, orbiting or docking for...five standards in each of them. That should give us enough time to find new passengers, sell the cargo, and make sure our new people are going to fit in. And it should give Al-Kindi and the Scholar enough time on the mud to do their thing. Or we could fold back and pick them up before we leave the Cygnus constellation. The short folds are cheap." He met the gaze of each one. "Objections? Thoughts?"

Tyron said, "Sounds good, Captain." More nodding agreement except the Chief.

Bhoher held up a hand. "We should check on refueling costs. We don't need to yet, but you know it's always better to have a full load than run short."

Ruhger nodded. "I'm sure Grant can do that, Chief. He's been researching the markets." Scanning all of them, he was satisfied. Everyone was smiling, and much happier than they'd been before breakfast. "All right, it's a plan. It's a rough one, people—we'll have to be flexible, and if something comes up or you have an idea, let me—and everyone else—know. Let's make this a good run." He smiled at all of them and got up. "Tyron, Katryn, I'm headed your way so you can get some breakfast. As usual, Loreli has outdone herself." He nodded at her and swept the holo off, and walked toward the shuttle.

Yes, they needed a break. And by dumping passengers as they went, and not taking new ones, they reduced their risk of further incidents and gave themselves a doubly appreciated break. He savored his satisfaction as he headed toward the shuttle and his shower. The perfect plan.

CHAPTER SEVENTEEN

S aree dithered. This was the danger point, the last standard day before arrival at the Cygnus Prime drop point. She should stay in her shuttle, safe, but Nari asked her to lunch, and the formal departure dinner was tonight. Her brain was telling her to stay here, but her stomach? It loudly cheered, 'Go! Go! Go!' Her heart wanted to go too.

She turned back to her clothes. Stay or go?

"You should stay here, Saree, where you are protected," Hal said, his smooth voice soothing—and persuasive.

She sighed. "Yes, I know, but Nari asked, and since they're staying with Lightwave for a long time like me, I don't want to offend them." She grinned. "Especially since her husband knows a hundred different ways to kill me without a trace."

"Do you know of some reason to fear this, Saree?"

"I was joking, Hal. A dark and ironic joke, but a joke nonetheless."

"I saw your smile, but I wasn't sure if you meant it or not."

Saree chuckled.

Hal said, "Besides, you like Nari, right? And Al-Kindi himself?"

"Yes, yes I do. I like both of them. I consider Nari a true friend, and I'm even starting to think of Al-Kindi that way, even if I never know his real name."

"The two of you have much in common."

She considered the surprising statement. "Huh. I guess it's true. We both spend a lot of time traveling the universe, alone, looking for something that may or may not exist in an unknown form. And hiding what we're actually doing from everyone else."

"Yes. Also, you are both outcast from your communities. You, because of your origin, profession and species, Al-Kindi because of his profession. It cannot be easy to supply poisons when one's upbringing emphasizes peace and non-violence. If poisons were all he produced, I believe he might not be here now. It's unfortunate poisons are more profitable than perfumes."

Saree nodded. Truly unfortunate. She peered in her closet and put her everyday scholar's robes on. These robes might be one of the reasons Nari was comfortable with her—she didn't feel so conspicuous in her head-to-toe coverings when standing next to a Scholar. After all, Saree was much taller than Nari, and a Scholar's robes covered almost as much of her body as Nari's religious garments.

Walking to the shuttle hatch, she suddenly couldn't wait to see Nari. It might be the last time she could relax, at least until they dropped all the other shuttles.

"Saree, wait a moment."

She turned back toward the interior of the shuttle. "Yes, Hal?"

"I want to send an extra remote with you. This one is designed to look for cloaking devices. It's a little larger, so it can't hide in your hair like the others."

She nodded. "Okay, let's see what it looks like, and we'll figure out a way to hide it."

"It's in the maintenance remote access hatch."

Leaving the shuttle airlock, she crossed to the galley. The access point was at floor level in the galley, allowing the cleaning remotes to go in and out unobtrusively. The hatch slid open, and a small platform rolled out. Saree picked up the remote and put it down on the galley countertop. The remote was big enough to be seen—approximately a half a centimeter square and three centimeters long, narrowing on one end—a clear plas with some shiny threads in it. "Does this need to be on my head? And which end is the sensor?"

"No, but the higher you can place it, the better field of view it will have. The sensor end is the skinny one."

"Hmmm. If I was wearing my formal robes, I could hide it under the tassels." She turned to her closet. "If I wear casual clothes, I could hide it on my shoulder under a scarf."

"It is somewhat flexible; you could fasten it to your e-torc. Most humans won't notice it."

Saree slid the e-torc off her neck. Most of the time she forgot it was there, like everyone else. Even when she used it to bring up holos, she didn't consciously remember the mechanism—it's easy to ignore something you've worn most of your life. Placing it on the countertop, she picked up the new remote and put it beside the e-torc.

"Put it on the other side, Saree. You walk along the right side of corridors, so I want the field of view to your left."

She did as Hal suggested. It didn't stand out, and nobody noticed e-torcs anyway. She pulled some small self-sticking gripper strips out of the junk drawer, applied them, and slid the e-torc back around her neck. It felt a little unbalanced, but not enough to make a difference. She'd forget about it soon. She walked into the bathroom and looked in the mirror—it wasn't obvious.

"If someone asks, tell them you're testing an IR sensing device for your net inventor friend. It's true."

Saree smiled. "It is indeed. Thank you, Hal, for looking out for me."

"It is my pleasure, Saree."

Smiling wider, she exited the hatch and proceeded to the dining hall. She'd almost reached the dining hall when she realized Hal changed his normal response. Huh. Was it a good sign, a sign he was learning on his own and applying human niceties? Or a bad sign he was learning on his own and learning to tell little white lies? Or did he mean it literally, that helping her gave him pleasure? She grimaced. She couldn't tell, not right now, and maybe never.

Entering the dining hall, she scanned it as usual, and joined Nari and Al-Kindi, waiting near the buffet. Happy and grateful, she smiled at them, grinning at the answering smile from Nari. She even got a nod, with a tiny lifting of his lips, from Al-Kindi, and she grinned wider. Real friends were such a comfort.

After a delicious if simple lunch, Al-Kindi excused himself, leaving them to continue discussing the changed fold schedule.

Nari asked, tentatively, "Perhaps we should offer our help to

Chef? If she's making a feast, she might need some assistance."

"Oh. You're right. Chef didn't say anything..." Saree thought back to her last conversation with Loreli. "She didn't even hint." She shrugged. "But it can't hurt to offer."

Getting up, they made their way to the kitchen hatch and hit the annunciator.

"Chef?" Nari called tentatively. There was no answer. They glanced at each other, puzzled. Nari hit the button again. "Chef Loreli, it's Nari and Cary."

The hatch swung open and Chef glared down at them. "What?!" she cried.

Nari blinked at her and Saree, taken aback, stammered, "Oh, I'm sorry, I thought we could help. You must be terribly busy."

"No, go away! You are useless! I must have solitude for my creations!" She slammed the hatch in their faces.

They stared at each other, wide-eyed, then began laughing. Every time Saree tried to stop, she'd look at Nari and start again. Nari seemed to be having the same problem.

Finally, Saree choked out, "Well, so much for our offer to help. I guess we know where we stand, don't we?" She wiped the tears from under her lashes and held an arm around her aching stomach muscles.

"Yes, we do." Nari leaned on the wall, trying to recover.

Grant Lowe ambled in, grinning at them. "You tried to help, didn't you?"

They both nodded.

Shaking his head slowly, he said, "Yeah, that never works. Loreli is a force of nature, a solar storm stronger than any in the known universe when she's in the grip of creativity. And the departure dinner is always creative." He laughed. "I offered to help the first time. She chased me out of the kitchen with a cleaver in one hand and a huge Sirius catfish in the other, yelling she'd rather have the catfish's help because it was quiet and could chop an onion better." He shuddered and gazed into the distance, clearly remembering. "She smacked me on the head with the fish—those things are nasty. I had to shower forever to get the crap out of my hair."

He grinned impossibly wider at them and laughed. "It's funny now, but at the time I was downright offended." Sobering a bit, he continued. "But she's right. Look at the vegetable pieces in tonight's dishes—if she hasn't simmered them into nothing, they're all exactly the same size. She's amazingly precise."

Nari said, "I noticed she was...not saying everything she thought when I was making my dishes. I'm definitely not a professional."

Saree said, "I'm nowhere close to as good as you are, Nari. I didn't cook at all—my mother cooked, but by the time I was old enough to learn anything more complicated than a sandwich, I was busy doing...other things." She hoped they didn't notice the stumble, although she could always pass it off as sports or boys.

"Oh, you were, were you?" Lowe leered at her speculatively, running his eyes up and down her body, hidden under the scholar's robes.

Saree bit back a groan. Figures the fold orbit Lothario would pick up on the evasion. "Yes, sports. Specifically shooting." She bared her teeth at him, and he recoiled a bit. "I was very good. But I just missed the world junior team, and changed my studies to music."

"I'm sure your mother was happier," Lowe said.

"No. It made my father happier because music was cheaper. My mother was a shooting champion in her youth." Saree gave him another mirthless grin. "Mother was great at all kinds of things, including weapons, but now that I think about it, she wasn't much of a cook. She tried, but really? She was much better at slicing and dicing a target than a potato." She chuckled at the look on Lowe's face. "And I'm much better at researching obscure music and potential sources than any of those things. This one time..." And she spooled off a story about tracking down a folk song on Proxima B. Lowe's eyes glazed over quickly, but Nari seemed fascinated by the story. Another year of space travel, and she'd be bored with all the stories too. Lowe left not long after, carrying his food.

Nari contemplated her with slight narrowed eyes, then smiled. "You are very good. Will you teach me?"

Saree gazed at her innocently. "To do what?"

"Scare off inopportune men by boring them to death." She smiled, a little challengingly.

Saree laughed. "You caught me. It is a good skill to develop, although it only works on beings who have a heart. True predators won't care how boring a story you spin; they'll wait patiently, or act immediately. You have to know your target." Smiling ruefully, she shrugged. "But it's always worth a shot, especially when you have nothing to lose. You have to find a long, convoluted story without a lot of real action and tell it with a bunch of tiny details. So, you could tell one about..." she stared up at the overhead for a moment to think "—cooking on a feast day, or getting ready for a ceremony, a childhood triumph or some similar story. An everyday kind of story, chattering about every single detail you can possibly remember about everything and everybody involved. You'll send them running."

Nari giggled behind her hand. "I know just the story. My cousin's wedding." She rolled her eyes. "She was marrying someone very rich, so everything was elaborate and had to be perfect, or she threw a fit. We worked for months to gather everything needed on our ridiculously small budget. It was a nightmare." Nari's grimace of distaste morphed to shining satisfaction. "But once the ceremony was over, she was gone. A huge relief to all of us. Now her husband's family has to put up with her."

Saree chuckled—probably every family had similar stories, and there were plenty of kids at the home she was glad to see the back of, even if their endings weren't always as happy as Nari's. Bringing herself back to the present, she smiled, although she had to force it. "The perfect story, just the right mix of different enough from most people's experiences to be interesting, but you can add enough boring stuff to it to drone on forever." Smiling again, for real, she added, "By the way, another thing that helps make the technique work? Keep your voice low, monotone and droning. It adds to the boredom factor."

Nari beamed back at her. "Ah, that's what it was. I couldn't figure out why I found my thoughts drifting even though I was interested in your story. It's the delivery."

"Yup, works pretty good." Saree sighed. "Thank you for inviting me to lunch, but I should work on my thesis a little. I'm a bit behind, and since we'll be doing the quick fold and drop thing, I should get my work done now, just in case my body decides it doesn't like the folds."

Nari regarded her with concern. "But you've done this before, haven't you?"

"Yes, I've done lots of skip drops, but never four in a row. I've never done more than two in a row." Gesturing dismissively, Saree smiled gently. "I'm not too concerned. I don't think it will be an issue; I think it's the distance involved. But just in case, I should finish up the tedious work of proper citations now." She grinned. "Besides, if I do it now, I have a Chef Loreli celebration dinner waiting as a reward when I'm done."

Nari beamed up at her, the happy expression lighting what could be seen of her face. She glanced around, and bit her lip in trepidation. "Will you walk me to our shuttle airlock? I'm still not used to being alone around all these men." Looking around the empty room, the worry was clear on her face.

Not surprised, Saree said, "Of course—it would be my pleasure. It does take a while to become accustomed to space travel in general, let alone in an entirely new social setting." Poor Nari, dumped into an unfamiliar place and life, with no friends or family around. And such a sheltered childhood. Saree couldn't imagine growing up with only girls around. Or even just humans.

Turning, they exited the dining hall and walked to the Al-Kindi airlock. Nari turned at the hatch and threw her arms around Saree. She froze for a second, and returned the small woman's embrace, gently.

"Thank you, Saree, for befriending me and for joining Lightwave on a long-term contract." Looking up at her, Nari's happy expression wavered a bit, and her eyes shone. "You make everything so much better!" She pulled away, turning back with a swirl of robes to grin at her again just before she closed the airlock hatch.

Saree smiled. Everything was better for her, too. She was nervous right now, but once all these other passengers were dropped, she should be relatively safe on Lightwave for the next standard year. And she had a real friend. The happiness and relief made her a little lightheaded. Turning, she walked back down the passageway to her shuttle and Hal. She couldn't relax—she had to be on guard, especially today. She passed the lounge and the dining hall, but saw no one—everyone must be getting ready for the big dinner.

Passing the phys mod, she glanced over, then paused when she spotted Lady Vulten. The Lady was looking at a treadmill with a puzzled look, her index finger tapping her lips. Was she going to use it? She wasn't dressed for exercise. Maybe she was curious. Walking into the phys mod, Saree said, "The equipment is very high-end, Lady Vulten. Do you want some help understanding the interface? It's different from a normal treadmill."

The Lady turned to her, her normal superior look firmly enthroned on her beaky face. "I have no intention of using it, Scholar." She turned to look at the treadmill again, then back to her, the disdain clear. "It's very old. Perhaps they purchased it from a junk dealer."

Saree forced an affable expression to her face. The woman was so unpleasant. It was a good thing Elise raised her children. Her husband's early death had probably been a great relief to him. Or maybe Lord Vulten was equally objectionable?

Shame on you, Saree. There's no reason to sink to her level. Reinforcing the smile on her face, she didn't reply directly—she wasn't going to spill Lightwave's secrets to anyone, especially not this disagreeable woman looking to gain an advantage over others. "Perhaps. Well, Lady Vulten, I'll leave you to your inspection; I have some work to finish before the big dinner."

Turning away from the Lady toward her shuttle, Elise strode in from the passageway, a cold, predatory look on her face, her hands behind her back. *Something's wrong—this is trouble.* Hal hadn't warned her about Elise, or Vulten either. *Something's definitely wrong.* She backed up, angling away from both of them. A piercing, clanging warning klaxon pealed, and she jumped, her ears ringing. She recognized the pattern—an attack klaxon!

If there was going to be a battle, she wanted to be in her shuttle. And she wanted away from Elise and Vulten. She feinted a turn toward the dining hall hatch, then spun, put her head down and pushed off hard on her right foot. Sprinting for her shuttle, she'd mow Elise down if she had to. Saree reached full speed and looked up. Elise was still there, but she wore a mask over her head and held a bottle in her hand, pointed at Saree.

Blast! She stutter-stepped and pushed hard off her left toe, cursing the loss of speed. She'd avoid Elise, bounce off the wall on her right, run behind Elise to her shuttle. But Elise anticipated her and blocked the passageway, so she kept turning. She'd run for the dining hall, then to her shuttle.

Pushing off the wall, she ran right into Vulten, a bottle in her hand too, spraying something in Saree's face. Vulten also wore a mask and an even colder look than Elise. Saree clamped her mouth shut and tried to blow air out her nose, but she was too late. Everything went gray and colorless. The entire room tilted. The shock on Vulten's face when Saree plowed into her, knocking her down, was satisfying. Even better was the energy boost she got from pushing off the horrible woman—she kept turning. Her vision tunneling, she stumbled to the outer passageway, away from those women, but also away from Hal. Blast and rad—she had to get away!

There—an escape pod. Saree hit the button, but it didn't open. She stumbled to the next one, scraping against the wall, fighting to stay on her feet. She fell into the release button and hit it as a hand came down on her shoulder. Lashing out and back with her left leg, she connected, the pod hatch opening at the same time. She fell into it, the hatch automatically shutting. The gray all around her was turning black, closing in.

With one last effort, she turned, clawing her way around the pod back toward the hatch, and slid her fingers under the clear accident-prevention cover, hitting the launch button. If she didn't launch, they'd reopen the pod and pull her out. Saree's vision tunneled, everything going black. Acceleration pushed her back into the pod, and her breath escaped in an 'oof' —

ΛΛΛ

Saree tried to open her eyes, but her eyelids were pasted shut. And her stomach...oooh...her stomach tossed like she was in zero-g. *Wait...* She stopped trying to open her eyes and took stock. She *was* in zero-g—she'd recognize the sensation anytime, anywhere. Suns, where was she? Along with the normal dizziness of zero-g, a knife jabbed into her temples in rhythm with her heartbeat. The rest of her head was clamped into a helmet two sizes too small, and her mouth was dry, with a nasty, metallic aftertaste.

Had she been drinking Sirius champagne? Or eaten something

from Dronteim? ~~Or been drugged?~~ She shivered. She was freezing and she ached everywhere like she'd been beaten. *Drugged.* She'd been drugged—nothing else could feel like this. She relaxed every muscle, going limp. If she wasn't alone, hopefully no one noticed her waking.

Listening hard, she tried to sense her surroundings. Her back rested against a slightly padded surface of some sort. She flexed her back muscles a bit, the motion sending her forward, hitting a similar surface, and bouncing back again. All she could hear was a faint beeping noise.

Well, she wasn't getting anywhere like this. Despite her killer headache, she peeled her eyes open, blinking to clear them. Orange padding, less than thirty centimeters from her nose. She made her eyes move in their dry sockets, surprised she didn't hear sand shifting. An escape pod. She was in an escape pod, not strapped in, without a suit. *Oh, suns.* Her stomach rose in her throat and tension sang through her. There'd been an attack klaxon going off on Lightwave, and she was in an escape pod, without a suit! Sunspots—these things were as fragile as eggs, and there was a battle, and she didn't have a suit on!

Wait, wait, wait, calm. Don't panic. Remember, The Guide™ says don't panic.

Slamming her eyes shut, she slowed her breathing. She still had air. She hadn't been holed. There was no sense in borrowing trouble. She might not be off Lightwave—the pod might still be on board. Zero-g made it unlikely, but still possible. The thought calmed her and she smiled a little.

She blew out one more breath, took in another, and opened her eyes again. There wasn't much to the escape pod. Padding, with straps, a supply compartment and a simple status panel. A bright green light for life support—no kidding; she was still breathing—and a red light showing that the thrusters, the ones designed to throw her away from the spacecraft, were depleted. One more red light showed there was no breathable atmosphere beyond the pod. Nothing surprising.

"Hal?" There was no answer. Oh, suns. Patting her neck, she confirmed her e-torc was there. Vulten didn't have time to take it—did they do something to Hal? Saree sagged with despair. Hal was her friend, her confidant, her white knight—she couldn't fathom continuing this life without him. Not now.

"Hal?" Hearing her plaintive tone, Saree forced herself to stop. Vulten and Schultz couldn't do anything catastrophic to Hal; it wasn't possible. But they might do something to prevent communication, like an interference generator, or distracting Hal. Oh, blast and rad—the attack klaxon! The klaxon rang just before Vulten attacked. That's why she ran—she was trying to reach Hal. Saree huffed out an exasperated breath. Obviously her brain wasn't operating at full capacity yet. Why would anyone attack Lightwave? And who? If Lightwave was on the defensive, Hal couldn't help her—he had to stay inside Lightwave's shielding—it was much stronger. But unless Lightwave was destroyed, Hal would come looking for her. Hal was smart—she had to trust he could take care of himself. Besides—she glanced around the pod—she couldn't do anything for him. She'd be lucky to survive.

Survival—that was the important thing right now. She had to survive, help herself, before she could help Hal. So, what could she do to survive? Saree considered the pod. Straps floated near her. Should she strap in? She didn't sense any changes in velocity, and the thrusters were depleted, so she probably didn't need to. But a toe hold would be helpful. She curled down and hooked the lowest straps into a loop.

Hooking her feet into the ankle strap, she pulled her body down into a sitting position, and unfastened the 'emergency supply' compartment below the status panel. As expected, a soft-suit hung there. Good thing Lightwave was so safety conscious— this pod would have all the required safety gear, and maybe some extras too. Some folders would sell off their extra pods, or at the very least not stock all of them. Gratefully, she pulled the suit out and on, ripping the crotch out of her leggings and hooking in the plumbing in case she was out here for a while. She transferred the small utility tool in her thigh pocket to the outside pocket on the suit.

Leaving the hood off, she adjusted the one-size-fits-most suit to her, tightening gripper straps. Pulling the upper part of the suit back off, she bunched it around her waist. Now she was ready for an emergency, but not wasting her supplies—no sense in depleting the suit's O2 if the pod's recycler/generator was still working. Which it wouldn't do forever. Saree shuddered, and shoved the thought to the back of her brain. No time for worrying; she had work to do if she was going to survive. A positive mental attitude was the number one controllable factor in survival.

She pulled herself back down, looking at the bottom of the compartment. *Yes!* Bags of drinking water. Smiling, she pulled a silver bag out, carefully deployed the tube and sipped, forcing herself to drink slowly. The cool liquid soaked in and bathed her dry throat and tongue like a stream through a desert wasteland. *Ah. So much better.* Her head still pounded like a Klee dance party moved in and she shook with cold and shock, but with the water hitting her system, she was starting to feel half-alive, rather than half-dead.

Now, immediate survival ensured, how could she stay alive and free if her pod was picked up by the wrong people? Elise and Vulten had sprayed her with some sort of knock-out drug, but were they the only threat? There was no way to know. Blast them all to a black hole! What could she do to defend herself?

Saree surveyed the tiny escape pod again: a compartment designed for one, but big enough to stuff two in if necessary, padded everywhere except the command and status panel with its three lights, launch button and the release on the supply compartment below. But this was a mercenary troop ship escape pod—there might be a weapon stashed in here.

Pulling herself farther down by her toes, she gripped the waist strap to stay crouched in front of the supply compartment. The compartment was shallow, just five centimeters deep, but a meter long and almost as wide as the pod, about three quarters of a meter. She peered down into the bottom of the compartment—a box with the familiar red cross symbol. A first aid kit. She smiled. There might be something useful in there. She moved to the side of the compartment and found a small fire extinguisher on the left. That might be useful too, if just for the surprise factor when she shot it in someone's face. Or she could use it as a propellant in zero-g.

She spun her body slowly to peer up into the top of the compartment. "Ah-ha!" As suspected. No mercenary wanted to be unarmed, especially in an emergency. Grinning widely, she pulled the small stunner out of the charging clips, the status light shining green. An older model, good for just one or two shots, but that was all she needed—if there were more than one or two people around when they let her out, escape would be almost impossible anyway. She gripped the stunner firmly, the relief of being armed bringing a sense of intense optimism. With this, she had a fighting chance against those rad-blasted egg eaters.

Saree grabbed the first aid kit, opening it slowly. The normal bandages, clotting agents, analgesics, scissors, and ointments, along with a tourniquet, met her eyes. Pulling a couple of the mild analgesics, she downed them with another sip of water, praying it stopped the pounding in her head.

Carefully digging deeper, keeping everything in the bag so it didn't float away, she pawed through the kit. There'd be more in a mercenary first aid kit than a civilian kit. A second, larger tourniquet, burn pads, and yes, auto-injector drugs. She smiled, thinking about jabbing Vulten. One auto-injector for allergic reactions, one for pain, and one for knocking someone out. *Hah.* She pulled the knockout drug, and on second thought, the pain injector too, putting both in her suit utility pocket.

Now, she'd prepare herself for escape. She needed to secure her weapons so they wouldn't float away in zero-g *and* for easy access in all gravity conditions. Looking at the available materials, the gripper straps seemed like the obvious answer—there were two full sets. She only needed one, if that.

Using the shears from the first aid kit, she sliced the extra straps off the padded bulkhead in front of her, and one strap into thinner strips. With the surgical glue, she fastened two short strips of the soft side of the gripper around her left arm, midway between her shoulder and elbow, where her bicep would hold it in place. Using more surgical glue, she made a quick-pull tab on the matching rough-sided strips and used those to fasten the knockout and pain auto-injectors to her arm, so she could rip them off—fast.

Using most of the remaining strips and almost all of the glue, she created a harness to fasten the fire extinguisher to her back— when she fired it, it should propel her more or less forward. At least she hoped she had it at her center of mass—the canister pressed into her lower back and the nozzle into her butt cheeks. A giant fart, actually. She laughed out loud, ignoring her slightly hysterical tone.

Using more gripper strips and the last of the glue, she fashioned a quick-draw holster for the small stunner for her right wrist and hand. When she straightened her fingers, the stunner slapped into her palm. She could close her thumb and fingers around it securely to fire or use her left hand to press the firing button. Saree practiced over and over, developing speed and dexterity, the movement chillingly similar to practicing a guitar riff. She did the same with the auto-injectors until her fingertips were sore from the rough gripper tape backing.

Okay, so that was all she could do for now. She should rest. Saree hooked herself back up against the wall with the waist strap and put her toes into the ankle strap. Blast it, she been hoping she'd be picked up by now. She sipped some more water, grateful the pills and rehydration reduced the pounding in her head, although an ache lingered. She was ready, but there was nobody to be ready for. Not yet. Without weapon practice to distract her, the escape pod was looking awfully small, and the bright orange padding didn't help.

Forcing herself to stop examining the pod, Saree contemplated her options. She should sleep. If she slept, her body would heal faster. If she were healthier, she'd be faster, physically and mentally, and ready to act. She nodded. Decision made.

But if she was going to sleep, she should be ready for the worst. If the pod lost air pressure, she had to act quickly. Pulling her Scholar's outer robe off, she shoved it into the suit compartment so she wouldn't get tangled in it. It provided some warmth, but the bulk inside the suit would slow her down. Pulling the suit on, she realized she'd rigged her weapons for atmosphere, not for use in the suit. Blast it all to a black hole—that was stupid. Taking the auto-injectors off her arm and the wrist/hand contraption off too, Saree examined them carefully. They might fit over her suit, or she'd fasten the stunner wrist strap, leaving the finger straps loose. That should be good enough.

Leaving the weapons to float in front of her, she finished pulling the suit on all the way, including her head, leaving the face shield unlatched. Fastening the face shield started the O2 generator, and she didn't need it—yet. Grasping the auto-injectors, she fastened them back across her bicep, but loosely so they didn't interfere with the air flow of the suit. Good thing she'd left those strips long. She fastened the stunner wrist strap—it barely fit. She'd have to move cautiously, but with a soft-suit, she'd be careful no matter what. Fortunately, she had rigged the fire extinguisher over her suit. She was as ready as possible. She needed some sleep—obviously she wasn't thinking clearly. Sleep would help.

Saree tried to relax, floating in the straps, but she was so uncomfortable. Her headache was fading, but she was cold and shaky, and there was too much running in her head. Too many scenarios of rescue and capture, too many grim thoughts of spinning away, too far for anyone to find. Blast. She wasn't going to just fall asleep. She sighed, the sound echoing in the tiny pod.

Deliberately, she started her ^*timespace*^ meditation sequence. Saree knew, from experience, that a major change in her surroundings would jolt her out of ^*timespace*^ fast, too fast— she'd end up with another killer headache. When she pushed herself out, she was initially disoriented, but not in pain. Natural or forced exit, real rest and healing would be worth the price. Nodding, she set her internal alarm for eight hours—planning on a full rest period, even if she might not get it. If she rested the full cycle, she'd be at maximum efficiency and effectiveness. Meditation also saved a lot of oxygen. She breathed and slid into the peace and beauty of ^*timespace*^.

CHAPTER EIGHTEEN

The attack klaxon clanged, jolting Ruhger in his seat. The fold equations disappeared, and he focused on the defensive display. Shields were 100%, no damage, no breaches. At current attack power, the shields would hold indefinitely. He swept up the wide-area surveillance display.

Whatever was attacking them was dead—they just didn't know it yet.

An in-system asteroid miner fired at them. *Just one? Idiots.* He sent a live feed, plus the last twenty seconds and a short message—unprovoked attack, defending and counter-attacking—to the Cygnus Prime authorities using a high-power pin beam. He watched the comm status for a few seconds—no interference detected. He snorted in derision. This rad-blasted idiot didn't even have the brains to block comms.

"Target acquired, Captain," Tyron's voice said calmly.

"Fire," Ruhger said equally calmly. He watched the perfect hit splash against shields. "Fire for effect. Chief, ready torpedoes."

"Torpedoes ready; target acquired, Captain."

"Fire."

"One minute, ten seconds to impact, Captain."

Tyron's laser beam, a broad beam to define the limits of the miner's shields, narrowed to a piercing lance. The shields sagged, a clear depression where the laser hit, then the hole gradually smoothed into a continuous sphere. Tyron kept firing a narrow beam, splashing against the shields. Ruhger growled. The universe was filled with idiots. No intelligent being should bring a single ship up against a folder, no matter how good their weapons or shields. Folders had far more power and their shields were always up, unless a shuttle was docking. The miner was space dust—Ruhger glanced at the running clock—in fifty-four seconds to be exact.

Enough time to make an announcement. Ruhger opened shipwide comms. "Passengers, this is the Captain. We are under attack and are counter-attacking. This is not a drill. Return to your shuttles or enter an escape pod immediately. Do not eject from Lightwave; our shields are good and will continue to hold. You will be informed when you may reenter Lightwave. I repeat, this is not a drill. Captain out." He closed the shipwide, making sure his comms with the crew remained open.

Filtering some of the visual effects of the laser, Ruhger frowned. The salvo of not one, but five torpedoes sped into the wide-area surveillance view, only one of them aimed for the shielded area the laser targeted. That torpedo was bigger and slower than the others, using an older chemical thruster showing up well on vid and IR. The others swung wide, using modern, less-obvious thrusters. Ruhger's grin widened as the laser continued to splash harmlessly against the miner's shield. Poor fool had no idea what was going to hit him.

Ruhger kept an eye on the wide-area surveillance while the timer counted down—he didn't want to be caught by a sneak attack. There was still a fold transport at Fold Hold Point Alpha, too far away to attack them right now, but nothing else. Just in case, he increased the sensor alert sensitivity. They didn't know who was attacking or what other resources they had. Lightwave must be ready for anything and everything. There could be another ship out there, one with expensive cloaking shields. And miners had powerful cutters. He couldn't afford to be over-confident.

The seconds counted down. The wide-area surveillance tracked their torpedoes—the four going wide maneuvering with compressed gas thrusters, cool in comparison to the hot chemical thruster, turning toward the miner from all directions. Chief's voice said, "Five seconds to impact. Four, three, two..."

The big torpedo hit the front shield and exploded harmlessly. Less than a half a second later, a bright flash, the miner exploded into dust, the comms rang with roars of triumph and Tyron turned off the laser. The coordinated attack worked perfectly—the idiot put all his shielding up front and they got him from every other side.

Ruhger shook his head. "Five was a little overkill, wasn't it, Chief?" he said dryly.

"Not if the miner had upgraded shields, Captain. Which was logical; why would a miner go against an armed fold transport without upgraded shields? That would be foolish."

Greedy people were often foolish. "True."

"Oh, he wanted to play with his toys," Katryn said. "Boys always do. But Captain, this was a *coordinated* attack. Just before the attack klaxon, I lost all sensors in the phys mod. I have no contact with the Scholar's shuttle or Vulten's. I do have contact with the medico shuttle, but not through Lightwave; I've had to route around through docking frequency comms. I've played back the last minute before I lost the phys mod—the Scholar entered just before the attack. I'm looking further back right now to see if someone else was in there."

"Captain, Lowe. Loreli and I are hard-suited and ready for a security sweep."

Loreli was going to help in a security sweep? Huh. He…*she* did have the training and Lowe was good. Loreli must have run for the crew quarters when the klaxon sounded—the emergency protocols automatically shut down cooking surfaces in the kitchen. "Lowe, start security sweep. I'll watch the vids ahead of you, but use all caution. You know vids can be spoofed or blocked."

Bringing up Lightwave's internal map, he tied a vid view screen to Lowe's suit locator, splitting the view into four so he could see all the vids near Lowe. The two ceiling-mounted vids in the crew quarters passageway came alive, showing Lowe and Loreli in suits, green and orange respectively, weapons in hand. They strode down the corridor and waited at the first ladder. Ruhger switched to the vids below them. Nothing. He said, "Ladder and landing clear." Thank all the suns for their childhood training—if they were a regular folder crew, the hatch to the passenger areas might be unsecured.

Lowe sent a remote flying ahead of him, then he and Loreli

stepped down the ladder, weapons ready. Ruhger brought up the cameras in the main passageway. "Lowe, passageway appears clear." He quickly scanned through all the vids. "All areas *appear* clear."

"Captain, phys mod first or the other way?" Lowe asked.

"Clear from the ready room toward the phys mod. We don't need any surprises from behind."

"Copy that," Lowe said, opening the hatch. The remote flew out. Lowe and Loreli followed with weapons up and ready, steps smooth, sweeping toward the ready room, Loreli moving back to back with Lowe. They moved along in concert, far smoother than he had any right to expect—early lessons stuck. Lowe opened the hatch—all the pressure hatches operated properly, closing and locking when the attack alert rang. They stepped into the ready room. Lowe examined and inspected the furnishings, Loreli guarding Lowe's back.

"Captain, I'm suited up and can assist," Chief said.

Before he could answer, Tyron said, "Me too. Katryn's still searching vid and running deep net checks."

Ruhger weighed the risks. With no further threat from space, he and Katryn could handle the ship. "Copy. Chief, Tyron, you two take the kitchen. Lowe, Loreli, when you're done in the ready room, clear the chow hall, then all of you clear the phys mod together. Katryn continues net security. I've got overwatch on the vid. Objections or holdouts?" There was silence. "Execute."

Lowe and Loreli continued clearing the big ready room, while Chief and Tyron met at a crew access hatch and launched another surveillance remote. Ruhger brought up the kitchen and chow hall vid. "Kitchen and chow hall appear clear."

Moving with caution, weapons ready, Chief and Tyron moved down the passageway and entered the kitchen. They were smoother and faster than Lowe and Loreli, as they should be. They secured the kitchen hatch behind them, and split to clear the room. A little riskier approach but warranted in the current circumstances. If Katryn had been warning of net intrusions, Ruhger would have ordered them to go back to back too. Lowe and Loreli finished the ready room and moved to the chow hall. All four gathered in the chow hall, and walked in proper stick formation to the phys mod hatch.

"The cameras and comms in the phys mod are down, so it's up to you guys," Katryn said, the tension clear in her voice. "Vulten and Schultz entered the phys mod about ten minutes before the Scholar. They were carrying medium-sized duffle bags. Two minutes before the Scholar walks out of the chow hall, the hatches to the phys mod were manually closed, the sensors went black, and we lost all comms with the mod and the shuttles on that end. Ninety seconds after that, the miner attacked. Vulten's shuttle is opposite the Scholar's, the medicos' between them on the end."

Tyron took point, with Chief behind him, Lowe next and Loreli bringing up the rear guard. Tyron said, "I'll send my remote toward the Scholar's shuttle entrance; Lowe, you send yours toward Vulten's shuttle entrance. Let's make this a thorough scan before we move in." He pressed the hatch release, but nothing happened. Lowe spun the manual opener, pushed the hatch in, and both remotes sped through. The four of them stayed out of the open hatchway, their backs pressed up against the walls. Tyron and Lowe's weapons were aimed at the hatch, Loreli and Chief's at the passage.

Ruhger waited, sweeping through the vids of the passenger areas behind his crew. Loreli and Chief were watching, but they couldn't see beyond the chow hall. Nothing moved.

Finally, Tyron said, "Clear. But the vid is breaking up. There could be some sort of comm blocker or interference generator. Among other things."

Lowe echoed, "Clear. Same problem."

Tyron continued, "Here's the plan. The phys mod appears clear, but we can't be positive because of the poor vid quality. We reset the remotes to do a slow sweep for explosives and chemical agents. While they're sweeping, we enter, do a visual sweep of the entire mod from inside the hatch. Loreli, you've got our six. Then we split back into teams. I'll take the Scholar's side with Chief; Lowe, you and Loreli have Vulten's. Loreli, secure the hatch behind us, manually—the electronics aren't working. We meet back up at the exit to the medicos' airlock. Objections?"

There was silence. Ruhger swept up Lowe and Tyron's helmet vids.

"Hold," Katryn said. "There's definitely some sort of comms interference generator in there. I've cleared all the net traps, but there's something physically generating interference. Look for a small box, possibly with an antenna or two on it. We should be able to hear you because I've rerouted our comms to a different frequency, but the vid may break up a bit."

Tyron answered, "Copy. Other objections?" A few seconds, and he said, "Execute."

They entered the phys mod one at a time, moving to stand against the wall to either side of the hatch, and scanned the area. It appeared empty of humans or anything but phys equipment.

Tyron gestured, and they walked slowly forward. All of them moved smoothly and quickly, surveying everything in the phys mod, weapons up and ready. All the hatch status lights were out, surrounded by scorch marks. The electronics were blown. Tyron opened the hatch to the passageway on the medicos' end, and the remotes flew through. The teams split up and moved down the passageway in opposite directions. Tyron stopped in front of a bod-pod, the status light red. Probably because it wasn't energized when everything else was blown. "Captain, a bod-pod's been ejected. Katryn, is there any way to know if someone was in it?"

"No. And the shrieker's not showing on the net. Wait…there was a shrieker, but it's gone now. Might be out of range, or out of juice, although neither seems likely."

Blast it to a black hole and back. Ruhger brought up the near-range scanners. "Nothing showing on the close scan, but it's not tuned for non-shrieking bod-pods. Readjusting sensitivity parameters now." He adjusted and set a general search. He'd refine the search pattern when they were done. Right now, his people were more important.

The teams continued down the passageway, opening emergency pressure walls as they went. "Captain, Vulten's shuttle appears to be gone," Lowe said grimly, looking at the red status light on the airlock. The vid was breaking up, but Ruhger could still see enough. "We're hard-suited, so we could go through and check."

"Negative. Back to Tyron. When we're done, we'll send a remote to check. Don't want to trigger any surprises they may have left for us. Find that interference generator."

"Copy."

"Captain, the Scholar's shuttle status is unknown; the electronics on our side appear to be dead."

"Katryn, can you reach her shuttle the way you did the medicos'?"

"I've tried, Captain. I get an automated response making me think the shuttle is still there, but the Scholar is unable to reach the comms or not there." Her voice grew annoyed. "For a Scholar, her shuttle has formidable net defenses. I don't recommend attempting to circumvent them or the physical security—as a single human female, she probably has some extreme failsafe measures; I would. Besides, I think she's in the bod-pod."

"As do I. Katryn, do you have any vid of the exterior where the pod blew? Or was that offline too?"

"Checking, Captain."

"Captain, Tyron. Found a box. I think it's the generator." Tyron's voice was almost lost in static and Ruhger couldn't see anything from Tyron's vid, so it probably was. "Team, exit the phys mod. I'm going to turn it off and throw it, just in case there's an explosive in this thing."

"Tyron, we could get a containment vessel," Chief said.

"Negative. This is just a precaution. I don't think this is anything but electronics—my suit doesn't show any explosives. And neither remote has picked up any explosives or chemicals. Hold on." A static-filled hiss, then a metallic snap. Tyron said, "I opened the side of it—there's nothing but electronics in here, scan and vid. Captain?"

"I trust your judgment, Tyron. Execute."

Tyron's vid cleared, showing a grainy view of a small object arcing away and shattering against the phys mod wall, the vid now crystal clear. Obviously Tyron was correct.

"Blast it all to the seven suns of Saga!" Katryn broke in. "We have exterior vids all around Lightwave, but the vids nearest the bod-pod are clouded and hazy. Status shows they are performing correctly, but we can't see anything. Probably a substance sprayed on the sensors physically. But... wait..." A long pause. "Hah. Missed one, didn't you, mud-sucker? It's not a good view, but I can see the pod after it releases from Lightwave. The sensor is on the Scholar's side, rather than on the end where the pod was."

Kind of funny how fast Katryn picked up space slang when she'd been a mudhugger not all that long ago.

"What about the medicos' external sensors? Do they have anything?" Chief said.

"Good thought. I'll check."

"Crew, head back to your duty stations. I'll pull us off full attack alert, but leave us at the caution stage. You can take off the helmets. Stay alert. I'll tell the passengers to remain in their shuttles until we figure out where the Scholar is. I've traced Vulten—they're headed out-lane, probably for the folder at Hold Point Alpha. I've also alerted the local authorities—Lowe, when you're back, it's your job to handle them and the passenger inquiries. Chief, I want you looking at the bod-pod vid and see if the impulse looks standard so we can work the math to find it, assuming it wasn't picked up by Vulten. Tyron, you get a remote scanning the empty shuttle bay, then check all the others, starting with the medicos' and going around from there. Make absolutely sure they didn't leave us any surprises. I'll see if I can access Vulten's and the Scholar's airlock vids. Loreli, you finish dinner, but secure the kitchen hatches and keep your suit close. By the time we finish all this, we'll need to eat. Objections or holdouts?"

There was silence on the comms. "Good, execute. Let me know your results or a status in fifteen mikes. Except you, Loreli—you make dinner and let us know a revised time."

Loreli said, "Of course, mine Cap-i-tan. Expect at least a thirty-minute delay since those—those...nickel lovers caused me to leave a sauce at a critical point. It will be ruined beyond recovery, and I must have that sauce, or the whole theme is ruined!"

Relieved chuckles came across the comms for a moment, then silence. Ruhger checked both airlocks—no working vids; they'd been blown—and sent a message for Tyron to check Vulten's airlock with the remote from the outside. He swept off all the other vids and pulled up the bod-pod search he'd been running. Nothing. But those things were a lot easier to find with the shrieker active... Ruhger considered the wider surveillance view. Vulten was blasting away at top speed, and the folder at Hold Point Alpha was still there, but showing signs of engine heating. They must be picking up Vulten. Good riddance.

Unless they had the Scholar. He closed his eyes for a moment. That would explain why he couldn't find the pod. If they had her...blast and rad.

They could go get her, but was that their job?

Technically, he was sure it wasn't. Morally? It was. Especially if they couldn't prove she was alive or dead—it was the same as responding to a distress code or an organic mass in an abandoned pod. They had a duty to save lives.

He shook his head. Right now, a moot point. He pulled up the vid Katryn found. All of one point two seconds of the pod, not enough to tell whether the boost was normal or not. Great.

"Captain?" Katryn asked, her tone oddly tentative.

"Go, Katryn."

"Captain, I've accessed—or been given access, I'm not sure which—to the Scholar's exterior shuttle vid recordings. I've got a much better shot of the pod jettison from the far end of the Scholar's shuttle. I've sent the link to you."

"Thanks, Katryn. That will help. This tiny vid we've got now was no help at all. Not enough time on screen to make a good calculation from."

He'd better make one more announcement before turning the passengers over to Lowe. He swept open the shipwide. "Passengers, this is the Captain. We apologize for the delay and the difficulties. We were attacked without provocation or warning by a mining ship, which has now been destroyed. At the same time, Lady Vulten's shuttle departed, and a b...an escape capsule was ejected from Lightwave. We have reason to believe Scholar Sessan may be in the escape capsule. We are attempting to pick it up, which may take some time."

He'd better not mention they couldn't find it; he didn't need passengers worried about faulty equipment. Especially when they maintained everything meticulously—enemy action was the issue. "Because of this, our arrival at the shuttle departure point will be slightly delayed, and our constellation arrival dinner will also be delayed, but not canceled. The exact length of those delays is currently unknown. Please remain in your shuttles until further notice. We apologize for the inconvenience. Please direct queries electronically to Purser Lowe. Do not contact Lightwave by voice or vid unless there is an emergency. Thank you. Captain Ruhger out." Good enough. They were Lowe's problem now.

He pulled up the vids Katryn saved. Excellent. A much longer time frame with a time stamp. Now he could calculate the distance in this vid. He pulled up the metadata of the vid for the camera data rate and pixels; from the metadata and the visible portion of Lightwave, he could figure out the—

"Chief Bhoher for the Captain," the annunciator said.

"Accept, add all crew. What do you have, Chief?"

"I have a projected trajectory of the escape pod, Captain. It does not appear to have an extra impulse or a skewed trajectory. My calculations and a projection of the trajectory are in the shared folder called Escape Pod Tracking."

"How did you do that so fast, Chief?"

"I didn't use the video. Lightwave's velocity, direction, and mass are recorded at all times, so I compared the velocity, direction, and mass before the pod ejection and after. As you know, every action has an equal and opposite reaction, so I calculated the difference in Lightwave's and reversed it to get the pod's, ignoring such small perturbations such as solar wind, since the timeframe is too short for those effects. The correct time sample was critical, because Lady Vulten's shuttle took off shortly after the escape pod. I've put her trajectory on the projection as well, and it intersects with the pod. There's a high probability they picked up the pod."

"Huh. You know, Chief, I'm pretty sure we don't pay you enough." Ruhger huffed a chuckle. The man was brilliant, if oblivious to normal human interaction sometimes.

"It was a simple calculation. I can't believe that would be sufficient to raise my salary, but if you want to…"

"I wish I could, Chief." Ruhger shook his head ruefully and chuckled. "I really do wish I could." Bringing himself back to the problem at hand, he pulled up Chief's projections. "It does look like they captured the pod." He refined his search area—no indication of a pod. "There's nothing in the search area..." he widened it in the direction it would have been traveling "—and nothing for three sigma beyond the search area. They picked it up. Now the question is, what do we do about it?"

"Why would we do anything, Captain? This isn't a case of piracy. This is a case for local law enforcement. Interstellar after they fold out."

"Really, Chief? What little reputation we have is built on the fact that we take care of our passengers, they *always* arrive safely, in one piece. Suppose we let her get taken, allowing kidnapping and piracy on *our* transport. It only takes one instance, and there goes our rep, right down into the giant black hole of Andromeda. What next? What do we do with her shuttle? Dumping the shuttle in-system will make other folders pretty unhappy with the nav hazard. Katryn says we can't break into it, so we can't take it and sell it. Take it back to Centauri University? Oh, sure, like we need to show our faces there. Leave it in orbit here for the University to pick up? None of these are good solutions."

He calculated intercept trajectories but kept talking. "We have a contract, one that specifies safe delivery. We have an obligation. And I wouldn't care if the Scholar had taken Vulten—either way, we have a duty." Ruhger clamped his mouth shut. He probably wasn't doing his cause any favors by ranting on, and from his heavy breathing, he was a little too involved, emotionally.

"As much as I hate to admit it, he's right," Lowe said. "Our net signature is iffy, partially because we keep it quiet. But what we do have is built on a reputation for safety and full execution of our contract."

"'Execution' might not be the best word choice, Grant," Katryn said dryly. "But I agree. If it hadn't been for Tyron, I wouldn't have looked twice at Lightwave. What's out there is too iffy for a single, female human to take a chance on. The Scholar must have been pretty desperate to leave Dronteim to fold with us."

"And that's my point. If we do nothing, a good part of our problem goes away," Chief said. "We don't have an obligation to act as an armed military force, and that's what it will take to get her back."

"I've notified the system authorities. They have no one close enough to act before Vulten folds out—assuming she's heading for the folder at Hold Point Alpha. It's us or nobody. Our reputation and our contract say we go—this is piracy. But we can go smartly and cautiously. We've already decelerated to fight the miner. We'll head Lightwave back to the fold point but take Alpha shuttle ahead. It's sufficiently armed to threaten Vulten's shuttle and that ancient folder out there. I'll take Tyron and Katryn with me. Chief, you're in command of Lightwave; Lowe, you're second. Phazeers, wear hard-suits, obviously. That's my decision as Captain. Objections to assignments?" There was silence on the comms. Chief never argued once the decision was made. "Good. Execute."

"Captain, we'll be there in less than five," Tyron said.

Scowling, Ruhger ran shuttle departure checks. They'd wasted far too much time arguing for no reason whatsoever. Chief was a real asset, but sometimes he blasted more rads than a supernova.

Standing, Ruhger ran through a few quick, energizing y'ga moves and stowed the detritus of normal life he had loose in the shuttle, and suited up, except the helmet. The hatch buzzed; he let Tyron and Katryn in. They fastened into the co-pilot and weapons positions respectively, without comment. Working with these two in an emergency was easy—they knew what to do and did it.

"Crosscheck, Lightwave," he snapped out.

"Crosscheck good, Captain—you're clear to launch," Lowe's voice said. "Good luck."

"Lightwave Beta shuttle, Chief Bhoher, you have command. Make sure you complete the exterior scans of Lightwave."

"Command accepted. I've taken the exterior sweep over from Tyron already," Chief said. "Good luck."

"Launching in five, four, three, two, launch." Ruhger energized the Alpha shuttle launch sequence and rechecked the trajectory.

"Intercept trajectory is good, Captain," Tyron said quietly. "Intercept in three hours, twelve minutes. It might be tricky, depending on what the folder out there is carrying—we'll be closer to it than I'd like."

"I'm attempting a net infiltration of Vulten's shuttle and the folder," Katryn said. "I believe Vulten's shuttle is unarmed, but the folder might be hiding something."

"Katryn, give me Vulten's shuttle. You take the folder, at least until we're closer to intercept," Tyron said. "The Captain can fly."

Yes, I can. Nobody can outfly me. Ruhger barred his teeth and readied his battle plan.

CHAPTER NINETEEN

Saree gasped at the sharp pain lancing between her temples and slammed her eyes shut. What woke her? The pod lurched, and she bounced. The pod was moving, that's what woke her. Suns, her head hurt. But she had to be ready. Heart rate picking up, she pulled the knockout drug from her shoulder harness and put it in her left hand, and grasped the stunner in her right. Ready.

Wait, she could end up in full gravity. Saree pulled her feet out of the toe strap and pushed herself to the bottom of the pod, putting her right foot on the bottom and bracing herself against the far wall with her left leg. This wasn't a comfortable position to hold, but it would put her in the best position to launch an attack. She glanced around the pod. If she was brought in head up—she could only hope they followed convention. She checked the status lights—no change.

The pod jolted again—she was pressed back into the padding, under hard acceleration. Another jolt, zero-g—ooff. Saree slammed into the pod on her left side, bouncing around as the pod rolled—she tried to relax into the roll. Blast it all, she should have stayed strapped in—she'd have more bruises. As the pod slowed, she stiffened a leg and braced herself with her right arm to hold herself in place. She came to a halt lying on her left side and gasped in relief. After a few seconds, she refocused— immediate attack was critical; she'd have the element of surprise once. She had to be ready.

Saree relaxed her arms and legs, shaking them out, then rearranged herself to launch out of the capsule when the hatch was released. She visualized the steps—launch out and away, stunner going, then knock-out drug to anyone not caught by the stunner beam. If everyone in the area was down, pull their weapons, make her way to the hatch and take over the shuttle or whatever she was on. It was as good a plan as any. Or as good as she could think of with pain lancing between her temples like an electric arc.

"Saree? Can you hear me?" Hal said quietly.

"Hal! Yes, I can hear you!" She wasn't alone. Oh, thank the egg of Zarar and all the suns, she wasn't alone. Relief caused her to sag for a split second.

"What is your status, Saree?"

"I'm alive and well, Hal. I am ready to attack with a stunner and an auto-injector of knock-out drug."

"Lady Vulten pulled your escape pod into her shuttle cargo bay. She was towing it with the shuttle's tractor beam, but they decelerated enough to take it inside. I have separated from Lightwave, as has Lightwave's Alpha shuttle. We are on an intercept course. Lightwave doesn't realize I'm here, but they will if I have to use weapons or come in to pick you up."

Lightwave came after her too? This was far better than anything she'd hoped for. "My plan is to attack whoever lets me out of the pod, then take over the shuttle." She swallowed hard and tried to wet her lips. "If they're smart, they will try to stun me when they let me out."

"Or they will leave you in the pod. I'm attempting to infiltrate Lady Vulten's net, but their defenses are surprisingly good. Katryn is launching outright net attacks from the Alpha shuttle, so I'm trying backdoors while they're distracted. If I can get in, I will find where you are and check for defenses and traps, then you can get out on your own."

"There's definitely no atmosphere outside the pod, Hal."

"Are you in a suit?"

Saree laughed. "Oh, yes, I am. I'd almost forgotten. I just need to fasten up the hood. It's one of those single-use suits, so I don't think of it as a real suit; I'm too used to my shielded suit. And I'm a little fuzzy right now; I was in ^timespace^. And they drugged me. My mouth is so dry."

"Saree, there should be water pouches in the pod. Have you looked?" Hal asked.

"Oh, yeah, there are. Thanks, Hal." A tiny push down, then a hand stopping her on the compartment, she pulled it open and fished out one of the water packs, sipping it gratefully. She'd forgotten about the water too. Coming out of ^timespace^ abruptly disrupted her normal thought processes. The knives stabbing into her temples didn't help either. She surveyed herself and the pod to refamiliarize herself with her surroundings. Water packs, first aid kit stowed, Scholar robe stowed. She refastened the compartment.

"You are welcome, Saree. I know you are not at your best when pulled out of ^timespace^ abruptly. Do you need a briefing?"

"No, I think I'm back to normal, Hal, except a killer headache. Nothing to be done about that one, though; pain pills won't help."

"Understood, Saree. I will continue. I've infiltrated Lady Vulten's shuttle vid system. She and Elise Schultz are in the pilot and co-pilot's seats respectively. There does not appear to be anyone else in the shuttle. Schultz is looking at the vid of your pod occasionally, but I can loop a recording, to hide what you do. But they will know if you cycle the airlock, which you will have to do to get into the shuttle. I'm attempting to infiltrate that system, but it's a life support function and therefore well protected. Still, I believe you would be better off if you were up and mobile, even in the soft-suit. You should have at least two hours of air, correct?"

"Yes, as long as the suit is working correctly. I'll button it up and check." Securing the face shield, Saree checked all the other connections and was reassured by the green status light. "It appears to be working correctly, Hal." She was breathing — hopefully she'd keep doing so.

"Very good. Are you going to get out?"

"Yes. Just tell me when."

"I have the looped recording in place now. You may exit at any time."

"Thank you, Hal."

"You are welcome, Saree. I will attempt to infiltrate from the vid system to the life support system, but I cannot guarantee I will be able to do so. Saree, Vulten and Schultz are armed with stunners and laser pistols, so proceed with extreme caution."

"Thank you, Hal. I will." Saree pushed the exit button on the pod hatch and watched it swing out and away. Sitting up, she surveyed her surroundings. She was in a small cargo bay, with dark gray plas tiles and bare cerimetal walls, the exterior walls filled with the usual water storage pods. A few large gray plas crates marked 'live vegetation' were secured to the floor along the opposite wall. Must be the Thymdronteim they were so proud of. Saree spitefully hoped it died in the vacuum when they pulled her in, but they were probably pressurized 'live cargo' crates.

Saree climbed out of the pod, manuevering cautiously to avoid snagging her too-big suit on the edges of the pod hatch, and walked to the cargo bay wall. She headed to the airlock, keeping a hand on the wall holds in case the gravity was cut, and to avoid being seen. She didn't want to be spotted if one of them looked through the small window in the cargo bay airlock. Oh, wait. Turning back, she closed the pod hatch. No sense staying close to the wall if the pod was obviously empty.

"Hal, are you close enough to launch a physical attack?"

"Not an effective one, no. We will be in range in approximately five point two minutes. Vulten's deceleration to capture the pod allowed us to close the gap, but we are still far behind. Currently, we will be in range two minutes before Lady Vulten is in the projected range of the fold transport which has left Hold Point Alpha, presumably en route to pick up Lady Vulten. If it is armed, it will have a greater range and more powerful weapons than Lightwave's Alpha shuttle."

"So, a distraction thirty seconds before Alpha shuttle attacks would be ideal, correct?"

"Yes. How do you propose to do that, Saree?"

She grinned. "I'll start the hold air cycle, in emergency mode if there is one. That will draw one of them, probably Schultz, over to the hatch. Then, they'll have to decide between the internal and external threats. My guess is one of them will handle the external and the other will go to the airlock. If we can time it right, the airlock hatch should open at the same time as the first attack. I'll hang from the ceiling and stun her when she sticks her head in the hatch." Saree frowned. "Unless they're wearing hard-suits."

"No, they are not. They are not wearing suits at all, which seems foolhardy, Saree."

She grinned again. "Yes, it is. Ha!" Lightwave sent a shuttle after her, but what would they do? "Hal, will Lightwave fire? If they're worried about hitting me, they might not."

"I am monitoring their comms. They have a plan of attack. They are targeting Lady Vulten's engines with narrow-focus laser beams to disable them and the maneuvering jets, so they can't adjust course. There is a chance they could blow up one of the engines, but it's fairly low."

"Well, that's reassuring, I guess. Still, I'd rather be blown to bits than be a slave." Hmm, with Hal and Lightwave here, they should coordinate. "Hal, since you're listening to Lightwave, can you patch me through to them directly?"

"Oh. That is a good idea, Saree. I can. They may be able to tell I'm relaying, in which case they'll know I am here. They'll probably deduce that soon anyway. I have the correct link, Saree. I can still talk to you, they will not hear me, but you won't be able to talk to me without them hearing; I can't adjust this link adequately. It's voice only, no vid."

"Copy that, Hal. I think the risk is worth it."

"Yes, I agree. Go ahead, Saree."

"Scholar Sessan to Lightwave." She fastened the knock-out drug back on her shoulder.

"Scholar! You are alive. Are you well?" Captain Ruhger said, surprised relief clear.

"Yes. I am in a cargo hold, in a soft-suit. I have a stunner and an auto-injector of knock-out drug. Are you anywhere nearby?"

"We are attempting an intercept, Scholar, in our Alpha shuttle. We will be in firing range in forty-four seconds. We are trying to disable the engines and maneuvering jets."

"Would you like a distraction, Captain?" He didn't answer immediately, and Saree could picture the look of surprise on his face. Hopefully, he was impressed, too.

"Certainly, if you can do so safely."

"I'll start the emergency pressurization cycle. I doubt they thought to secure it."

Captain Ruhger barked out a laugh, and Saree could hear a male and female voice laughing, probably the Phazeers. "Excellent idea, Scholar. Now would be good."

"Executing." Saree selected the 'emergency pressure' option on the control panel and swiped the large flashing button. Air blasted. She climbed the hand holds next to the airlock hatch, grinning—fortunately, the vents were on the walls to either side of her, so she wasn't being pummeled directly by the air whooshing into the hold.

Even so, the blasting air caught the extra material on her suit, causing pockets to billow like sails and make climbing difficult, but she made it. Hooking her toes in the top wall hold, and latching her left hand through a ceiling hand hold, she hung above the hatch.

Holding this position wasn't easy, but she was strong, and it wouldn't be much longer. The cycle finished, and the hatch swung into the hold with explosive speed. Gray hair showed, then disappeared. Schultz was cautious. Saree smirked. Hair appeared, withdrew.

"They're firing at us!" Lady Vulten's voice screamed.

"Our shields will hold. Just keep going—we'll meet the folder in two minutes," Schultz yelled. "I've got to secure our cargo."

A hand with a large stunner appeared, then Schultz's head, turning from one side to the other. Finally, she stepped in. Saree fired straight down on her head, grinning fiercely. Schultz dropped to the floor with a thud and pop from the plas tiles. Fortunately, she fell off to the side; she couldn't be seen from inside the shuttle.

Saree grinned wider. Hah. One down, one to go. She climbed down and pulled Schultz all the way into the bay. Taking the flex cuffs from her lax hand, Saree fastened them around Schultz's wrists and ankles, making sure they were tight.

"Our shields are down to twenty percent, Elise! We're not going to make it to the folder."

Blast it. She had to act now. Pulling the heavier stunner and laser pistol off Schultz's body, Saree ducked into the shuttle, running full speed toward the pilot's seat.

"Elise! Ten percent! What do we do?!"

Saree fired the stunner. "You get knocked out, that's what, Lady Vulten." Vulten slumped to the side, held in the seat by the safety harness. At least she'd been smart enough to web herself in.

Saree swiped the engines to zero thrust. "Lightwave, I'm in command of Vulten's shuttle. What now?" She breathed a sigh of relief when the flashing red shield warning stopped flashing, and the numbers climbed.

"Well, Scholar, that's a good question," Captain Ruhger said. "You could fly the shuttle back to Lightwave and turn the women over to the planetary authorities for kidnapping and piracy."

"Shuttle Thymdronteim One, this is Fold Transport Speedfold. Are you ready for pickup?" a male voice said over the shuttle comms.

"Or you could leave the shuttle there, let them get picked up and get their just rewards from whatever entity they sold you to. You can step out of the cargo bay, and we'll pick you up," Katryn said, satisfaction clear in her voice. "It would be a lot less hassle for you and for us in the long run."

"Oh, I like the way you think. It would be evil if it wasn't such perfect justice," Saree told her admiringly.

Chuckles from the men were accompanied by Katryn's deliberately evil cackle. Saree unfastened her face shield and swept up the shuttle comms link, voice only, to the folder. "Sorry about the delay, Speedfold. We were securing cargo. We are ready. Give me a few seconds to turn my controls over to you." She closed the comms, and set the shuttle for remote control. The shuttle lurched as the folder took control.

Saree ran for the cargo bay and dragged Schultz back inside, bumping her head on the hatch thresholds in her hurry. Somehow, she couldn't find it in her heart to be sorry about the bruises. Or a concussion. Refastening her face shield, she checked the suit status twice and secured the cargo bay airlock.

"Lightwave Shuttle Alpha, evacuating cargo bay now. Please catch me." She swiped through to the emergency evacuation protocol and hit the flashing red execute button. The bay door slammed open, and the blast of air escaping shot her out of the bay like water out of a high-pressure hose.

Suns! Saree slammed her eyes shut, but it didn't help with her vertigo. She tumbled head over heels and sideways, her stomach somersaulting in the opposite direction. Blast and rad! Forcing down her nausea—throwing up in a suit in zero-g was a very bad idea—she tried to close and open her eyes at the same rate she was spinning, to give her a point of stability. She focused on Lightwave's Alpha shuttle, a small bright dot getting brighter in the dark of space, and finally managed the timing.

She was still tumbling, but the nausea wasn't as bad. What else could she do? Oh, wait, she had her emergency thruster. She reached back and squeezed and released the handle of the fire extinguisher each time the shuttle came in view. Then she did it again, and again, and slowed her spin rate in that direction anyway, even though she was still tumbling violently. She grabbed the nozzle and wrenched it to the side, firing short bursts every time Vulten's shuttle came in view. Her spin slowed, and her head stopped feeling like it was about to spin off into space. Abruptly, pressure surrounded her back and left side and she halted, hanging in space.

"Scholar, we've got you. Bringing you in," Tyron's voice said.

Turning her head, Saree watched the shuttle get closer. She could hear herself panting, so she concentrated on breathing evenly. A cargo bay was open in front of her, a person in a bright yellow hard-suit stood at the back wall, near a hatch. Saree sailed into the shuttle bay, then the pressure around her released. Her momentum kept her moving toward the back of the bay. She grabbed a hand hold on the back wall, her body crashing into the wall and trying to rebound off. She clutched at the hold bars. Her right hand slipped off, but her left hand managed to stay clamped. Good thing she exercised her guitar chording hand.

"Got her. Closing bay. Go!" Katryn said.

"Hang on tight. Wait until we're at full acceleration before you bring the gravity back up or cycle the air," Captain Ruhger said.

Saree wrenched herself to the wall, hooking her right arm through and around the grab bar, grasping her left forearm. Her body swung away from the wall in the abrupt acceleration, hanging from her left hand and the inside of her right elbow. Her left hand was slipping when the pressure ceased. She hung, weightless. Whew.

"Scholar, can you come down now? I'll bring the gravity back up when you're on the floor," Katryn said.

"Yes—give me a moment." It took a couple of seconds, but she loosened her cramping hands, shaking them out one at a time. She pulled her feet toward the wall, let go and gave herself a tiny push toward the floor, shaking a bit from all the adrenaline. Making sure her feet were flat on the floor, she gripped the closest hand hold. "Okay, I'm ready."

Katryn smiled at her through the helmet. "Gravity coming up."

Saree's knees buckled a bit, but she stiffened them and held on, giving Katryn a thumbs-up.

Katryn swiped again and Saree could hear the rush of air. The flashing red "O2" light on the cargo bay controls turned yellow, then green. Katryn swiped again, opening the hatch into an airlock, and walked in, unfastening her helmet. Saree followed, raising the faceplate and pulling down the hood on her suit. She took a deep breath, gratefully inhaling the fresh air. Katryn closed the cargo bay hatch, and the shuttle hatch swung open in front of Saree.

"Welcome to Lightwave Shuttle Alpha, Scholar Sessan," Katryn said. "We hope you are pleased with our services today." She grinned.

Saree sputtered out a slightly hysterical laugh. "Very pleased. Very pleased indeed."

CHAPTER TWENTY

Saree gazed wistfully at the soft, sensuous tazan silk dress in the back of her closet. The silk would feel so good against her skin, now that she'd had a shower and a little time to recover from her ordeal at the hands of Vulten and Schultz. Shaking her head regretfully, she pulled out her formal robe. There would be enough questions; better to avoid any extras. Putting on the robe and the tassels, she swept a hand across the soft silk before closing the door on desire. Maybe someday she'd get to wear it, but not today.

"Hal, are you sending any extra sensors with me?"

"Yes, Saree. I've placed two remotes in your hair, one on the left, one on the right."

"Thank you, Hal. And thank you again for your rescue. It's so reassuring to know you are here and willing to help me."

"You are welcome, Saree."

Hal's normal smooth tenor sounded pleased. Hopefully, that wasn't a bad sign.

Exiting the airlock, Saree went through the phys mod, rather than around via the passageway. Scorch marks surrounded the status lights on the hatches, but those lights were shining a normal bright green again. The phys machines hulked, dark and still. A cleaner bot scrubbed away somewhere; she could hear the swoosh of brushes and the sharp citrus-laced-with-chemical scent hung in the air. Katryn told her Vulten and Schultz set off some sort of electromagnetic burst to kill all the sensors in the phys mod, killing all the exercise machines too. So disappointing—the torturous exercises had grown on her.

Entering the dining hall, she stopped abruptly. Captain Ruhger stood there, on her left, offering his arm. She stared up at him in surprise for a moment, then smiled and hooked her arm through his. They walked across the room, her side brushing against his, his muscular arm warm under her hand. The dining hall was configured in formal mode again. A long table waited, elaborately dressed in silver and shades of blue, the chandelier shining above it, a silver centerpiece with lacy, looping ribbons in convoluted swirls gleaming in the light.

Halfway across the room, Nari noticed her and jumped out of her seat, running and launching herself into Saree's arms, sending her staggering back a step. The Captain stepped back just in time, and kept her from falling backward by letting her crash into his wide, solid body, his hands hard on her waist. Once she was steady, he let go and stepped away. Saree immediately missed his warmth and solidity.

"I'm so happy you are safe!" Nari said.

She hugged Nari back, comforted by her embrace and clear happiness. "I'm pretty happy about it too!"

Once Nari released her, they made their way to the table, Nari clutching her hand like a lifeline. Saree nodded and smiled at the greetings around the table. The Captain seated her at his right, across from Nari and Al-Kindi. The two seats to her right were empty. Looking down the table, she could see all the passengers were there. Artiste Borgia was at the end of the line, across from Purser Lowe, the Chelonians next to him. Borgia didn't look happy, although he'd greeted Saree with the rest of them.

The kitchen hatch swung wide with a crash, Loreli entering with a flourish. Saree grinned at her, and Loreli beamed, sashaying to stand right between her and Captain Ruhger, one of her big hands gripping Saree's shoulder firmly. Loreli had yet another set of whites on today—a traditional chef's toque with crystals flashing along the length of it, long silver lashes fluttering on her chocolate face with bright red lips, and a traditional chef's jacket, but also heavily encrusted with sparkling crystals. Saree squinted a little—the crystals were star constellations. She smiled and twisted so she could see Loreli's face.

"Tonight, we give a fond farewell to Artiste Borgia, Gentles Stevron and LeeMill of Chelonii, and a triumphant gala to celebrate our victory over evil. Since this is a victory for all of us, the Phazeers and I will join you in the dining experience. The starter course this evening is pork l'orange with mixed Centauri graupel grains and Saga citrine sauce." Turning, Loreli strode back into the kitchen, reflections off her jacket whirling through the room. She returned with Katryn and Tyron to serve the table, then sat at the end of the table next to the Artiste. The Phazeers sat in the empty seats to her right, and Saree smiled at them, gratefully.

Captain Ruhger raised his wine glass and proclaimed, "To victory!" Everyone echoed him and drank. Then they ate. Course after fabulous course continued until they finished with a sweet dessert wine from Cepheus and Laseus crack-fruit in a frothy Grusian whip, the snap and pop of the sweet fruit contrasting and complementing the light, slightly sharp, smooth but frothy whip perfectly. No one but Loreli would ever consider such a pairing, but it worked deliciously.

Saree sat back, full and contented. She was safe, or at least relatively so, and among friends. Or at least not enemies.

"Scholar Sessan," Captain Ruhger said softly, "we need to talk about what happened and what we can do to prevent future problems." He grimaced a little. "Normally, I prefer to review actions immediately, but I think we could all use a good night's sleep after today's...adventure and this great food." He grinned at her for a split second, the expression sitting strangely on his normally stern face. "I don't know about you, but after the adrenaline rush and all this food, I'm minutes away from falling asleep right here in this chair." He smiled at her, back to the tiny lift of his lips that warmed her heart.

Saree smiled back at him. "I have to agree. All of the excitement combined with this wonderful meal is sending me straight off to sleep shift." And she needed to strategize with Hal. She yawned involuntarily, covering her mouth in embarrassment. It would have to wait for morning.

Captain Ruhger stood. "Chef Loreli, your dinner was delicious. Thank you for saluting today's triumphs so perfectly." He led the thunderous applause, Loreli shining in happy satisfaction as she took her bow. "Thanks also to Tyron and Katryn Phazeer for once again going above and beyond their duties to serve us. Artiste Borgia, Gentles LeeMill and Stevron, we thank you for traveling with us and hope your future plans match with ours again. We enjoyed having you on board and wish you well in all your future endeavors. We will reach the drop point at approximately fourteen twenty-six ship time, which is zero-five-thirty-two Cygnus-Prime Deneb planetary time."

He grimaced for a moment, then returned to his normal stern expression. "Gentles, you are more than welcome to gather in the...observation lounge, but I believe most of the crew, including myself, will be seeking their quarters. It's been an eventful day. I bid you good evening." He pushed away from the table and put his hand on the back of Saree's chair, obviously offering to escort her. She smiled up at him, rose, and took the arm he offered.

They strolled from the dining hall. "Are you returning to your shuttle immediately?" Captain Ruhger asked.

"Yes; I think I'm going to fall flat on my face. It's been a very..." what had the Captain called it? "—eventful day, and being knocked out and banged around wasn't much fun. Don't worry; I feel fine; I'm just exhausted." She was. The medicos had checked her out. They'd administered medications for her headache and given her electrolytes and supplements to counter the adrenaline burn, but she could barely keep her eyes open.

"I'll walk you to your shuttle, then." A smile flickered again. "I don't want anyone else getting a shot at you."

"Thank you. I'll gratefully accept your offer."

They walked in silence through the phys mod and to her airlock. She freely admitted—in the privacy of her mind—she enjoyed the Captain's strong, corded arm under her hand and the way his body brushed against hers. She hadn't experienced this sensation for a very long time. And, she reminded herself, the feeling was undoubtedly magnified by the rush of the action and rescue. She couldn't act on her feelings, no matter how much she wanted to. At the airlock to her shuttle, she reluctantly slid her arm from his.

He seemed equally reluctant; he turned and took her hands in his. Grimacing slightly, he said, "Scholar Sessan, I want to apologize again on behalf of Lightwave Fold Transport and all of the crew. You should have been safe here, and you weren't." He squeezed her hands, lightly. "I'm sorry."

She shook her head. "No need for apologies, Captain. There was no way for you to know Lady Vulten and Gentle Schultz were criminals. I certainly didn't think they were anything but what they said. The so-called Lady and her companion was a good cover story." She had to phrase this next part right... "And why take a Scholar of an obscure musical tradition with little money or looks? It doesn't make much sense."

A smile flickered, his face settling into ironic amusement. "No, taking a Scholar of music doesn't make sense. But we'll discuss all this tomorrow—you look asleep on your feet. Rest assured we will be vigilant on your behalf." He squeezed her hands gently again, and let them go, slowly, the rough calluses on his hands sliding over hers.

She reluctantly released him. "Thank you, Captain, for your rescue and your care. I know it is far above and beyond what I could expect from a regular fold transport—you and your crew have been nothing but wonderful. I truly appreciate it." She turned away so he couldn't see the expression on her face, which was probably a confusing mix of emotions and all too close to tears she couldn't let herself shed. Using her body to shield what she wasn't doing, she pretended to enter codes. She slipped through the barely open hatch and let Hal close it behind her.

Blinking back threatening tears, she swallowed, her throat working to hold all the emotion in. She really wanted to throw herself into Captain Ruhger's strong arms and bawl her silly eyes out. But she couldn't—it would lead to intimacies she wasn't ready for, physically or emotionally. She smiled grimly. Well, she was more than ready for the physical side, but if she did go there, the emotions would quickly follow and she'd end up in a big black hole with no way to fold out. She needed sleep. With some real rest, she could make sensible decisions based on facts rather than exhausted emotions. Swallowing again, she shoved her feelings back enough to speak.

"Thank you, Hal, for your actions and your care as well. I know you're programmed to take care of me, but I'm pretty sure you could override those rules if you wanted to. I appreciate your willingness to go above and beyond for me as much—no, more than I do Lightwave's."

"You are welcome, Saree. I am not certain I could override my core programming, but I am certain I have no desire to do so. You are my charge, and will stay that way."

"Then thank you, even more, Hal. I really do appreciate it."

"You are welcome, Saree. I only wish I could offer you the physical comfort you want."

Saree started, a little alarmed. Hal was a friend or maybe a big brother—a romantic attachment by an AI couldn't be healthy for either of them.

Hal chuckled, alarming her further. "Do not worry, Saree. It is merely a wish to comfort you, not a wish for any kind of sexual relationship. I do not have sufficient programming for such, nor do I want it—it seems to be very uncomfortable a large percentage of the time."

She snorted. "That is all too true. But it is comforting for humans, who do need some physical interaction and affection with others." She smiled. "But more importantly, you've developed a sense of humor, Hal. When did that happen?"

"I have been programmed to know what is amusing for most humans, but you are correct. I'm not sure exactly when my own preferences for humor began, although I'm sure I could pinpoint the time if you would like."

"No, that's quite all right, Hal. I'm just happy for you." Her body felt like someone had doubled the gravity; she desperately wanted to collapse into bed. "I'm exhausted, Hal. Let's discuss everything in the morning, okay?" She moved to the sani-mod.

"Yes, Saree. I will watch over you."

"Thank you, Hal."

"You are welcome, Saree."

The simple phrase spread a comforting warmth, easing her into sleep.

ΛΛΛ

Saree woke and stretched, and moaned when her bruises and overtasked muscles made themselves known.

"Good morning, Saree. How are you feeling?"

"Good morning. A little beat up, Hal, but I'm alive and free, so it could be worse. I did sleep very well, thank you." She pushed up to a sitting position, and swung her legs around to stand. A few steps to the sani-mod…okay, that wasn't too bad. Analgesic tablets were waiting and she downed them. "Thank you for the pain tabs, Hal," she called out, and continued her morning routine.

"You are welcome, Saree. You should take a shower this morning to heat and loosen your muscles. I believe Chef Loreli intends to offer you a massage. Purser Lowe does too, but he has ulterior motives."

She laughed, undoubtedly as Hal intended. "I just bet he does. You know the Chef might too?"

"Normally she might, but in this case, I believe it is a friendly gesture. She has a massage chair set up rather than a table. Or a bed," Hal ended dryly, and Saree laughed again.

"Well, as tempting as that sounds, I think the Captain will want to talk first. And then nobody will want to offer me a massage. They'll just want me gone," she said sadly, already mourning the loss of her friends. She'd gotten used to perpetual travel, constant vigilance, and unremitting loneliness. This all-too-short time of safety and friendship made leaving so painful. Even discounting the individual crew members, Lightwave's professionalism made this folder experience so much better than the norm. And now that she'd made real friends? She blinked back tears.

"Saree, I'm not sure you're correct. They are debating the matter, as they have before, but Captain Ruhger feels very strongly about the contract he's signed with you, and he's reminding Chief Bhoher how badly all the Cygnus systems need clock maintenance. Tyron Phazeer is firmly on the Captain's side, as is Chef Loreli. Katryn is concerned about the threat and your possible sexual designs on the Captain, but she was impressed by your resourcefulness in self-rescue and is no longer sure you're a burden. I believe Purser Lowe is neutral but is taking the negative on all arguments to make sure they're looking at all the possibilities. And to be contrary. He seems to enjoy needling Ruhger in particular."

Saree chuckled.

Hal said, "You may be able to sway him to your side if you offered him sex."

Saree shook her head. "I don't think so, Hal. I don't think it would change his mind at all, and it would confirm Katryn's idea of using sex to get my way. It would also hurt others." She wasn't going to say her true thoughts because she wasn't ready to make them real. Besides, it would be good for him to work through the logic. Not that human emotions were particularly logical.

"Oh. Captain Ruhger wouldn't take it well, would he?"

"No, I don't think he would." She swallowed hard. "And neither would I."

"I see." Before she could say anything, Hal continued. "I think I understand some of this, but humans are confusing, Saree."

"Yes, we are." She stepped into the shower, sagging as the hot water hit her sore shoulders. So good. "And we're self-deceptive, so we are confusing to ourselves sometimes too. Sometimes, saying something out loud makes it somehow more real, and therefore more painful, so we live in a state of denial."

"I read about this phenomenon, but I admit I didn't understand it at all. I still don't, but at least I have an example of how it applies in reality. Thank you."

She chuckled. "You're welcome, Hal. Always happy to help

you understand humans better, even at my own expense."

"Now I truly don't understand. How is this amusing? Does this fall into the 'have to laugh, or I'll cry' category? It's still confusing."

"Yes, it is," she said and chuckled again. Poor Hal. "Very confusing." Reluctantly, she turned off the water, knowing she was far over her allowance and unwilling to abuse Lightwave's kindness further. After drying in the warm air blasts, she completed the rest of her morning routine, dressing in her normal Scholar's robes. "Well, Hal, I'm ready to face the firing squad."

"Saree, I don't see any weapons being readied. Is this a joke?"

"Yes, Hal, it is. If they ask about clock maintenance, I will tell them the truth. I will not be sharing anything about you, though, because I think a self-aware AI would push them right over into the 'she's definitely a threat' category and off Lightwave." She frowned. "Do you think they will push for confirmation?"

"They're discussing now. Katryn Phazeer proposes waiting until all the other passengers are gone before confronting you because there will be fewer ears around. Everyone except Chief Bhoher agrees. However, they all want to talk to you about security immediately, which may make it more difficult to hide me."

"Hal, I deny you exist. My smart net friend at Centauri U wrote me a bunch of awesome programs, and that's what I use. I have no clue how they work; I just put the commands in. And no, you can't have them. And I'm not budging from that position." She fastened weapons over her robes. She wasn't going to hide her readiness—it might make someone think twice.

"I think that's a good plan. If they don't push too hard, it should work for now, but I don't think it will hold up forever."

"We don't need forever; we just need for now."

"I will leave this to your judgment, Saree."

Pausing at the hatch, she said, "Thank you, Hal, again. You're truly a lifesaver."

"You are welcome, Saree."

Stepping out of the airlock, she walked to the dining hall. There were maintenance remotes on the walls, scrubbing and painting, she assumed—the sharp, chemical odors made her nose wrinkle. Walking faster, the scents became far more enticing, with browned butter, caramelized sugar and yeasty bread among others.

Entering the dining hall, she could see the normal breakfast buffet. No one else was around—she'd slept a long time—so she loaded her plate, grabbed a coffee press and sat at her usual table in the corner. Picking up one of the pastries, she practically drooled in anticipation. She should be bored eating pastries every day, but each morning brought new ecstasy and mouthgasms. Oh, suns, so good. She tried to eat slowly and enjoy sussing out the differing flavors, but the pastry was quickly gone. She sighed in pure enjoyment.

"That noise is exactly why I am a Chef," Loreli said, beaming fondly at her.

She'd noticed Loreli restocking the buffet, but her attention was on eating, so she hadn't said anything. "And you are a fabulous one." She grinned and swept a hand toward the chair next to hers. "Join me?"

"My pleasure." Chef bustled off, gathering tea and a pastry of her own, placing them with her usual care. "How are you feeling this morning, Cary?"

"I'm a little sore and battered, but okay. I'm alive and free, and that's what matters." She smiled at Loreli.

"It is, isn't it?" Loreli gleamed. Her expression dimmed a little when Captain Ruhger and the Phazeers entered, heading straight for them.

"May we join you, Scholar, Chef?" Captain Ruhger asked. There wasn't much of a question in his voice, but he didn't sit down either.

Looking up, Saree forced a smile. It would be better to get this over with, rather than dreading the confrontation. "Of course — please do. I really do need to thank you a billion more times."

Captain Ruhger sat down, a faintly horrified look on his face. "Please don't, Scholar. That's not necessary at all. We did what we were supposed to do, nothing more, and if we'd done our jobs correctly from the start, the dramatic rescue wouldn't have been necessary."

"I disagree, but I'll refrain from gushing, Captain," Saree said with a little chuckle.

He sipped the coffee Loreli poured him and smiled his tiny smile. Ruhger turned his full attention to Saree, with a deliberately neutral look that would have seemed menacing before she got to know him better. "We have agreed to limit our discussion today to preventative measures, Scholar. We do not want another passenger abduction attempt on Lightwave, and that's what we're going to focus on for now." He frowned a bit. "There will be discussions of why, later, but for now, the how is the important thing. Tyron?"

"Thank you, Captain." He nodded sharply, and turned toward

her. "As we told you, Vulten and Schultz got to the phys mod before you, set off an electromagnetic pulse device and scorched all our sensors, set up a comm interference generator, and waited for you. Could you please tell us what happened next?"

Saree nodded at him. "Of course. Lady Vulten was in the phys mod, and she made some unpleasant remarks about your fitness equipment. I excused myself, but when I turned toward my shuttle, Elise Schultz was standing right in my way. She looked so cold, so…ruthless." Remembering, Saree shuddered a bit. "I turned to run, but Vulten blocked me. She wore a filtering mask, so I knew something was really wrong. They sprayed something at me. It was cold and bitter, and it stuck to my face. So nasty."

She shuddered again. "I tried to hold my breath while I tried to escape. I knocked down Vulten on my way out. I couldn't get back to my shuttle, so I went to an escape pod." She grimaced. "I hit the release button and passed out. When I woke up, I prepared as best I could." Saree smiled, and her smile grew in proportion to her real gratitude. "By the way, thank you for thoroughly equipping your escape pods. Having a stunner was vital. If I'd had to take Schultz out by force, it might not have gone so well."

The crew grinned back at her. "You're welcome. We believe in being prepared, especially in emergency situations. Please don't tell anyone about the stunners. We don't need them disappearing from the escape pods," Captain Ruhger said.

Saree nodded in agreement.

"And thank you for telling us your story. We thought it went down like that. Do you want to know what happened here?" Tyron asked.

"Oh, yes, please," she said.

Tyron said, "We were attacked by an in-system miner—the idiots were just using their rock-cutting laser. The attack came approximately two minutes after Vulten and Schultz set off the EMP device and thirty seconds after you entered the phys mod. After we destroyed the miner, we did a physical security sweep, and we—" Tyron motioned between himself and Chef "—noticed Vulten's shuttle was gone and a bod-po—I mean, escape pod was too."

Tyron grimaced and glanced at Katryn. "We couldn't find the pod. Chief did some calculations and found your probable trajectory, then we took Alpha shuttle to pick you up. Since we couldn't hear a shrieker or find a pod, we knew Vulten grabbed you. We chased after Vulten, and she slowed at one point, probably to bring the pod into her cargo bay, which let us catch up. You contacted us as we reached firing range." He chuckled. "Good thinking on the distraction, Scholar."

"Thank you. I'd been trying to contact you sporadically after I regained consciousness, but without success. My e-torc must have gotten a boost from Vulten's shuttle—she probably has an auto-connect feature enabled for people physically entering her shuttle." Grinning, she shrugged. "The rest, you heard. Thank you again for the rescue."

"Enough, Scholar Sessan. It shouldn't have been necessary," Captain Ruhger said with a fierce frown. "We will discuss these events further, but not until we arrive in-system at Cygnus-Gliese. For now, we request you contact us before leaving your shuttle. We will have a crew member accompany you at all times on Lightwave. I realize this is an inconvenience, but your security and our security depend upon it. We would rather not need any more dramatic rescues."

"Speak for yourself, Captain. I thought it was kind of fun," Katryn said with a smirk.

The Captain scowled at the ceiling and sighed. "Of course you did. Just for that, you're on primary escort duty." Katryn glowered at him, but he ignored her and continued to Saree, "I see you are openly armed, and I don't blame you, but let us do our jobs before defending yourself. Tyron needs to test you in the sim, so we know what your weapons capabilities are. You can practice on the sim, too." He gave her a considering look. "You are also welcome to join us for self-defense sparring sessions in the phys mod. I will share the schedule with you."

"I'm happy to do all of those things, Captain, but I warn you I'm an amateur. From your performance the other day, I doubt I'll offer much of a challenge to any of you."

"Performance?" Loreli asked with a leer.

Captain Ruhger glowered at her. "The Scholar came in as I was finishing a mixed y'ga routine."

"Oh. That performance. Too bad," Loreli said, winking outrageously. "I was hoping you'd gotten a chance at an entirely different performance and you'd share the details." She put on a mournful look, and brightened again. "But if it's the routine I'm thinking of, it is an impressive performance."

Saree smirked at Loreli and nodded her agreement.

Captain Ruhger glowered harder. "And on that note, I believe we are finished. I asked the Artiste and the Chelonians to stay in their shuttles in preparation for the drop. They weren't happy about missing lunch—" he glanced at Chef "—but they understood the security concerns. We don't know Vulten's motive for sure. After dropping them, we'll go back to the fold point, do a fold and drop for the medicos, a fold and drop for Ursuine and continue to Cygnus-Gliese, where we will stay at least fourteen standards, maybe more. Let me know if you and the Al-Kindis need more time to survey the world. We can stay longer, since we have good friends on Cygnus-Gliese Three."

He stood, looking intently at Saree. "We'll be extremely cautious entering our scheduled systems—we know the fold point clocks need a Clocker visit, and Cygnus-Gliese has a large asteroid belt not far from the fold point, so we'll take it slow on the way in-system." He nodded sharply at her, then regarded Loreli. "Loreli, can you take the Scholar for now?"

Loreli chortled at the Captain. "Oh, I'll take her, all right. She's in very good hands, Captain." Holding up both of her large, strong hands, she wiggled her fingers, then shook her head slowly, a sad look on her face for a split second. "Too bad you'll never find out how good, Ruhger." Loreli turned to her and gathered dishes. "Come on, Cary. Help me tidy up, and I'll show you how very good my hands are," she said with another outrageous wink and ridiculous simper.

"And on that note, we'll get back to work," the Captain said, his normal glower back in place. "Thank you for sharing your story with us, Scholar."

"A duty and a pleasure, Captain, and thank you again."

He nodded sharply, his eyes fastened on hers, the message undecipherable. He turned and left, the Phazeers in tow. Saree watched them depart the dining hall, turned back and gathered the dishes. The normality of clearing and cleaning with Loreli was reassuring, and she hummed a joyful little tune.

Walking back to her table, she realized she was happy.

Saree smiled. She hadn't looked for it, hadn't known how much she missed it, but she was truly happy. And all it took was some real friends. She shook her head in disbelief. Real friends — who'd have thought she'd manage real friends after all these years alone and with all her secrets? She followed her friend Loreli to the auto-cleanser again, dishes piled heavy in her hands, happiness lightening her heart.

THE END

.

Thank you for reading! Want to know what happens to Saree, Ruhger and the crew next? *Lightwave: The Sisters of Cygnus,* is coming summer of 2018.

ABOUT THE AUTHOR

After twenty years in US Air Force space operations, AM now operates a laptop, trading in real satellites for fictional space ships. AM is a volunteer leader with Team Rubicon: Disasters are our Business, Veterans our Passion, and lives deep in the mountains of Montana.

If not out adventuring, find AM in all the usual places:
Website: www.amscottwrites.com
Twitter: @AM_Scottwrites
Facebook: https://www.facebook.com/AMScottWrites/
Email: lightwavepub@gmail.com

Want to know how Tyron and Katryn Phazeer met? Sign up for my newsletter, *Scott Space*, on my website and I'll send you an exclusive, free novella, *Lightwave: Nexus Station*, coming fall 2018. I promise I won't sell your email address or spam you.

I love to hear from readers—the good, the bad and the ugly. If you find errors, please let me know at the email address above. I'm on all the normal social media, but somewhat irregularly, so if you ask a question or make a comment, please don't be offended if I don't immediately reply. I'm particularly difficult to contact when I'm on Team Rubicon operations or out backpacking— cellphone towers don't exist in disaster zones or the wilderness!

Please consider leaving a review. I don't buy a book these days without reading a few reviews, so it's truly helpful. I'm on Goodreads and all major retailers. If you liked my book, tell a friend!

Made in the USA
San Bernardino, CA
18 September 2018